You and I and Someone Else

Advance Praise

You and I and Someone Else is both a lyrical, bittersweet love song to the South and a careful study of love itself, using that recognizable—but in Schachner's capable hands, amazingly fresh—territory of the family. In Frannie's world, love is not a birthright; it must be learned. I cried when Schachner's characters failed and cheered when they succeeded, having felt their epiphanies as if they were my own. This is a book that redefines parenthood and responsibility, and does so unapologetically. I admire it for its insight, its sly humor, and its careful, hopeful heart. Make this your next read.

—Joshilyn Jackson, *New York Times* best-selling author of *The Opposite of Everyone*

In the tradition of Alice Munro, Anna Schachner explores the mysteries of family with unflinching humor and a poet's ear for language. Driven by an intricate and compelling plot, *You and I and Someone Else* develops complex characters and relationships that reveal the emotional and psychological truths of secret-keeping. If this is her first novel, I'm already waiting for the second.

—Karen Abbott, *New York Times* best-selling author of *Liar, Temptress, Soldier, Spy: Four Women Undercover in the Civil War*

You and I and Someone Else is a wonderful novel, with incandescent characters, brilliant writing, and a heart as wide as the sea, where the story begins. Schachner has created a warm and intricate world in which we share souls and dreams. You will absolutely love this book. I did.

—Philip Lee Williams, author of *The Divine Comics* and *The Flower Seeker: An Epic Poem of William Bartram*

MERCER UNIVERSITY PRESS

Endowed by

TOM WATSON BROWN
and
THE WATSON-BROWN FOUNDATION, INC.

December 2017

You and I and Someone Else

To Ann Marie —

ANNA SCHACHNER

*Thank you for hanging around
me all these years! Happy
reading, now & always —*

Anna Schachner

MERCER UNIVERSITY PRESS | *Macon, Georgia*

2017

MUP/ P541

© 2017 by Mercer University Press
Published by Mercer University Press
1501 Mercer University Drive
Macon, Georgia 31207

9 8 7 6 5 4 3 2 1

Books published by Mercer University Press are printed on acid-
free paper that meets the requirements of the American National
Standard for Information Sciences—Permanence of Paper for
Printed Library Materials.

ISBN   978-0-88146-597-6
Cataloging-in-Publication Data is available from the Library of
Congress

For my father, in memory, and my mother, in celebration

The way I need you is a loneliness I cannot bear.

—Carson McCullers,
The Heart Is a Lonely Hunter

You and I and Someone Else

Prologue

Before my parents could give me their secrets, they had to keep them from each other. Little by little, one by one, those secrets came to live inside my house and, eventually, inside of me, the only things, it turned out, that ever would. But secrets have a way of forging their own identities. One day Rita appeared, her eyes lit from behind. She was small and wiry, and she had been Jude's first wife long before he hoped to make me his second.

I met her at a gas station in late fall, when the smell of the earth still tried to make its way past the new subdivisions built around the edge of Cornelia. Old mill towns once grew from the center out, unraveling like the cotton thread that made them, but Cornelia, heeding progress, had started to expand from its *edges* out. It's just that people got caught in this shift. Sykes Bowers, his gnarled fingers blackened by years of dripping oil and greasy handles, had been replaced by more steel pumps advertised as "Self," yet nothing had changed about the odor of grass, trees, and fresh soil. Rita must have known this, too. Both the front and back seats of her station wagon were piled high with cardboard boxes, each marked in thick, black letters as "French Erotica." Her license plate read Kansas. There's nothing, after all, like endless miles of wheat, the earth dutifully used, to make you think of sex, French or otherwise.

"Don't mind the boxes," she said when she caught me staring. "Not all of it is really erotica."

"That's good. There might be laws about transporting that much."

"Oh, the transporting is over." Beyond her left shoulder, across the road, stood Cornelia's one grocery store where older citizens still reminisced about Green Stamps and china sets accumulated one piece at a time.

"Are you new to Cornelia?" I asked.

"This time, no." She put the cap back on her gas tank and stepped down from the cement island that held the pumps. No more than five feet tall, she wore a choker made of ribbon frayed along its edges, and from it dangled a turquoise pendant that bounced against her neck as she spoke.

"You're moving back here?"

"No, I wouldn't say that."

"Passing through?"

"Aren't we all?"

I couldn't help but think of my mother, who once told me that the digestion of food was a metaphor for life itself. "The colon knows all," she had said. I smiled at Rita and went to pay for my gas. The attendant inside had fingernails as clear as the plastic cup lids stacked on the counter beside him. Rita waved as her car passed, a stiff hand held up as if she were stretching her fingers. She turned onto Justin Road, where gift shops that sold wind chimes made out of tarnished spoons and welcome mats in the shape of cats now claimed a row of shotgun houses. I hoped she would stop for a while. She seemed like a woman in need of a welcome.

Later, when we were fixing dinner, I told Jude about the strange woman from seven states away. I told him I had pictured her driving, imagining the knees and elbows of all those French lovers bumping against cardboard as she tried to stay awake late into the night. "I've never even met anyone from Kansas before," I said, peeling the papery skin of an onion. "I didn't know there were people in Kansas."

"All of them in red, sparkly shoes?"

"And striped tights," I added.

"I never understood those tights. Does a witch need tights?" He tousled my hair, leaving a piece of lettuce clinging to my bangs.

"I hope not." A single tear formed in the corner of my left eye, the one most sensitive to everything, including onions.

"Stick your head in the freezer for a minute."

"I keep telling you that if you want to get rid of me, it's the *oven*, not the freezer. The freezer will *preserve* me." I put the knife down and smiled at him. "Really, Jude. There was something familiar about her."

He stood still, his attention focused on the lettuce. "Was she small with curly hair?"

"Yes."

"Deep voice?"

"Yes."

"Rita," he said.

"Your Rita?"

"Sounds like it anyway." He pushed the cutting board back and moved to the sink. "She must be back for Evan."

I waited for a second so I could choose what to say. Jude's face was unflinching, but he pressed together the tips of his left fingers, as he always did whenever he mentioned his son. "How can she do that?"

"For *his memory*. She's back to make sure I remember Evan."

"How could you not?" I asked softly, so I wouldn't sound judgmental.

"I don't think she wants to remember him alone," he said. "It's too big a job for one person."

Barely more than a year later, Rita carried our unborn child low against her narrow hips. Sometimes I could only imagine the arrangement in terms of our three bodies. Her body was my body. Her body was Jude's body. Her body had been with Jude's body. The baby might be born a triangle, but better an isosceles than a secret.

Rita was defiant. She was her own country, her own entity, fiercely alone. I would see Rita around town, her thick hair pinned on top of her head and her purse strapped across her body like a row of ammunition. As her stomach grew, she walked faster and faster, the sidewalk or the parking lot disappearing beneath her, and she looked like she was being chased. She was, by most accounts, what with Evan dead and Jude just waiting for her to outsmart him. I should have known that I would come to need her, need myself, even if I didn't know who I was.

Chapter 1

The night my parents conceived me, my father had just returned from a four-month stint of Navy duty. My mother always insisted that men in uniforms had no effect on her, but she must have been somewhat taken in by the crispness of his trousers and the cap that sat on the back of his head, its bill pointing ahead. They were living in Charleston, so she cooked shrimp and okra, which they ate with their fingers, taking turns dipping both into sweet, melted butter. My father had only two days before he left port again. He had already decided to devote each of the forty-eight hours to matters of the flesh, food and otherwise, given that a wide expanse of sea automatically attends to the soul.

My mother described their apartment as long and lean, the outside of which was beautifully fortified with wrought iron. From the living room window, she saw my father walking up the street, his duffel bag slung over his shoulder and his shoes tapping against the cobblestone. Beside her on the sofa was her purse, and in it a photograph she had cut from a magazine of a young man standing in a doorway and waving. She kept him secret, her ideal man, the one whose name she would never assign. She liked knowing that she and my father were each other's challenge, while the smiling man who had just told someone good-bye would never make any demands. She understood love best as a demand.

She met my father at the door of the apartment, her hair freshly set and her waist an inch smaller than the previous month, when she had learned of his impending arrival and stopped drinking Coca-Cola and eating sweets. "I heard the ship's whistle an hour ago," she told him when he wrapped his arms around her shoulders, "and I've been watching out the window ever since."

"I've missed you," he said simply.

"Thank you," she replied.

"My pleasure," he teased.

They sat on the faded Persian rug because the furniture was still damp from my mother's cleaning, and my mother massaged my father's feet, which had been trapped inside official shoes so long he had forgotten the feel of soft, worn wool beneath them. From somewhere in the building, pipes clanked.

The next morning, my mother went out onto the balcony overlooking Teal Street and sat down to think. She was staring across the street, into the apartment of a couple in their seventies whom she often met on her daily walk to the market downtown. Through their living room window, she saw him gently kiss his wife on the lips. The woman tilted back and received his kiss with a slight rise of her chin. My mother was touched by such tenderness, such ease, after what must have been years and years of familiarity, perhaps even challenge. She padded back to the bedroom, which ran along an outside wall, and found my father just waking up, his hair still obliged to the curved indentation of his Navy hat.

"Madelane," he said, yawning, "it's good to be home."

"Yes," my mother answered, "it is. I mean I hope it is."

My parents did not leave the apartment until the afternoon, shortly after lunch, when my father felt compelled to visit his great-aunt Clarisse, who was mostly senile and ordered things from the backs of magazines only to send them right back. He went to visit, and my mother went for lemons, for iced tea. She had walked only about halfway to the corner market when she saw my father take a turn in the opposite direction of his Aunt Clarisse's, away from town and toward the shore. She followed him, drawn to the hastened pace of his walk, the way his arms swung casually at his sides as if obeying the rhythm of the wind and not his body.

She thought how handsome he was, how young they both were. With all that time in front of them, they would need something to fill it. They would need a child.

She followed my father to the water, sixteen city blocks, staying nearly a block behind him. When he disappeared into a gift shop, she had to wait anxiously outside. She closed her eyes for a second, to imagine what he was buying for her, and she nearly missed his exit, his arms, package-less, once again swinging at his sides.

At the water, my father entered a cinder-block restaurant whose sign advertised the best fried catfish on the eastern shore. He took a booth with a red vinyl seat and stared at the menu, his chin propped on his hand and his elbows on the table. He chose the catfish, which he ate with fried potatoes and green beans. My mother stared through a dirty windowpane, suddenly aware of how suspicious she must look, what with her black pumps and proper handbag. She walked the three blocks back to the main road and called for a taxi from a nearby pay phone. She was sliding onto the worn backseat just as my father was ordering a fresh piece of lemon meringue pie, a layer of clouds garnishing the top.

Back in the apartment the light had changed, and my father's Navy uniform seemed to have taken shape and personality. Her imagination at play, my mother watched the uniform exit through the front door, feeling the loneliness of months, years even, to come, there in those four rooms. She thought about the little restaurant by the water, seeing it rocking gently on the sea, my father sitting contentedly in the red booth and enjoying the distant view of the shore. More than that, she wondered why he would deceive her, even if it were for catfish and sweet tea served in mason jars.

Twenty minutes later, my father returned. He opened the front door and jingled the keys. "Madelane," he called.

My mother met him in the tiny dining room, her lipstick freshened and a kettle boiling for tea. "How was Clarisse?" she asked.

"Just fine," he answered, kissing her on the cheek and sighing. "Crazy but fine."

My mother looked at him. He was hiding the truth, she knew. There, with his square shoulders and green eyes in front of her, she felt each moment that she would be alone or doubtful of him as sure as she felt the thin ring of sugar that his kiss had left on her cheek. Why had she thought that marriage was some kind of end point, some destination, when she felt she had yet to arrive? She had gone to college, where she had read philosophy and memorized equations. What good was either now?

"Do you love me, Duncan?" she asked.

He put down the news magazine he had selected from the stack on the coffee table and gave her a quizzical look. "You can count on it," he said.

My mother sighed. "What do you think about when you're out at sea? What occupies your thoughts?"

"You."

"And?"

"And?"

"What else?"

"Just you," he said, sincerely, though the corners of his eyes were already suggesting a smile.

"Don't you think about the future at all?" she asked. In the apartment beneath them, the telephone rang, followed by a muffled thumping of feet. My mother removed the tea towel from over her shoulder and brushed a piece of hair back from her face.

"I think about the future all the time. Sometimes it's just difficult to separate the two. You," he said, raising an arm to open an imaginary door, "and the future. It's all the same, Madelane."

Not knowing what to say, my mother took my father's hand in hers, having placed the tea towel back on her shoulder. Not twenty minutes later, I was made, consciously on my mother's part, not so on my father's, the kettle whistling endlessly from the kitchen and any discussion of lemons long forgotten.

My mother's stomach grew like a gourd, oblong and almost pointed at her navel. She maintained her daily walks to the market, even in the winter, when she wore the brown swing coat she had cherished since college. My father went back to sea for six months, where he considered the future, his thoughts pressed to the porthole. Numbers were steady and sure, he decided, mysterious yet dependable. He would go back into banking after his duty was over. When he looked out across the sea, he felt frightened by its expanse, so he wrote my mother long, beautiful letters, more like stories. Once he described the continents as huge mats where people merely tumbled about, never sure if they would keep their footing.

Often times, at night, my mother would read his letters again and again, rocking her belly gently in the cane chair, creating what she thought was the rhythm of the ocean, the very same rhythm my father knew. Was marriage a bigger purpose than anything else? She wasn't happy being married. What was marriage? It was all the possibilities that her life excluded. It was reading women's magazines and not understanding such passion for cranberry-walnut relish or gingham. It was the tentative curve of my father's back as he sat on the bed those mornings home on shore leave, bent to coax his socks to his ankles. She rested her hands on her stomach, over mine as well, and wished that my life would be filled with infinities, with dancing and movement and change that sometimes took me by surprise.

Then she decided that she would try harder at marriage, try harder at love, if that was more apt, because there would be someone else involved.

One particular night, at the end of a day when her feet had swollen and she had not felt like leaving the apartment, she remembered following my father to the seaside restaurant. It was such a small secret he thought he had kept from her. So harmless and small.

Ignoring her feet, she took her cardigan sweater from the hall closet and called for a taxi, which arrived promptly in five minutes. She rode to the beach with her hands tucked inside her pants pockets, fingering the cork from a wine bottle, which she had saved for some reason she couldn't remember. She could smell the ocean as the taxi approached it, that strange odor of wet sand meeting a sky that hung just a little too low.

The restaurant was closed. Aside from the one street lamp that cast an arc of light across its roof, the building was as dark as the beach that stretched beyond it. The driver pulled to the curb, slung his arm across the stretch of seat separating them, and looked at her. When she said nothing, he asked, "Am I waiting for you?"

She felt flustered for a second, not sure of what she would actually do there, alone in a quest that would continue for years. "No, that's fine," she told him, and paid him with bills fresh from the bank that morning. As the taxi pulled away, its lights found one lone fishing boat tied to the wharf at the side of the restaurant, by the water's edge.

Heavy with me, my mother edged down the wharf and gauged the distance she would have to heave her newly rounded body to sit in the boat. She stretched one leg about two feet in front and then bent as best she could to catch her weight with her hand, which she flattened against the wooden seat stretched across the inside of the boat. The small craft bounced on the water. She held in her breath, waiting for it to steady itself, which it did, patiently receiving the waning slaps of water.

Then she sat and gazed at the restaurant, and the ocean, and the lights of Charleston dotted on the sea. The salt from the water and air settled heavily on her body, like the coat she wished she had brought along. There would always be a part of my father she wouldn't understand, she decided. She had known that when she married, and she would accept that. She would allow him that. She could better picture herself, her life even, if she had to work at knowing him.

But what frightened her was that her child, the one growing inside her, might be the same. How would she love someone she didn't understand, someone in whom she did not recognize herself, if that were the case, after all these months of waiting and hoping? I kicked hard, down near the rounded bottom of my own ocean, to assure her that the question remained.

When I began my slow entrance into the world three months later, my father was learning to crochet. It was another secret that he kept from my mother, driving to the weekly Saturday morning class at the arts center with the radio volume turned up, as if trumpets and saxophones pushing against the window glass could disguise his mission. That week he had secured a job at a bank, as planned. He was a Loan Officer. He accepted the title with some vague yearning that "officer" would honor his Navy history, although he knew that it couldn't, that the only honor he could bring to those months at sea was memory itself. Even his uniform had been relinquished. And of the mementos he brought back from various ports, only one remained: a necktie with bottles of rum splattered against a dark green background, a tacky gift from a nervous young woman who had handed it to him on a sidewalk in Cuba and then scurried away. So the desire to crochet, to connect small squares of cotton to small squares of cotton, offered no connection to his former vocation. He did not particularly like the necessary intricate movement of needles, but he knew that *creating* things (his job at the bank involved rearranging, not creating) was important. And he knew that my mother would never take on such tasks. He knew that if his child were to have handmade blankets and doilies on which, years later, she could place her trinkets, he would have to make them.

He had no doubt that I would be a girl.

My mother did. In fact, in perfect role reversal, my mother stared the nearly 50/50 probability straight in the eye and questioned the very suggestion of balanced odds. As she saw it, the fact that she had tricked my father into parenthood, having planned my conception without asking for his complicity, would tip the scales in his favor. I would be a boy, she was sure. "He'll probably look like you, too," she told my father. "He'll get those long, wasted eyelashes and come-hither eyes."

Nevertheless, the crochet instructor that morning stood over my father's busy hands and nodded in approval. My father was working on his seventh square, the size of two cigarette packages placed side by side. "This should be relaxing," he looked up to tell her.

But he was thinking of smoking, his time in the Navy given to losing bad habits, ironic given that some sailors used the time to acquire them. The instructor smiled at him and moved on to the other students, all of whom nodded politely as class dismissed, all of them older women in various stages of middle age, and slightly smug about their squares.

Other than smoking, my father thought of a lot of things that day as my mother's water broke. He thought about death. With another life so close, it was only logical. He thought about two of his boyhood playmates who had been hit by a car when they were ten. He had seen it happen, watching in horror from the front steps of his house where his mother had sent him to shine his father's shoes. One of the children, the boy, had cried out just before the car tried to slow, what sounded like the word "yes" to him. He didn't know why this returned to him as he sat, twenty-three squares to go. When he left class, he drove home to my mother, making only one stop, offering that same word when he arrived and my mother called out, "Duncan, please tell me that's you," feeling its usual optimism heavy against his tongue.

Someone had been busy. During his absence, my mother, restless from nine months and eleven days of pregnancy, began opening things. Slumping through the house, both hands on her buttocks, she had started in the kitchen and removed the lid of every jar and container first in the Frigidaire and then from the cupboards. On the bottom pantry shelf, she found a jar of pickles left behind by the previous owner, which smelled like turpentine when opened, but she persevered, a handkerchief held steadfastly to her nose.

When she was finished with the kitchen, she moved to the bedroom and opened the lid of the trunk at the end of my parents' bed. She opened all five drawers of the mahogany dresser inherited from my grandfather on my father's side, a carpenter, exposing all sorts of attire. This included the waist-high cotton underwear she had worn all her life, serving as testament to her underlying practicality, which she had always, unfortunately, mistaken for monotony.

From the kitchen, she moved to the nursery, solemn in its anticipation of my arrival. She unscrewed the lid of every baby product on the new changing table, even the Vaseline, which was as hard and brown as stale bread when the time came to use it. She opened the door to the wardrobe where five or six blue sleepers hung from tiny wooden coat hangers. She removed the lid to the plastic diaper pail, admiring its cleanliness, soon, she knew, to be a thing of the past. She opened the window to chilly April and invited the squirrels to crack open all the acorns they could find. "Let them fill your cheeks," she said, some vague memory of a poem encouraging the words. It would have been hard for them to decline, for my mother, very, very pregnant, was a commanding presence.

Opening things to summon unborn children was an old wives' tale, she knew, but for week after bloated week, she had felt like an old wife, that title still as odd to her as any. She untwisted the top of a jar of molasses she had left waiting in the kitchen and saw a tiny black bug crawling around on the surface. "I hope you get fat," she said, and meant it.

When my father came home, my mother stood in the hallway under the Renoir print, the floor darkened behind her where her water had landed. With great effort, she had changed into clean maternity pants and a light blue shirt, the one she had always hoped she would be wearing when I arrived. "The baby has requested today as a birthday," she said, her mouth a straight line.

"Today?" my father said, after two seconds' hesitation, staring directly at my mother's stomach in hopes of seeing my quick progress downward. He didn't voice it, but the fact that it was a Saturday did not seem right. Babies should be born during the week, he felt, so that schedules, jobs, lives, were rightfully interrupted.

"Does that not suit you?" my mother said, rolling her eyes.

"Is the back door locked?"

She nodded yes. He reached for her hand, and they walked side by side through the front door, down the steps of the duplex, and along the sidewalk to my father's car, where he had hidden in the trunk a suitcase full of new pajamas, magazines, and my mother's favorite chocolate to surprise her.

Sixteen hours later, I came, almost a week late, and in the middle of my father's favorite television program, *Gunsmoke*. My mother had always wanted to be a gypsy, so she let my father be a cowboy, at least for an hour a week, when he sat with his expression fixed to the television screen, the contemporary world—where problems were solved without guns—forgotten. But not that week. Not that night.

That night he watched my mother. He tried to imagine her pain but could not think of more than her two knees, rounded like lumps of bread dough from all the extra water. One vein rose to the surface of her forehead, a thin, blue line of effort that my father noted, worried it was some other demarcation, some division between two things that should never come into contact.

Two days later, my mother carried me home wrapped in a snowy white blanket and wearing crocheted booties with cloth spurs sewn onto the back, the very first of my father's projects, despite the fact that I was indeed a girl. He had pulled them over my chubby feet when my mother went to use the restroom, the very first time he held me without her fussing over his shoulder. When she brought me home and unwrapped the blanket, her first thought was that she had claimed the wrong baby.

"Spurs?" she shrieked from the nursery, so tired and hormonally imbalanced that the house might just as easily have been spinning. "Duncan, come tell me if this one's ours!"

My father appeared in the doorway, not the least bit sheepish for having been discovered, and said, "Lane, I would think you would have noticed earlier if she wasn't 'ours.'"

She wasn't convinced.

He reached over, pulled the blanket away from my face, and ran a finger under my three chins. I grimaced, my whole body shuddering in only the way that a newborn's can. "She's ours," he affirmed and smiled. "She looks just like you."

"Do you think so?" my mother asked, moving closer. "Do you really think so?"

The truth was that my father had wanted a son. He never so much as said it, but everybody, including my mother, knew it. To compensate, she attracted as much drama to me as she could. Her first idea was to get me onto television, and she signed me up for an audition without telling my father, who wouldn't have approved of such an exhibition, the very thing he didn't want for me. It was 1961. Television was black and white, so my mother was sure the producers would not be concerned about my small bout of jaundice that had turned my entire 29-inch body the color of weak saffron.

I could have been a child star, yellow but famous, had my mother been able to relinquish me to the bubbly twenty-one-year-old actress portraying a diaper-challenged mother. When the woman held out her arms to take me, the camera blinking red in the background, my mother's fingers leaked glue from the tips—a skill she later told me that all mothers had—and she was unable to peel them from under my head and bottom.

"Do you have children?" my mother asked, her arms still stretched out in front of her, parallel to those of the actress.

"No," she replied, tossing her eyes toward the director as if to say, "Is all this really necessary?"

"Then you've got no right," my mother said, pulling her arms in and clutching me. She walked out, back straight, head high, her heels staccato against the shiny, tiled floor.

From the set, we drove in the white Ford Falcon that sounded like a go-kart, to my father's office. We walked in past his highly efficient secretary and surprised him as he was coming out of his conference room.

"Oh, my goodness," he said to my mother, which she indicated was the improper thing for a new father to say to his baby and the woman who carried her.

"Would you please take us to lunch?" my mother demanded more than asked.

Supposedly, without even a word, my father grabbed his suit jacket from the back of his chair and led my mother (and me) by the elbow out of the office building and two blocks deeper into downtown Charlotte, to the best Italian restaurant he knew. On the corner of Tryon and 5th, waiting for the light to change, my mother slowly handed me, arms outstretched, to my father and said, "She won't be in film after all." Again, for a brief second, I was suspended between two worlds. My father took me and tucked my tiny feet into the fold of the blanket that he himself had ironed the day before.

"She doesn't look enough like you anyway, Lane, but I'm glad you see it my way," my father said, rubbing my mother's forearm, taut from carrying me.

My mother did not answer, for in moments of great despair she imagined nothingness, the opposite of joy.

"She's got enough to worry about just being a girl," my father said a few minutes later, buttering his bread, seated with his back against an enormous fish tank filled with all sorts of algae and ceramic castles with fish-sized passages.

My mother sighed and rolled her eyes at what she thought was a jab at her own excessive primping. But she somewhat agreed. "What good is a famous baby, Duncan? This is what I asked myself. All those people standing around watching to see if my baby was good enough."

"What people?" my father politely asked.

"Well, they"—my mother caught herself and then continued—"there would have been the directors and the actors and the makeup people. People needed to make the whole thing look real."

"It's gotta look real," my father said.

"That's just it," she said, rocking the bottom of my carry-all cradle, which sat on the table beside the parmesan cheese and Sweet and

Low, despite the waiter's scowling disapproval. "I don't want to have to make it look real. I don't want to be a mother from the outside in."

My father put down his bread knife. "How do you want to be a mother? Inside out?"

"Don't laugh at me, please." She dipped the corner of her napkin in her water glass and dampened a strand of my hair, which she then twirled around her finger so that it finally rested against my forehead like an S. "I want to feel it before I think it, that's all."

"It?" my father said.

"It," my mother said, and she ended the conversation by dipping her spoon into his Italian sorbet, which was the color of the inside of a pumpkin.

After a four-course meal, my father and my mother, carrying a sleeping me, paid the bill at a counter that also served as a display case. Inside was an Italian ceramic tea set with birds and flowers hand-painted on the cups and teapot in brilliant blues and yellows. My mother made my father buy it, not for her but for me, when I was older and could appreciate such "female things," as she phrased it to my father, the very man who secretly crocheted.

Back at home, when she had finally placed me into my small, wooden crib for my afternoon nap, she unwrapped the tea set from its layers of tissue paper and put each piece away in the tulip-lined shelves of the butler's pantry. She told herself, a sigh tugging at the back of her thoughts, that when the time came—perhaps an unexpected toothless smile from me in the baby bath, even my first defiant "No" as a chubby toddler—she'd recognize love, and seize it. When her unpacking arrived at the very last piece, a teacup that, in keeping with the set's handmade origin, was just a tad smaller than the others, the glue from earlier in the day reappeared. Her fingers stuck to the handle, breaking it off with a soft clicking sound. She put the cup alongside the others regardless, wrapped the tiny handle in one sheet of tissue paper, and placed it in her jewelry box where it forever remained as she learned about herself from the inside out.

My father, however, was a man of action. That evening, after the Italian lunch and on his way from the bank to the small duplex, my father made a stop that resulted in nothing more than a few unanswered knocks on the door. It was the same stop he made the day of my birth, the same address, the same objective. So I'll start with what happened just before my arrival, when my father, as always, followed his heart, or at least a slight panicked feeling that he was doing something no one else would.

As my mother was feeling the first of many contractions, he drove, never challenging the speed limit, to a neighborhood just off the interstate. Charlotte was small then, and its circumference felt to him suddenly like a big piece of elastic waiting to be stretched. The city would grow, banking money encouraging it, he knew. It was inevitable. But now the line of trees just beyond the shoulder was intact. The cement was the color of pancake batter, still clean, cracked from the weight of trucks, but clean enough. The older neighborhoods, where brick ruled out over wood, were regal, or just beginning to deteriorate. He took exit 58, toward the west, and sighed. He checked his watch, careful not to be gone longer than two hours, the window of time that he and my mother had agreed upon that morning when he didn't tell her he was learning to crochet.

The apartment complex was quiet when he parked between two sedans, although he knew that there were dozens of children living there. He had seen them, riding bicycles in the parking lot, climbing the weathered wooden fence around the trash dumpsters. Once a little girl had asked him for a quarter as he passed the area that held vending machines. She bought a package of watermelon bubble gum with it and offered him a piece. He chewed it for just a few seconds, surprised by the excessive sweetness, and then threw it away, careful to wrap it back in its aluminum packaging before tossing it in the garbage.

The day I was born, he climbed the slatted stairs and knocked lightly on the door of 42E, not a full-force knock but not a timid one either. A woman answered the door, as he expected. "Good morning,

Melissa," he said, and stepped inside where the light hit the worn carpet in half-cones as it filtered through two narrow windows that looked out over the empty, discolored pool.

"Duncan," she said, kissing his cheek the way that my mother had already stopped doing, "thank you for visiting."

"I can't stay long. The baby could come any minute."

"Yes," she said, simply, and swept her arm toward the sofa so that he would sit.

My father wasn't sure, but he thought Melissa to be under twenty, or maybe just twenty. He had never asked her age, preferring other details—what her favorite fruit was, if she watched television for the company of voices, if she had always planned on being a mother. Yet she moved slowly, like an older woman whose bones were adjusting to less flesh. He watched her cross the room, a comma-shaped scar on the front of her calf, just below her skirt.

"Is Hugh sleeping?"

She nodded yes and smiled. "He's about to walk."

"And how's the drugstore working out?"

"It's fine," she answered. "Just fine."

He thought of Davies, Melissa's husband, how he methodically stirred his coffee in the mornings at breakfast, the sailors lining both sides of a long metal table, the ocean defining them. They had become fast friends, and my father respected Davies's good humor, his conviction, even if he could be cocky, so sure of himself. Davies could keep a poker face better than anybody, and he made my father consider the difference between a secret and a lie. Still, that was in the context of a card game, something to pass the long nights at sea. It wasn't life, which only happened when they returned home, which is why he tried to forget, among other indiscretions, that he had seen Davies with a strange woman in a bar when they were docked in Baltimore. The woman was not pretty, but she was vivid, colorful, dressed in jewel tones, sliding a row of bangles up and down her arm. She laughed with her mouth wide open, a musical laughter that my father nevertheless resented.

Three days after Baltimore, Davies died from a bad heart, a condition undetected by the Navy's initial physical. My father couldn't attend the funeral, but when he heard that it was in Charlotte, where he had planned to return, he knew that he would look up Davies's wife. He knew that he would offer her what he could—consolation, support, an ear, but not remembrance. He would help her move ahead, not look back, and that meant doing what he could for the baby she had yet to deliver. He did not allow himself to think what she might offer him, for my mother was his life. His life was depending on him.

"There's a teller position at a branch of the bank over on South Boulevard that will be opening up," he told Melissa.

She looked at the carpet. Her straight brown hair fell forward against her chin. "I don't know. I'd have to sit still all day and smile at people I don't know."

"You get free checks," my father said hopefully.

"I don't know, Duncan. I'm telling you, I feel restless. Without Davies here, I just feel restless. Like I used to."

"You've got Hugh."

She nodded again. "I know it. He's my Cracker Jack prize."

My father stood. "You know you can call me at the bank if you need anything."

"Tell your wife that you forget about the pain. There's plenty of other pain a lot worse than having a baby."

My father didn't say anything. He gave Melissa a squeeze on her forearm and opened the door. He thought about the baby boy sleeping in the room down the hallway. Boys had a surer course in the world. Maybe it wasn't right, but they did. Still, the child would need some kind of father, someone to remind him of that course.

"Okay then," he said to Melissa, smiling, and then he left. Outside, he could breathe again. He felt a kind of control waft away from his body. He thought for a second. He hoped my mother would release me as easily as a sigh. He hoped that I would be truth delivered.

If I had been there with him, instead of pushing my way into the world, I would have told him that truth is bittersweet and fleeting, like just about anything else worth having.

Chapter 2

I wanted to love Jude the first time I saw him, but I wasn't sure I could. Beside a little boy whose mother wouldn't let him ride alone, Jude straddled a red pony with a painted-on green mane on the carousel in front of Value City Discount Center. He sat, stoic, a grown man going in circles. His back was curled like a capital C. His hands gripped the metal bars, and his feet were turned outward on the steel perches beneath them, his knees pushed up to his shoulders. As the mother looked on, the little boy smiled and clung to the blue pony's yellow mane, so excited that his whole body seemed to vibrate. Jude's eyes were moving, watching the cars angle in and out of parking spaces in between glances at the little boy. It was Saturday in Cornelia, and there were tube socks in packages of ten, jumbo jars of peanut butter, and pre-paid phone cards to buy. But Jude wasn't buying. When the ride ended and the boy's mother peeled him off the pony, Jude stayed on, putting another quarter in the metal box. He needed somebody to get him off that carousel, so I stood on the sidewalk and watched, wondering if it would be me.

"You look familiar," he said, as he passed me the fifteenth time. "Have I seen you fourteen times before?"

"Possibly," I said, trying not to smile.

"Fifteen's the charm," he said over his shoulder.

I counted six more revolutions before another little boy with a runny nose came to stand beside me, watching and sniffling until his mother called him away.

On the next revolution Jude said, "I think I might have vertigo."

"Does it feel like the world is going around and around?" I asked, moving a foot or so closer.

"Yes," he answered. Then he swung one leg over the pony so that he sat sidesaddle, his feet crossed out in front of him and suspended a few inches over the platform. Then he added, "Indigo. Flamingo. I can't think of any more words that end in go."

"Me either," I said, although "ego" came to mind. "Maybe that's an omen." I waited to see if he understood my flirt, but he didn't change expressions. At least the back of his neck, the slight protrusion of his ears beyond the mass of thick, brown hair, didn't change. He held up his hands up in the air, waving his palms, showing me that he was sure of his balance, that even price-slashing and curious strangers could not break his focus. I thought his hands were beautiful. Everybody else's seemed copycat fakes.

"Do you need another go round?" I asked when the ride stopped. I looked from him to the four empty horses. All were in need of paint—a smile that actually turned up, nostrils of equal size, or ears still pointed at the tips.

"I'll wait," he said, fighting a grin. "I just ate a bunch of popcorn. I don't want to throw up my allowance."

"Oh." I reached into my purse and found two quarters. I placed them on the flattened nose of the pony and smiled at him. "Just in case," I said. I wanted to see how he would unfold his body from that position, how that much melancholy could be gathered up and taken away.

He nodded. He slid the quarters toward him and then smiled back at me. "Money from strangers. My, my, my."

"Have a good ride," I said. When I came out twenty minutes later, he was gone, but on the way to my car, I passed him sitting in his, studying two photographs in his wallet as if he were preparing for a test.

I discovered Jude's bakery my sixth day of living in Cornelia. It had a wide storefront wedged between the weathered brick buildings of downtown, all eight blocks of it. Café curtains hung from brass rods along the bottom half of the windows. Black and white photographs of the town from earlier years decorated the eating area. But the best part was on the right side of the building, next to a small alley that attracted Cornelia's one shy graffiti artist. Here, through a thick pane of glass, a pedestrian could see straight into the kitchen. Here, I stood and watched Jude, mindful of the last man I had sex with, months earlier, when I decided that I would never act on lust again if something else didn't accompany it.

I started imagining the kind of man who would own a bakery. *What can I fix?* he would ask. And the answer would be hunger. He might consider "sugar biscuits" (otherwise known as scones), rhubarb tarts, and wedding cookies in perfect rows behind clean glass as offerings, chaos undone. Then he would dismiss all such nonsense and submerge his hands in dough, work to be done, whatever sad thoughts had driven him to that carousel no doubt creeping in.

There were two young men in the kitchen with Jude, both with sharp noses and white aprons tied in double knots around their waists. It was not quite a kitchen, not quite an office, with the obligatory pots and racks and a huge roll-top desk, a stoic beast with an enormous mouth full of paper. I watched Jude speak, his eyes blinking rapidly at what I suspected were the ends of sentences, when the other two bakers peeked into an oven or searched for a spatula in the wide drawer beside the sink.

A few minutes later, he tapped me on the shoulder from behind. I acted surprised, so that he wouldn't know I had been waiting for him.

"If you can't afford to come in, we thought we'd offer you something sweet on the house." He held out a plate of mini pecan pies.

"Thank you." I took one and rested it on my palm.

"Aren't you the woman from the store?" he asked. "From the carousel?"

"Yes. Frannie."

"I'm Jude. I owe you some quarters. You kept me a cowboy, remember?"

"I remember," I said, not sure he even meant the sexual innuendo. "You had the tame horse of the bunch."

He watched me eat, smiling, and then pointed to a crumb of piecrust trapped in the corner of my mouth.

"I'm saving that for later," I said.

"Beauty *and* practicality," he said, but it sounded almost wistful, like he was doubting one of the two.

We met for coffee that night, out of the rain, in the bakery. We sat at the table by the window, sipping from black porcelain mugs. Jude had closed early. A heavy-set man came to the door, jiggled the knob, and shot us a curious look. Jude only smiled and mouthed, "Sorry." The lights flickered on and off, which Jude said happened periodically when the tenants in the upstairs apartment used their state-of-the-art stereo equipment. Outside the window, headlights bent around the curve leading toward the interstate and then disappeared.

"When I was a child," he said, nodding his head toward the candle on the table, "my mother let us burn candles as part of a lesson. She used to tell us that electricity was expensive so we'd learn to turn out lights and not watch so much TV. For the longest time, I thought you bought electricity at the store, like meat or bread. Or it came in cans that had to be opened carefully so that none of it would spill out."

"Maybe that's why you own a bakery. So that nothing will go to waste."

"What about you? What did you think electricity was?" he asked.

"I thought it was piped in by some men turning a huge crank at the power station down the street from our house. Like an old phonograph player. I had seen one of those at my grandparents'. We used to pass the power station on the way to the grocery store. I'd always look. My mother would say, 'Look, there's where your lights come from. And the round and round of the attic fan. Aren't you glad that people are working so hard for you?'"

"Little people with tired hands."

"Yes, and hair that stood straight up on end."

"It took me a long time to realize that batteries weren't some evil plot," he said, shaking his head.

"It took me a long to realize that batteries even existed. My parents believed in effort, not convenience." *I* was proof of that, but I couldn't expect Jude to know it.

Jude smiled. The electricity returned suddenly. Music from a radio somewhere in the back of the room drifted toward us, and Jude tapped its rhythm against the table. I tried to count the specks of gray in his hair.

"Is that why you moved out here from Charlotte? Convenience?"

"Sort of. Is that why you rode the carousel? Trying to stay ahead of all those evil plots?"

"That would be impossible," he said quietly, leaving the last word suspended between us.

If houses did not hold spirits, I might not have ever moved to Cornelia. My house on Euclid Lane in Charlotte held the spirit of five failed relationships, one for each finger on each hand, one for each of the senses, not counting the sixth. I could chart the pattern, bad to worse, thumb to pinky. The first relationship, with a handsome man named Greg, ended in a Chinese restaurant that looked like a brothel, with fortune cookies so stale they could only tell the past. And after that was Edwin, a smart, shy man my mother nicknamed Ed-loser when he stopped calling me after a weekend in the mountains. The next two were practically interchangeable, Ted and Fred, nothing particularly poetic about the way I felt when each left me.

The last was Charlie, and I nearly loved him. He called every day, showed up when he was supposed to, and brought me small, eccentric gifts. One week longer, one more sentimental note pinned on the back of a vintage handkerchief, and he could have folded me up and kept me in his pocket alongside whatever plans he had for leaving. Because that's what he did—he left on a Monday morning, after a big breakfast of banana pancakes and orange juice. I went to take a shower, and when I came back to the kitchen, he was gone, although he had washed and dried his own plate and placed my silverware across mine, the way my mother had always insisted on. He was the first man who made me start imagining what our child might look like, so when he left, he took an olive-skinned, green-eyed baby girl with him.

All of these men lived in my house, their wrongness propping its elbows on my dining room table, its smelly feet on the couch. It just took me a while to understand that it wasn't their five spirits, but mine. Five different variations of my spirit, all staring back at me, hair tousled, eyes reddened, in the medicine cabinet over the bathroom sink, suspicious of each other, competing against each other, wondering when circumstances would change. Circumstance. It is the reason so many things don't get done. If you leave your life to circumstance, you leave your life.

I left my house instead. I sold it on a Monday, after three months of strangers walking through, three months of cleaning every day until I could see myself, more and more myself, reflected, sometimes tall and thin, sometimes short and squat, on any surface, like a house full of carnival mirrors. Then I had an estate sale, when more strangers walked through the rooms, claiming the velvet loveseat I had bought from a thrift store, clicking the iron floor lamp on and off so that all those spirits, all five of them, were cast not only in dispersion but in fickle light. When the last person left and I had tallied the sales— $1496—I got in my car and drove to Cornelia. I bought the second house I looked at that afternoon. My real estate agent, a thin, nervous man with paisley suspenders, was stunned that a woman who started saving for retirement at eleven could be so impulsive. "Once, at a restaurant," I added with a smile, "I chose Thousand Island salad dressing without knowing my other options."

The house was small, with casement windows that opened outward. Each room I walked through, I went directly to the window and turned the iron handle until the aged paint released the metal frame, imagining the entire room breathing one huge sigh. Eight sighs. Eight long, earned sighs, for it had been empty and shut up tight for almost a year after the elderly owners moved to Arizona to find air that wasn't fat with humidity. Outside, there were flowerbeds that bordered both sides of the deep backyard. Hydrangea bushes that I would revive, whose blossoms were brown and brittle as old paper. Clumps of monkey grass that looked like green pom-poms with withered ends. A double clothesline with eight wooden clothespins clipped down its middle, a row of strange, permanent birds.

"It makes me want to wash a whole bunch of white things," I said to the agent.

He rubbed his chin, not commenting.

"I want to buy the house, though," I added, "before I hang out my laundry. I think that's better, don't you?"

"You Southerners do like things in their proper order," he said. "I'll write the contract."

When I moved in a month later, I imagined one long white sheet stretched down the center of the yard. I would start at the farthest end and wrap my body in it until all the white belonged to me, until only the smallest edge trailed behind me, like a hesitant ghost, or a wedding veil.

My mother came for her first visit the morning after my date with Jude. She parked her sedan in the driveway behind my car. She believed that only relatives could take such liberties with driveways, while the curb was for strangers, repairmen, or friends, whichever the case may be. I stood in the doorway and watched her. As she followed the sidewalk to the front steps, she let her eyes scan the grass and then turned to find the mailbox. She did not believe in plastic mailboxes. Milk, CDs, makeup, all of it fine in plastic, but not the mail, which was the most dependable thing she knew.

"You should have brought Daddy," I said, kissing her cheek so that I wouldn't smear her lipstick.

"He's under the weather. He'll come next time."

"What's wrong?"

"Oh, I think it's just a touch of that stomach flu." She patted her own and then looked me up and down. "You appear to be a homeowner," she said.

"I was a homeowner before. What's different?"

She shrugged and climbed the last step to the landing. "I don't see what was wrong with Charlotte. Your job was there."

"My job is wherever the computer is. I've been working at home for months now. The only difference is home is now Cornelia. I needed a change."

"Well," she said, the word that chronicled all. Her signal that we had reached a place in the conversation where going further might disappoint her.

My parents never asked about the missing parts of my life. They must have filled them in all on their own, dodging the inherent discomfort. They must have given me a husband who never worked weekends, a man's man for my father, someone who lifted and protected, and a gardener for my mother. They must have said, "Two children, two children is fine," a little sister for the protective older one. They must have assigned me higher cheekbones and ethical standards to match. All these things could be shared. It was what they didn't talk about that was most important, lying beside each other in bed at night, pillows propped behind them, blaming each other for what they weren't able to give me.

"I haven't met any of the neighbors yet," I told her. "I hope they're nice."

"There are nice people and nice houses everywhere."

Inside, she rubbed my arm, unbuttoned the top of her jacket, and began her examination. I let her wander through the house alone. I counted her steps—three in the kitchen to the refrigerator, which she would open and shut with quick observation, mindful of eggs rolling dangerously in the produce crispers, three kinds of cheap beer on the bottom shelf. Five steps in the front bedroom to the closet to see if the winter coats were wrapped in plastic, if the block of cedar, a yearly gift in the Christmas stocking my parents still hung for me, was indeed deterring moths. Seven steps in the office to the far bookcase to see if the photograph of me at the zoo when I was nine, the last year I could get away with horizontal stripes without joining a posse of clowns or Weight Watchers, still sat on top. It did—I had made certain.

"It's a fine house, but your father would want a second bathroom," she said, from the hallway that was wide enough for the upright piano I had seen in an antique store. On the inside leg, someone had carved "Yes." That one word alone.

Her heels clicked back toward the living room. She was wearing black pants that stopped at the ankles, sporting little cut V's at the hem, and a plaid shirt with the same light brown as her hair. I had her thin body and long limbs, but not her obedient hair, which grew with the ends curled toward her neck in perfect symmetry while mine hung coarse and straight. "Your mother's hair looks like a punch bowl. Always has," my father said to me at my cousin's wedding as he stood over one, dipping into something mixed with ginger ale that made him want to dance.

"And he wouldn't like that electric stove. Gas is better."

"Don't tell him," I said, teasing. "I'll draw flames around the burners."

She stopped in the doorway and returned her purse to the crook of her elbow. "I believe that he is having me followed."

"Daddy is having you followed?"

"There's a man in a big blue car three houses down. It was behind me when I pulled onto the street and it stopped and parked. The driver's just sitting inside."

"Noooo," I said, shaking my head.

"Yes," she said curtly.

"What are you doing that would make Daddy have someone follow you?"

"Don't mock me," she said quietly. "You don't know that I'm not up to something."

"Please don't be up to something. Please tell me that this is just one of those things that he does every once in awhile for whatever unknown reason he might have. Like the carnival or those crazy glasses."

She stared straight at me and then added, "It's my turn to be up to something."

"It's nobody's turn," I said. "I'll go down there and talk to the man in the car."

She looked stunned. "He's not going to talk to you if he's following me."

"Mama, that's crazy talking."

She thought for a second. "We'll go together."

"Okay. That sounds like a semi-crazy plan."

I hoped that all neighbors I hadn't yet met were watching from their windows, watching the new woman with the mismatched furniture and trim, nervous mother strolling down the sidewalk. Elbow to elbow, we passed two houses without speaking, both sets of our eyes fixed on the blue car at the end of the street, parked across from the house with one shutter that hung crooked as a smile.

My mother stopped and pulled me to her, and for a second I thought she would turn around and go back. We were a few yards from the car, whose driver folded over the edge of a newspaper to stare at us. "There's someone in the backseat, too," my mother said sadly.

It was my father. He wore the corduroy cap left from his days right after the Navy, when photographs captured him dressed like a foreigner, someone who wanted to fit in but couldn't. I left my mother standing on the curb and marched up to the back window, which he rolled down with the exaggerated motion of a man caught. He was already a small man, but the absence of things—his briefcase, maps, mint packages—that cluttered his own car made him even smaller. And the car was a Lincoln, the closest thing to the length of a ship that still rolled.

"Daddy," I said.

"Frannie."

"Whose car is this?"

"I tried to rent a limo. Then I changed my mind and got the Lincoln. It's a rental car, and this is Mr. Brewer, my professional driver." He nodded toward the man behind the newspaper, who pivoted his body to tilt his head in greeting. The radio was on, turned down so low that it didn't really count. A car passed slowly in front of us.

By now, my mother had moved to stand behind me. I could smell her hairspray. She moved in closer and rested her head on my shoulder so that she could get a better look at her husband.

"Lane, you look pretty," he said. "I like that scarf."

"I like this scarf, too," she said, without lifting her head so that I could feel her chin bumping against my shoulder.

I knew that my father was not following my mother, had no deception in mind, although he had probably charged the Lincoln on a third credit card with the highest interest rate yet, one my mother did not know he had, just to make himself pay it off. And he didn't have a stomach ache after all. There was a pervasive pain, a kind of aching that had bothered him lately, never really settling anywhere, obliged to nothing. But he could explain that. In fact, he had come to explain that, assuming my mother was off on her usual list of Saturday errands, which he didn't think included a visit to me. The Lincoln was an afterthought, an excuse to be decadent. A distraction.

"I came to surprise Frannie," he ended. "I want to take her for a ride to celebrate her new house."

"Usually people do that *in* the house, and with a gift," my mother said.

"Well," he replied.

All in all, my mother took the announcement with her usual fortitude, never asking to tag along, and walked back to her car. She passed us and waved, and we waved back, as did Mr. Brewer, although he didn't seem to mean it.

My father opened the door for me and slid to the far side of the backseat. "Is your house locked? Want to go for a ride?"

"I'll go for a short ride. Where to?"

"Charlotte too far?"

"Okay. Can we stop and get a mop? I need a mop."

"I can get you a mop," Mr. Brewer said, not missing a beat, and started the car.

When I was a child and all I knew of my father outside of our house was that he was a banker, I used to tell him that his mind was filled with numbers I could see when I looked down into his ears or up into his furry nostrils. I *heard* them, rattling around, bumping into each number, multiplication through proximity. From then on, from time to time, he would shake his head and then say, "Numero uno," his nickname for me. And the game spilled over into his very speech. "Chances are," he'd say when my mother asked about the weather. "The numbers are good," he said when he sorted laundry and triumphed with pairs of socks, each mate just like the other. "You bet," he said when he was asked if he was coming, caught lagging behind in the grocery store, at parties, or overdue for dinner.

Words, those things I corrected in my work, proved to be fickle, but I knew that numbers were tough. Tough and true. My father knew this, too. That's why he started with them.

"Frannie, I've always regretted that you were an only child. But the number one is the leader number, the most defiant number there is. Numero Uno. It's made you strong."

"Or isolated."

"Strong," he affirmed.

"What's wrong, Daddy?" I asked. "You seem very worried."

Mr. Brewer turned up the radio and the thick, long notes of R&B filled the car. Outside, the world moved slowly and predictably. The stoplight would change on the count of forty. The group of kids waiting to cross would disperse, two by two, at the far corner. The Mini Mart would charge three times what it should for a pint of milk.

My father reached in his back pocket and extracted his wallet. He waved a $20 bill in front of me as we pulled out into the Saturday shopping traffic on Grand Avenue. "See this?"

"Twenty dollars."

"I've had it for eighteen years."

"The same bill?"

He nodded. "It came from Greg Meadows."

"My prom date in high school?"

"He didn't get a limo for you, and when he brought you home, I went out the back door and met him at his car. I made him give me twenty dollars, a quarter of the price of a limo for the night." He looked proud of himself.

"No way. Besides, he ran from the door to the car. I saw him."

"I told him," my father continued, "that one day I would rent you a limo so that you would have the experience."

"That's pretty sad. That you thought I wouldn't ever get the chance again."

"You won't get the chance again for the prom."

"I hope not," I said. "Did you really get that money from Greg Meadows?"

My father offered his best half-smile and folded the bill. "No. I thought about it but decided that it would embarrass you. I did, however, have a chat with him at the car."

"Daddy, I never even liked him. He looked like some forgotten country music singer. His hair was as spiked as the punch and he chewed gum the whole night."

"He told me he was afraid of you." He looked apologetic, the corners of his mouth set.

"What about me could possibly have made him afraid?"

"Your confidence perhaps. The fact that you're beautiful and smart, too."

"He was just trying to squeeze out of an uncomfortable situation. Neither one of us had a good time, and we were both ashamed."

He sighed, which meant he had something he wanted to say, but didn't.

"God knows that was a long time ago. Still, you should have had a limo for the prom."

"Or a Lincoln." I patted the seat between us. Mr. Brewer glanced at me via the rearview mirror and winked.

"Or a Lincoln." There was a hollowness in my father's voice, and I realized that he was disappointed, truly disappointed—the prom had actually meant more to him than it had to me. I had gone only because I had wanted to impress my mother, to wear a long dress, to pin up my hair with barrettes overlaid with real roses her friend Martha cut from her garden. My father had taken photographs, I remembered, but at the time I thought it was something he did only to appease my mother, who stood behind him motioning me to smile.

We came to another stoplight. Mr. Brewer waved at the man driving the car next to us, allowing him to pull into the lane in front of it, the Lincoln's silver hood ornament catching the glint of the sun. "Go on then," he said, finally tapping his horn and motioning one more time for the car to pull ahead before singing a few words from a song I didn't recognize.

"Would you like to go downtown?" my father asked. "Downtown," I knew, meant my father's office, as if the entire center of a city had compressed into a twenty-by-twenty space with gray carpet and mediocre art where my father still talked numbers.

Twelve miles of concrete and twenty minutes later, we glided into the parking lot adjacent to my father's building, which towered shiny and new, like most of downtown Charlotte. He got out and sat on the front bumper, the cap still on his head and the city's skyline just over his left shoulder. "I have given in to nostalgia," he said. "I think the only other time you've ever been down here was a few times as a child," he added.

I thought about it and nodded. "There was that time when Mama was sick and you took me to work."

"I remember that." I followed my father's eyes to the side of the parking attendant's small brick house. With spray paint someone had written, "Keri loves you all night long." My father leaned closer to read it.

"Keri needs to spell her name right," he said.

"She's too tired to spell. She's been up all night."

He chuckled. "Let's sit here for awhile." My father nodded toward a bench outside the attendant's building and sat down. He was beginning to sweat, and he unbuttoned his shirt one button. His usual plain white T-shirt, which he ironed each morning standing in his boxers and reading the newspaper spread out on the counter beside him, was not underneath. In its place was a light gray T-shirt, words barely visible across the front.

"What's that, Daddy?" I asked, pointing to the V of his open shirt neck.

"Oh," he said, looking down, clearly remembering our game. "That would be some script." He pressed his oxford shirt, "blue for banker," as he always described it, to his body.

I squinted and tried to read the black letters through the fabric of the button-up. "What does it say?"

"It says, 'Where did the carnival go?'"

"Good question," I said.

Up until the last five or so years, my father had a summer dalliance with a traveling carnival, something my mother and I had never understood, at the very least, and long resented, if the truth be told. "Where'd you get it?"

He brushed some dirt from the spot next to him and patted his hand there for me to join him. "A friend gave it to me." He did not smile, not even the plastic smile he used with people he didn't like.

"Okay," I said, sighing. "So, what's up, Daddy? What's going on?"

Behind us, Mr. Brewer shut the car door and started walking across the parking lot, his hands thrust in his pockets, the edge of an afro peeking out from under his cap.

My father spoke slowly. "Frannie, I've got cancer."

"You're sick?" I felt my heart drop, like a bad elevator.

He nodded.

"What kind of cancer?" I imagined someone else—someone with her own father to answer, not mine—asking the question.

He took out a comb from his back pocket and quickly ran it through his hair, which had always curled in S patterns in the summertime. "I went to the doctor's," he said, placing the comb back out of view, "for the second time this week. They had some tests come back and, well, it's in my lungs, both of them, and it's right bad."

"Lung cancer?"

"Yes, that's right."

"Are they sure? I mean, it's for sure?"

"Yes."

"What about an operation?"

He nodded and uncrossed his legs. "They'll do that. And chemotherapy."

"When?"

"Next week. I'll be admitted on Monday."

I nodded, forcing tears to stay put. "You don't deserve this."

"I have a list of herbs to try," he said. "I'm going to combine the traditional with the non-traditional. There's got to be a happy middle."

"A happy middle." He had been attempting that position as long as I could remember—how odd that he needed it to happen now. "Have you not told Mama yet?"

"I'll tell her tonight, but Frannie, I don't want her to know how bad it is. Not right away." He sternly shook his head.

"What do you mean? You have to tell her."

"I'll tell her I have the cancer, but I don't want her to think I'm going to die."

"You're not going to die." I said it with conviction, the only deterrent I knew for tragedy.

He shuffled his feet under the bench, exposing a caravan of ants. "Yes, I think I am."

"No," I said. I looked around me, as if the woman scurrying across the parking lot to her minivan was going to stop and cast the deciding vote, agreeing with me, declaring him immortal.

"Okay," he said, rebuttoning his shirt.

"Do you want to die?" I said it mean, landing hard on each word.

He shrugged his shoulders. "It doesn't really matter one way or the other," he said quickly. "The world will still go on."

"Then why the operation and the chemo and the herbs?" I asked, realizing I was angry at his answer.

"Because I owe that to you."

"And Mama?"

"And to your mother."

He stood up slowly and walked toward the building. "I'm not giving up, Frannie. But I know that I don't control it."

"You're going to have to tell Mama," I called out after him.

He turned just slightly. "I'll work on it," he called back.

I sat back on the bench, stunned, and watched my father disappear beyond the double glass doors. I spent the next ten minutes thinking of all the things mightier than cancer and hoping one was my father, another me. When he returned, two folders under his arm, I told him about another. "Daddy, I've met a man," I said.

"Oh?" He leaned toward me. "A nice one?"

"A nice one. His name is Jude."

"Jude? What kind of name is that?" This was a question typical of my father. The noun could be anything—"Subaru? What kind of car is that?" or "Amstel Light? What kind of beer is that?"—as long as it was something new for him to consider.

"It's short for Judson. He's a baker."

"It's serious?"

"Well, he makes a living off it."

My father smiled.

"No, it's not serious," I said. "I just met him. But there's a lot of potential."

"Well, that's nice, Frannie." He put his hand over mine on the bench, and then tapped the top of it several times, as if it were a cantaloupe. "I'll get to meet him, won't I?"

"Maybe," I said.

"Good."

"He's shorter than you," I said.

"Is that a worry?" He puffed out his chest.

"No, it's something that just occurred to me."

"If I do meet him, let's not tell him yet."

"About the cancer."

"I think it might be nice for him just to meet me, not the disease. One at a time."

"Okay," I agreed.

"Besides, it's been a long time since you've brought anyone to meet us. I'm out of practice."

"Just tell Mama no photos for the boyfriend album."

"Now *that* I'll tell her."

"Would you let me drive the Lincoln?" I called out to Mr. Brewer, who appeared from the back of the parking lot with a Coke in his hand.

"I can't do that, I'm afraid."

"I have not been drinking, and I only speed when I'm running late, which I'm not. And I just want to drive for a couple of blocks."

"Can't do it," he said again. He did not sound sorry.

I half-jogged to where he stood and looked up at him, remembering to smile. "My father has cancer, and I want to drive him around the block or so in the Lincoln Town Car. Please."

He stopped sipping and looked hard at me, no doubt not accustomed to that kind of announcement, given that luxury rental cars are generally for happier occasions. I waited while he thought. "If you hit something, I reckon I'll be working for my cousin Will, cutting grass and raking leaves."

"You will not be working for your cousin Will, I promise."

He tossed his can into a metal bin and adjusted his hat. "I'm going to let you drive for a maximum of nine blocks. That's one mile, according to most calculations. I will be counting."

"I hope that you will be in the back seat counting," I said. "But thank you."

We walked one behind the other back to the car. "I get to drive," I told my father.

"Why's that?"

"Because I want to."

"But you haven't been upstairs yet." He wiped his forehead with a handkerchief that he pulled from his pocket.

"This is your place of work," I said. "We are not interested in work right now."

He got in the passenger seat without saying anything else. I started the engine and caught Mr. Brewer smiling when I glanced in the rearview mirror. He waved his fingers at me and looked away.

"Don't hit anything, Frannie," my father said.

Two days later, when I drove my own car back to Charlotte, to talk to my mother, I still had not hit anything, although I had kissed Jude and admired the future and decided that the best way to scare off death was to remind it of what it wasn't. When my mother, who, despite my father's efforts, had already figured out the gravity of his illness, suggested that I move back, I refused, thinking of Jude. When she put a hand on either of my shoulders and stared me so hard in the eye that whatever little bits and parts of me were floating around unattended finally merged, she said, "Have a baby, Frannie. It will make him happy, give him something to look forward to," I agreed, thinking first of my father and then of Jude, working my way to myself.

Chapter 3

My mother sat me down at her kitchen table, my father asleep in his recliner in the den, and excused me from the larger moral constraints she had taught me my whole life, which included everything from using Woolite on the gentle cycle to the conventional cycle of events that led to a family. "We will assume that the child will eventually have a father," she said. "But for now, I believe you will be just fine."

"Thank you," I said. "From what I understand, I'll have to have sex to get a baby. Do I have your permission to have sex?" Twenty-five years earlier, she had given me an abbreviated biology lesson, using a glue stick and napkin ring. When I worried about the glue, she said, "Til death do us part," a joke I almost understood that very day. But right now, she was a woman who could not tease or be teased.

She glanced toward the den and lowered her voice. "Not necessarily. There are sperm banks. It makes sense. Your father, after all, has always placed his faith in banks."

"He's placed his faith in the ocean, Mama. Or he left it there and has not gone back to get it."

She looked hurt and then added, "That still doesn't change our plan."

I didn't correct her about the "our" because, as far as I understood it, one person and one person only carries and delivers a baby. I didn't tell her that if there was going to be an "our," it would be the baby and me, although Jude did keep making cameo appearances in my imagination. Instead, I took her hand and led her to the doorway between the kitchen and den, where there were still faint indentations from my father's pocketknife, his annual records of my growth. I nodded toward my father, turned slightly on his left side, one cheek flattened against the brown leather. "Mama, that is a man to whom you need to give your all right now. Your all and my all are separate and different. And not equal." I meant it as a compliment, but she looked hurt anyway.

My mother had not applied makeup that morning, and her mouth had tiny lines emanating from all around it, like a childish depiction of a sun. She let go of my hand and walked back to the kitchen, suddenly nostalgic. "When you came along, you changed everything."

"That's a baby's job," I said.

She took the coffee filter from the machine, stuffed it into the disposal, and flipped the switch beside the sink, squinting as the disposal grated. She was as thin and willowy at sixty-one as she had been as a young woman, but her body was hardening vertically, softening laterally. Her long torso now tilted slightly but stiffly forward, perhaps, now that my father was sick, leaning into the future to see if she could get a look.

She turned off the disposal and said, without looking at me, "That's why people have children. To help them find where they should put their faith."

"I don't think most people think it through all that much, Mama. That's why this is a little overwhelming. It's not very thought out. A week ago I didn't have a huge plan. I didn't have a plan at all."

"It's always good to have a plan," she said, smoothing the front of her pants.

"I don't think I should tell Daddy about this until it happens. *If* it happens."

"Of course not," she said.

I knew that my father, like my mother, believed in order, even if it had to be interrupted from time to time. "Daddy might want me to have the good ole nuclear family."

"Your father hid under his desk in elementary school the last time he heard that word," she said. "But he does believe in tradition."

"Who knows?" I said, moving further away from the door. "I could meet the perfect man, and he could be the perfect father." I tucked all of Jude into that statement, afraid to use his name.

"No such thing," my mother said decisively. At that, we ended the conversation, falling back on what we always had: silence, absence really, which had lived like a guest, unnamed, in our house for so long that I nearly loved it as my own.

I was about to turn thirteen when my mother had the baby who would have been my sister. Two days before Valentine's, when I was still hoping to be asked to the school dance, I came home to find my mother sitting in the living room with a stranger, a door-to-door broom salesman with a walrus moustache and a bald head. He held out his hand and said, "Jim Marble" when she introduced me as her oldest daughter. She had been saying for months that the baby was a girl, although it was before sonograms replaced intuition.

My mother sat on the couch, her stomach protruding a foot or so in front of her. She was nearly eight months pregnant. Her thick ankles were hidden under stretch maternity pants that could have doubled as a tent. But while her body had rounded, expanded, and shifted, week by week, her face had not. Her cheekbones were as defined as ever, and the double chin she had complained she had acquired with me never happened. It was as if she had told her body that all signs of pregnancy must stop at the neck.

"Frannie," she said, "the baby is going to change this house, so I'm buying lots of new things to go along with it." She patted her stomach. "Including new brooms with no germs." The Beatles were playing on the stereo console.

Mr. Marble held out a red-handled broom to me. "Try it. It sweeps itself, it glides so smooth."

"Smoothly," I said under my breath. I took the broom and walked over to the edge of the carpet, running it a few times across the hardwood floor of the hallway.

"Very smooth," I said, handing it back to Mr. Marble. He made me feel uncomfortable, even though my mother seemed happy.

"That broom craves music. That's why I asked your mother here to put on a record. With music, that broom practically seduces the floor."

At this, my mother sat upright and raised her eyebrows, the very same expression she would wear when I told her about my first date. I moved toward her on the couch, but Mr. Marble caught my arm as I walked past. "Do you dance, Frannie?"

My mother began to rock herself to her feet. Mr. Marble turned and held out his hand. She took it, hesitantly, and wrapped an arm around my shoulder when she was upright. "Frannie's never really learned," she said.

"Well, anybody can learn," he said. He held the same red broom out in front of him and moved two steps to the right, counting, "One, two, one, two." He swept his free hand in front of him. A thick gold bracelet fell out from beneath his jacket sleeve. I wanted my mother to tell him to leave, and then I wanted us to go upstairs and work out our strategy for the school dance. Would I go alone? Would I finally get up the nerve to call the boy who lived two streets over and had occasional sneezing attacks?

"This is not even the way we dance," I said.

"Come on," Mr. Marble said. "It all translates."

I followed his steps. In front of the velvet-covered couch, my mother moved slowly in a square-like pattern, the corners of her mouth loose, her right hand gripped around the handle of the broom, and her left one poised in an imaginary shoulder. "I haven't danced in forever," she said, more to herself than either of us. "It's not easy to move this much stomach. Good thing my partner is so skinny."

I watched the two of them, strangers to each other, dance, until the stereo needle found the scratch on the album. My mother stopped, leaned her broom up against the console and reached down inside. But the record kept going. I spun around and saw my mother clasp both hands to the console, lowering her weight down to her knees, her head bowed toward her stomach. Her knuckles were purple.

I rushed to help her up as Mr. Marble looked on in stunned dismay. "Mama?"

She did not lift her head to speak. Instead, she collapsed on her side. "The baby."

Mr. Marble bumped my arm as he leaned over to touch my mother's shoulder. "Are you all right? Aren't you all right?" He must have asked her seven or eight times, but she never answered. I raced to the kitchen to call my father.

He arrived a few minutes later, his tie crooked and his jacket absent, more stunned and disheveled than I wanted him to be. Mr. Marble had disappeared, but in his place were two ambulance drivers with a stretcher scurrying up the sidewalk. From the steps, I saw my mother reach a hand out from under the white blanket. My father held it as the men carried her to the ambulance. He walked the ten or so yards alongside her. Then the stretcher disappeared into the ambulance like a baking tray into an oven. My father shouted, "Frannie, you stay here. I'll call you. Stay here."

I nodded. I spent the next two hours sitting in the living room, making a list of all the reasons I should go to the dance but wouldn't. It became, however, a list of all the reasons the baby might not have wanted to be born, which began with dentist's visits and ended with me.

When my father came home about ten o'clock, he walked to the refrigerator, put his palm on the handle, and then took it back. He extracted all the contents of his pants pockets—money, mints, slips of paper—and placed each item on the counter in front of my mother's flour and sugar canisters. The last was a bottle of hospital hand lotion.

"How's Mama?" I asked, my back pressed against the countertop.

"She's going to be okay, Frannie. But she's going to be sad." He stood beside me and pressed his back against the Formica, too.

"The baby died," I said softly.

He turned to look directly at me, although I didn't think he really saw me. His eyes had been replaced by dull gray. "Yes, the baby died. A little girl," he said, barely aloud.

"What happened to the baby? Where is she? Did she cry when she was born?"

"She was born dead, Frannie." He slapped his hands on the countertop and then tapped his fingernails several times. The fluorescent light above the sink flickered. A small gasp escaped his mouth. I waited for him to hug me, or to squeeze my shoulders, as he often did to show me he approved of some decision I had just made. But he didn't. He walked out of the kitchen and into his bedroom. The door clicked shut. The house waited. The silence crept in.

The next morning, he knocked on my bedroom door and said, without opening it, "No school today, Frannie. You can go to the hospital to see your mother."

"Okay," I called back. I lay in bed and thought about what I would say to my mother. *I'm sorry. I'm sorry that I wasn't enough and will now have to be enough.* My adolescent bravado aside, I never said these things to anyone but myself.

My father drove us to the hospital with all four of the windows cracked. My mother was asleep when we arrived. I watched my father stick his head in the door and then dig in his pocket for a dime. "I'll be right back," he said, disappearing down the corridor into a mass of sea-green bodies.

I crept into the room, the thin slits of light seeping through the pulled blinds. My mother immediately lifted her head and said, "Frannie." She was pale. The oxygen tube in her nose made it appear as if some invisible hand was flattening it.

"Mama. You're awake. I thought you were asleep."

She half-closed her eyes and barely shook her head. "No. I was faking it."

"Why?"

She gently ruffled the ends of my fingers. "Oh, my," she said. "I suppose I didn't want to talk to your father."

"Daddy?"

"I can see it in his eyes." She pressed the sheets tight against each side of her body. I looked at her stomach, which was only a little smaller than it had been the day before.

"Where is she?" I asked quietly, not sure if it would make her angry or not.

"She'll be buried. Just like anybody else."

I nodded my head in understanding. "I'm sorry, Mama."

With this, my mother began to cry. "Yes, I'm sorry for you. For you and for me." I reached for and held her hand until my father returned. When his face appeared in the door's rectangular window, she sniffled, raised herself up in bed, and ran her fingers around her eyes. "You're my only girl, Frannie," she said, reaching to hug me. "My only girl."

That night, my mother called me from the hospital to tell me she would be coming home the next day. "I want you to think about the dress you want for the dance," she said.

"Nobody's asked me, Mama."

"You need to be prepared just in case," she replied, her voice stretched thin. When I didn't respond, she added, "Because you're my girl," and ended the conversation. I replaced the receiver and listened to the sounds of my father in the bedroom next to mine, what had been the guest bedroom transformed into a nursery. He was taking down the crib and the bassinet, hauling them piece by piece to the basement.

Ten minutes later, the telephone rang. It was a boy from my school calling to ask me to the dance. Eric, the one who worked in the biology lab and had dirty fingernails. I told him yes, although I didn't like the way he wouldn't look at me when we had talked. It must have been his style, for when we danced that Friday night, with red hearts suspended by ribbon from the school cafeteria ceiling, he held me far from him, a continent of empty, wasted space. "You could be my girl," he said once, awkwardly, during a slow song, but I pretended I didn't hear him. I silently counted the tiny flowers printed across the bodice of the dress my mother had bought me the day she returned from the hospital. At the end of the dance, he plucked a red heart from the ceiling. I thought he might offer it to me, but instead he tossed it to the floor, already crunchy with trash to be swept up the following morning.

I discovered that my own quiet street in Cornelia had a gauge against which to measure just about anything, and it was called motherhood. I was apart from it, outside it. Because it wasn't yet mine, I studied it. In the late afternoons, when chickens were roasting in ovens and the first stream of after-work traffic returning from Charlotte began challenging the four-way stop sign four blocks from my house, mothers, with their babies strapped into three-wheeled strollers or wedged against their hips, gathered in front of the house two down and across from mine. These women had shoulder-length blonde hair or dark hair with bangs and layers that effortlessly framed their faces, and thin bodies that seemed hardly capable of having held another human being. They stood in a circle, intimate but not solemn. Occasionally, one would point down the street, and they all would look, squinting eyes, one foot turned out to support the baby lifted with practiced ease. How easy it all seemed—the responsibility of life—when so much of it was clumped together, for I seldom noticed much about one lone mother maneuvering her child up the sidewalk.

But in numbers, as my father could tell you, everything changed. In numbers, mothers' fears of illness, of mediocrity, were softened, hidden in the soft folds of so much baby flesh. In numbers, their triumphs and defeats co-mingled, one complete spoken sentence or successful potty session trumped by a day of preschool where ducklings, talking trains, and all things tender sometimes weren't. There was so much motherhood, so much compared to my one tiny decision to join them, that I couldn't imagine walking up to the group and infiltrating, expecting their automatic approval without having earned it. It didn't seem right. But I could imagine a baby. A baby seemed right. I didn't realize how much of my life revolved around longing until the possibility of a baby arrived, giving that longing substance, as if the child—

a prodigy even before conception—had taken the prettiest crayon from the box and colored me in.

But I would not visit, or even walk past, a sperm bank. I made a list of men whom I would consider as a father for my child. I was still a list maker, my whole life a stack of accumulated experiences with no theme in sight. This new list was much more directed; it contained two people, a man I had known since childhood, and, of course, Jude. I went to Hugh first, surprising him in his studio on a weekday morning, when a whole set of dinner plates was baking in the kiln and a train was passing outside the beveled windowpanes where kudzu had built its empire.

My father must have been impressed with Hugh, who grew to be very much like his father Davies had been, tall and solid, built like an old oak tree. But Hugh was not drawn to, and would not be lured to, water, and thought "ship" was a better verb than noun. He was not good at being passive, sure that the world would follow his command, which it generally did. He had always kept his light brown hair in a ponytail. When we had met as children, it was long in the back, the best rebellion he could manage. A few years later, when we attended the same high school, the ponytail became defiant, and even years after that, I once caught him removing a rubber band from two stalks of broccoli at the grocery store so that he could keep up the tradition.

That was the night he spent at my apartment, my first apartment as a working woman out of college, set for the future, sure of myself. I would complete the picture with, a bold act of casual sex. It had been years since Hugh and I had sex for the first time when I was eighteen. Afterward, I decided once again that it meant nothing, that it didn't even feel right, although the ease of always being able to go to Hugh was there. We spent the rest of the night discussing the ways that we were and were not connected, not including the very recent sex. Our lives had overlapped for years, but only we knew this. If, long ago, my mother had suspected that Hugh was my father's child, we always knew that he wasn't. Still, as children we made a pact to keep our relationship secret from our parents—what began as a childish power play grew into a friendship that never conceded to change. It was something so familiar that, even as an adult, I liked its secrecy, how I could, in some ways, keep Hugh all to myself.

Hugh heard me slam the metal door and turned from the work-table where he was mixing glazes. It was nearly as cold inside as it was outside. He hadn't turned on the industrial heaters that hung from the ceiling like big boxes wrapped in tin foil.

"Hey," I said.

He smiled and stood to kiss me on the forehead. "Hey," he replied, dragging it out to almost two syllables, making fun of an accent I didn't think I had. He brushed off dried specks of paint from the stool next to him and motioned for me to sit, pulling out the imaginary back and then pretending to push me in toward the table.

"I didn't call first."

"No, you didn't. But you never have. If you called first, I'd feel obligated to think about what I should do before you got here. I'd have to make fondue or something."

"Or shave?"

He looked around the studio and shrugged his shoulders. "The kid next door said I looked like a Chia pet. Why would I mess with that?"

"You wouldn't," I said, trying to look stern.

He bent down to tilt the bucket of glaze, his St. Christopher medal swinging forward.

"Did I catch you in the middle of an order?"

"Nah. Just stuff for a show next month."

"The one in Florida?"

"Yep." He studied me for a second. "I like your hair longer."

"You've still got two or three inches on me." I had been thinking a lot about Hugh's hair, probably because I knew that soon, with the chemo killing the good along with the bad, my father would have little, if any.

"You still unattached?" I asked him this question every time I saw him, even if *I* wasn't, and he always answered the same.

"Pretty much so. I told you," he said, "that after the divorce, I might be single forever. I'm not good at undoing." He put the cap back on a tube and wiped his palms on his jeans. He was the kind of man that women would stare at on the street, not so much because he was handsome but because he was earnest. He was ever present.

"Somebody'll snatch you up again."

"Snatch. Is that a real word?"

"Yep," I said. "As real as anything else."

"What's wrong? That's a Frannie segue if I've ever heard one."

"Hugh, Daddy's sick," I said.

"What kind of sick?"

"Cancer."

He leaned toward me, one palm planted on his knee. "Is it bad?"

I told him everything, highlighting the good news, how the operation had taken nearly three hours and the doctors emerged from the swinging doors to describe the cancer as "contained but extensive." My mother said that sounded more like a wildfire. I said thank you and didn't bother with interpreting. My father had come out of recovery, awake and punchy, even winking at one of the nurses who had been especially kind to him. He told her she was too pretty to have a tattoo, which she did, on the inside of her wrist, a little star whose five points were no bigger than dots.

Hugh shook his head. The telephone rang, but he glanced at it and then at me, swishing his hand when the machine picked up. "Is he back at home now?"

"He will be tomorrow."

"Does my mother know?"

"I'm not sure. But that's not why I'm here." I waited for him to look at me, which he did, hopefully, curiously. "I came to ask you if you would consider having a baby with me."

He jerked his body back, nearly toppling the stool. "Did you say baby or Bombay, as in martini?"

"I did not say Bombay, although if we have a baby, I would prefer a martini over a cigar."

"Dry, with an olive branch," he said, cocking his head.

"You think I'm making peace with my father?"

He shook his head. "I think you're making peace with someone. Not sure who. Maybe death."

"I'm afraid he's going to give up, Hugh. He wants it for me, a baby, I know he does. But a grandbaby would give *him* something to look forward to. It's not like he's got other kids. I'm it. Unless we count you."

"He's not my father."

"Not really, no, but sort of."

He tugged at his collar, classic Hugh thinking mode. "Why me?"

"Because I know you. Because in some weird kind of way, it seems to make sense."

"So our first pact's still on or off?"

"The first pact doesn't seem so necessary anymore," I said quietly. "The first pact was always dubious. Or maybe frivolous."

"Oh, and this one isn't?"

"Maybe. But the good news is that with the paternity pact, you're my backup. I'm asking you as a backup only. If I'm not pregnant in a year, will you do it?"

"I'm not good enough to be Plan A?"

"There's no hierarchy here. I'm trying to be practical, that's all. You know how hard that is for me."

"Your father will still be okay in a year?"

I nodded. "The doctors think so. With chemo and all." As far as my mother was concerned, the "all" meant the baby. I wasn't so sure, though, that there wasn't another "all": my mother and me.

"So what's this year thing? Is there some new paternity club or service I don't know about and you pay by the year, like some reverse..."

"Do I have your sperm that you'll do it?"

He laughed. "I feel like I need to top that joke or I'll drop down to Plan C. Okay, how's this: That's *ejaculately* what you have. My

52

sperm all swimming, dreams of gold medals galore, upstream to make you a baby, if you still want it in a year."

"I just want a baby. Your duty stops there. And I promise your little sperms that my awesome eggs will meet them halfway. At the rest stop with the clean bathrooms."

"Or a hotel," he said, grinning.

"Not a hotel," I said. "That would be seedy."

Hugh bit the corner of his lip and let his eyes wander down to the kiln and then back up. Then he bowed in front of me. "Ah, Frannie. I dream of being Plan A. What's his name?"

"A year," I said, not ready to share Jude with him, and raised his hand so that I could kiss his knuckles, tasting a hint of the clay that he had already given form.

I did not, as my mother had done all those years ago, as Hugh would have me do if the responsibility became his to share, plan any further. When I thought of the baby, I thought first of my father. When I thought of my father, I thought of him as a younger man, the one who would not get old and die. I thought of his shoulders rising just above the curved ridge of the front seat that separated us those long hours on the yearly drive to our family vacation at the beach. I thought of the top drawer of his dresser, inches above my child's reach, where he kept his loose change, unusual pebbles, and other small treasures, all collections to be continued. I thought of myself, reaching, always reaching to see if the piles had grown larger.

Thinking of Jude was different. When I let myself think of Jude, I imagined sex with him, the inevitable tangle of arms and legs and the other less visible tangles that followed. I imagined my new house with his things in it, wondering how I would reconcile his Lazy Boy with my silk chairs. We had been on six dates, each one a little longer, until the last totaled seven hours and ended on my couch. He had kissed me like he meant it, the best kind of insistence. I felt a kind of fluttering inside, wrapped around a kind of warning. I thought I was getting closer to understanding what that insistence was—whose it was—when he surprised me with an invitation to a beauty pageant.

"I have been asked to be a judge," he told me when he called. "And it only just occurred to me that you might like to see my scale of beauty."

"Oh, yeah? What are the required credentials for judging a beauty pageant?"

"A tuxedo and a libido. And a small business you want to grow in a quirky little town with a mean memory."

"And what will I do while you're judging?"

"Well, I would guess that you could sit and be pretty all to yourself."

"I'll practice beforehand," I said, already pondering what I would wear, thankful it wasn't going to be a bathing suit and a banner.

The Miss Iredell County pageant was held the night before my half-birthday. I was as close to thirty-seven as I was to thirty-six, a fact I did not tell Jude for fear that he wouldn't understand such attention to age. The competition was an extravaganza lurking somewhere between fantasy and fact, televised on the local public access station, held in the brick Civic Center the day after the ATV show that left beer cans strewn in the parking lot. There were pumps that pointed at the toes and lip gloss that made a mouth into a luminous attraction and lots of taffeta. I was suspicious of beauty pageants, but I was even more suspicious of a man who couldn't see through such artifice. I stood beside Jude, dressed in my best silk skirt and drop earrings, wondering how much of me he saw. I wanted him to undress me, but taking skin and bone, too. I wanted to see if he would stick around to see what was underneath.

Jude wore a tuxedo, rented. From his apartment in Cornelia, he had driven to a mall in Charlotte and, in the formal wear shop next to the luggage store, chosen a basic black tux with a black cummerbund, perfect for a prom.

"Where were you twenty years ago when my father tried to extort money from my prom date?" I whispered to him, the buzz of conversation growing louder as we made our way to the front of the room.

He slowed his step and turned to look at me, fighting a smile. "Really?"

"Well, not really. But sort of." I shifted my purse under my arm to wave at Mrs. Greene from the drugstore. "It was more like a fine for not liking me more."

"How did he determine what was enough?" Jude asked.

"What do you mean?"

"That the guy didn't like you enough? I mean, maybe I should go ahead and write him a check 'cause I don't think enough is ever enough for a father, even in my case." He circled an arm around my waist. I kept my stomach, or maybe my breath, held in until we reached our seats, suddenly afraid of what sticking around would require from both of us.

Because Jude had to sit with the other judges, I did not sit with him but rather two rows behind him, on the center aisle, next to a thin man whose left knee shook. I couldn't see much of Jude except for his hair, which was fine. Ever since my father's hair had started falling out from the chemo, hair was my favorite part of Jude.

In the row of judges, Jude sat near the end, clearly the youngest. He was next to the former North Carolina lieutenant governor, whose three chins were stacked one on the other above the edge of his tux's starched white shirt. To his left sat a middle-aged woman who had been first Miss Iredell County and then Miss North Carolina, just twenty-five years earlier. Her profile was elegant and refined, but Jude wasn't distracted by beauty, hers or the contestants', I could tell. He felt a heavy responsibility at the pageant, not to choose the prettiest, or the smartest, or even the most capable woman, but to be fair. He had told me that, if you got right down to it, fairness, judging, offered some control in an otherwise chaotic world. Choice was powerful, so when the young women paraded, high heels clicking against the stage in front of him, he turned to look at me instead.

I could barely see his face, but I knew to lean into the aisle so that he could see mine. He mouthed, "Which one do you like?" three times before the woman sitting one row in front of me not quite whispered, "Tell him Miss Cornelia."

I shrugged my shoulders and smiled.

The evening gown competition swished and swirled in front of us. It was late October. Jude could no doubt see the last signs of tan lines. He could no doubt see practiced smiles and whitened teeth. The young woman from Mooresville, contestant number four, smiled at him, probably mistaking his friendliness for an early and unexpected advantage that came to no fruition. Behind him, the audience mumbled as another contestant approached the ramp. I was beginning to think that they all looked alike when something extraordinary happened. Miss Spring Lake fell. The very edge of her gown caught under the heel of a pump, and she tore a hole in the train the size of a football before landing with a thump, her chin hitting the wooden stage so hard that blood splattered the front of the former lieutenant governor's tux. The sound of her muffled whimpers made the entire audience cringe, everyone that is except for Jude.

Jude did not move. He was frozen. A judge without judgment. An action figure undone. Recoil recoiled.

The lieutenant governor pushed back his chair hard enough to scrape the wooden floor, edged around the corner of the judges' table, and rushed to Miss Spring Lake. "Are you all right?" he asked, keeping his voice low, as if that would help disguise the spectacle she had just created. The other judges followed. Only Jude sat, the tips of all his fingers lined up like he was about to type some solemn letter on the surface of the table.

"I am going to have to get glasses," Miss Spring Lake said, and tried to raise her torso before her head dropped toward the floor, her hair's black roots hinting at her evening's disappointing ending. Outside, the shrill of a siren was getting closer. I pushed my way past several people to stand beside Jude. He had not yet moved, but I could see the pleats of his white shirt move up and down with the force of each breath.

"Jude," I said, rubbing his shoulder. "Jude, what's wrong?"

The lights were now turned all the way up, and the audience was no longer tidy rows of heads but an organic, fidgety mass of black and white. Jude placed his left hand over mine on his shoulder and held it there for several seconds, without speaking. Then, with his eyes fixed on Miss Spring Lake, he said "She could have won."

"She's probably going to be fine, Jude," I said. "I'm worried about *you*. You look stricken."

He nodded. He removed his hand from over mine and stood up. I wondered who this man was, where Jude had gone. He said, "Excuse me," edged between two chairs, and scurried up the aisle as I watched, baffled and somehow hurt.

He returned a few minutes later, offering me a squeeze on the shoulder and a weak smile as he walked back to his seat, having missed the drama. Miss Spring Lake had been carried, draped between two men, off the side stage, so the competition resumed. At the end, Miss Huntersville won, although her ventriloquist act was more an exercise in lip-synching and her walk down the runway exaggerated and silly, as if it had been practiced in one of Charlotte's strip clubs (Cornelia had one, too, only it was Mandy Perkins, backlit in her bedroom window). Jude didn't say anything about why Miss Spring Lake's fall scared him more than it did her, but he agreed with me that Miss Huntersville wasn't the best. "Her answer to the question was ridiculous. The military does not need an arts program," he said. "Soldiers do not fingerpaint." I worried about them both—Miss Huntersville and Jude.

Nevertheless, Miss Huntersville went to the Miss North Carolina pageant, and Miss Spring Lake went for medical tests. I went for gynecological reassurance, putting my feet in metal stirrups, riding the riskiest horse in town. My father went for poison, pumped into his veins by a nurse named Inez. Jude went for a new display case for the bakery, putting his faith, after all, in appearances.

I didn't hear from Jude for long enough that I began to acquire that look, the one that women get when they're hurt but too mad to tend to it. On me, it drooped the edges of my mouth and straightened my eyebrows, two dark lines that would not let my dreary thoughts descend to my lips. I knew that rejection and silence were one and the same. I was used to silence. I made do with silence. Whatever had frozen Jude in that auditorium had wormed its way into his heart, which I suspected I might have been winning, a competitor after all. Only he had chosen silence, too. What we didn't say to each other, what I imagined saying to him and what I imagined he said to me, filled something in me, took its place alongside other regrets. I didn't call him, or walk by the bakery, the same way that I hadn't asked him what frightened him so the night of the beauty pageant.

I drove into Charlotte nearly every day to see my father, who now watched television or read the newspaper with a bedpan, thanks to the chemo, between his knees. So I imagined him healthy, practicing his putting on the living room's Persian rug while my mother stood in the doorway, worried. I thought more about Hugh, imagining him pulling award-winning ceramic sippy cups from the kiln. I saw everything and everyone as they should be. Except for myself.

Then Jude drove up to my house the next Wednesday afternoon and parked his car in the driveway. I was going after a batch of new leaves with a broken rake I had found in the basement, cursing each time the row of metal teeth came loose from the wooden handle but determined not to make a trip to get a new one. All of the neighbors were inside making supper. The mail had arrived early that day, and mine was still unopened in the box—two late half-birthday cards, including my father's, which usually came every year after the one my mother sent, and with a twenty-dollar bill tucked inside. This year, however, the cards arrived on the same day. It was nearly dark, which seemed appropriate for Jude's surprise visit, his more surprising opening remark.

After he crossed the lawn, walking clear around the biggest pile of leaves, he said, "I've only worn a tux once before last week. At my wedding."

I held the rake so that it formed a horizontal line across my body. "But you didn't come to talk about your wedding, did you?"

"Rita. She left me. I didn't tell you that part."

"I'm sorry," I said. I thought about the local newspaper's front page photo of Miss Spring Lake being carried off that stage. Behind her was the audience, including me, hundreds of people whose faces I would never have to distinguish. They would forever remain a conglomeration of people who shared a slightly tragic experience, the one thing that seemed to have separated Jude from me. "Sad things happen, Jude. I see them all the time. Happening." I twirled my hand in front of me. "I don't understand it. I don't. But I'm sorry she hurt you."

Jude cleared his throat. I felt a heaviness settle over me, and I kicked a pile of leaves in a bad attempt to be light-hearted.

Jude took a deep breath and started talking. "When our son fell, he fell toward me, Frannie. I was way too far from him to catch him— he fell from a piece of scaffolding, if you can believe that, from a house being built next door to us. But I saw him through the dining room window and I remember thinking that he was coming straight toward me. He was trying to make it to me." Jude pressed his thumb against his pointer finger, lost in thought. We stared at each other for a few seconds. He knew when to quit talking, too.

And I knew then why Jude had been on the carousel. I knew why he had frozen when the woman, all her beauty in spite of her, fell. I knew that his son was dead and that small towns could keep secrets, too, if they didn't trust you yet. I knew so much that my body felt weighted and full, even though the gynecologist's office had called that morning to tell me the kind of fullness I hoped for would very likely never come to be.

Chapter 4

Five years before I met him, Jude met a stranger in a tackle shop on the edge of Lake Forman just outside of Cornelia where cement gives way to pine straw, carpeting the ground in what, from above, must be a near-ring around the lake. Jude had always loved a pine tree. Though it was tall, its history was short, he said, and dutifully scattered each fall before other trees scattered theirs. Jude also loved the surface of quiet water, any water. He could skip a rock five times across a lake when the sun lay flat against it, and he taught the stranger the trick, a subtle flick of the wrist that earned him two extra skips. They were just two men out for the day, boys really, since most thoughts of their lives were tucked away at the very bottom of their tackle boxes, under the tiny things better at luring men than fish.

It was five months before Jude's son, Evan, died.

The stranger, my father, might not have ever thought again of Jude, for he was busy planning how to re-enter his life after several weeks away. The encounter was brief, chance at its best, that incredible cusp of time that fits snugly back into history. But Jude remembered, if not all the details, the way my father looked as his boat was headed back to shore. His responsibilities were almost visible as he wore the same look he must have acquired while the Buick's hood swallowed the white lines of whatever highways had brought him home from the carnival all those summers.

The day before, Jude had taken his son to the park to practice soccer. Evan was just six, small for his age but quick. They had grown bored with chasing a ball and gone for ice cream. Chocolate for them both. Jude had returned to the lake alone because Evan and Rita had left that morning for Massachusetts to visit her sister. In celebration of his temporary bachelorhood, Jude had worn the same shirt and stopped for a second chocolate ice cream cone on his drive to the lake, feeling the need for repetition. Without the responsibilities of father-hood and husbandom, all the world, North Carolina especially, was new again, like a photograph he hadn't looked at for a long, long time. The wildflowers that grew in sporadic patches down the middle of Interstate 77 were losing their color, but he doubted there was much color left elsewhere this late in summer. He doubted all the new sub-division construction in Charlotte could compete with just one stub-born clump of black-eyed Susans. He and my father mentioned this: that only the South could produce a flower whose beauty was linked to violence. The South could drop a hint like nobody else.

Jude had been a responsible but not necessarily serious person for most of his adult life. He did not think much about violence or tragedy or even flat tires, but something about Evan had struck him the day before. They were practicing kicks. Jude sent each ball back to Evan a little bit faster until finally Evan had to run for the last one, a shoe-string trailing behind him. The ball bounced up, and Evan jumped to meet it squarely with his right toe. Jude saw that his son had his straight shoulders, and his hands fluttered in the same way as they traveled to push his hair back from his eyes. He had Jude's practiced stare, the one that had first attracted Rita. Jude watched Evan the way he had watched him a thousand times, with the proud but tired eyes of a parent who loved his child with absolute ease. The split second that Evan was in flight, propelled by the passion that all healthy children have, Jude suddenly realized something.

"He's not mine," he had said out loud, and then caught himself. He does not belong to me, not even in the most innocent of ways, and he never did, he thought. Oddly, there was a celebration in that reali-zation, though he couldn't tell Evan it was the real reason for the ice cream. He just knew that he wanted to celebrate. So, first ice cream and then, the next day, ice cream again, followed by fishing.

In the bait shop where Jude had once rented a small outboard motorboat years ago, there was not one to be had. Most customers had checked the fishing forecast; Jude, like my father, had just wanted to be near water. My father, in fact, had taken the last boat out, and though he did not know him, Jude watched him from the rickety pier where he decided to try his luck with the fishing rod that Rita had given him for Christmas. He caught nothing, his grasp loose on the rod and the fish no doubt taking him for all the minnows that he was worth. As he cast, he sent Evan out into the world in a hundred different ways, careful with each rendition not to expect him back, at least not completely, not in the unchanged way he always would have wanted him back. These thoughts were practice, as with the soccer ball, only more important. He wondered if Rita had ever done this, and he was glad he was a man so that he would never really know the kind of separation after childbirth. What he had discovered at the park was painful enough.

No matter how provoked, these kinds of thoughts cannot be self-contained on a pier outside a bait shop on a Saturday when the sky is the best blue of early September. Jude began to reel in his line and, to his surprise, pulled in a lovely, sleek bluegill about the size of a shoe, its open mouth announcing what had brought about his demise. Or could have.

Like Jude, my father was not a wholehearted fisherman that day, and he steered the little outboard motor boat back in less than an hour. He had one fish in his cooler. Jude watched him, his image somehow entangled in all those releases of Evan.

As my father tied the little boat to the pier, he and Jude had the usual exchange about bad luck and smart fish that all amateurs eventually master. Jude confessed to me that he was too proud to say that he really didn't come for the fish. He was too proud to admit that he loved his son more than he ever had but suddenly from a distance that he was just beginning to navigate. My father must have been too proud to say that after two weeks working with the carnival, away from my mother, he couldn't quite stomach her quiet resentment. He must have been too proud to say that he didn't know what I thought of him, not really. They both swallowed, and they swallowed hard.

They were strangers, after all.

They did walk back to the bait shop together, chatting about earlier times at Lake Forman. My father could remember when there was only one marina, when the houses on the periphery of the water were few. Jude could remember when there was only one lake, when he swam there as a child and it seemed big enough to be the only lake in the world. My father was the one who suggested that they throw their fish back. Jude agreed, and they turned back to the pier.

"It's not about the fish, is it?" Jude said to my father, who was remembering why he had wanted a son.

"In most cases, no," he replied.

"Is that something we're supposed to keep secret?"

"You mean from people who don't fish?"

Jude nodded. He would teach Evan to fish, he decided.

My father stopped and motioned for Jude to drop his fish into his bucket. "We're throwing the fish back, aren't we?"

It was another question posed as an answer. The metal handle of the blue plastic bucket caught the sun's glint as the two fish arced into the water. The strangers waited for the two splashes, which happened so close together that they might have been one.

Such was the coincidence revealed when I took Jude to meet my parents. I made him drive from Cornelia to Charlotte, so if he did change his mind about me along the way, at least he could let me out on the side of the road where I could call the state patrol and get a free ride home. I wanted to flaunt Jude, make my father think that Jude might stick around, even if I wasn't sure he would. I wanted to make up for the fact that there would be no baby now, a loss that only seemed the least bit real when I was with my father, watching him for signs that he was giving up. It was four months into my relationship with Jude, almost three months into my father's chemo, which was taking his energy but not his memory. My father recognized Jude.

But it was my mother who reminded me of our plan, her whisper breathy against my ear: "You see. Forget the sperm bank. Now everything's falling into place. Your father and Jude are already connected. You just need a baby for a better segue."

"I'm the segue," I whispered back. "There's already a segue."

"Then a tangent," she added. "A cuddly little tangent."

Something inside me shifted. I had not shared my bad news with her, those weightless seconds with the phone pressed to my ear after I heard the message on my machine. My doctor was not optimistic. There were two more tests to be done, but the reality was that one ovary was bad and my uterus scarred. "Scarred or scared?" I had said, because it was as ridiculous as his diagnosis, and made the appointment for the tests, writing it in Sharpie on my calendar.

Outside the French doors, my father was introducing Jude to our family cat, Layla, who was almost twenty and could still chase squirrels, although she never caught one. I gave Jude a long, hard stare. I still waited for some omen, a quickened pulse or anxious heart, when I saw him. I wanted a pang, its edges sharp with desire. But it hadn't happened. When he told me about Evan's death, I knew there was a part of Jude I might never reach. But I was going to try, I had already decided.

For support, my father leaned on a "cane," one of the walking sticks he had been collecting for as long as I could remember. He wore his favorite green V-neck sweater, which now draped loosely over his arms and stomach. "Is Daddy eating?" I asked my mother.

"Little bits. A lot of tapioca pudding. French fries."

"French fries? He's a baked potato man."

"Not anymore," my mother said. She rinsed the tips of her fingers and then dried them on the dish towel slung over her shoulder. "He's a keeper," my mother said, nodding toward Jude.

"I wanted you both to meet him while Daddy was feeling pretty good." I was careful not to say "*still* feeling pretty good," which offered its own prediction.

"They would have liked each other even if he wasn't feeling good," she said.

Jude appeared in the kitchen doorway and flashed me a smile. "I have asked your father permission to take you out."

"You've already taken me out."

He walked over and wrapped an arm around my shoulder. "Then apparently we are doing everything in reverse."

"If only you knew," my mother mumbled under her breath, and walked into the den to take my father some tea. I kept a solemn face, my eyes focused on Jude.

"Do your parents know about Evan?" he asked.

"I told them you had a son. Who died."

He nodded. "I thought your father had that look. More so than your mother."

"What look?"

"A little bit of pity. Or something else. Helplessness. Whatever it is, it's normal."

I hesitated before I spoke, moving to sit on the bench by the door so that Jude's arm was no longer around me. I was angry, and I couldn't quite reconcile that anger with the Jude who had baked me a pie decorated with a crossword puzzle, a hobby I had inherited from my mother. "Maybe it's empathy, Jude, not pity."

"No, it's always pity first. You have it, too, ever since I told you. But it's okay, Frannie. It's a hard thing to take on." He squeezed my hand and went back outside to join my father, edging past my mother with a smile.

My mother waited until the door was closed and then announced, "He's quite handsome. In the true sense of that word."

"Yes, he is," I said. "And beguiling."

She handed me a small canvas bag full of perfectly folded kitchen towels. Visit by visit, she was offering me stockpiles of things, mostly domestic. Last time it had been light bulbs, every wattage and size available. From soft white to motion-detected, all light in my house now came from my mother. Before that it had been three sets of measuring cups that fit one inside the other, and one extra half-cup that she said—too seriously, I thought—did not play well with others.

"I have some cheese spreaders, too, if you want them," she said. "They have little ceramic fruit on the ends."

"I don't have anything to spread, Mama. Thank you, though."

"You just spread one thing, missy, when the time is right." Her eyes grew huge. She shook her head and tapped her lips several times. "Listen to what circumstances are making me say." She had started calling my father's cancer "circumstances" when we learned that complete remission was unlikely.

"Did you just say something?" I smiled and rummaged through the bag. "Fourteen tea towels. I'll have to dry a lot of dishes to go through these." I looked up at her.

"What?"

"You're hoarding for me? I used to be able to hoard all on my own, and now you're doing it for me."

"You stole things. I'm giving you things. I see a big difference."

It wasn't meant as an accusation, but since it was a long overdue reference to my childhood criminal past, it felt like one anyway. "Just baby food." I lowered my voice. "And one jar at a time."

"It's almost as if you knew," my mother said.

"I couldn't have known, Mama. How could I have known?"

Soon after my mother had told me I was going to be a big sister, when her stomach began to show beneath her tunic shirts, I asked for permission to cut through the woods behind our house to go to the 7-Eleven. While most girls visited the 7-Eleven to occasionally sneak a Tootsie Roll or Double Bubble gum into their pockets, I stole Gerber's carrots and turkey, spinach and peas, hiding the jars under my bed in boxes I took from the garage. The day my mother came back from the hospital without the baby, I had twenty-nine jars.

By the summer, when our famously beautiful sixteen-year-old neighbor Betsy rode The Swamp Fox roller coaster at Myrtle Beach twelve times in a row with twelve different boys, I had forty-eight jars of Gerber's and two breasts that would still fit into any one of them. Betsy would be famous for her purity gone bad; I would be famous for *puree* gone bad. But until I earned that fame by being caught, I had my very own secret to keep from my mother, who, in her sadness, turned her attention from me to Betsy.

My mother and I would sit on the screened porch and watch the neighborhood settle into the night as my father took his nightly jog. She would braid my stubborn hair into pigtails, again and again if I wanted her to, the results always earning a sigh from her. After he jogged, my father washed the dishes, something he insisted on after the baby, while my mother and I stayed on the porch, encased in aluminum screening, backlit from the tiki torches my father bought to entertain mosquitoes.

"That Betsy sure does have it," my mother would say quietly whenever Betsy strolled by, her ponytail bouncing against her back or her strappy sandals click click clicking against the sidewalk. Betsy's mother did not allow her to wear makeup or the halter tops that catapulted her into fame. "Betsy Wetsy," the boys called her at school, rubbing their crotches and laughing. She managed to wear her bandanna halter and purple eye shadow only when her mother was off shopping or running errands or the Saturdays when her displaced father drove across town to take her to lunch.

I was thirteen and still looked like the tomboy I knew my father wanted, so my mother sometimes invited Betsy to visit to try out new makeup. Before my father got home from the bank and before I began my homework, she and my mother would spend fifteen or twenty minutes in my parents' small bathroom with the peach-colored wallpaper. I was never officially invited in but would usually sit outside the open door, perched on my parents' bed. When Betsy emerged, my mother smiling behind her, she would be transformed into a cover girl, her green eyes outlined by pencil and her cheeks sculpted as perfectly as my mother's. When my mother sent Betsy home, clean-faced again, I'd follow her for a few houses and then turn to walk to the 7-Eleven to slide the smooth, cool glass under my shirt when the cashier wasn't looking.

I had always suspected that my mother found the baby food jars, so I was surprised that she was confronting me now, so many years later. "It was just something I did," I said, not knowing which was harder—explaining it to her or to myself.

"I guess it was an adolescent exhibition," my mother said.

"Betsy or the baby food jars?"

"Both, I guess."

"Did you ever tell Daddy?" I asked.

"No," she said, putting a finger to her lips and glancing into the den where my father and Jude were now watching a baseball game. "I kept your secret, but I should have given you a speech about doing the right thing."

"You should have," I said. The right thing. It was all I had ever wanted to do if someone would have just said how.

When we left my parents' house, Jude and I drove back to Cornelia. It was dark, and the new ramps being built to connect the two interstates were lit for the road workers, dark figures in hats and orange vests that still reminded me of my childhood painting smock tied on the sides with my mother's lopsided bows. Jude never liked to talk much while he drove. He played with the heat control, opening and closing the vents, occasionally saying, "You okay?" His car was clean on the inside, but the windshield wipers had made two arches on the grimy glass. I ran my fingers along their edges, tracing, and he said, "That's kind of sexy."

"Are you going to ask me if my engine is revving?" I teased.

He glanced in the rearview mirror, switched lanes, and winked at me. "My engine is revving," he said, "if I may speak bluntly."

"That's metaphorically, not bluntly," I said.

"Well," he said, his tone suddenly turning serious. "Let me be blunt: I carry around a lot of baggage, and I can't do anything to change that, Frannie. I'm not even going to apologize for it."

"I didn't ask you to apologize for it."

"I know you didn't." He reached over to stroke my hand.

A few minutes later, he pulled into my driveway, the porch light flickering. All the neighbors were asleep, their houses dark every night at eleven, before ten if their kids were under ten. Jude put the car in park but didn't cut the motor. He looked at me and arched his eyebrows. It had been almost four months. He was waiting.

A more modern woman would have seduced him a long time back. She would have gone to the mall and bought something that doesn't wrinkle or quite reach her thighs. She would have conceded to a Brazilian, a euphemism if there ever was one. She would have *been* a euphemism, what the world usually demands of women.

Suddenly, my body was way ahead of my heart, but that competition was never fair. "Please stay," I said, and leaned over to slowly kiss him.

"That's a good idea," he said, opening his door before our lips were officially separated.

We nearly jogged up the walkway. When we got inside, Jude hung his coat on the doorknob of the front door. "I like to do this in case I need to run," he said, smiling. "Or sometimes I leave it on."

"Do you take off your shoes?"

"I make my harem take them off."

"Should I meet the others first?" I shrugged my coat from my shoulders and placed it over his, the folds of fabric crumpled on the floor like awkward feet.

"There are no others," he said, serious again, as earnest as I had ever heard him.

Just Evan, I thought.

I did not pad to the bathroom for my diaphragm. Instead I removed every piece of clothing, one by one, and draped each over the coats. I removed my bra last, turning to hook it around the lump of clothes, oddly human-shaped, so that Jude could see me from behind, the disobedient skin of my thighs, the vacation plans of my butt, its eye on Florida. As an afterthought, I took off my socks and stuffed them into the cups of the bra, finally achieving a balanced set of breasts, even if they smelled like old wool and sweat. "There," I said, "are some breasts." I was surprised at my own ability to tease him when I felt so terrified, naked to the core. "I have built you a woman, and please note that she came first."

"Me next," he said.

I nodded, wrapped my arms around the real things so as not to distract him, and thought about how silly my body was not to be able to capitalize on what was sure to follow.

Jude started with his watch, tucking it into his pants pocket and arching his eyebrows. Then he snapped his fingers, called "Girls," waited a few seconds, and with just the right amount of melodramatic reluctance, undid his laces, throwing each shoe to the floor with a definite thump. Then he unbuttoned his shirt, removed it, and, looking quickly around the room, secured it around the lampshade behind him. I had to look. His stomach was perfect, slightly rounded but firm, all those bites of pastry courteous and diplomatic, and when he bent over to tug off his pants, it barely rolled over the top of his boxers. He arranged his pants under the shirt on the table that held the lamp. He took off his boxers and swayed them between us. "A hundred percent cotton."

"I can tell," I said. "Polyester is slicker."

"That's right." He turned around and worked his pants through the two openings of the boxers and pulled them about halfway up the legs. "Sometimes he needs help in the mornings," he said.

One of the good things about lust is that it is its own boss. I didn't think. I kissed him instead, on his stomach, finding the indentation of his navel with my tongue. He kissed me back, all over, without a definite plan, his mouth map-less but bold. My body was responding just fine, and then I started thinking. I couldn't not send mental commands to Jude's DNA, telling it, despite whatever irony might be lurking in my body, to send in the troops. I even added, *Do it for Evan, too.*

We ended up choosing the guest room, with the bed from my childhood, an old iron headboard with brass lions' heads and a mattress that once had a work ethic but no longer did. This bed was the closest to the living room, where the people we had designed for each other were polite enough not to leave.

After Jude did leave the next morning, I drove back into Charlotte for my doctor's appointment, passing the bakery with its late breakfast crowd, its street address written out in silver metallic paint. I thought about stopping but decided against it, afraid that Jude would be able to read me, well aware that sex changes nothing and everything at the same time. Jude had waited long enough, never pressing me, another kind of tacit agreement reached: our relationship required patience, which meant it might just last.

Then, within hours, science confirmed what I had felt to be true the night before when I willed Jude's sperm up the down alley to my egg, naming the hypothetical pair Betty and Jake and then un-naming them, afraid of the specificity alongside such doubt. There would be no baby.

"Sometimes," my doctor said, as if he, too, had been there with Jude and me the night before, his stethoscope hearing all my secret thoughts, "sometimes this kind of news recreates sex for women. It frees them."

"I do not feel free," I said, my paper gown crackling as I crossed my arms over my chest.

When he left the room, I untied the gown and blew my nose with it. As I got dressed, I wanted to call Hugh, take my comfort where I usually found it. I should have told him that the pact was off, but I couldn't face him yet, flawed and useless as I was. I thought about calling my father to hear him say "Hallo," his voice slightly inflected. I thought about going to get my palm read, or at least my wrist tattooed, so that I would have something permanent and concrete to mark a loss that was not. But what I did instead was call my mother and simply ask her to join me for coffee.

At our usual meeting place, my mother had arrived ahead of me and chosen a booth. Venus was really a restaurant, but it served "continuous coffee" for a dollar. Neither of us made good use of the deal. My mother was convinced that caffeine was correlated to cancer, and I had already had three cups.

"How's Daddy?" I asked first.

"He's very nauseous today. Your uncle Jim's there visiting. What did you want to talk about?" She smiled at the waitress and dunked her herbal tea bag in hot water.

I sighed. "I can't have children, Mama. I just found out today for sure. A bad uterus to begin with and some endometriosis after that."

She looked stunned. "Oh, Frannie. Oh, Frannie."

"It's a setback, Mama. Just a setback. I have to get used to the idea—that's all."

She slapped her hands on the table. "How can that be? You would have known before."

"How would I've known? I knew about the endometriosis. But I've used birth control for years. I never really tested the idea of getting pregnant before Daddy got sick."

"Oh, Frannie," she said.

"Do you want to punish me for having sex?" I added and tried to smile.

"It's simply not fair."

"I'm Mrs. Brandon," I said quietly.

Mrs. Brandon had been our neighbor when I was a child. She was a large, single woman in her fifties with a house set behind a tall wooden fence covered with ivy. She died suddenly, after which, from my bedroom window, I watched people carry covered casserole dishes into her house, sad that she only had visitors *after* she died. After a moving van hauled away all of her things, I discovered that the back door to her house was left unlocked. Inside, everything smelled like cleanser and Windex. The entire house was empty, but in the closet of the back bedroom, I found dozens of tiny, empty baby clothes hangers. And then in a box on the floor was a small collection of miniature food items, the kind that a kid younger than I would have played with. Canned soup. Broccoli with a chip in the stalk that revealed the original opaque white of its plastic. A loaf of Wonder bread. A package of lemon Jell-O with the O rubbed off. "Jell," I said out loud. I carried the pretend food to the kitchen, where I put it on the counter next to the refrigerator that wasn't humming. When I confessed to my mother that I had been next door and told her about the hangers and toys, she said, "Mrs. Brandon never had children. That doesn't make sense."

But it made sense to me now. Adults could play make-believe, too, only their version started with denial. So I slowly told my mother about the doctor's visits and the tests. The restaurant was noisy, and I could hear my own voice like background music. My mother listened, her eyes growing wider and her worried lines pointing more fiercely away from her mouth. Mine was not the kind of news that invited chitchat.

"So," she finally said, brushing sugar off the table, "we won't tell your father about this."

"Well, there's always us to keep him wanting to fight," I said. "There's us."

"No, I meant let's not worry him with the news right now."

"Okay, but the other thing, Mama, is that Jude might not stick around if I can't have children. A lot of men might not want me if I can't have children."

"A lot of men don't count." She folded her hands on the table and looked me in the eye. "Don't worry yourself about a lot of men."

"I just need one," I said, trying to joke. I crossed and uncrossed my legs while she took five dollars from her wallet and put it on the table.

"Let's go shopping," she said.

"I don't feel like shopping right now, Mama."

"Let's go," she said, standing.

There were pages of work at home and the obligation to tell Jude the news—maybe not now, but sometime—so a distraction was good. I followed her out of the restaurant and several blocks down the street, wondering what kind of shopping was left in this part of Charlotte, not close enough to downtown to be rejuvenated and far too outdated to have a shopping center. She walked quickly, all those classes at the Y paying off in strong legs that tried to match her will.

We stopped in front of a dress shop, the kind that almost no longer existed, where old ladies in trim suits with belts sold hats and trim suits with belts. Apart from a fancy set of pajamas, my mother had never worn a belt in her life. The only hat she owned was a visor that she wore at the beach, rusted around the metal clasp but embossed with seashells.

"What is this?" I asked.

"Plan B," she said. She looked past me into the store.

I didn't know what she meant until I looked up and through the window saw a woman coming toward us. I realized it was Melissa, although twenty-five years had passed since I had seen her, and every one of them suddenly felt as complicated and heavy as water.

Chapter 5

My mother pushed open the door to the dress shop and then reached up to still the small brass bell, un-announcing our arrival. Melissa did not smile. She looked from my mother to me, moving just her eyes, which were Hugh's eyes, green and round like pennies. "We're having a sale," she said, sweeping one arm to her right. "The red tagged items are thirty percent off. I assume that's why you're here."

"We'll look," my mother said. She wrapped her arm under mine and tugged me toward the first rack, full of polyester blouses and skirts with anchors or pineapples around the hems, tugging hard enough for me to know that I would have little say in what was going to happen.

"How are you, Madelane?" Melissa asked as we passed. "It's been a real long time."

"Doing well," my mother said, a tinge of hostility in her voice.

"And Frannie. Look at how the little girl grew up." She slowly shifted her gaze to me, dragging years with it.

My mother had taken me to Melissa and Hugh's house on a Saturday when I should have been in dance class at the Y. Before we left our home, my mother had written my father a note and taped it to the cabinet where he kept a bottle of Dewars for his after-work cocktail. But she ripped the note off, read it again, then shoved it way down in her pants pockets and studied the air for a few seconds. "Let's go," she said to me, as if it would be an ordinary trip to the grocery store.

It wasn't. In the station wagon with the faux wood, we passed through neighborhoods where the houses were closer and closer together until we turned onto a street with gravel driveways, where yards that hadn't been raked, full of pine straw and leaves, also had trash and the occasional sofa or chair.

"Where are we going?" I asked just once.

"Your father has a lot of friends," my mother said, and left it at that.

She parked the car on the curb and told me to act "like there's glue on your bottom," but, after only a few steps toward the house, she came back and opened the passenger door where I sat, wide-eyed and unsure. "Frannie, I want you to forget this after it's all over," she said and waited while I slid across the seat toward her. We walked, hand in hand, up the cracked cement sidewalk. My mother knocked on the front door. "Please don't say anything," my mother said, seeming to forget I was only ten years old and seldom spoke, at least to strangers. But I realized later that she meant to my father; I shouldn't say anything to my father.

A woman answered the door with the metal chain still intact, allowing only two or three inches of gap, to peer out at my mother and me. "Madelane?" she said, her eyebrows pushed together above her nose. Her pink fingernails clamped the edge of the door above the handle. She looked at me and smiled, and, had my mother's eyes not been so dully focused on her, I might have liked her. Something inside of me told me to like her.

"May we come in, Melissa?" my mother asked. I let go of her hand and turned around to see a large dog on a chain lift its chin and stare at us.

Inside, the house smelled of cigarette smoke. The living room had little furniture, but it all tried to match via muted flowers and stripes. A cotton rug was crumpled under the coffee table where someone had left a plate with a paper napkin balled in the middle.

"What's wrong?" the woman asked. "Is Duncan alright?"

My mother pointed to a door off the living room. "Is that somewhere where we can talk?" she stated more than asked. I looked around. I spread my arms and tried to do one plié the way my ballet teacher had shown me, with my toes pointed out like a duck's. I did another and another, but I knew I was not graceful, my toes better for kicking balls than pointing. I also knew that my mother was upset and that we were not supposed to be in this house. The woman's face at the door was familiar because I had seen it, along with a strange man, in a photograph in the top drawer of my father's desk as I was looking for a pen.

I was growing more and more anxious by the time a boy a little taller than I was emerged from the hallway with the peeling wallpaper. I stopped. I looked in the opposite direction, hoping my mother would reappear.

"Who are you?" he asked.

"Frannie," I answered, politely.

"Who would name a girl fanny?" he said, laughed, and then shot from the room. From somewhere in the house, my mother's voice rose and then waned again. I looked around the room, where nothing suggested a child's life—no toys, no juice boxes, no concerned adult asking him where he was going. So I followed him.

I slid out the front door and tiptoed down the side of the house. Two flats of pansies, their faces long gone, lay on the ground next to a hoe and a pair of dirty women's sneakers. Near the back of the house, the boy sat on a bicycle with handlebars in a high V and fringe hanging from the bottom, which he ruffled while watching me.

"Is that lady your mother?" he asked.

I nodded. "She knows your mother."

"My mother works in a store," he said, as if he had practiced it.

"What about your father?"

He gripped the handlebars and made the bike do a wheelie, although he had to steady his balance and the bike's when he landed. He bent over to spin one of the pedals, and I saw that his hair was matted in the back, a comb as much a stranger to him as I was. "My father is dead. We have Duncan instead."

I froze. I understood that every morning my father went to work, where the bank claimed a part of him I never saw, a serious part with worry and conflict that he took out of his briefcase many nights after I went to bed. Suddenly, this strange boy had convinced me that there was another part of my father I didn't know.

"That's my father," I said sadly. I sat on a plastic yard chair and rested my elbows on my knees.

"He's great. He takes me shopping and buys me the stuff my mom won't."

"What's your name?"

"Hugh Jenkins."

I glared at him, feeling something inside of me shift. "Does he let you call him Duncan?"

"Yep."

"How old are you?"

"Eleven," he said, proud of the double digits. "Twelve before you know it. Duncan's your father?"

I nodded. I didn't have a chance to speak more because my mother appeared in the back door window and motioned for me to come inside. I considered not obeying. I knew something about my father that she didn't, which almost never happened. The last time it had, it was because my father had taken me on a secret "excursion" to a horse farm where he talked to a man about buying one and then changed his mind.

"I have to go," I finally said to Hugh, when my mother started holding up fingers and counting. "Do you go to Green Hills School?"

He nodded, and I walked back to the house. My mother gave no commands, but I followed her to our car anyway. "There's a boy in the backyard who knows Daddy," I said, an announcement with such fast bravado that it felt like a hiccup.

She stopped turning the key in the lock. She pivoted and stared at the house, thinking. "Come on," she said, holding a hand behind her for me to take.

We crossed the street and walked down the side of the house, past an old wheelbarrow so rusted along the handle that it felt like a hundred of my cat's tongues. Hugh was lying on the metal chaise, even more rusted. He popped up like a jack-in-the-box and said, "You're back."

My mother stared at him. For a second, I thought she might cry, but she didn't. She wrapped an arm around my shoulder and pulled me toward the car once again while Hugh shouted, "Can't she stay and play?"

My mother was calmer on the way home, although at the first long traffic light, she muttered, "The boy in that wheelbarrow was a fairy tale gone bad." She tapped her fingers and then added, "But not *your* Grimm Brother."

"His name is Hugh. He was fun," I said simply.

"Let's keep this to ourselves, Frannie," she said, not knowing that was exactly what I would do, keep Hugh to myself so I could keep finding out things about my father that even she didn't know. She focused her eyes squarely on the car in front of ours and turned on the country radio station. We drove through Charlotte with the wood peeling from the station wagon, watching the fathers driving home from work and the mothers turning around at traffic lights to tell their children to be quiet, to be patient, to act right.

I overheard my parents that night, their voices sharp. They were arguing about Mrs. Jenkins. It took me several years to put together the pieces, years when I gave up dance classes and having my mother braid my hair and sitting on my father's lap to hear about his days in the Navy. But I had Hugh.

Now, my mother sashayed to the side of Melissa's store and began browsing a rack of dresses, sliding each one along the metal bar and holding one up to her shoulders to check her reflection in the full-length mirror. When I moved just an inch or two, I could see three angles of her, and in every one she looked like a different person and not once my mother, the woman who created an idea of me before she created me. "Frannie," she said, holding up a salmon-colored dress, "it's your color."

"But not for me," I said. I glanced at Melissa. For almost thirty years, Hugh had promised that he never mentioned me to his mother, and I felt a good deal of shame for standing in front of her now, pretending I didn't know she had once loved a dog named Amber, stolen ten dollars from a woman on the bus next to her when she couldn't pay the electric bill, and allowed her son to grow up thinking his father had died a superhero.

Melissa, without looking at either of us, said, "She's too young for these clothes." She picked a piece of lint from her own dress, which had box pleats and a pocket trimmed in ribbon. It seemed right for a woman with her hair in a bun, a butterfly barrette holding the coils of gray in place. "You've turned out just fine, Frannie. Quite fine."

"Thank you," I said. Fifteen years earlier, her comment might have been appropriate, but it seemed silly given that I was thirty-six. "But you don't really know me."

She leaned against the counter that held the cash register and didn't speak for a second. "I know of you."

"From my father?" I asked.

"Yes."

"What did he say?" I meant to sound sarcastic, but I couldn't keep years of curiosity from surfacing. "Did he tell you that he was proud of me?"

"Of course, he's proud of you," she said. "You're his whole heart."

At this, my mother began humming. It was her way of getting attention, quieting a room. Some people cleared their throats; my mother filled hers with half-song and warbled.

"Let me select some items for you," Melissa said to my mother. She chose several polyester blouses from the rack and made her way to the back of the store, the assortment swinging in front of her. She waved my mother to the curtained dressing room. If my father were there, he would have held his mouth to the quarter of an inch of space down the middle of the panels and said, "You look good in everything, Lane. I don't see why you don't just buy it right now."

And my father essentially *was* there. My father was why we had come.

My mother held up a blue sweater for Melissa to see. "Duncan's favorite color."

It was a bold move, and I waited to see what Melissa would do. She merely took the hanger from my mother and nodded in agreement.

"Mama, I've had a hard day, and I would like to go home." I reached for the sweater from Melissa and hung it on the nearest rack. "Tell her about Daddy. If that's why we're here, then just tell her."

The three of us stood for a second. I looked at the one clump of spider veins on the front of Melissa's right leg, thin, blue circuitry visible through her tan hose, a color my mother hadn't worn in ten years. The first night we had sex, Jude had discovered a tiny spider vein on the inside curve of my left knee. In my pants pocket my fingers found the piece of paper with my earlier doctor's appointment written on it, and I thought how I might have made both of these women grandmothers.

"Melissa," my mother said, "Duncan is sick with cancer."

Melissa held a hand to her chest. "Oh no."

"He hasn't told you?"

"No, not a word," Melissa said.

My mother draped the other blouses over the top of the counter and took out the small black calendar that she carried in her purse. She opened it to the last week of January. "In two weeks he'll have his last chemo treatment for this round." She pointed to the date. "But I believe that he could use your support as well."

Melissa looked at me and then back at my mother. "What do you want me to do?"

"I'll let you know," my mother said. She put the calendar back in her purse and zipped it shut.

"Is he going to die?" Melissa asked.

I had already begun moving toward the door, my eyes fixed on an old hardware store across the street with a huge "GOING OUT OF BUSINESS" sign. But I turned around. Melissa looked stricken. My mother's eyes roamed the shop before stopping at me.

"Is he, Mama?"

She set her jaw even firmer. "Not if we all can help it." With that, she nodded good-bye to Melissa, slipped her hand into mine, and pulled me to the door.

As we walked up the sidewalk, I glanced behind us to see Melissa flip the sign that hung on the door to "Closed" and then stand in the window, so still that she might have been a full-figured mannequin.

"I remember going to see her when I was a kid," I told my mother. "That was more than twenty-five years ago." She let go of my arm and raised a hand to adjust each of her two gold earrings. Strangers passed us, the sidewalk busier than just a few minutes earlier. "But what I can't tell is if you've seen her since." I chose carefully what I said next, aware that I was in the precarious position so familiar from my childhood where I had to gauge one parent's knowledge against the other's. "I feel very certain that Daddy has."

"I haven't seen her," she said, "although we've talked a few times." She rubbed a fingertip around her lips and then reached into her purse for lipstick while I decided that Melissa, tempting her fate, must have called my mother. "Melissa hasn't aged well," she said, looking into the compact mirror I had given her years and years ago, the powder long since gone.

"Maybe her life has been hard." My mother knew, and I knew, that lonely women do strange things, and Melissa must have been lonely even before Davies died—leaving the Midwest for the South, following a man who already knew its lazy seasons and its rigid boundaries. Davies also knew water, the ocean, joining the Navy without expecting Melissa's disapproval, which followed him anyway, like a lazy reputation.

According to Hugh, in Iowa, his mother had always liked the ocean, too, pictures of it in encyclopedias and on television where it was made more predictable, more knowable, than it really was. She hadn't liked it so much in reality, when she finally got close to it, when it borrowed Davies for months at a time and stared back at her without apology. It probably would have been easier if he had died in the ocean. If I had been her, I would have wanted to be able to blame something other than his heart.

"Whose life isn't hard?" my mother asked, indignant. "Look at you—you just found out some sad news, and you're being strong and brave. You were strong from the day I had you, but you're learning brave."

"What if you hadn't had me, Mama? What do you think would have happened with you and Daddy if I never came along?"

She stopped walking to reapply her lipstick, its case as sleek and shiny as a new bullet. "I will not waste my time thinking like that. Your father's body, the one that helped make you, has turned on him. I feel like I am competing with that cancer."

"That cancer's got nothing to do with you."

She stopped walking. "Of course it's got something to do with me. After thirty-eight years, he can't blink his eyes without it having something to do with me."

"*I Dream of Genie*," I said.

"What?"

"On that show where Barbara Eden was the genie woman, when she blinked her eyes, she could do anything. She had pointed-toe slippers and all the power she wanted."

"Magic," my mother said, "not power."

"And great abs," I added.

Ahead of us, my father's office building, its two rows of glass windows, reflected the late afternoon sun. I counted six floors up and five windows over to the left. Underneath the building was a parking garage with an empty space reserved for his Buick. He had refused having his name painted in the space, arguing that he didn't deserve such celebrity.

"How, you know, close do you think she and Daddy are?" I asked my mother, when we had already covered a block, snack bars and electronics stores interspersed in the spaces that had once held department stores with coffee shops. Neither of us had mentioned Hugh yet.

"Not that close, as I understand it," she said, hollowing out her voice, "but close."

"So you think that you and Daddy and Melissa will all be fine together? You think it's worth the awkwardness? 'Cause it was pretty awkward in that shop. And it might make Daddy feel awkward, which is not what we want."

She didn't answer. We had walked almost another block, my mother's sedan in sight, when she finally did. "I think it's what your father has wanted all along. He's just not good at knowing what he wants."

"Which is why he has us," I mumbled and kept walking, still unsure how I felt now that things once hidden no longer were.

The flowers began to arrive on the following Monday. The delivery boy did not ring the doorbell, but knocked, the screen door already pulled back and his toes against the stoop so that answering the door was more like agreeing to dance. "Flowers for you," he said, "and cookies. I'll accept one of them instead of a tip, if you want."

I took the arrangement and twirled it around several times. I hoped the neighbors would see that I was being sent flowers, delivered by a hippy boy in the kind of van I tried not to associate with child abductions. There were astromerias, purple ones with white tendrils that looked like lashes around one large eye, and stems of green fern with leaves of endless V's stacked against each other. There were also five cookies on sticks, in the shape of tulips, each one decorated with that extra sweet icing you buy in a tube if you're anybody but Jude, who had a bumper sticker that read "Pastry Power."

"Let me get you a couple of dollars," I said and found my purse. I had the habit of tossing my money to the bottom alongside receipts, hand lotion in little bottles from hotels, and enough pens to last through a nuclear winter.

When he left, I put the arrangement on the dining room table and looked for a card, but there wasn't one. I removed all the cookie flowers, one by edible one, and discovered that Jude had signed his name on the back of each, under a sprout made of green plastic wrap. I bit into the top of the yellow one and worried nonetheless. I knew that a man who's lost a child would imagine the future, and if he's able to do that much, he might as well imagine a future that was lovely and right and full of possibility. A man who's lost a child would want another. So I didn't call Jude to thank him for the flowers. If I had, it would have been a lie. It was easier to eat the evidence of him and later tug on my jeans inch by slow inch than it was to call him.

Every day that week I got a different arrangement with a different flower cookie. Every day that week I told myself that I had to tell Jude I was damaged goods, yet I didn't. Every day that week the scruffy courier took his three dollars and said, "Thanks," not meaning it, traveling back down the street so slowly that I ran after him on Friday and gave him a daisy with the black icing chipped in the middle and let him keep the money, too. His brazen request earlier in the week had annoyed me. In just four short days, I had turned annoyance into maternal pandering. If he hadn't already been able to drive, I would have taken him for new school clothes, or at least a vaccination.

Then, on Friday night, Jude personally showed up at my house with the last arrangement. He handed it to me and sat with me on my front steps while he ate two of his own cookies, complimenting himself on the roses, which were clearly his best work. When he finished the last bite and I still hadn't said anything, he tapped me on the shoulder and said, "I love you."

While he wiped a dab of icing from his lip, I started breaking the words down into syllables, only there was just one syllable in each word, not enough to stall.

"Thank you," I said.

"'Thank you'? I didn't just open the car door or pay your bar tab for you. I just told you I love you. You should say something equally weighty, like you have a third nipple—which I know you don't—or you have to get back in your spaceship."

"Mothership," I said weakly, ironically.

He clapped his hands together, saying, "Beautiful, just beautiful." Then he stood up, angry, which did not look any better on him than it did on anyone else. I watched cookie crumbs trailing behind him as he disappeared inside. I watched the kids across the street drawing with chalk on the sidewalk, their faces turned toward the ground in intense concentration. I watched two-doors-down Mrs. Greene shoo the Biggerses' cat from her yard. I heard the television come on.

I went inside because Jude hated television more than I did. I stood behind him as he sat on the couch. He wore my favorite shirt, a worn, almost-slick chamois that he always tucked in at the beginning of an evening and untucked within half an hour. I tousled his hair, but he pulled away. "I loved the flowers and the cookies, Jude. You know that. Thank you again."

"You thanked me already. You keep thanking me for things. That's why I'm in here pouting."

"Okay."

"Okay."

I put my hair behind my ears, even though it made my face look long, halfway to a pout, too, an expression I was determined not to make. I sat beside him, the couch's thick cording digging into the back of my thigh. He pointed the remote and turned up the volume on *Jeopardy*.

"I need to know about Rita," I said, cupping my hands around my mouth in mock announcement, then fluttering my fingers.

"Why does she matter?" he shouted back, and then he lowered the volume.

"I just need to know about her. If you love me, I need to know who else you've loved."

"Is it a contest?"

"I want to know what happened. If you resent her." Sometimes I thought my parents resented each other, but they were both so busy pretending they didn't that they forgot all about me.

"I don't resent her." He frowned. "I can't think of anyone I resent right now except for you."

"I deserve that," I said. I waited while he changed the channel to the evening news. "Do you blame her for Evan's death?"

He leaned back and rested his head on the top of the couch, where the cats used to sit at night before he spent so much time there, sending them into the linen closet to leave clumps of hair and tiny translucent cat fingernails. "Why would you ask me that? I just learned your middle name a few weeks ago."

"Marie."

"Yes, I know," he snipped. "*Thank you.*"

"I'm sorry if I offended you. It's just that you have this whole life that was undone and against your will, and I'm trying to understand how I fit into that."

"Why do you have to understand it? Wouldn't it be better to know what you feel?" He leaned up and pushed back the coffee table a few inches. "You're reluctant, Frannie. That's the pretty word for it. But 'scared' is the better one. The real one."

"You've got to give me some time, Jude." I made sure that my tone was not whiny. "Lately, every time I thought there was someone else, it turns out there wasn't, and I was left with just me all over again. I keep showing back up. I'm like my own drunk relative at Christmas."

He got up and turned off the television, forgetting that he held the remote. He pulled on his sweatshirt, his face popping through the hole with his eyes shut. "I'm going," he said.

"If you leave, my night will be lonely and sad."

He started to say something but changed his mind. He gently untucked a clump of hair from behind my ears and smoothed it against my cheekbone, letting his fingers linger. "We should make an excursion soon. There's someplace I need to show you," he said.

Then he left, and the rest of the night was just as I had predicted.

That night, instead of sleeping, I lounged in the bathtub for three hours, replenishing the hot water five times, even though it made me feel decadent and wasteful. I thought about Jude's body, even as my own was shriveling. I called him at 2 a.m., feeling needy and guilty. At

2:20, we were having sex. At 2:48, I was just about to tell him that he had chosen a damaged woman to love when he started talking about Rita.

"You should know," he said, rolling to his side to face me, "what happened."

He had returned home from work one day to an empty house. All the furniture was gone. Standing in the bedroom was the antique four-poster bed that he and Rita had been given as an anonymous wedding gift. Jude heard a motor running and followed the sound to the kitchen. On the counter the hand-held mixer was whirring, the two beaters' rotation so fast that it was barely visible. There was no food in sight. The refrigerator had been unplugged; the pantry held only cans of soup and plastic bags of dried beans. The tin foil had been removed from under the burners on the stove. Even the broom and dustpan no longer leaned in the far right corner.

Rita had moved to the middle of the country, or at least that's what the memo said on the answering machine when Jude finally heeded the red blinking light. The divorce papers came two days later, when she must have been just about to Oklahoma. He said he knew her route because it would have been the opposite of their honeymoon route. Rita believed in symmetry.

"It had been coming for a long time," Jude said, pulling the sheet up over us. "Without Evan, we didn't know who the other one was."

"Are you sorry she left?"

"Not anymore," he answered.

"Do you ever talk to her?" I wriggled closer to him, smelling flour, which I liked to imagine explained those specks of gray in his hair. I didn't like to think of Jude growing older.

"Not anymore. We used to talk from time to time, but that stopped a while back."

"That's sad," I said. "To love somebody and then not know anything about them."

He rolled over on his side. "I appear to be good at it."

I let a few seconds and the sarcasm pass. "When are we going on that trip?" I asked.

"Not tonight," he said into his pillow. "But sometime in the mere future."

"Near future, you mean."

"Mere. As in it doesn't count for much yet."

Hurt, I got up and padded to the kitchen for a snack. I made Jude partake, too, plumping his pillow against the headboard when he sat up to glare at me. We ate every last one of those cookies in bed, sleeping with the crumbs like disobedient, spoiled children. Every passing second indeed brought the future, and nothing, not even Jude's eager love, could stop it.

The next morning, I pulled down the wooden steps from the hallway ceiling and climbed up each creaky one of them, ashamed for not doing it before I had moved in and committed to the bank what I couldn't commit to Jude. There was a strange odor in the house, and by process of elimination, I had determined that it came from the attic.

I found the body of a squirrel. At first I thought that June Carter or Emmylou, my cats, had gotten it, but I knew there was no way they could have pulled down the ladder and climbed up there. The squirrel lay in the middle of the floor, centered perfectly, still fleshy, but every bone demanding recognition. There was no mystery really. Death could be tidy, and private. I stood for a long time, staring, hating bones for being permanent, hating permanence.

I left the squirrel where it was and climbed down the stairs, backwards, having to find each step below me, like a bad dance routine. I walked back to my office, where Emmylou had taken my seat. I stood for several minutes, unbending a paperclip, and then I dialed the numbers to my parents' house so quickly that I had to start over, afraid I had accidentally called some faraway place like Michigan or The Netherlands. No one answered.

My father cannot die, I thought as I counted eight rings before the machine picked up. *He cannot die when there is so much about me he would never get to know.* Melissa had said he was proud of me, but I couldn't be sure. I hung up the phone, put my hands on my hips, and thought some more. I couldn't change the inevitability of my father's death, but I could change me. I needed to get busy, and Jude would be part of that.

When the doorbell rang, I stood up to look out the window. The florist's van was in the driveway, and the passenger door was wide open. Jude still loved me. Time was on my side; my Southern wild-flower book said he had 206 varieties to go, if only there be sugar to coat them.

This time I met the delivery boy on the sidewalk. He shook his head and whistled. "You got 'em coming from all over the place. This one's from somebody in Charlotte named Hugh. I took the call and wrote the card, too." He looked at me, waiting for a response, and then held up the hydrangea. It was the color of just-about-ripe blue-berries. My favorite—the hydrangea and the blueberries. And, if I thought about it, Hugh.

A few minutes later, I was following the florist's van down the street, making my way toward the interstate and to Hugh, who deserved some sort of update on his own future. If I hadn't needed gas, allowing the needle to move all the way to empty before stopping at the BP, I would have missed the strange woman at the gas pump with the weighted-down car and outdated jewelry. But there Rita was, turning down a three-dollar car wash, fully aware that if you do go home again, uninvited and almost defeated, it's better that you not preen, that nothing, your car included, be too pretty or too clean.

Chapter 6

I chewed three pieces of bubble gum, one thumbnail, and a straw I found in my glove box while I drove to Hugh's, worried. Melissa must have called him. Or maybe he wanted to remind me of our pact. At first, I decided it was selfish of me not to have updated him on the probability of his being a father: zero. At least via me. And then I decided I was a coward; I had been cowardly. I didn't want him—Hugh, the last person who would ever judge me—to know what the doctors had confirmed. Why, I wasn't sure. And now I would have to tell him about Jude, too, which meant confessing that he probably wouldn't have been my choice for father regardless. It was either that confession or the hydrangea that worried me most. Hugh had never conjured romance for me before. There hadn't been any romance, just sex, and not much of that. Even the card read, "From: Hugh." That delivery van could have been carrying a new printer or a set of bath towels, or even an artificial Christmas tree—Nature slighted, not doing the slighting—and the same card would have worked.

The studio was dark. I got out of the car and banged on the metal door just in case, but no lights came on. I edged around the back and took the stairs up to the apartment over the studio. Hugh had built it himself after his divorce. One huge room, loft-style, it had wide windows that looked out over the old train trestle, and Hugh had placed his couch facing those windows. So I could see him, sleeping, a book opened across his chest, a floor lamp creating a circle of light. I started to tap on the window but stopped myself. What would I say to him? Don't send me flowers? Don't reach out to me? Don't send an announcement that you're Hugh, all Hugh?

I didn't need an announcement—he had always just been there. He was Hugh, my adolescent confidante. The first man I had sex with. He had always been there. And I always knew where to find him. I had tracked him down in a S&S cafeteria, where he sat having lunch all by himself and reading the free car magazines, looking at photos of 1970s convertibles, his cornbread growing cold in front of him. Another time I found him in his favorite spot at Freedom Park stretched out on a blanket in the sun, squishing dandelions. And there was the one dive bar where he would go alone, sitting in the booth under the window with the ancient metal blinds whose edges were as sharp as scissors. I knew where he liked to be, and up until my move to Cornelia, he had known the same about me. The fact was that I had always needed him more than he needed me. And that suddenly worried me.

I tiptoed back down the stairs and cranked the engine, hoping it wouldn't wake Hugh, sending him out onto the deck to inspect. I backed up the driveway, watching, but no Hugh. I drove back to Cornelia, feeling a little sad and not understanding exactly why.

Back home, my kitchen was warm and steamy from boiling water, for pasta, even with the fan over the stove whirring and Jude swatting his hands in the thick air over the pot. He had taken out his contact lenses, replacing them with a pair of wire-rimmed glasses that he now took off and rubbed on his shirt, removing the steam.

"Where've you've been?" he asked, kissing my forehead. "It's spaghetti night."

"Sorry I'm late. I drove over to my parents," I lied. "But I think they were all settled in for the night, so I didn't stay."

"Yeah? Your dad feeling poorly?"

"He has been ever since this last round of chemo. Hey—I met the most interesting woman at the gas station."

I told him about her, French erotica included, and he listened. Then he said her name, a complete sentence, which is when I said it was too big a coincidence and he said there was no such thing and I said then how do you explain our meeting and he said destiny. It was a ping-pong game of a conversation until he held up his hands and insisted, "Here's my proof," reciting every bumper sticker she had, although I only remembered a few. That's when I began to worry about why she had come back—who has the nerve to say "Divine Goddess on Board" if they can't back it up?

"Are you going to find her?"

"No."

"Why not?" I asked him. "Don't you want to know how she is?"

He shook his head. "Not really. You can't *find* Rita anyway," he said. "She has to come to you. Some people are just like that."

"You're going to run into her, Jude. Considering this is Cornelia, probably tomorrow."

"Probably so," he said, "if she really is back to stay."

"I wish you had seen her, too."

"I'll see her soon enough."

I didn't want to annoy him, but I had more questions. "If you can't find Rita, as you say, how did you ever marry her?" I asked.

"I loved her."

"I know, but what was it that drew you to her?"

"I don't know exactly," he said, shaking his head.

"How could you have loved someone and not be able to say why you loved her?"

Jude turned off the burner with a dramatic click. "I'd rather not remember," he said, ending the conversation.

It would have been much easier to forget about Rita, or to hate her, or to just feel sorry for her, reducing her to nothing more than someone overcome by tragedy. I couldn't be sure, but I had a feeling that Rita had run from Evan's death, not from Jude, situating herself in the very middle of the country where nobody without an aerial view could spot her. If she had returned to Cornelia to assure Jude's memories of Evan, as he seemed to think, then she was going to have to show herself. You can't make memories from far away, and, as I understood it, the best way to keep a memory was to create another alongside it.

If death is a kind of leaving, a departure of departures, then my father had already had his share of practice. There had been his ship's debarkations, of course, each one distinct from the other. Once, he told me that he used to stand on the deck, his hands thrust in huge sailor pockets wide enough for him to extend all five fingers, look at the receding land, and wonder if he would remember what he was leaving. "The farther away the ship would get, the smaller all that land was. It was just like forgetting something," he said.

"Me," my mother had said, under her breath, careful that only I would hear. I was an adolescent at the time. I said nothing, knowing, even back then, that was the safest thing to do.

Now, after months of cancer and three rounds of chemotherapy, my father's body was tired. It was shrinking, muscle losing definition, his back forming a small but definite slope. His hands shook when he tried to pour himself a glass of orange juice or use the remote control. And, after the last round of chemotherapy, his fuzzy eyebrows began to fall out first, becoming patchy, stray ones sticking straight out like antennae. My mother volunteered to fill them in with her eyebrow pencil, every morning if she had to, but my father said his face felt lighter without them—even if gathered together they would weigh less than a wish. His hair, however, put up a more determined fight. It had stopped falling out in patches. Instead, when he ran his fingers through it, a fine dusting fell around him.

My father's response to these changes, ironically, was activity. He started attending events, inviting me to accompany him to tile grouting or electrical work demonstrations at Home Depot, or to films at the art museum, or to talks by writers stuck somewhere between religion and science at Charlotte's huge new bookstore. While I usually went, and in just two weekends could hang a ceiling fan and banter about Buddha, it was grocery shopping that he most often requested. He called me to accompany him to the grand opening of So Fresh Market, the one with the delicatessen that made the ethnic food aisle redundant. He called me to go to the closing of Charlotte's last Winn

Dixie, somebody finally accepting that Dixie had not been won and probably never would be. He called me as he cut out coupons for the grand opening of Ingles, which he pronounced the Spanish way, having visited Cuba and Mexico and, once as a civilian, Venezuela.

The Saturday afternoon after I saw Rita at the gas station, my father called me, a last-minute request. "Feel like a little grocery shopping?" he asked. "I want to check out that new Harris Teeter out your way. They're having a grand opening. It will be you, me, and your mother. She is trying to control the cancer, or actually me, through food." He cleared his throat. "We'll let her try."

It was true. Apart from whatever responsibility she had assigned to Melissa, or taken from me, my mother's most recent cancer fighting strategy involved whole food and nutrients, my father's strategy (apart from the French fries) from the beginning. She had decided what my father could and couldn't eat, replacing his fairly mundane diet of meat and salads with vegetables and seeds, and some whole wheat bread, if he asked nicely, with butter on top. She didn't have the medical prowess to read his medical chart, but she sure could read a thermometer pulled from an organically fed turkey breast.

"I don't think I can make it today. I've got a date with Jude in just a couple of hours," I said. "And I'm going to need some time to get ready." After nearly five months with him, Jude sometimes still called and asked me, formally, for dates, and I reciprocated by planning my outfits, curling my eyelashes, and trying out high heels.

There was a pause. In the background I could hear golf on the television, the announcer's hushed voice, the same way my mother sounded when she gave me updates about my father, as if whispering about how he pushed himself up from the armchair, his mouth clenched and his eyes closed against the pain, erased it.

"You can come ready for your date, and we'll have you back home on time," he said. "It's not that much to ask."

I moved the phone away from my mouth, stunned at his harsh tone. Then it occurred to me it was the first time since he had been sick that I had denied him anything. Other than a grandchild, although he didn't know about that.

"Okay," I said. "I'll take a shower now. Can you give me an hour?"

"Lather, rinse, don't repeat," he ordered, the humor back in his voice. "And don't take your mother's side when she and I argue in the cookie aisle. I am changing strategies. Now I want pleasure from food, and that's it."

He could attribute the grocery store excursions to resisting my mother, but I knew they were throwbacks to those Saturday mornings of my childhood when my mother would have her hair teased and sprayed at the salon and my father would take me to the A&P. The store had become famous for employing a pair of Siamese twins as baggers, the brown paper sacks crunching as they were unfolded, one hand from each of the twins creating a pair that worked in unison. Their hips were joined, their shoulders and faces perpetually turned toward each other, but I wasn't allowed to stare as I wanted to. In fact, I suspected that my father turned shopping into a world excursion to keep us both distracted; he was as intrigued by them as I was.

As we wandered the aisles, he would assume the role of a tour guide. We bought German chocolate, Thai coconut milk, Italian sausage, frozen Swedish meatballs, Mexican chili peppers, and a steak sauce from Jamaica that he would sprinkle on hamburgers and say, "Reggae, reggae good," after which my mother would check the expiration date. Once, he let me buy a package of éclairs filled with white crème as thick as the paste we used at school. "Frannie, I want you to know about the world," he would say. "Sometimes I worry that you'll grow up thinking it ends with us, your mother and me. With Charlotte. The world does not end with us or with Charlotte. You know that, right?"

I nodded. "There are people in other countries. Is that what you mean?" Back then, I had already planned which countries I would visit first: Spain and Brazil.

He shifted his eyes to the side. "Yes, that's part of it."

At the end of the lesson, we would proceed to the checkout where Shirley and Eugenie stood waiting at the end of the counter. My father would smile at them and then look away. Once, I whispered to him, "They are sisters forever and ever. They can't ever leave each other," and he answered, "More like being married."

My father was a good student, a student still, because when my parents picked me up that afternoon, it was the first time I could remember in a long while that the two of them drove to my house together. My mother tooted the horn, and through the window I saw my father open the passenger door. Before I got in, I gave him a quick kiss on the cheek, which, thanks to the chemo, felt as smooth as glass, as smooth as the top of his head. He wore his corduroy cap, a humble tenant of the coat closet where my mother's infamous tiger-fur cape hung. Stacked on the backseat were at least a dozen baseball caps, some actually advertising sports teams, others computer software or motor oil. "He won't wear any of them," my mother said, when I held up a couple for examination.

"I'm not a little boy," he mumbled.

"I'm going to buy you a fedora," I said, leaning forward, my elbows fitting perfectly between the two headrests. "It's more your style."

"Fedora," my father said absently. "I wish I had a fedora." Looking at my mother, he added, "Doesn't that sound like a good name for a cat? Should we get another cat?"

"Not with the goat," she said.

"Goat?"

My mother put the car in reverse and started backing down my driveway, opening the driver's door because she didn't trust rearview mirrors. "Your father has bought a goat to cut the grass for him."

"Does it have horns?"

"Like a marching band," my father said, smiling.

"It bleats. The Shumans are not pleased. It bleats under their kitchen window. They think it's hungry. So we are the neighbors who are starving their goat."

"It's not hungry," my father said.

"How can you have a goat in the city?" I asked. "The city is no place for a goat."

"It's only for a week. I have rented a goat for a week."

My mother nodded. She bent her arm back toward me and fluttered her fingers. "It's not a mean goat, just stand-offish."

I sat back against the seat, the leather cool against my arms. For my date with Jude, I had chosen silk pants and black heels, and I felt, perhaps for the first time, that I was worthy of my mother's car. My father had always bought practical cars, sedans with four doors, the same number of people he thought appropriate to inhabit a car at any one time, perhaps some ironic ratio left over from his time on a ship. But my mother had always been lavish with her cars. For every piece of classic, practical clothing she owned, her Lexus offered a gadget. Hidden sunglass compartments, seat warmers, stereo speakers surrounding the interior like a well-trained military unit.

"I'm tired of cutting the grass, too," I said. "I want a goat."

"Take ours," my mother offered.

My father turned to wink at me.

As it was, the grand opening of Harris Teeter felt quite different than any other grocery-shopping event with my father, partly because I was overdressed and conspicuous, partly due to my mother's presence, or impending presence. She dropped the two of us at the curb, slowly maneuvering her car up and down the busy rows while we hurried inside to the coolness, the electronic doors making us feel lazy.

"We'll start with the sweet things first," my father said. "A pie, maybe. Blueberry." He pulled a metal cart from three or four stuck together and rolled it forward a few times, watching to make sure the wheels didn't stick. "Cancer will do that to you," he added, maneuvering slowly around the floral department—which made me think, a little wistfully, of Hugh. Small groups of people were everywhere, blocking the aisles, tasting free samples of cheese served on toothpicks, and accepting coupons from strangers.

I walked beside my father, aware that the ritual of long ago had changed, maybe not so much by time but by "circumstance," to quote my mother. My father was not looking for the exotic; he was looking for the normal, the very thing over which he had lost control. "Jude says owning a bakery is like being a psychiatrist," I told him. "People want to feel better. They prescribe themselves sugar and butter."

"I am no longer interested in order, in what should come first or last," he said. He stopped walking to let several old women pass us. To our right, rows of tiny sprinklers sprayed water on the lettuce and spinach.

"So go ahead and tell me," I said, trying not to sound frustrated.

"Tell you what?" He placed a mango in the cart and nodded toward it. "A young woman showed me once a long time ago how to eat one of these without having to change clothes, but I could never master it."

I grabbed two more mangoes and put them with the first. "Keep practicing," I said. "Now tell me."

He rubbed his forehead. "Frannie," he said, "if I die, before I die, there are some things you should know." He thumped a few melons and handed me the smallest to put in the cart.

"You're going to tell me now? In the grocery store with my mother still searching for a parking spot that's not next to a truck or an SUV?"

"I'm not telling you now. I'm only trying to tell you that I recognize there are some things I will need to explain."

"Such as?" I thought about the long-ago pact with Hugh, how much he and I both had wanted to know my father, to keep him.

He paused, looked around to see if anyone was watching, and then adjusted the sign over the lemons. "Well, I'd like to be cremated and cast to the ocean, for one. There's that."

"Oh, Daddy. It's not time for this talk. Don't tell me it's time for this talk." I would not let myself cry in front of him. Or in front of dozens of suburbanites so used to excess that they wouldn't even notice. I was determined that my father would see me stoic and steadfast, reinforced by my second-best date outfit. In my imagination, his death had always required my ability to be strong, but I wasn't sure I would be.

"Frannie, there are other things." He looked past me. "I will need you to help your mother understand some of the decisions I've made in the past."

"The carnival?"

"Not that."

"Melissa?"

It suddenly occurred to me that there might be other things I didn't know about, or want to know about. I wondered if all these years my father had another life beyond even Melissa and Hugh, and then I realized it was the carnival.

He nodded. "Well, sort of. Hugh. It was always more about Hugh."

I tried not to look surprised. "Her son, you mean?"

"Davies's son. In a lot of ways, he's so much more his son than hers. And that's what worried me."

"Why? Why was he yours to worry about?" I wanted to say that Hugh had grown into a man who sent flowers for no reason—that he was kind and good—but I couldn't. I wanted to tell my father that he never should have worried about Hugh, especially since there were my mother and me to worry about. But I didn't.

"His father could be reckless. Melissa, too. I didn't want Hugh to turn out like that, too. I wasn't sure Melissa was up to the challenge." He put both hands on the cart for support and shifted his weight.

"Did you think Mama was up to the challenge? All that wondering and anxious speculation?"

"It wasn't fair to anybody, especially your mother."

"We went to visit them. Years ago when I was just a kid." It felt so good to confess that I just kept talking. "The house was really poor, and Hugh was playing in an old rusty wheelbarrow. And he teased me, but he asked me to stay and play." I stopped. "I thought he was nice. I liked him."

"I heard about that visit from your mother, Melissa, and Hugh," he said. "Everybody's version was different. But Hugh's was the best because he talked the most about you."

"That was a long time ago, Daddy," I said, not ready to have this conversation either.

"Ahh. Not so long, says the man with cancer." He smiled. "Frannie, it might turn out that, later, Melissa and your mother could be friends. If you can, encourage your mother to pursue that."

"I don't think Mama would want to be friends with Melissa, Daddy," I said, thinking of their stilted interaction in the dress shop. "I really don't."

Over my father's shoulder, I saw my mother standing by the flowers, peering down the aisle. I waved to her, but she pointed behind her and scurried off. "I'll be right back," I told my father, intent on getting my mother and him to talk, to put some history in its place.

I scanned five of the nineteen aisles until I finally saw her, perched on the bottom shelf of the cereal section, reaching up for a box of bran flakes. She stretched and stretched, unsuccessful, until she finally asked a teenaged boy for help, which he gave with a nod of his head. She didn't see me until I called to her, using my father's nickname.

"Lane!"

"Where's your father?" she asked after glancing toward me.

"He's in the seafood section, Mama," I said, speculating, out of habit, where he might have headed next, what his intentions were.

She looked horrified. "He'll buy farm-raised if I don't get over there. They feed those fish excrement."

"Actually," I said, "I think he was going to the health food section. Let's head that way."

Of course, he wasn't there. He was probably eyeing the red velvet cakes and disrespecting Jude, who thought buying a grocery-store cake put you on the path to moral ruination. I kept my mother in the health food section as long as I could, checking sugar grams on boxes and praising chickens that had been raised cage-free. It seemed odd that a chicken could accomplish what I couldn't—because even though I wanted my parents to establish some trust with each other while they still had the chance, I had no idea what I would do with that kind of freedom.

Later, after Jude called to cancel our date—too much work at the bakery—I spent the evening wobbling around the house in my high heels, alone and all too free.

I still needed to talk to Hugh. So the next morning I called him four times, left three increasingly frustrated voicemails and then, finally, my impersonation of Bellsouth calling to disconnect his phone because of lack of use. While I waited for Hugh to call me back, I walked to the bakery to see Jude, but it was the after-church lunch rush. He could only wave in between making sandwiches and working the register.

When I got back home, Rita sat on my front steps. Her head was bent toward a clipboard, the surest indication that she was selling something, but she looked up, her gaze traveling the straight line of the sidewalk to me. She stood up, slowly, unfolding her body as if it were a napkin. She wore faded jeans rolled up at the bottom and a blouse with flared sleeves and lace around the collar, caught somewhere between Victorian and bohemian, an era yet to be named. She was lean and tan. I would have envied her if I had not been so busy trying to figure out why she was there. She was, in fact, prettier than she had been at the BP. The difference, I decided, was that she had a purpose; any woman who shows up at her ex-husband's new girlfriend's house would. And I knew from watching my mother these last couple of weeks that purpose adds color to cheeks, definition to muscle, at least to the heart.

"Frannie?" she asked as I pulled my keys from my purse.

"Yes?"

"Frannie," she said, this time as a statement, no exasperation or expectation included. I had to fight the urge to ask her if I could come into my own house.

"You are Frannie, aren't you?"

"Can I help you?" I asked.

"Au contraire," she said. "It is I who can help you."

"You're Rita." I stopped on the bottom step, wishing I had cleaned the house like I usually did on Saturday mornings, my mother's ritual now mine. "We sort of already met at the—"

"Yes, that's right." She cocked her head and smiled at me. "Jude's ex-wife."

"At the gas station."

She nodded. "I remember."

Rita wouldn't be the person to change the phrase "awkward silence" into "graceful silence." She looked me up and down a few times but didn't seem to have anything to say, so I said, "You wanted to meet me more officially?"

She laughed. "This is Cornelia. We don't do official here."

"A clipboard is very official," I said, nodding toward hers.

"Not this one." She tucked it under her arm and held out her hand. "There's no reason for us to set off on the wrong foot. I'm Rita Dawson."

"Dawson like Jude is Dawson," I said. "That's official."

"Speaking of Jude, I saw him this morning at the bakery. I had a muffin." Rita rubbed her stomach. "Banana nut," she added.

I held up the white paper bag that Jude had sent with me. "He made me a sandwich. Pimento cheese. With lettuce and tomato and a special pickle."

"Well, the special pickle makes you the winner, doesn't it?" She winked, only it wasn't playful the way a wink should be—it was lethargic. A lethargic wink is not a wink.

"Were you just curious about me? Is that it?" I edged past her to swing open the screen door, my key in hand.

"I'm curious about everything," she said.

"But you're back in Cornelia for good? Curious or not."

"Yes, for good. Since the 'for better or for worse' part didn't work out, then it's fair to say that I'm back for good. Somewhere between the two."

I lowered my voice, given that neighbors' windows were open and a porch in Cornelia was as good as a stage. "I know that you and Jude share a sad bond." Her eyes flashed, not with surprise but with anger. Maybe this far past the grief she had found anger again. I saw it in Jude, too, but he was better at quieting it.

I unlocked the door and instinctively held up a foot to barricade the cats, but they were nowhere in sight. I was, after all, about to let a stranger into the house, and yet she didn't feel like a stranger.

Rita peered past the door, squinting her eyes. She was so small and narrow that it was hard for me to imagine her pregnant. "Cute house," she said. She hadn't moved yet, although her eyes hadn't allowed anything to go unchecked.

Inside, the telephone was ringing, but whoever it was could wait. If it was Hugh, I'd call him back, still unsure of what to say. If it was Jude, he would be seeing me soon enough, explaining how Rita knew where to find me, how he had fed her and then sent her over here like an ambitious stray dog.

"Would you like to come in?" I asked.

"No," she said, shaking her head. "I only came to tell you that you and Jude are okay. The pickle. The sex. Everything. It's okay with me."

"You're giving me permission, is that it?"

"No, my blessing. There's a difference." She pushed her hair back, finally wrapping all of it to one side so that it reminded me of a mermaid's tail. I tried to imagine her twelve years earlier, when Jude had met her, but it was hard to think of her as younger, or older. She was the kind of woman who would age suddenly, wrinkles and worry lines the last to arrive. And she was the kind of woman who would barely notice.

"How do you even know anything about me?"

"Jude told me a little bit. At the bakery just now. He's taken with you. Really taken with you." She didn't sound jealous, not the least bit. If anything, there was a touch of surprise in her voice, or maybe a little suspicion.

"Jude and I are getting to know each other," I said. I shifted the bakery bag in my hand and lifted my chin. A strong chin, my father always said, is a sign of character.

"Well, that's how it starts."

The phone rang again. "I should probably answer that," I said, thinking it might be my parents. The screen door swung closed behind me. I turned to look at Rita, and that's when I saw the resemblance to Evan. Jude had two photographs of him attached to his refrigerator with magnets from the local real estate company. Rita had his eyes and his heart-shaped face. Or he had hers.

"Okay." She looked past me to the street and sighed. "Well, I'll go. My car's at the bakery, and I know the way back. We should all walk while we can. It's not like I-77 won't eventually plow through Cornelia. Although in the years I've been gone, it's not like anything has changed in Cornelia at all." She sighed again. She was like a deflating balloon with an agenda, only I didn't know what it was.

"A lot has changed in Cornelia," I said. "For example, I'm here." I listened as the answering machine came on, but whoever was calling didn't leave a message.

She turned back around to face me. "Oh, yes, you are," she said.

The screen door must have made me feel protected because I said what I had been thinking for the last couple of months, something I had never even said to Jude: "You left without explanation. Or without even saying good-bye. I guess I don't understand how someone could do that."

"It's hard to know," she answered matter-of-factly, "who left who first. There's all kinds of leaving."

I nodded, wondering why she wasn't more hostile, or coy, or even crazy—the way Jude made me think she would be. As she walked away, her shoulder blades a pair of parentheses beneath her cotton blouse, it occurred to me that she hadn't even mentioned Evan. She was just Rita, not a real visitor. She hadn't come in my house, or even sat on the top step to gossip, as my neighbor Brenda sometimes did. She did not ask to use the bathroom, or the telephone, or, as a very strange handyman did, my blow dryer. She had not slept in my bed, as Jude had, the sheets pulled up to his ears.

Yet she had made me doubt Jude.

As if to prove this, she took her time strolling down the sidewalk. It took me a few minutes to decide that she hadn't come back for Jude and Evan, but to somehow challenge me.

After Rita's appearance, I spent a couple of restless hours trying to work on an article about historical landmarks in the South. Then I cleaned the bathroom. I couldn't talk to Jude. I thought about leaving a message on his machine at home, something a little sarcastic. Then he called me, and I ignored his voice coming through my machine, watching his number on the caller ID and adding up the digits all the way to thirty-two, no doubt somebody's lucky number, but not mine. I held my cats, rubbing their smooth stomachs, making myself think of life without him in it, which I decided would be sad and lonely. Still, Rita had rattled me. She had made me feel less sure about him, which made me less sure about me, and whenever I was less sure about me, that meant talking to Hugh.

I turned off my computer, fed the cats, and drove to Charlotte.

After we met, that first afternoon when my mother had confronted his mother, I didn't see Hugh for at least a year, but then he transferred to my school and was on the playground one day, calling me Fanny and then apologizing for it. He was a year ahead of me, so we only had one year at the same junior high, but it was time enough to figure out that we shared my father. Hugh took on the role of telling me about him, although in those early years it was more private eye-inspired, two children trading information about their parents. He told me what kind of kite my father had bought him for his birthday, or what kind of pizza he and my father had ordered after playing baseball. He couldn't have understood that the time he had with my father was time I didn't have—back then, I barely understood it. And I was proud that Hugh liked my father so much. He pronounced both syllables of "Duncan" as if they were marching steps.

But by the time we were teenagers, there was less information to share. Hugh spent more time with friends than my father, and I was ashamed to talk about my father's absences and how angry but quiet my mother had become, especially after the baby died. Our secret friendship was confined mostly to high school, where we had short conversations in the noisy hallways. Hugh told me less and less about his mother's relationship with my father. I knew that once my father painted a screen door for her, and she had thanked him with just a quick hug and a sad smile. I knew there were other men in Melissa's life; they came and went while my father remained consistent. While Hugh suddenly grew out of his need for my father, I had years of practice at not needing him. I was sure that whatever happened with Hugh and his mother happened because of some deficiency with my mother and me. But I never told Hugh this.

When I got to Charlotte, the studio was closed up as tight as it had been on my last trip. I could tell from the top of the driveway that Hugh's truck was not pulled parallel to the high cement wall where it usually was. I had teased him that he'd never get married again because nobody could get in or out of his truck on the passenger side. I parked in his spot so he would see my car if he returned while I was there.

I knocked a few times on the metal door, brushing the rust off my hand as I walked around the back of the building, the railroad tracks twenty yards or so from me, running straight through the state, splicing it, dividing it. The small ravine between the building and tracks was covered in kudzu, millions of green hands grabbing for anything they could. One of Hugh's kilns was near the back, set up on cinder blocks the way someone else might have done a tired car. I put the tip of my finger to it, but it was cold. I saw the beauty set when I bent to pick up a penny, face-up, which my father had always said was good luck.

There were three small pieces. One, the comb with clay teeth as thin as toothpicks, was unglazed, the baked clay somewhat rough beneath my finger; another, the brush minus its bristles, was lightly glazed and nearly slick; and the last, a hand mirror whose warbled glass was no wider than two inches, was glazed with an earthen green, finished and dry to the touch. They were clearly Hugh's work, each perfect except for the crack across the widest part of the mirror's handle, as if someone had gripped too hard. For several seconds, I couldn't move. If a train had come by, I wouldn't even have been able to wave.

I heard Hugh's truck as I was placing each piece back onto the overturned plastic bucket where I had found them. I stood still, meeting his gaze across the weeds and gravel, until he walked up and stood beside me. "I came to visit," I said.

"You know where the key is. You could have gone in," he said, rubbing my back as a hello.

"I came to see you, and you weren't here."

"You were waiting for a train to come by like you always do," he said, smiling.

"Maybe. You doing okay?"

"I'm doing okay. That's a good word. Okay."

He hadn't shaved that morning. The beard at the tip of his chin had one gray patch that looked like a crescent moon. He nodded toward the beauty set. "There you go."

"That's not your usual pitcher or bowl."

"I've been stocking up in case, well, in case I become a father. You caught me." He seemed embarrassed.

My heart felt ridiculous and old. It had never occurred to me until I saw those three tiny pieces that Hugh would be anything but relieved he wouldn't have to finish our pact. Ours was such a desperate agreement, the desperation all mine, or so I thought. I suddenly understood I was going to disappoint him. "That's why I came, Hugh," I said, keeping my voice as even as I could. "I need to tell you something."

"So tell me."

"Well, all this time I just assumed that when I wanted to have a baby I could have one, and it turns out that's not the case. I've been told that I won't be able to stay pregnant, carry a baby to term. Not ever."

"Jesus, Frannie." He wrapped his arm around my shoulder.

"You think you've had female trouble," I mumbled into his shirt.

Several stray cats that had lived around the studio for years darted onto the top of the kiln, meowing, paws swiping at air. Hugh swished them away. Then he hugged me, dedicatedly, both arms wrapped tight. "I'm sorry, Frannie. That's rough news for you."

"Well, I guess this means our pact is off."

"Yeah," he said softly. "Well, disregard the flowers then."

"I've been wanting to ask you about that."

"Just something I felt like doing," he said, releasing his arm and sending the cats, who had crept close again, scampering back into the kudzu.

"Thank you," I offered.

"You don't have to thank me." He did that shuffle thing that men do when they're trying to make a getaway. "Listen, I've got a bunch of work to do."

"Yeah, sure." He had never tried to get rid of me before, but I deserved it. I nodded and looked toward the tiny mirror. I would have held it up to see my horrible self reflected if Hugh hadn't already done such a good job of that.

Chapter 7

I got up early the next morning and drove slowly through sleepy Cornelia, partly on the run from the silence of my house—although inside my head was loud with thoughts of Hugh—and partly on the lookout for Jude.

Jude walked to work in the mornings. He would leave his loft on the top floor of what had once been Cornelia's secondary mill, the stand-in mill after a fire shut down the main one, and head down Benders Road, take a right onto Main, and stride toward the bakery. He usually had a newspaper tucked under his left arm, all headlines muffled against the sleeve of his T-shirt. He talked to passing dogs, not necessarily to their owners. If the school bus sputtered by, with the twin boys from Anderson Road positioned in the far back seat, their faces turned toward the rear window, he silently counted the heads in the seven windows stretched down the side, his lips moving like a lazy ventriloquist. But he always came up one short.

I knew all this because after our first night together at his loft, I had walked with him. "Let's do the walk of shame together," he said. So we had, allowing Cornelia a no-sneak preview of us. At the bakery, I ate my breakfast croissant in the same clothes I had worn the day before, with no makeup on, and Jude told Mrs. Horton that yes, I did look different without it. That was the day Jude started his tradition of bringing me the bill penned on the outside of a white paper bag with more food inside. This tally, no matter what I had eaten, always read, "Amount Due: Your Complete and Utter Devotion for Eternity." In return, I started my own tradition: I left a tip. I applied the lipstick that I carried in my purse (but almost never wore) and kissed one of the napkins from the metal dispenser, leaving it draped over the old brass cash register with the numbers that popped up in a window.

All of Cornelia talked about this at first, but as the months accumulated, Jude'n Frannie passing through that stage of novelty and excitement and settling into routine, the town had something else to talk about: Rita. So Cornelia talked, and I stayed away from Jude because I was afraid I would be careless with him like I had been with Hugh.

I drove that morning but didn't find Jude, although I heard in the dry cleaners that he had lost two of his bakers to Harris Teeter, who paid fifty more cents an hour and had, necessarily, a good dental plan. Jude could have told me this news if I had answered the phone the nine times he called. But I hadn't.

The next morning, I showed up at the bakery before he did. At 6:00 a.m., a good hour before Jude usually arrived, I stood with a white apron tied around my waist and questions about Rita making me fat because I had swallowed them whole. Jude's head baker, a short woman who said little, let me in the back door, nodding her head at the apron.

"Budget fashion?"

"I'm here to help out for the morning," I told her. "I heard two people quit."

"Suit yourself," she said, "or don't." She looked hard at the apron again before closing the door behind me and turning on the huge mixer so no conversation could begin.

I took a quick survey of the kitchen. Stainless steel bowls were stacked feet high beside the sink. I counted eight bricks of butter sitting on the countertop. A row of croissants was cooling on a metal rack. I peered into the ovens, all three of them, and saw Jude's famous sugar cookies, though in predictable round shapes, no stems attached. Then I went into the front dining room where the long pastry cases were empty and yesterday's doilies waited. I stood by the window, watching for Jude. I got bored with that, so I ran my hands under the shelf that held jars of biscotti and got the key to unlock the front door. It was still dark outside.

When Jude appeared around the edge of the bank, I stared him down. He stared back at me. He let his eyes travel the length of my body, stopping at my shoes and moving back up past the apron to my pink lips, decorated like it was date night.

"Nice apron." He shook his head and kept walking. "I can't get you to even pick up the goddamned telephone and you show up like the Pillsbury dough boy in drag at 6:30 in the morning?"

"I want to work in the bakery today. I heard you were short on help."

"Why?"

"I like baking. You know that."

"Why, Frannie?"

"Here's another why: why did Rita come back?" I stopped so that he would, too. Only he didn't. He kept walking, so I had to jog to catch him. "Why did you send her to my house?"

"I didn't send her, Frannie. I just told her about you. I told her that I had moved on, that I had found someone I cared about who could give me a whole new life."

"You want a whole new life?"

Jude handed me the paper, a photograph of Clinton waving from Air Force 1 on the front page, and bent over to pull a weed from one of the huge cement planters that flanked the entrance to the bakery. "That possibility comes with any new relationship," he said, standing up to look me in the eye.

"What if we were 73?"

"Then we'd be card-carrying AARP members in practical shoes." He looked down. "Like the ones you have on today." He swirled his hand in the air, demanding a smile from me, but I didn't oblige.

"What if the chance of being a father again was completely removed from the equation?"

"You don't do math on the weekends, remember? We are not an equation."

"We sort of are," I said. "You minus me is just you. Me minus you is just me. You plus me is something we don't even know. Those are all very different values."

Jude did not look convinced. Even I wasn't convinced. A woman in a borrowed apron talking algebra was dubious at best. And beyond that, beyond Jude and me, there was Evan.

And now Rita.

Jude hooked two fingers over the top of the apron pocket and gently tugged. I shuffled forward. "How long is your shift?"

"I'll work through lunch, and then I'm going to visit my father."

"How is he?" Jude asked.

"Weaker, according to my mother. The same, according to him." We were face to face now, close enough that I could see where Jude had nicked himself shaving.

He took the paper from me, rolled it, and tapped me on the butt. "The President has just kissed your ass."

"Finally," I said.

"So, Frannie," he said slowly, "are you saying that you're not interested in having children?"

I sat on the window ledge and pouted. I said nothing for a few seconds, those seconds before I lied via omission. "I've always wanted a family. Always." I did not tell him that I couldn't have a child of my own.

Jude nodded. "I could see you as a mother. You'd be good at it. Even the part where you have to give kids the freedom to be themselves, which is the hardest part."

"Why do you say that?"

He shrugged. "I don't know. You're such your own person, I just figure you'd be good at letting somebody else do that, too."

"How am I my own person?"

"You're just Frannie wandering around Frannie land. I don't know. You're different than other people. I feel better about everything when I'm with you."

"Really?" I wondered if Hugh would agree with him. After the broken pact, I was sure that our relationship had been damaged, maybe beyond repair.

"For real."

"Thank you," I said, not sure what else to add. And then I remembered. "I didn't mean to be flippant. I wasn't referring to—"

"You're welcome."

For a moment, there was only the sound of a few cars driving slowly past. Then he reached down and extended a hand to me, which I took, rocking myself up against gravity, just another force I didn't understand. It wasn't even seven in the morning in Cornelia, so there was no music to be had, what with the bank not yet open, its Musak tucked silent and waiting behind speakers, and the crossing guard's transistor radio audible only to herself as she pedaled her way down Walnut Avenue, ear plugs and safety intentions intact. So we couldn't dance. Instead, I put my nose to Jude's neck and sniffed for his aftershave, one of the rituals that we had already established. This time he did the same to me.

"I miss that Old Spice thing you had going on," he said. "You know, when I rubbed off on you."

"That was Old Spite," I said, smiling. "Which leads me to my next question: how did she get my address?"

He let go of my hand and sighed. "I don't know. But it doesn't take much to find out where somebody is around here. You know that."

"Did she tell you why she came back?"

He shook his head. "She doesn't have to say it. The only reason she'd come back is Evan. I don't think she can live with the absence. So she has to fill it with something else. Maybe it's me. Maybe it's here, Cornelia, I don't know."

"And what about you?" I asked.

He sat on the ledge now, square in the middle, so that I couldn't join him. "I don't love you because I no longer have Evan, if that's what you mean."

It wasn't what I meant. Jude must have wanted another child. If I hadn't just deceived him, I might have outright asked him if he did, but I couldn't bring myself to ask the whole truth of him when I couldn't offer it in return.

On the other side of the windows, the head baker stacked muffins, lemon tarts, and cinnamon bums (as Jude called them) in the cases and then wiped the countertops. Jude tapped on the glass and gave her a thumbs-up before checking his watch.

"Come on," he said. Taking my hand, he led me around the side of the bank and to the bakery's back door. "The staff comes in here," he said, sweeping an arm in front of him.

When we stepped inside, standing beside the rows of shelves was my father, wearing a baseball cap and the one pair of madras plaid pants he had ever owned, acquired when he took up golf on a whim over fifteen years ago because he had read that it increased IQ. My mother and I had both told him that a pair of pants on which you could play a game of chess was not a good thing, but he insisted, executing a sloppy golf swing for backup. He was much thinner now, and the pants were baggy.

"Frannie," he said, clearly surprised.

"What are you doing here, Daddy?"

"Well, I came to see Jude's bakery." He reached to the shelf beside him and half-heartedly shifted a large can of walnuts.

"You came in the back?" I asked. "At seven in the morning?"

"Hi, Duncan," Jude said. "You doing okay?"

My father shrugged and said, "I'm up and out."

"Does Mama know you're here? Where's your car?"

"Something smells good," my father said, lifting his chin. "The car's across the street at the drug store. I'm just out for a drive. I can't sleep these days."

"Mama knows where you are?" I asked again.

"Your mother was up at six, cleaning out the coat closet." He looked down at his pants and sighed. "Which is why I'm wearing these. She put on the cape and I put on the madras."

Jude leaned over and whispered, "Is this about to get kinky?"

"You know about the cape?" I asked my father.

"Some," he answered. "I know it has something to do with your mother's romantic past."

"My mother has a famous cape that she tries on from time to time," I said to Jude, without taking my eyes off my father.

My mother's college boyfriend had been an abstract artist obsessed with stripes. His car sported bright Mexican serapes, and he wore striped shirts each day of his life. He gave my mother a cape made of faux tiger fur, which he insisted she wear to a party. It was their last official date. Two days later, Baylan dropped out of college and went to live in Europe, in Romania, my mother said, where gypsy women would bathe him as he stood naked and somewhat anxious in a metal tub. She never saw him again, but he claimed mythic stature in our house.

When I hit adolescence, my mother started removing the cape from the old armoire in the attic, where it was wedged between my father's raincoat and her holiday sequined jacket. It hung well below her waist, and her hands appeared tiny and hapless from beneath the folds of animal flesh, fake as it was. Once, my father, who returned home unexpectedly early, scowled and said, "Fe fi faux fur" when he saw my mother in it. Finally, she stopped wearing it unless she had something like a new manicure or "Neighbor of the Month" to celebrate. Then she and I would each try it on, preening for the other while she invented stories about Baylan and the gypsies and bracelets stacked up arms like too many options. The cape became code for my mother's warnings about men, about settling, about rushing, so, of course, we didn't let my father in on the game.

"Do you have a cape, too, Frannie?" Jude asked, raising his eyebrows.

I shifted my body away from Jude and looked at my father. "I always thought you bought the pants for golf," I said.

"Who's the daddy of stripes? Plaid. Plaid is the daddy of stripes."

I laughed. "Is that country club rap?"

"Golf is for sissies," Jude said, too seriously, trying to find a way into the conversation.

"Yes, it is," my father agreed. "Anybody with any sense knows that a real sport requires you to leave the ground, not attach yourself to it with cleats."

"You got that right," Jude said, winking at me.

An hour later, when my arms were submerged in soapy water nearly up to my shoulders, Jude came and stood in the doorway. I could hear lots of voices coming from the front, so I knew that the bakery had attracted its usual morning flurry of customers, mostly men in dark business suits about to make the drive into Charlotte. Progress liked its asphalt sprinkled with sugar.

"You're good," he said, smiling in approval.

I wiggled my butt, the only part of me that was completely dry. "So what did you and my father talk about over breakfast while I was soaking in Palmolive?"

"Not much, really."

I turned the faucet off and lifted my arms from the sink, flinging water at Jude, enough to make him duck back into the mop closet. I could tell that he was lying. He threw the word "really" onto the end of anything he didn't quite mean. "What did you talk about, Jude? Come on. He didn't drive all the way out here to sample the coffee cake."

"Well, if you must know, he wanted to know why I became a baker."

"What did you tell him?"

"That I liked making things. That I liked to eat. That food is a celebration of life."

I dried my hands on my apron. One of the counter girls stuck her head through the door and motioned for Jude.

"Was that all he wanted to know?"

Jude took my apron strings and tied them into a huge lopsided bow that not even a preschooler would claim. He lowered his voice and added, "He also wanted to know if my intentions were honorable in regard to you. He wanted to know if I loved you and if I planned on a future with you."

"He's getting ready to die," I said, forcing out the words. "He wants to make sure I'll be taken care of."

Jude didn't say anything. He moved back toward the door and brushed his hand across my shoulder. "Do you want to know what I told him?"

"Not right now, Jude. Right now I need to finish these dishes." I didn't look at him. "Because if you said yes, I won't know whether to be happy or sad. Or for whom."

"I'll tell you later," he said curtly, "but the answer rhymes with 'guess.'" I heard him slap the door open and then turn on the coffee machine that gurgled and puffed out steam for lattes.

I didn't finish scrubbing the pots. If I had been named employee of the month, my photo taped to the front window, as Jude did in rotation with each employee, then somebody would have been obligated to draw a big, fat mustache, bushier eyebrows, and nose warts on it. I didn't even tell Jude good-bye. I just untied the apron and went to look for my father.

I didn't go far. I had only driven a few blocks past the end of Main Street, a half-mile or so before the turnoff to the interstate, when I looked, as I always looked, for the train tracks that the town was threatening to displace in favor of a condo complex. They were the same tracks that ran behind Hugh's studio and all the way down to Georgia, past Atlanta somebody had told me once. For now, the area was an open space, open to the sky, which always appeared beveled above it, bordered along the back by a thin row of water oaks and pines. There had probably been crops there at one point, maybe peanut plants, with shallow roots and a tangy odor that the ground could never release. The tracks ran parallel to Main Street, with one crossing and one guard rail for a narrow, cracked road that ended past the trees. I slowed, listening for a train. A black dog ran across the far left corner of the field and disappeared into the trees. My father's car was parked between several clumps of tall, gangly pines.

He sat on the front bumper, his arms folded across his chest, elbows pointed out, leaning forward. He was very still. He was facing east, although the trains always came from the west. I honked and waved at him. He turned to look but didn't wave. I couldn't see his expression from that far away, but when I pulled up beside his car, he looked slightly embarrassed.

"Are you waiting to hop one of those trains about to come through?" I asked, rolling down the window.

He looked across the tracks. "Frannie, I don't mean to sound dramatic, but another train is coming for me. And not one I want to hop." He stood, pushing up with his hands, the usual grimace giving him chipmunk cheeks.

I got out of my car and hugged him. He was so thin that my right hand met my left elbow. Jude must have noticed, too. On the front seat was a white bag full of muffins. "Take Mama some breakfast," I said. "Go home, Daddy."

He nodded and pulled the keys from his coat pocket.

"Take care of yourself. And Mama, too. I'm going to be fine," I assured him. "I am going to be just fine."

I drove away first, but I stopped down the road and waited for his car to pass, some five minutes later, followed by the train's whistle, which sounded strangely weak and low, like a father's signal for a child to come in from play, to come in right now.

When I was not quite seventeen, my father disappeared for nine days one summer, in late August, that time when nobody really wants to admit that summer is over, but it is. Gone are long days and strolling neighbors with complaints about the heat. It was also the summer when my mother began studying wind patterns, a wistful meteorologist with Kmart decorations for instruments. She staked in plastic sunflower pinwheels among the holly bushes and hung wind chimes in the lowest branches of the weeping willow tree. While the sunflower faces spun merrily from time to time, the wind chimes in our front yard never rang out. It was as if the metal bars, rather than bumping, delicately touched each other and said, "Shhhh." Having placed each of the three sets of chimes herself, my mother often commented on this curiosity, looking up from whatever she was doing to note first the wind and then the lack of music thereafter. She'd cock her head, then say, "Nothing, absolutely nothing."

"Why would Daddy leave like that?" I asked the morning when we awoke to discover him gone, a note stating that he needed a trip left folded on the kitchen table.

But she didn't answer. She stood in the doorway behind the screened door, listening.

I took the silence—hers and the wind chimes'—as a bad omen.

After two days, my father called, just once, from a gas station food market, or at least that's where he told us he was. He said he had bought a cup of bad coffee and a road map. He said he would be home in a week. During those seven days, my mother and I did not mention him; we talked around him, as if he were some strange phenomenon we didn't quite understand, like money on trees or cars with wings. We tried on the cape. We ate expensive finger food, shrimp cocktails and tiny quiches the size of the one fifty-cent piece in my piggy bank. We did not do the dishes, such heedlessness mocking my father's recent home improvement projects, including a pair of curtains in the bathroom made out of jute. "Jute, otherwise known as the cat's scratching post," my mother said the third night, all humor gone from her voice.

When he returned with no excuses, no apologies to either of us, I watched my mother greet him in the driveway. Casting her eyes first toward the wind chimes, she took his favorite windbreaker from the crook of his elbow and said, "It was rainy wherever you were." He did not answer. Then I heard her say, "Nothing, absolutely nothing." My father bent over the back seat, his face turned downward. When he stood back up, his lips were slightly pressed into an O, as if he were on the verge of some subtle but meaningful surprise.

As I watched from the other side of the living room window, open to the night sounds of crying babies and TV news, he pulled a candy apple from a bag and handed it to her. I was surprised, but she took it right away. She held it upside down and let it swing back and forth a few times. Then she wrapped it carefully in the windbreaker and handed it back to him. She walked to the house, her arms folded across her chest.

He entered the house backward, pulling a worn, nylon suitcase up the one step from the porch into the house. "Where've you been, Daddy?" I asked.

"Frannie," he said. He looked tired, tired and old the way I didn't want him to be.

"Where've you been?"

He surveyed the living room behind me. "I've been away, Frannie. And that's all I'm going to tell you."

Later that night, my parents went to sleep in their usual routine, although my mother spent an unusually long time in the bathroom. I stayed up because in my teenage bravado I thought I could solve the mystery. But all I found was the candy apple lying forlorn and forsaken in the thin strip of grass next to the driveway. I didn't hear my mother until she came up behind me. I turned quickly. She still had on her green dress, the one that was cut like an A with a belt of gold coins that dropped just below her waist.

"Mama," I said quietly.

She opened the driver's door and sat behind the wheel of my father's Buick, one leg in the car and the other flat-footed outside on the pavement. I thought she looked like a rebel, but, more realistically, I knew she was preparing herself for what was going to be a hard ride ahead. "Your father is attempting to rewrite the Bible."

"Just how is Daddy rewriting the Bible?" As far as I knew, my mother had never paid much attention to religion, to anything so abstract that an update or makeover couldn't improve it. She would have listened to Jesus' story and considered a better ending.

"You know." She nodded her chin toward my hands. "Adam offers Eve the apple. Eve refuses because Adam has already left the garden. That story."

From the faint glow of the streetlight, I could see that she was wearing her full face of makeup. Her gardenia perfume drifted toward me with the breeze, ignoring the wind chimes along the way.

"Where was he, Mama? He must have told you something."

"Your father has been working at a carnival." She said this last word as if it were a long-lost memory. "As a magician."

My eyes widened in amazement. I felt my lungs expand.

"All along your father has been able to do magic, and I never knew." She shook her head slowly from side to side. "Magic, and I never knew it for what it was," she repeated.

"What kind of magic?" I asked.

My mother turned her body and placed both feet on the pavement outside the car. She was wearing the shiny black pumps she had worn to every funeral she ever attended. While most women had rows of shoes lining their closets, my mother had always owned only seven or eight pairs, in basic colors and very classic lines. "Gorilla woman."

"Gorilla woman?"

"Yes. He was part of the act where a woman turns into a gorilla." She ran her palms around the circumference of the steering wheel.

"Women don't turn into gorillas," I said. I leaned against the back door of the Buick, my feet stretched far in front of me.

"Oh, I think they do." She turned to face me. "They just need someone to make them believe. Like an announcer. He was the announcer."

"How is that magic?"

She gave me an incredulous look. "You hold a microphone and tell hundreds of people that a woman is about to turn into a gorilla and that's not magic? You set it up so convincingly that people stay, actually pay good money, and that's not magic? Mystery is magic, Frannie. What you don't say is more important than what you do say. This, I know."

I tried to picture my father in his dark business suits standing in front of a crowd with a microphone. Then I remembered how once as a little girl I had asked him to take me skating, and instead we had gone to the local county fair. Inside the arena, elbow to elbow with hundreds of others, we watched the gorilla lady—three shows—and ate cotton candy until our faces were sticky and white from the sugar.

"I can't believe it," I said. "Not Daddy. It just doesn't seem possible."

"What doesn't seem possible, Frannie," my mother said, "always is."

From then on, my father disappeared every year, in late summer when my mother had already begun her autumn planting and catalog Christmas shopping. If she had ever protested to him about it, she stopped. Instead, gorillas came to be a joke in my house the way snoring or adolescent crushes were in others: "Monkey business," my mother came to call my father's second career; "King Kong," she referred to him behind his back; "It needs a little more gorilla, no, vanilla," she'd say, tasting my latest baking project. Time drug its knuckles through the year. We abandoned family vacations. My mother wore her makeup and gardenia perfume. I went off to college.

But *that* summer, the summer my father first discovered the carnival, I discovered something else. Hugh and I made our first pact: we would not interfere in our parents' melodrama. And we sealed the pact with sex—my first time with anyone—in the garage my father had built himself, on some old quilts, awkwardly and clumsily, our bodies not as compatible as we seemed to be otherwise. I had called him to talk, about my father, to see what his theory was. Then he showed up, after my parents drove away, out for dinner with friends. The sex just happened; it wasn't planned, although its possibility must have always been there. Maybe we wanted to do what our parents hadn't, for Hugh swore that my father's relationship with his mother was innocent enough. I believed him. Still, it was a melodrama. Melissa and Hugh, the carnival—my father's secrets all suggested one unavoidable truth: that my mother and I were not enough.

Hugh left before my parents came home. I took a cold shower and sat on the porch in the August heat until my father's headlights bounced up the driveway, music seeping from the house next door because our neighbors, like my parents, preferred open windows to air conditioners. I didn't know what I was supposed to feel or do after the sex, but during it, I had felt much of my anxiety about my father sweat away from my skin, calming me. As always, Hugh had been there to make me feel better. And every time I thought about telling my father about Hugh, and didn't, I swallowed that silence whole.

And silence was what I still knew best. After my father came to the bakery to verify Jude's intentions about me, which were so honorable that I would have to be *dis*honorable just to challenge him, I didn't tell my mother about it. I didn't run to Hugh, although I wanted to. I squelched any further conversation about who would or would not make sure that, going into the future, that fickle friend, I would be okay.

It didn't take Jude long. The next afternoon, in my mailbox, I found an envelope with one of his personal checks inside, made out to me for $48.92, although I had no idea what hourly wage I had earned, or if he had let me claim myself, woefully, as my only dependent. I wrote him a resignation letter, printed on stationery with my name embossed in gold. It said that I needed fifty-one weeks of vacation a year, a private parking space, and soup stock options. But I couldn't let that one bad joke stand alone. I ended by writing that I didn't need hot water and cheap detergent to wrinkle my hands when time had already offered, thank you very much. Then I paid Lacy Dennis, a girl down the street, to walk the letter over to the bakery.

As I suspected he would, Jude showed up at my house that night, right around suppertime. "You can't resign when I already fired you," he said, swinging the letter in front of me and smiling.

"I don't recall that you fired me."

"That check was severance pay. You have been severed."

"That makes me think of body parts," I said, stepping out onto the porch.

"I like where this is going." He darted his eyes back and forth from my breasts to my face.

I laughed. "That's fine. The girls and I"—I gave him a stern look—"have already found another job."

"You take them everywhere you go, even to work?"

"Everywhere," I said.

"Good for you."

"And *you*."

"And me, me, me, me, me," he said, grinning.

I couldn't help but hug him. Then we sat side by side on the steps so that the neighbors wouldn't miss any more developments in our relationship. Sometimes I wondered if all of Cornelia knew more about us than I did. More specifically, I wondered if Rita did; after all, she had a history with Jude that I could never share.

I pulled my knees up to my chest. "I saw Rita today," I said.

It wasn't the first time. After her visit to my house, I began seeing Rita around town. She was always walking, striding, really, as if she were one step ahead of being angry. But she smiled a lot, too. She smiled at everything, it seemed. Once, as I sat in my car waiting at a stoplight, I saw her emerge from the hardware store, a hammer in one hand and a small brown paper bag in the other, smiling. Maybe she had traded up from French erotica to handymen in tool belts.

"Walking around town?"

I nodded. "She's interesting, Jude. And intense and child-like all at the same time. I feel kind of drawn to her."

"I can understand that," he said. "She always was a little quirky. After Evan died, that quirkiness turned hard, if that makes sense." He tapped his thigh against mine three times, a sad attempt at flirting, and then looked disappointed.

From inside the house, the alarm on the oven sounded. I was making carrot soufflé, one of the recipes my mother gave me when I moved to Cornelia. I had previously lived as a mature and independent woman in four other houses or apartments in Charlotte, with appliances and mixing bowls and even the savvy to swap out ingredients, but she only started sharing her recipes when we were no longer sharing zip codes.

"I've got a soufflé in the oven," I told Jude, standing. "Are you staying for supper?"

"Do you want me to stay for supper?"

"Let's see what the soufflé looks like." I reached for his hands and helped pull him up. He lifted one of mine and kissed it, so I lifted one of his and did the same.

"God knows we don't want it to fall," he said, kissing my other hand. "I would not want to be with a woman with a fallen soufflé on her record."

"Moral dilemma?"

"The worst kind."

He followed me through the living room, past the dining room, and into the kitchen. The whole house smelled sugary and decadent, and through the window of the oven, I could see that I had done my mother's recipe proud. It should have been a happy moment, Jude nodding his head in approval as I lifted the puffy soufflé from the oven to the counter, "All Things Considered" on the kitchen radio and the Williams boy tossing a football in the backyard next door. And no bad jokes about things deflating or not rising to their potential or, even worse, carrots being the root vegetable of all evil.

Sure I had told my father I was going to be fine, a theory I had to believe, Jude or no Jude, I opened my mouth and owned the cruelest joke I knew: "Jude, I can't have children. If I go forth and multiply, it's only because I'm doubling a recipe or figuring out the triple discount points at the carwash."

"Only on Wednesdays," he said slowly, staring so intently at me that I should have *divided* into a billion parts, my very own diaspora, "and they don't count toward the wax option."

Chapter 8

I took a fork from the drawer and dug it into the soufflé, blew on the steaming bite I pulled from the very middle before I ate it, and stared back at Jude while I swallowed, waiting for a real response. All he did was point and open his mouth, so I dug out another bite from the middle and blew on it before I gently slid the fork into his mouth, lifting the handle as I pulled it out. He pursed his lips and puffed out his cheeks, waiting for it to cool, and then finally swallowed.

"If you think about it, I just gave you your walking papers," I said.

"No," he corrected me. "You just announced your walking papers, the ones you wrote for yourself." He took the fork from me. "The soufflé, by the way, is excellent."

"I fed it to you like a baby," I said sadly. "Did you notice?"

"Give me thirty or forty years, and you might be doing that for me three times a day every day, Frannie. Or I might be doing it for you. And there might also be diapers involved. It all…"

"Depends," I murmured.

He turned off the oven, took a step to the side, and pushed himself up on the counter. "That's what I meant when I assured your father that I would be there for you."

"Yeah, but you didn't know that I was, and here's a word I hate, barren, when you told him that."

He didn't say anything, so I scooted the soufflé to the left and pushed myself up on the counter beside him. "Speak. Talk. Pontificate."

"I'm not the pope."

"I'm awful," I squeaked out. "You're not the pope, and I'm awful."

"Listen," he said, tapping his fingers on the tile. "I wasn't expecting you to tell me you couldn't have children, but I get it now. My heart's dancing around on my sleeve, and yours isn't, so there had to be a good reason for you to be holding back. Now I know what it is."

He believed it so much that I almost did, too. "I just found out a few months ago," I said, trying to make him realize that it wasn't the gynecologist's grim assessment that made me reluctant. I still wasn't sure I loved him. That was what made me awful. Only an awful heart in an awful person could listen to a proclamation of devotion that reached so far into the future it bumped up against a box of adult diapers and still not be convinced.

"What is it exactly?" he asked.

"A broken uterus. I can get pregnant but not stay pregnant."

"And they're sure?"

"Conclusive, to quote my doctor."

"Well, I'm sorry," he said.

"For me or for us?" I asked. I didn't say it, but my "us" always included Evan.

"Both," he said, "if you want me to be honest. I can't say that I haven't thought about having another kid. But then I can't say that I haven't thought how much it scares me, too."

"Which one do you think about more?"

"I don't know, Frannie," he said, tenderly, too tenderly, so that if *he* didn't know, I definitely did.

I nodded. Outside the window over the sink, a floodlight on the back corner of the Williams' house came on, and then there were children's voices and a football that arced from one side of the window to the other. It was too coincidental, too rehearsed—the cosmos or God or even a lowly pontificating pope should have opted against such synchronicity, such blatant underscoring. Jude winced, and I saw a little of the man I had seen on the carousel.

"Did Evan play football?" I asked, trying to be brave. The more I knew about Evan, the more real he became.

"No," he said, shaking his head. "Rita wouldn't let him. Not even Peewee Football. Because she knew it would lead to more football."

"I should have been a boy," I said. "My father wanted a son anyway."

"No, he didn't," Jude said, wrapping an arm around my shoulder. "All fathers want a little girl to spoil." When I shifted forward so he couldn't see my face, he understood what he had said. "I'm sorry—I'm not saying that I want a little girl. I just wanted you to feel better."

"It's okay." I reached underneath my knees and tugged open a drawer. I handed a fork to Jude and then took a bite of soufflé with my own, and then another and another until Jude did the same. It was a simple, honest, egalitarian supper. And far far away in another zip code, my mother and father were probably sitting down to their dinner, my mother having schemed her way through another healthy recipe, my father accepting each new meal like a day on the calendar, the future arrogantly pending.

My mother was, in essence, rebuilding my father's life. She had started with food and, like the very cancer she wanted to thwart, was working her way to other areas. She ordered an entire new wardrobe for him, each pair of pants a good size smaller than what he used to wear, either accepting or rejecting the fact that he was shrinking in front of her. She threw out all his toiletries, from Band-Aids to toothpaste, and spent over $100 replacing them, each suddenly assigned a specific spot in the bathroom, her regiment as close to Navy life as she could come. She had Goodwill bring a truck to collect the old stereo console whose lid opened to reveal an actual record player, which spun like bad thoughts in front of her; then she went to an electronics store all on her own to purchase a CD player with five slots for discs. She changed her hairstyle, after nearly fifteen years, deconstructing the orderly bob and adding loose layers that made her appear disorganized, or, at the very least, relaxed. She bought a cell phone and called me to report all this, a sad journalist with a sadder story. She even hired a cleaning woman.

Her name was Brevna. She was an Indian woman with the traditional *bindi* on her forehead and fingers that were stubby and wrinkled. She spoke as if each word was its own architect, separate and complete, without other words around it. She drove to work in a dented, small pickup truck that she parked a good two feet from the front curb, which I witnessed the next time I went to visit my father, the image of him on the crossing rail still as clear as the tracks running South to Georgia.

From the front door, my mother and I watched Brevna move up the sidewalk as if there were a skateboard hidden under her sari, which was the color of eggplant and trimmed in gold metallic thread. A shopping bag, bulging with a hard-edged something, bounced against the folds, TOYS R US written in fat black letters across the top of the plastic.

"She's very exotic, isn't she?" I said. "I bet she was beautiful when she was younger."

"She has nine children and twenty-two grandchildren," my mother said. Her hair fell across her forehead now, and I couldn't see the arch of her eyebrows.

"Like the Gradys," I said, referring to my old neighborhood's most notorious family, "brazen pagans," as my father called them, who turned their front yard into a haunted house every Halloween, populated by three generations of themselves wearing outrageous clothes and bad makeup, which really did little to distinguish them from any other day.

"No, not like the Gradys," my mother said, but did not elaborate. "And she judges me."

"How so?"

"She clucks her tongue, and she talks with your father in a lowered voice so that I can't hear."

"At least you've hired her. That's a start." I tried to make my voice perky, a technique I was perfecting whenever I talked to my father. "That's a big step for you."

When I was a child, a stream of older black women would appear on the neighborhood sidewalks in the mornings and again, walking more slowly, in the late afternoons, moving to and from the bus stop at the corner of Park Road. But back then my mother would have none of it, claiming that anyone who couldn't clean her own house shouldn't have it in the first place. So I spent the Saturday mornings of my youth following my mother through the living room, dining room, kitchen, and bedrooms as she assigned chores. During those years, my father was exempt from cleaning. It was a strange way to ostracize him, but that's what it was.

"I hired her to entertain your father," she whispered. "The carnival come home."

"Being from India is not a sideshow," I whispered back. "You can't conflate them."

"It's not about where she's from. You'll see," she said and opened the front door. "Good morning, Brevna," she announced, smiling. "This is my daughter Frannie. Frannie, Brevna."

Brevna nodded curtly, almost smiled, and held up the plastic bag so that it was even with her hip.

"For Duncan?" my mother asked.

"Of course," she answered and kept walking across the foyer, stopping at the coat closet to open the door and then close it again, as if to make sure no one was hiding. The smell of mothballs escaped and lingered.

"She brings stuff for Daddy?"

"Little things to amuse him," my mother said, coyly, liking the suspense. "Things other people don't have."

I kicked at the small Persian rug that had been in front of the door for as long as I could remember, squaring its edges against the wooden frame. "She sure seems to know her way around the house."

My mother rubbed the top of my arm. "Your father likes her, drawn as he is to unusual things."

"Are we not unusual enough?"

"I think we aren't," she answered.

"Okay, what about Melissa?" I said. We hadn't discussed our visit to the dress shop, and I still wasn't sure what she had or had not told my father about it. I wasn't even sure that my mother's Plan B hadn't already been executed.

"Melissa is not all that unusual either," she said, coy still, although at that point I was almost sure that she and Melissa had been in recent contact.

"Are we going to talk to Daddy about Melissa? Can you let me in on what's going on?"

"Brevna, you mean. Brevna's going on. Let's live in the moment."

I did not know how to fight her. "Okay, so what does Brevna clean?"

"I don't know," my mother said wistfully. "I swear when she leaves, the house isn't any cleaner, and she *stirs up* a lot of dust."

I looked at her. "What does that mean?"

"Her husband runs a pet store," my mother said, ignoring my question. "I met her when I went in to cuddle the bunnies." She looked stricken and then pressed a palm to her chest.

"It's okay," I said before she could go on. "Just because I can't have a baby doesn't mean you can't publically cuddle bunnies."

"Oh, Frannie," she sighed. "It's so unfair."

Suddenly, from the den, we heard my father say, "Well, look at that!"

At the end of the foyer, positioned squarely in the middle of the doorway, was a lizard the size of a serving platter, its pink tongue flickering in and out, its eyes cast sideways, and its tail curled into an upside-down number six, my mother's unlucky number, or so she always said.

My mother screamed first. "A lizard! Someone get this lizard out of the house."

At that, Brevna scurried to the doorway, a towel draped over her arm, purple bedroom slippers now replacing her heavy black shoes. "Skink," she said. Then she reached down and scooped it into the towel, a hand under its belly and another beneath the tail. Its body appeared to stay stiff, but its legs moved wildly beneath it, what its heart, trapped inside a prehistoric body, probably couldn't do. I remembered, as a child, once asking my father if my cat loved me, and he answered, "She's domesticated, so yes."

My mother clamped both hands onto my left arm. "Are lizards mean?"

My father's head appeared behind Brevna, and he edged his way around her. He stuck out an arm, thin beneath the expanse of shirt sleeve, and tapped the lizard on the head a few times, saying, "Skink, skink, a little green skink."

"Skink, skink, the skink is in pink," I said, tugging at the towel and offering my father an inquisitive look.

"Whose towel is that?" my mother asked.

"What does it matter?" I said. "The better question is what's a lizard doing wrapped in it?"

My father did not look well, did not move well. When he walked toward me to hug me, his steps were deliberate and heavy. "Brevna brought it to entertain me for the day now that the goat has been returned."

My mother rolled her eyes and looked at Brevna, who stood with the skink stretched across the bridge of her arms. "What happened to the Hindu board game?" she asked, her voice hovering somewhere between frustration and confusion. "Gods and goddesses, lots of invisible and well-intentioned gods and goddesses," she added, looking at me.

"Her name is Sylvia," Brevna said.

"She only meant to entertain me," my father corrected, casting his eyes sideways in poor imitation of Sylvia.

"It's a girl?" my mother asked.

"May I?" I asked Brevna, extending my hands. She wrapped the long edge of the towel around Sylvia's tail and lifted her to me. I studied the skink's webbed, flat toes and wiggled my nose at her. When her weight settled against my arm, she was as heavy as a good dictionary, her flesh firm and smooth. I handed her back to Brevna and rubbed my palms against my jeans.

My mother stood silent, denied whatever reptilian rapture my father had experienced. "I had a camp roommate named Sylvia so many years ago," she said. "She loved horses." Then she looked sadly at my father, who patted her on the shoulder and sighed. "Brevna," she added, "shall we get to those shelves?"

Brevna nodded curtly again and followed my mother out of the room, holding Sylvia in front of her, her arms stiff, her back straight.

My father leaned one shoulder against the wall, anchoring a leg beneath him. "Who knew?" he said, although I wasn't sure what he was referencing or why.

I answered anyway. "Nobody," I said, and kissed him on the cheek.

"I've talked to Melissa about you," he said, as I turned to follow Brevna and my mother.

I stopped, ran my fingers along the edge of the table where my parents had always left their car keys. "Recently, you mean?"

He nodded and, with some effort, put one hand on each of my shoulders. "Perhaps when I die, you will get to know her."

I wanted to tell him that he wasn't going to die, that any one of us could begin a sentence with "When I die" the same way we could with "When I was born." Even Sylvia, who could not be protected by organic lettuce, or by having the name of a long-suffering poet, or even by Brevna herself, would die. I thought of Evan. I wanted to have known him, but I knew Jude without him, which was the closest I would ever come.

"Why?" I asked instead.

"It seems right," he said, thoughtfully, "and I have a feeling that she'll be able to be a good friend to you. And she might need your friendship, too."

"Doesn't she have her son?"

He pursed together his lips and reached one hand to the doorknob for support. "She has Hugh, yes, but that's different."

"He's a good guy. Hugh." It was only a half-confession, although as soon as I said it, I felt guilty. I couldn't think of Hugh now without feeling guilty.

"Yes, he is," he said, but he didn't ask me how I knew or to what extent. He shifted his weight, grimacing. When I reached to help steady him, he swished a hand in the air and shook his head. "Speaking of good guys, Jude loves you."

"You sure?"

"Sure like numbers," he said using one of his code phrases that I hadn't heard in a long time.

"He told you this?"

My father nodded, almost smugly.

"I think that makes you happier than it does me," I said.

"You don't even know," he said, as my mother called for him to come take his vitamins.

A few minutes later, I met Brevna coming out of the bathroom, where she had sequestered Sylvia in a metal tub she found in the basement. She shook her head several times, slowly, her lips drawn tightly against her cheeks, scolding me, for what I wasn't sure. When I didn't answer, she leaned in toward my ear and whispered, "Your father does not want a clean house or healthy food. He wants comfort. He wants to be involved in the world. You tell your mother that." She pulled away from me, nodding her head in a I-told-you-so kind of way. "They move like this, your parents," she said. She held out her arms so her body made a T, leaned from one side and said, "This is your mother," and then she leaned to the other side and said, "This is your father," the whole time flapping her hands. When I shifted my eyes from her face to her hands, she added, "This is you," and she straightened, centering her imaginary T, to demonstrate where I was.

"You just met me," I said.

"I listen," she said, tapping one ear. "And today I have heard and seen enough to know."

I stared at her, a little stunned. Such bossy-pants nerve, right in the middle of so much anxiety and fear. She was direct and simple and even honest. Most of all, she was right. Everything she had said was right. She had stepped into our house and done what I couldn't—because I was afraid that to ever be just Frannie meant choosing my mother over my father or my father over my mother. And then what would we do? But Brevna didn't give a skink's tail about all the secret pacts and plans and partings dirtying up our house: she got straight to work. She cleaned. She assessed.

"Yes," I said, ashamed, "I see what you mean. They might as well live in separate houses." I thought for a second as she bent to rub an ankle, her bracelets jingling against her hand. "What will you bring my father next?" I asked.

She looked at me, no longer scolding, but not sympathetic either. "Next I will bring a bird. From the rainforest. Your father is interested in the rainforest."

I nodded, knowing that my father would never get to the rainforest to see one himself. "Bring the prettiest one," I said.

She nodded and went back into the bathroom. I heard metal scrape against tile, and then she emerged with Sylvia in the metal tub, my mother's lacquered nail polish tray minus the nail polish covering the top. She carried Sylvia past me, into the den where my father was watching the weather station, and set the tub on the floor. Then she lifted Sylvia and placed her in the glass terrarium waiting on the coffee table in front of my father. I moved to the doorway so that I could watch Sylvia, the ragged edge of her jowl moving up and down, as she ate the organic lettuce Brevna fed her. Then I watched my father, who looked slightly amused but otherwise so weak and wan that it made my whole body hurt.

My mother wheeled the silent vacuum cleaner past me, the cord rattling behind her. I followed her into the laundry room. "He looks really bad," I said, stretching my arm to stop her. "I don't like how bad he looks. Let's get Plan B—or Plan C—going. Let's get on it, Mama."

"Don't say that," she said, her hands shaking. "Don't say how bad he looks."

After that, my mother began bringing in Brevna every other day, and she gave her specific chores in addition to trying to keep my father alive. So, four days later when Brevna was cleaning my old room, she found seven jars of baby food from the collection I had stolen, one by one, from the 7-Eleven. They were buried in a box, covered by a stack of magazines—*Teen Beat* and *Tiger*, pages and pages of music and makeup and advice about boys—in the cut-out alcove of the attic, accessible by the small gnome door at the back of my closet.

I thought that I had thrown away all the jars years ago, as the house began to resettle around the three of us, and the baby, whose name we never said, slowly disappeared, her presence pushed out by each piece of office furniture that my father moved back into the nursery. My mother's stomach resumed its flat, hard surface, but my father only touched her at the small of her back, as if he were nudging her forward.

I was in the kitchen making a milkshake for my father when Brevna, her bedroom slippers flapping against her heels, came to the door and pointed for me to follow her. I did, without a word, passing my father in the den and avoiding his curious expression, half-question, half-suspicion. The doctor had called the day before to say that the tumors were still growing, though slowly, which had kept my mother in the den, talking to the bird that Brevna had brought instead of to my father, listing all the birds she could name, as if to convince it she could be trusted via her many and close bird relationships. It was a macaw with a striking red beak, at home in a metal cage whose top was rounded like my mother's hair used to be. My father had smiled when he saw the bird and positioned the cage on the coffee table so that it directly faced him, clicking its tongue whenever he moved.

Brevna led me upstairs and down the hall to my old closet door and then stood, the cardboard box in clear view, positioned between my six bridesmaids' dresses on one side and some old suits of my mother's on the other. Behind the row of clothes, pinned to the wall, was a drawing of my father that Hugh had done years ago, as a birthday gift for me, although I couldn't remember which one. In it, my father's face was turned to the side, his jaw line more defined than it actually was, Hugh's pen assuming its macho duties. He had drawn another portrait of Melissa, just to show me, he said one day at school, but he let me keep the one of my father.

"What?" I asked, not sure which Bevna wanted to discuss, the box or the drawing.

She bent, reached into the box, the glass clinking as she did so, and retrieved a jar of stewed carrots, which had turned a greenish-brown. She squinted and moved the jar closer so that she could read the label, the same way my father read all his prescription labels. "Vacuum-sealed," she said.

"It's a good thing," I said. "It's over twenty years old."

"Your mother told me that you were a good daughter."

"I am," I said, meeting her challenge.

"It's yours?" she asked, pointing to the jars.

"It's mine. Was mine."

"So whose is it now?" she asked, her chin tilted down and her eyes locked on me.

I had to think. Anything twenty-plus years past its expiration date belonged to no one, claimed no status.

But Brevna wouldn't allow it. "Whose?" she demanded.

Using my fingers for effect, following the example of my father, who was downstairs doing his own sad math, I did mine. My sister would have been twenty-four, not long out of college, inviting men to her first apartment, regretting that she hadn't studied abroad or regretting that she had—in a country she loved too much. I would never be able to do calculations for my own child, but it felt good to think about *her*, to give her a life, to imagine how her bedroom would have been next to mine, how close we might have been.

I wasn't sure how Brevna felt about crying, so I wiped the corner of my eye. "I stole these when I was younger. Years ago. Before my mother had her baby, my sister, and after the baby died."

Brevna nodded, as if she were fact-checking rather than listening to something so solemn that I had never been able to say it aloud before. My father must have told her.

"I had a lot more, but I guess I got rid of all the other jars."

She nodded again. "Take them back."

"What? To the store, you mean?"

"Take them back," she said again, and this time she smiled.

"What would I say?" I asked, bending to inspect the other jars, all of the contents crusty and puke-green.

"Take your mother with you. She should have made you do it a long time ago. Children who aren't disciplined stay children." With that, Brevna left the room, although she returned a few seconds later with the plastic Toys R Us bag, which she held open as she stood in front of me, her gaze a laser burning into my conscience.

Without looking at her, I placed each of the jars into the bag. They clinked and settled into the plastic, bulging now with the weight. She cupped a hand under it and hoisted it to me. Then she called, "Miss Madelane, Miss Madelane."

My mother appeared, with grease marks on her cheeks and her hands in rubber gloves. She looked from Brevna to me. Then she looked at the jars of baby food and said, "Those?"

Brevna did not say a word. She left the room, closing the louvered closet doors as she did so. I let my eyes sweep across the patchwork bedspread before lowering the bag to the carpet.

"I'm going to return them," I said to my mother. "To the 7-Eleven."

She did not look surprised. "They won't be able to sell them now," she said, such disappointment in her voice.

"No, I'm going to return them because I stole them, Mama. I stole them."

"That was so long ago," she half-whispered.

"Will you go with me to the 7-Eleven?" I asked.

"Okay," she said, thinking. "Your father has Brevna. And the bird."

I touched my finger to my cheek to show that hers were dirty, but she only removed the rubber gloves and placed them, one precisely over the other, on my old bed. "I'll get our coats," she said, "and tell your father we're running an errand."

Five minutes later, we were walking up the sidewalk toward the 7-Eleven, which still stood next to an apartment complex where my mother and I once returned a stray poodle to its family. The trail behind our house that I used to take as a child had long ago disappeared, as had the woods, both replaced by three new homes with copper gutters and bay windows without a bay to overlook. My mother walked briskly, and I tried to keep up, the bag clutched to the middle of my chest. As we turned the corner onto Park Road, my mother said, "It was something your father and I never got past."

"The baby?"

She nodded. "You either. I stole one once," she said, "to try to understand. To see how it might have made you feel."

"And?"

"I felt guilty. Is that what you felt?"

"No. It was my secret. It made me feel more important. At first, it made me feel like I was more important than the baby."

Her pace slowed a little and she turned to look at me, pressing down the collar of her coat. "And then?"

I swallowed hard, afraid I would say something to hurt her. "And then it made me feel like I was more important than Betsy, that pretty girl down the street. I think, for a while, you replaced the baby *and* me with her."

"Maybe I did," she agreed. "Maybe I did."

I waited a few seconds and then made the best apology I could. "I couldn't have known, though. I couldn't have known."

"Who could have known?" she said, and set her stare straight ahead, past the line of cars and the distant steeple of the Methodist church where I had gone to summer camp and smoked my first cigarette.

I wrapped my arm in hers. We kept walking, shoppers in reverse. A man in a truck honked at us, and my mother, on second thought, shot him a mean glance, only he didn't slow down long enough to see it.

"I think I'll tell Jude about stealing the baby food," I said.

"I think you should tell your father, too," my mother offered after a second.

"And include that I'm barren?"

"That's a horrible word. You're not a wheat field." She stopped walking, and then added, "No, don't tell him anything just yet."

"I don't know," I said, considering the fact that he would worry about me again, worry that I didn't have my future all sorted out. "But even if I could have a baby, I can't have a baby for Daddy." I shifted the bag, and one of the jars fell onto the grass, rolling down the hill into some bushes. We stared at its path, the passing traffic blowing our hair off our faces.

"And I can't have a baby for you either," I finally said, almost wishing that Brevna was there to tap her other ear, to say that she had heard.

"Or for someone else," my mother added quietly, without naming Jude.

We crossed the parking lot and entered the store, where you could still buy a package of Camels and beef jerky at the same counter while eyeing the pornography behind it. My mother stood, looking from one side of the store to the other. It might have been her first time in a 7-Eleven, since convenience was seldom her priority.

"Let's get a Slurpee," I said, pointing to the machines.

The young clerk, who had "Brandon" written in black italics on his dirty blue smock, planted his hands on the counter and stared. There was no one else in the store. A life-sized cutout of a race car driver stood beside the door, advertising beer. My mother walked over to it and kissed his cardboard cheek. "I've always wanted to do that," she said over her shoulder, "but to the real one." Brandon rolled his eyes. Behind him, in copies of *Penthouse* and *Playboy*, all those perfect bodies sweated it out behind cellophane.

"My mother was a Playboy bunny," I said suddenly to Brandon. I turned to see her eyes widen in surprise, one hand still resting on the driver's shoulder.

"No way," he said. He was short and dark, with a goatee and an earring.

"How many bedrooms does the mansion have?" I asked my mother.

"Fourteen," she said, without missing a beat. "Not counting the secret one."

"Oh, yeah, the secret one," I said, impressed with her ability to improvise.

I placed the bag of jars on the counter beside the boxes of bubble gum and fireballs, pointed to the Slurpee machine, and said, "Two small mixed ones please." He nodded and took two cups from the stack on the counter.

I watched him draw the Slurpee, first blueberry and then cola, from the machine, and then I watched my mother take a long sip, blinking her eyes, drawing in her lips. "It's giving me one of those headaches," she said.

"Ha," the clerk said. "Get it? A Playboy bunny *with a headache*."

I gathered in my breath and looked him in the eye. "I would like to return this baby food. I stole it over twenty years ago."

"I wasn't working here then," he said, glancing down at the bag.

My mother walked over to the counter and took three short sips through the straw. "I told her that she can't go to the mall until all this is settled." She took another sip.

"I've been grounded for over twenty years," I continued. "I need some new training bras. And a diary with a lock. Please let me make it right." I tried to look desperate.

He smiled slowly, looking from my mother to me. "Y'all are good." He stuck a hand inside the bag and pulled out a jar of creamed spinach. "Shit," he said, reading the date on the lid. "You weren't kidding."

My mother bit the end of her straw and then said, "She missed the '80s altogether."

"I hope the mall still has some 8-track tapes left." I turned to scan the aisle behind me. "I'll pay you what the baby food's worth now, if you'd like," I offered.

He waved his hands in the air. "We're even. And the Slurpees are on me."

"Thank you," my mother said, and we walked out past the newspapers and tall PBRs submerged in ice, even in January.

"Nice Peter cottontail, if you know what I mean," Brandon yelled after my mother, laughing as the door closed behind us.

We walked past the blue payphone where a man was repeating a number out loud, scribbling with a tooth-marked pen. We walked past the dumpster where a mother cat and three tiny babies were patrolling, both of us stopping to see if we could coax them to us. We walked all the way home, a good five minutes longer than the trail had ever taken, and then we stopped at the end of the driveway beyond which a very clean house waited.

"What did you name her?" I finally asked my mother.

"Alice," she answered. She wiped an eye and put one foot and then the other on the slate stones my father had installed last summer.

I decided right then that when I told Jude about my day, I would begin with Alice's name, no longer secret, only beautiful and complete.

But I didn't. When I saw Jude that night, I discovered that I couldn't share her with him just yet.

My father returned to the hospital the next week, and his first request was that a ferret be brought to visit. "Brevna could sneak him in here," he told me when I stopped by to relieve my mother for a couple of hours, although she refused to leave. It was the hospital where I had been born, situated on a quiet street lined with old oaks and legal offices that used to be houses, the best law, of course, practiced in the home.

"How would she do that?"

"I don't know," he said, sighing and adjusting the IV tube that ran into the top of his left hand. It wasn't a serious request—he made fewer of those. He had developed an infection in his blood, from the chemo. My mother had found him barely upright and lucid in the backyard, on the redwood bench under the huge azalea bushes that he refused to clip, the laws of Nature and geometry battling it out. "He's not going to die now," my mother had said when she called, "but come see him. Be here as much as you can."

She sat in the hospital recliner, her arms folded across her chest as she watched the nurse back out of the room with his chart. "Grown men eating pudding," she said, shaking her head.

"It wasn't bad," my father mumbled.

At that, my mother stood up and rummaged in her purse for a pair of tweezers, which she held up to my father, and pointed to his nose. "Let me tidy you up a bit, since you're about to have company."

"The doctor doesn't count as company, Madelane. He has, after all, attached a tube to my private sector, so I don't feel like I have to remove the last hair in my nose or clean the bathroom."

"Not the doctor," my mother said. She sniffed the air like a puppy and wrinkled her nose. "I hate that hospital smell. People in hospitals deserve more pleasant odors."

"Who's coming?" I asked but then realized it could only be one person.

My mother had not even finished stacking the food containers on my father's tray when Melissa appeared in the doorway. She wore tweed pants and a cardigan sweater with thick wooden buttons. She looked like a senior model from the old Sear's catalogue, which my mother still kept on the top of her magazine rack. She stood, waiting for one of us to speak, her mouth opened slightly. My father looked surprised, but he was not the first to greet her.

"Hello, Melissa," I said.

"Come in," my mother said, "and don't mind us." The last part had some sarcasm attached, but that was to be expected.

Melissa smiled weakly and took several small steps into the room, her shoes squeaking against the floor. "Thank you," she said. "Duncan." She blinked rapidly and then lowered her eyes.

"It's good of you to come, Melissa,"

"Of course," she said.

My father moved his gaze to my mother. "You never cease to amaze me, Lane," he said, although I couldn't tell if it was a compliment or a sudden and painful realization.

"Duncan," Melissa said, "Madelane called me. She thought you might like a visitor." She walked to the side of the bed and rested her hands on the steel bars. "I'm sorry you're going through all this."

I listened for hesitancy, since Melissa was in front of the most critical audience. But all I heard was concern and tenderness. I watched her hands as they busied themselves in her coat pockets. She must have known that with my mother in the room she couldn't smooth his sheets or plump his pillow. I watched her eyes darken when my father shifted his weight and grimaced. And I understood what my mother must have known all those years ago, what Hugh never said because he couldn't betray her: Melissa had spent a good deal of her life wanting something from my father that she never got. It was suddenly clear to me that she had a lot in common with my mother; no wonder my father wanted them to be friends.

"So how are you feeling?" she asked, finally placing her hands on the bedrail.

"My blood's infected, and I just ate pudding with a straw. Other than that, not bad." He patted her hand. "Thank you for asking."

For the next fifteen minutes, until the nurses ushered all of us out in order to let my father rest, small talk prevailed. We were just a family and an old friend catching up. The dress shop was closing, and Melissa didn't know what to do next. My father knew the weather. My mother knew the nurses' rotation schedules for the next week. I knew that Jude was waiting on me back in Cornelia, a movie already in the VCR. And I knew something else: I didn't mind that Melissa was now a visible, real part of our lives—it was better that way. But I wouldn't allow her into the events of one particular day that I had been imagining for months: the day six months ago when my father received his cancer diagnosis and disappeared before telling anyone. So, as the three of us left my father's room and walked past the receptionist to exit the hospital, I made a pact with that story. It was my Plan C, and I liked its ending. I replayed it once more in my mind.

It had been a clear day, both in Charlotte and at the beach, the northern tip of coastal Carolina that spawned pirates and the invention of flight and the velvet memories of my father's childhood summers. I imagined him driving there straight from the doctor's office, in his seersucker suit, five hours along darkening interstates and unambitious two-lane roads. He checked into a motel about a mile from the beach, where he could begin to smell the salty air, where the humidity occupied the room like the previous guest. In spite of it, he remembered the crisp blue gown from the doctor's office against his skin, the heaviest of uniforms. He opened the door to see the headlights from the highway—to remind him of direction, something the ocean did not demand.

Then he walked to the beach in the dusk, devoting the half-hour journey to his past: his parents. He thought first of his own father, quiet and remote, his wishes and disappointments tucked away like shirttails long before he died. Then he thought of his mother, dead for eleven years, envisioning the short string of pearls draped around her neck, worn smooth by nature and worried fingers. In death, beneath the white satin of the open casket, she had looked younger than in life.

Then he simply stood on the beach, the water shifting beneath a dark sky. Just ten quiet minutes before he turned and began the walk back to the hotel, where he would spend another hour with only the smell of the ocean—leaving it bit by bit—before driving again, the saltiness in his clothes waning with each mile closer to home.

But the walk back to the hotel, when the ocean was behind him, he devoted that to his future. He thought of me first—Frannie, the son he never had, the awkward child who had traveled away and away from him, all the while searching for ways to keep him close. And finally, his thoughts pushed inward until they found something familiar and true, someone beautiful, and he found himself thinking only of my mother.

Chapter 9

If my mother could offer Melissa, albeit in a practical cardigan and loafers, to my father, then I could offer Hugh, so I called him the next morning. It was a different kind of going-to-Hugh, though. I dialed the numbers with my pointer finger, like I did for pizza delivery companies or repairmen I had looked up on the Internet, reading each digit out loud. I would have had my secretary call him, if I had a secretary—that was how logical and efficient it felt.

His voicemail picked up after the usual eight rings, but I stopped myself from sighing at the beginning of my message so that he wouldn't come home to hear my disappointment, captured and accessible for all of time. Or worse yet, I didn't want him sitting at his breakfast bar, listening to a phone sigh as he was trying to decide if he would pick up because the person doing that sighing (me) had been so careless with him.

As it played, I mouthed the "It's Hugh—tell me something good" message that had been on his machine for years. Then I left my own: "Hugh, it's Frannie. My father's in the hospital, and I'd like you to go see him. With me. Maybe tonight, if that works. Call me." I hung up and went straight to my desk where the cats were sleeping on two articles waiting to be edited. I picked them up, one in each arm, and settled them on the bench under the window where the morning sun would hit once it edged around the Williams's new second-story addition, craftsman to castle in just four months. I worked for three hours straight while my phone did not ring, and then I called Hugh again.

This time I said that I would visit the hospital at 7:00 if he wanted to come, Room 472. I hung up and asked June Carter and Emmylou what they thought Hugh would do, but they, being cats with so many lives to worry about that they had stopped worrying altogether, didn't know. They both got up and wandered down the hallway, their tags clicking.

I didn't know either. All pacts would be off. I wondered if Hugh would feel that I had let him down again. But wondering about Hugh felt like wondering about string theory or Cool Whip—the complexity or simplicity of him, one of the two, made him difficult to predict, or so I was learning.

It had taken Melissa standing by my father's hospital bed for me to realize how much I wanted my parents together—not just living-in-the-same-house together but together like the pairs of socks my mother rescued from the back of the dryer, or together like the columns on the front porch my father had built four summers ago. Or together like that speck of a blink of a nanosecond when life and death meet up because neither one can turn back. To make that happen, my Hugh and my father's Hugh had to reconcile. It's not as if I hadn't already learned that keeping a man secret was harder than keeping a man.

I had a boyfriend right after I graduated from college, and I never told my parents about him. To be with him, I stayed in the small mountain town that housed the university like a strange relative, and I worked in a restaurant, serving overpriced dinners to hikers and skiers who drove up from the city to experience the outdoors. His name was Collins, and he spoke loudly. When I was with him, I shrank, silent, pushed back into myself by the mere volume of his words.

I met Collins in my last required journalism class, although poetry was his chosen art form. Collins did not have a major himself. He had been accumulating college classes for five years, working as a roofer and writing poetry on napkins. He lived in an A-frame house that he had built himself, with three rooms and a woodstove that boiled a huge kettle of water in less than five minutes. On winter weekends, we slept on a pile of sleeping bags and blankets that he dragged out from the bedroom and clamped together in front of the wood stove, his dog Jeffers curled beside us. As we lay on scratchy wool that smelled like rain, Collins taught me how to decipher iambic pentameter and how to kiss in small, succinct fashion so that the bristles of his moustache barely had time to tickle my nose. I kept my tiny apartment with its thrift store furniture, but I began to think of Collins's house as home, with the curl of the woodstove smoke ascending and all those words frolicking inside.

My father discovered my Collins secret, however. He drove up unexpectedly one Sunday, after a fresh snow made the North Carolina mountains into the work of a confectioner, and he pulled up in his Buick as I was returning from Collins's house to my tiny apartment, disheveled, the smell of sex still clinging to my hair.

"What's his name?" he asked when I went to hug him.

"Tom," I said, embarrassed enough for both of us.

"And does this Tom treat you well?"

"He writes poetry," I answered. "But I doubt if you'd like him. He won't be around long enough." Since I had lied about his name, at least I could voice one truth: I realized as I said it that Collins was not the kind of man who lasted. I had thought I could keep him all to myself by not telling anyone else about him. I felt safe in that secret.

"Then why give him a second thought?" my father said, backing away from the hug, his judgment made clear. "Don't cheat yourself, Frannie." Then he ended the conversation and took me to lunch at a new rival restaurant that specialized in appetizers.

That night, I couldn't sleep, what with Collins all alone with only an imposed pseudonym and my father's accusation—cheat—spiraling around me like smoke from the woodstove. In the dark, I drove back to his house, the A reaching toward the top of the pine tree that stood next to it, and walked in through the front door, finding it unlocked as usual. Collins was not there, although a woman's floral bathrobe was balled up near the woodstove. Jeffers came to lick my hand, a hapless apology for his owner.

I don't know what I was looking for, but I walked into the kitchen without stopping and opened each drawer one by one. In the third drawer, I found a napkin with scribbled words in neat, tidy lines that wrapped around the front to the back. Poetry. Lines that cited the wind and steeples and a woman's face so perfect that geometry emulated it. Me? I thought, holding a palm to my skin, searching for my mother's ridged cheeks that she hadn't passed on to me.

In the last drawer, the one where Collins kept the spatula, spoon, garlic press, can opener, and strainer that comprised his kitchen equipment, I found a single sheet of paper. My name was written in orange marker at the top, as if he were making a list of things about me that he never actually wrote. A list so secret that he didn't even know it himself. And his name, Collins Ryan, was signed at the bottom.

I left, stopping to write my initials in the ashes that had collected in front of the woodstove's heavy iron door. I made the s in Frances serpentine and defiant, the way my father did when he spoke my full name. Glancing in the rearview mirror as I headed down the long dirt driveway, I imagined Collins sitting in the lowest limb of the pine tree, eye-level with the peak of the A, watching me leave him.

My father never mentioned Collins, aka Tom, again, but a few weeks later, when I moved back to Charlotte, back to my old room, and in many ways back to the safety of Hugh, my mother found the paper with my name at the top that I had taken from Collins's kitchen. She threw it away, but my father discovered it in the trash, which he took out every night after securing the bag with a series of knots he learned in the Navy. He was holding the paper when I came for a glass of water.

"Who's Collins Ryan?" he asked.

"I don't know," I answered, pulling a glass from the cabinet. It was, and was not, another lie.

I must not have been convincing. My father took a Sharpie from the catch-all kitchen drawer and crossed through Collins's name. "I thought you seemed sullen," he said. He handed me the paper. "Frannie can stand alone, but shouldn't," he said. He picked up the trash bag and called out, "Right, Madelane," not waiting for an answer.

My mother's answer, maybe a few years too late, was summoning Melissa to the hospital, her way of announcing that she wouldn't be cheated, that she was tired of standing alone. Whatever lingering suspicion she had of Melissa, if it was hidden in "Plan B," Melissa's visit was as much a gift to herself as it was to my father. She might as well have worn a T-shirt that said, "No More Secrets," the sequel to my father's "Where did the carnival go?"

And I had to do the same with Hugh, who, without advance warning, did indeed show up at the hospital, room 471. I heard him across the hall, apologizing to a young woman who had just been wheeled back from an appendectomy.

"Wrong room," I said, opening my father's door enough to poke my head into the hallway.

He looked sheepish and did the Hugh scurry—a strut—toward me. "Word on the Duncan street, aka my mother, says that he's going to make it through this infection. Is that right?" He didn't bend to kiss my cheek, so I took a chance and rubbed a spot of clay off his. He let me.

"Yes," I whispered. "We think he'll be able to go home in another day."

"So?" He raised his eyebrows. "Why the urgency?"

"So, come on," I said, pushing open the door wide, not wanting to answer his question. "I told him you were coming." And my father was not surprised. If anything, he seemed relieved, like I was eliminating something from his to-do list. My father smiled first. Hugh was a little slower because he had to shrug off his frustration with me. When my father extended his hand but Hugh bent instead to give him a hug around his shoulders, careful to avoid the IV, I said the forbidden: "Daddy, this is my old friend, Hugh."

"Oh, he's not that old," my father said. "He had to grow up a little bit faster than most kids, that's all."

Hugh puffed out his chest, trying to keep the moment light.

But my father knew the moment for what it was, an opportunity he might not have again. "How do you think he turned out, Frannie?" he asked, nodding toward Hugh.

It was such a big question, full of even bigger unspoken ones coiled up inside: *How did I do as a fill-in father? Was it worth all the compromise? Could he have turned out this well without me?* I could hear part pride, part yearning, in his voice. I thought Hugh had heard the same until I caught him looking at me the way Jude had done the night I didn't say I loved him back. Hugh needed an answer more than my father. Hugh needed *me*.

"He turned out just fine," I said. But I couldn't really look at Hugh the rest of his short visit, instead studying the notepad on the hospital bedside table. What could even the most robust patient deem worthy of jotting down? How to keep ice chips from melting, how to make a tired vein more cooperative, how to encourage the nearly defeated heart to pump, pump, pump?

I had already figured out that Rita resented Jude for his relationship with me, so when I opened my door the next Saturday to find her standing, small and stoic, on the porch, the familiar clipboard tucked under her arm, my first instinct was to defend Jude. I said, "If you were wanting to find Jude here and offer more permission, he just left for the bakery about a half hour ago." I smiled, trying to look accommodating, but that was Rita's game, not mine. After a week of long hours at the hospital with my father, I wanted a quiet Saturday morning alone. I was still in my pajamas, the practical flannel ones with Dr. Seuss images.

She said, "No, that's not it. And good morning to you."

"Good morning. Sorry—I didn't mean to sound hostile."

She swished a hand to say that I was forgiven. "So, I want you to know that I have a nursing degree—I'm mostly a nurse. I went to college. It was a real college, not a technical college or a vacational college, either."

"Vocational," I corrected.

"No, Jude and I used to call them 'vacational' because they were so easy compared to the real thing."

"How do you know they were so easy?" I asked. "Ever tried to fix an air conditioner or raise a chassis?"

"Oh, I've raised a chassis or two." She slashed an imaginary strike in the air and grinned. "So I went to college, and I am only doing this until I can get a real job." She cocked her head and held up a tube of something. "Sample?"

"What is it?"

"Antagonism remover."

I leaned forward to look. It was a tube of something, all right. "With the built-in de-bitterizing ingredient?"

"Exactly," she said, unscrewing the top and rubbing a drop between her palms. "And the anti-jealousy compound, too."

I opened the screen door all the way and nodded for her to come in. "I'm not jealous of you, Rita."

"Not even if my pen writes pink?" She almost sounded wistful. "Not even if I have a tube of Very Cherry lipstick with your name on it?"

"Let's see what you have," I said. Last week, while not wearing my contacts, I had bought eight lint rollers and what I thought was a set of dishtowels from the very same catalog that nine different neighborhood kids pulled from their backpacks while standing on my doorstep, so I needed some lipstick to wear with my cat-hairless tube socks.

Rita stepped into my house, holding up her long peasant skirt with one hand and reaching for a small vinyl case with the other. "You're a winter," she said. She let her eyes scan the length of my body, the Cat in the Hat and the Grinch included. "You need warm, dark colors."

"I look good in black."

Without asking, she walked to the couch and set the case on it, her back to me as she unzipped a compartment and pulled out a plastic box.

"Okay," she said. "I'm not really selling cosmetics today."

"What are you selling?" I sat on the couch and looked into the case, open-mouthed. Inside was a variety of sex toys whose names I didn't know, although it wasn't hard to imagine what most of them could do.

"Did you say vibrate?" Rita asked, pinching her mouth to look prim.

"No, I didn't," I answered.

Rita smoothed her skirt underneath the clipboard, which had what looked to be an order form attached. "Too bad because my job is to set up Tupperware-like of parties in women's houses where all their friends come over, their Tupperware cabinets bare, and sell them adult toys which have nothing to do with Tupperware."

I pulled the drawstring on my pajama bottoms tighter. "It's 8 A.M. on a Saturday. If I didn't know better, I'd think you were here just to see what kind of information you could get about me. And Jude."

"Absolutely not." She clicked her pen a few times and looked so earnest that I nearly apologized.

"What about the Very Cherry?" I asked.

"I have it in lipstick and condom."

"What about something sweeter?"

She rattled some metal in the case and then offered me a sideways glance. "Lickorice? Spelled l-i-c-k. I'd suggest that one along with a motel right off the interstate, exit 48, that favors themes. I believe it has a *suite* with that very title."

"You know this how?"

"Jude and I went once. A long time ago."

I knew that Jude wouldn't want her offering this kind of information. He had never asked me about my sexual past, and now that his was sitting on my couch, I realized that part of him didn't matter to me. Sex was the easy part—to know that, all I had to do was think about Hugh, and I was trying not to think about Hugh and how he had looked at me in the hospital.

"What did you and Jude do when you weren't in very overt hotels by the highway?"

"Well, we had a son," she said, lowering her eyes to the floor. "We made Evan in that very overt hotel."

"Of course," I said, tentatively touching her arm. "I think about him a lot. And then sometimes I feel guilty because maybe that's wrong. That's something you and Jude should share. I don't want to interfere. But I can't get Jude to tell me much about him."

"I figured you would want to know more about him," she said, sitting up straighter, able to look at me again. "Everybody wants to know more about Evan."

"It's not about curiosity, Rita. I want to understand what Jude's feeling, that's all."

"Good luck with that," she said. "Jude's got his heart welded onto his sleeve when it comes to everything but Evan."

"You don't have to explain Jude to me."

June Carter sashayed out of the kitchen and came to sit at Rita's feet, but she didn't seem to notice. "Ever since Evan died, I can't look at bodies as things that have to get better or function with some kind of objective—I'm a nurse, you know." She put the clipboard and lipstick back into the case. "I can think about sex because it seems both so frivolous and so remote."

"Okay," I said.

"I came to tell you what I was doing so Jude wouldn't have to."

An uncomfortable silence followed until she wiggled her hand inside the case and crinkled some of the plastic packaging. "Do Re Mi Fa So La Ti Dildo," she said, barely a whisper, raising her eyes to meet mine.

"Orgasmic gardening is healthier," I said, quoting my exhausted mother as she kept her vigil beside my father's hospital bed a few days ago, her feet propped up on the starched white sheets near his.

We both laughed, which I thought earned me some access. "So why'd you come back, Rita?" I asked.

She started shutting the case—I had overstepped my boundaries after all. I was surprised when she answered. "I guess part of it is that Evan's buried here. Other than that, I really don't know myself." She pulled her hair behind her shoulders, gathered it, and flapped it against her back, which must have been her nervous tic.

"Evan's buried here?"

She nodded.

I wondered why Jude had never told me that. More important, I wondered why I had never asked.

Jude did not have an impulsive bone in his body, and if he did, it had broken and healed improperly. He thought out everything. He thought out recipes before following them, when it would have been so much easier to take the cookbook's word. He thought out plots as he watched movies, nodding at the end when he was right. He thought out walking routes around Cornelia, how to get from the bakery to my house with passing only one stoplight, or making only one left turn, or passing two churches and one house with an awning.

He thought out my father's death long before I did, which is why when I confessed to him that I wanted my parents together and happy again while they still had the chance, he was way ahead of me.

"Your mother will become someone else," Jude said, and, of course, I thought of Rita after Evan's death. "You'll have to be ready for that."

"After my father dies, you mean? But I'm thinking more about now. Now. Now is better."

We were at a roadside vegetable stand outside of Cornelia. When I was a kid, my parents used to stop at the same stand every time we took our Sunday drives—to make the neighbors think that we were going to church, my father used to joke—and I would ride home with a huge brown paper bag of green beans.

Some of the fields had disappeared over the years, but there were still rows of corn, and peanuts in bushel baskets, and thin, wooden bins filled with tomatoes, cucumbers, okra, squash, and kale, organized like a government, from the top row down. Layers of onion skin had fallen everywhere, and I picked up one to crinkle it between my fingers. Jude came to stand beside me and moved his hand beneath mine to catch the falling pieces. It was cold for April, and he had worn his fleece jacket with the sleeves a bit too long.

"Now," he mused, "is the hardest place to be. For your mother, I mean." He sniffed the tips of his fingers.

"I know," I said, "and that's why I feel so worthless. My father seems to have a plan, which is ironic and sad and horrible, and God knows my mother has lots of them, but none of it seems to be pulling them back together. You know, I want to know that they love each other like they used to."

"Nobody loves each other like they used to. 'Used to' is Southern for *how I wish*. It's code for nostalgia. Or somewhere in the middle, I don't know."

"You sure sound like you know."

Early in my father's illness, Jude would comfort me by telling me that my father would get better, return to banking where the numbers spoke to him again, keep the funny triangle of our family intact. But now he talked directly about my father's death, putting it in front of me like a roadblock, something that he would lead me to and watch how I got around.

"Are you testing me?"

He looked surprised. "What do you mean?"

I thought about Rita's last visit. I still hadn't told Jude about it. "Maybe you aren't sure how strong I am. Or could be."

"Where did that come from?"

"It doesn't matter. I'm just anxious today." I took his hand and placed it on my hip, right where the flesh became the softest, or so he had told me once. "Thump me," I said.

He glanced over his shoulder at the too-tanned woman who was taking customers' money, but she was busy weighing onions, a cigarette wedged in the corner of her pink mouth.

"Go on," I said. "Thump me like you do all the melons."

He looked sheepish. "I'll do better than that," he said, placing his other hand on my opposite hip and using my body to help even his weight as he lowered a knee to the dirt floor. He let go of me and straightened his collar, which I had been waiting for him to do all afternoon, knowing that he would accuse me of being fussy if I did it myself. Then he checked the front of his shirt and jeans, the way that men do when they're anxious, or confident.

"That was thump, not hump," I whispered.

"The only thing I could hump from down here would be an eggplant, and it's not my type."

I laughed so hard that the attendant stacking corn turned down his a.m. talk radio program and stared down the aisle to see what he was missing.

"Okay," Jude said, tilting his head to look up at me. "This is not a real proposal, but it's a practice one."

"What?" I leaned down so that I was almost even with his eyes.

"Frannie, will you walk down an aisle with me in some undisclosed location in the not so distant future, put a mood ring or something nicer if you want on your hand, and say something like 'yes' or 'that sounds good,' or maybe even 'I could do that'? Would you?"

"Practice?"

"Practice run only."

I bit my lip and looked over the mound of corn to see a steel crane lifting a new billboard advertising the subdivision that had sprung up not a mile from my house, all the trees cleared in a single day. "That sounds good," I said. I stared at Jude. He stared back.

"It is good, Frannie. Love is a good thing. Join me in it."

I wanted to, I did. I felt my heart beating so hard I was afraid it would burst through my chest and land in the tomatoes, and then I'd have to buy it back, in proper working condition or not. "A practice proposal for a practice engagement," I said just to clarify.

Jude finally stood up, awkwardly for a man who liked to practice things first. "Sure. So the next time when we do that, when it's real, you'll know what to say and do."

"I guess I should kiss you. We need to practice that, too." I tried to look flirtatious, but Jude told me not to bother and kissed me right there with people from three different counties (according to the license plates in the parking lot) looking on.

"Let's get the goods and go straight home," he said, pulling away from me.

We filled paper bags with onions and squash and apples and kale and tomatoes, some odd soup the only possible combination. While Jude paid, I walked back to the car and opened both the passenger and driver windows so the air could move through. I turned on the hazard lights, although the only emergency was that my heart was still pounding. I sat in the passenger seat with the front visor flipped down, studying myself in the tiny mirror glued to the back.

"Is it an emergency beauty consultation?" Jude said when he walked up, six bags clutched in his hand, his wallet, stuffed so full with receipts and bills that it would barely fold, perched on one of the bags. "Why the hazards?"

I didn't know how to explain it to him, but I tried anyway. "I used to come here with my parents, Jude. On Sundays. We bought green beans."

"What's that story about the kid climbing the bean stalk?"

"Jack and the Bean Stalk. But this is my story."

"Doesn't it end with some giant?"

"What are you doing? This is my story."

"Now we're practicing being married. Because when you're married, all the stories converge and you forget whose is whose." He nodded for me to put my legs in the car, and then he shut the door.

I cut off the hazards, cranked the engine, and turned on the windshield wipers instead. "So finish it," I called through the open window. "You finish my story the way you want to."

He walked around the front of the car, waving his hands and tilting his head in unison with the wipers. Then he slid in beside me and turned the hazards back on, more drama than even the perfectly ripe melons deserved. "Hazardly ever after," he said. "Story finished."

But nothing was finished, nothing. "How long will we practice being engaged?"

"You tell me," he said. "I'm not going anywhere."

They were such simple words, and not much of a story, but I felt my breath ease, my stomach relax. I had never thought of Jude as being permanent, not really. Hugh, yes, but not Jude. "Maybe we shouldn't say. Maybe we should make the transition without the la-di-da title and all the fanfare." I reached into one of the bags and felt up three unsuspecting tomatoes before I found an apple and took a bite.

Jude nodded, mulling through the idea. The tires crunched through the gravel parking lot until we were on the road, heading back toward Cornelia. We hadn't even passed the turn-off to the trail we liked to hike around Lake Forman when he said, "We don't have any green beans to snap, but you can tell me about those Sundays."

I thought about it. "I was just a little girl. I would snap the ends off the beans all the way to Charlotte. If my father turned off the radio, snapping was the only sound in the car the whole trip back, except that every once in a while he would guess the number of beans I had finished, and my mother would say, 'Too high' or 'Too Low.' I was happy. It was before my parents weren't. Or maybe before I realized they weren't."

"That realizing is the tricky part," Jude said. "You might even say it's the whole story."

"My story," I said, but I couldn't ignore the man to whom I had nearly committed for life. "And yours now, too, I guess," I added, practicing the best I could, Hugh tapping on my thoughts like they were bare shoulders.

It was too soon to tell my parents that I was practice-engaged, a secret I could keep longer because Jude and I were safe inside it. Nobody but us had to know. I did worry that someone at the vegetable stand had witnessed Jude's practice proposal and that the news, vine-like, was spreading through Cornelia, from the grocery store to the post office, where the tangible fact of a letter or bill or invitation was challenged by the potential of gossip and rumor and speculation. I needed to mail three edited articles back to my clients anyway, so I decided to make the trip to the post office to find out if I was worrying needlessly or not.

I met my mother on my front steps, her car parked in the middle of the driveway, as if she wanted to keep her options open. "Mama? What are you doing here? Is Daddy alright?" The hospital had released my father the day before. I wasn't convinced he was well enough to go home, although I suspected my gauge was a little off since he would never be well enough again.

As she took the first step, she nodded and reached for the railing exhausted, obvious by the dark half-moons under her eyes and the fact that her purse did not match her shoes. "He's back at home with Brevna, who's distracting him with a toad. Before she came, he ate *all* his breakfast this morning."

"Oh, good," I said, relieved, about the breakfast *and* the toad (two weeks ago it had been a snake). "He didn't want to come with you?"

"He thinks I'm shopping."

"Are you?" I asked, raising my eyebrows.

"I'm trading—it's not too much of a stretch," she answered.

"What exactly are you trading?"

"My secrets about Hugh for yours."

I turned to unlock the front door, the envelope of articles tucked under my arm. "Daddy told you he came to the hospital, huh?" I asked, looking over my shoulder. "Come on in."

"Yes, he told me, but I always suspected you and Hugh saw each other, talked." She put the emphasis on "talked," too tired to find another word with more sexual innuendo. "Let's sit here and enjoy the nice trees," she suggested, lowering herself to the top step, which I did, too. I had planned on telling her about Hugh once my father returned home from the hospital, but I should have known my father would beat me to it. She had brought Melissa to him; it was his turn to bring Hugh to my mother, not to mention it was a nudge for me to do the same.

"Hugh and I have been tight for a long time," I told her. "Ever since that day we went to their house when we were kids. He's been a good friend. Some benefits, but in the end he was just someone I could always count on." And I told her most everything, except for the part about our first pact of not interfering in our parents' lives. Except for the part about how Hugh had looked at me in the hospital, an image that had stayed with me for days now.

My mother sat still during my short narrative. Finally, she moved her purse from her lap to her side and said, "I would just as well not have known about the sex."

"It was only a couple of times," I argued.

"It was only a couple of World Wars," she said, aptly. I looked away. She shifted her back against the railing and added, "Well, tit for tat," which made me smile, thinking of the leather get-up among Rita's wares, its name a much dirtier version of the same phrase. Then my mother offered her disclaimer—"This is not something I have ever discussed with your father"—and began her story.

Like a vulnerable heart, Hugh had once been stolen.

It was the day of my parents' wedding, the third Saturday of May. My father woke extra early and went for a swim in Lake Forman. He was so tired after his bachelor party, a four-hour ordeal that involved a lot of drinking and a failed attempt, on the part of a hired stripper, at erotic dancing, that he merely floated on his back. And floated and floated, until he barely had enough time to get to his own wedding. But he did.

At the church, he parked his car in the lot under the shade of an oak tree and climbed the front steps to face my grandmother, whose delicate chiffon dress did nothing to disguise her anger. My mother was nowhere to be seen, playing the bride's role as she was supposed to, after a brief cameo appearance.

As my father had raced to the church, my mother, with her hair in an elegant sweep but the dress yet to be raised around her, left the changing room to make sure the guest book with the gilded gold lettering had been put out. It had, and was already signed by dozens. The last was the name she was concerned about—Melissa, who had carried a baby cradle tucked into the crook of her elbow, and in it Hugh. Sixteen-days-old Hugh, his fingers curled and no idea of how much trouble he was causing. Melissa's back was to her, her hips still wide from a hard pregnancy and a harder delivery, but my mother recognized her because she had followed my father to Melissa's apartment the day Hugh came home from the hospital.

As my mother watched, a group of guests arrived, pushing Melissa and the baby closer to the door that led off the church vestibule. Melissa placed the carrier on the floor, her left foot touching the side, to speak to several old women with their hair teased stiff. And she kept her foot there except for twenty seconds, when the women entered the church and she crossed the vestibule to get a bag of rice from the basket near the front door. My mother did not have time to think. She darted from behind the door and grabbed the carrier. She scurried past the rooms where her bridesmaids were changing and out the back door to the parking lot. She had driven her brother's new Chevy and had left the keys in the ignition for him to drive home after the ceremony. That one detail might have decided her fate. Or Hugh's. Or mine, for that matter. Nobody recognized the car, and if they had, she would have appeared to be nothing more than a nervous bride driving away from her future.

The thing was, she was not prepared to be maternal. She was prepared to be married. There was a difference. So she only drove to the other side of the parking lot, made the one turn onto Queens Boulevard, her hand securing the carrier against the back of the seat, and pulled over to the curb, tears clouding her eyes. Hugh had opened his eyes and was about to join her in despair.

She looked down at him, a run in her off-white panty hose suggesting the state of her entire life. She was stealing someone else's child? To do what? Hide him in a tree trunk and raise him to speak only to animals? Drive him, eternally, from state to state, until he was old enough first to hate her and then to leave her?

"No," she said out loud. "Even if you are Duncan's, you're not mine." She didn't like Melissa, no doubt, but right then she liked herself even less. She looked at her engagement ring, the diamond in the shape of a pear, and knew the fact that my father had chosen her meant something. It meant everything.

There was no clock in the car, but she calculated only about half an hour until the organ music started. *If* the organ music started. There was the chance, she realized, gasping, that she would spend what would have been her honeymoon in jail, her lacy negligee traded for a hideous orange jumpsuit.

She drove back to the church, choosing the back entrance to the parking lot and avoiding the small crowd, a distraught Melissa in the middle, gathered on the sidewalk in the front. She parked the car near the back again, carried Hugh to the patch of grass that ran alongside the building, and she left him, the lid of his carrier pulled down against the sun, his pacifier securely in his mouth. She would have fed him, if she had a bottle handy. She went back inside and finished getting dressed. It was going to be hard to blush after having kidnapped a baby, but she would do it. She would do it beautifully.

Somehow, miraculously, foolishly, or just plain generously, my mother was never implicated. On his way from the parsonage to the church, the minister found Hugh. Melissa was so relieved to have her baby returned that she never bothered to call the police. Ever since her husband Davies had died, she didn't believe in fairness or justice anyway. So, as my mother made her way down the aisle on the arm of my grandfather, she spotted Melissa in one of the pews on the groom's side of the church, even though she had vowed to keep her gaze on my father waiting at the altar. Their eyes met, and Melissa quickly looked down to Hugh, who lay sleeping in her arms. She knew.

And later, when my parents, still enjoying their post-honeymoon bliss, studied a table stacked high with wedding gifts so that the proper thank-you notes could be written, my mother tried to match a gift to

Melissa's name on the guest registry. But she couldn't find one. My father shrugged and said nothing while my mother thought. She knew it wasn't a place setting in the Lenox Wymberly pattern she had so painstakingly selected. She knew it wasn't a toaster. She knew it wasn't a set of nautical napkin rings, an anchor for this guest and a captain's wheel for the next. She wasn't sure what it was, but she knew it would be with them for a long time to come.

What she couldn't know then was that the gift was Hugh, and he would be with me for a long time to come.

After my mother left, neither of us quite ready to admithow relieved we felt (although we did), I drove to the Cornelia post office. On Murray Street, in front of the Anders/Carson real estate office, I thought I saw Hugh's truck. It was parked behind Mr. Carson's Cadillac with its *My Other Car Is Jealous* bumper sticker. But I couldn't think of any reason that Hugh would be in Cornelia, since I was in Cornelia, and kept driving.

Five minutes later, he pulled up behind me, honking, as I got out of my car in the post office parking lot. He stayed in his truck, the window rolled down, his sunglasses on so I couldn't see his eyes.

"Where have you been?" I asked, trying to sound casual, stacking the three Priority Mail envelopes on the hood of my car while I searched my purse to make sure I had some cash.

"I had to go up to Virginia to do an arts festival." He unbuckled his seat belt and let it snap back up to its holder. "You 'bout to mail something?"

"No," I said, smiling. "I like to bring these envelopes down here and hang out, see what everybody else in Cornelia is putting through the US mail. Building up my courage to mail something myself."

"You're a horrible smartass," he said, with no humor.

"Was that you parked down in front of the real estate office?" I tucked a ten-dollar bill in my pocket and gathered the envelopes.

"Yes."

"You buying the old Crawford house so they can't turn it into condos or something worse? I know you'd never just buy a house because it's a house."

"I'm un-buying. Trying to get out of a contract." He let his hand hang loosely over the steering wheel, but his body was rigid, his back not even touching the worn seat.

"Un-buying a house in Cornelia?" I took the three steps between his side mirror and me and tried to stand firm against an oncoming jumbled but bad feeling.

"That's right." He wiggled his fingers. "I was going to move out here."

"Oh, Hugh," I said, placing my hand over my lips. "Because of the baby? Because you thought we were going to have a baby?"

"That's part of it, I guess." He shoved the gear in park and then changed his mind and shifted back to drive.

I thought he was going to tell me the other part, so I waited, even though I should have jumped in my car and stayed in reverse all the way back to that day at the church, the day my parents were happily married with a brand-new Hugh looking on. "Did you know that my mother stole you from your mother?" I asked him. "Before she decided that you didn't belong to my father?"

"No," he said. "But she must have given me back."

"She did. You were just a tiny baby."

"Why did you tell me?"

"Because I just found out." I paused. "And I think I know the other part of why you wanted to move to Cornelia and why you agreed to our baby pact in the first place."

"You do?"

"Yeah."

He lowered his sunglasses down the bridge of his nose and peered at me over the top of them, his eyes finally visible. "You mean because I love you and probably always have? That other part?"

I nodded, even though the whole world felt like a no. Before that moment, I thought that not being loved back was pitiful, but it might not have been as pitiful as being loved, plain and simple and known.

Chapter 10

Hugh did not stick around to practice loving me or to un-love me, either one. There was no need. He drove away, and I watched for as long as I could, before I felt so mean and horrible that I jogged to the post office door and stood in line behind somebody applying for a passport, accepting my punishment. When I made it to the counter, I paid for the shipping and shoved the dollar and change back into my pocket. I was bribing myself into thinking that I should use it for the cup of coffee and scone I had planned on having at the bakery before I saw Hugh. But I couldn't go there now. I wasn't sure I could practice being engaged and effectively self-loathe at the same time.

I got back in my car and flipped down the visor. I didn't look any different now that I knew Hugh—and Jude—loved me. That made two. I almost had a list. I leaned forward and turned my head from left to right, trying to find something extraordinary, but I came up short. I smeared on a thick layer of Chapstick and fluffed my bangs before cranking the engine. I wanted to drive. Maybe I would go to Charlotte and do what I had done at least a dozen times when some boy or man broke my ridiculous heart: tell my mother. Only this time, it was because *I* broke someone's heart, which was a very different thing, although the common denominator was me. It would complete my story about Hugh, and it might make my father happy. It turns out that I had been taken care of all along—I just didn't know it.

I didn't take the interstate. I wasn't in a hurry, and I didn't want to see any more progress than I had to. I drove past the bakery, for the drama, and then past the elementary school and then past the Habitat for Humanity store until I made a turn onto State Highway 26, two lanes that arced and swirled across the top part of Iredell County, of-

fering tiny houses with too many yard statues out front and an assortment of trailers that might have been there two years or twenty—a
home that can travel doesn't accumulate time like one that can't. It was
the road my parents and I had taken to the vegetable stand all those
Sundays, passing so many churches that we should have earned spir-
itual credit, even if the only service we stopped for was to get air in the
tires.

I had driven maybe two miles in a steady rain, surprised at all the
new houses, when a small figure appeared on the side of the road. I
knew right away that it was Rita, not because she was one of the few
people I could think of who would be walking from nowhere to nowhere, but because I recognized her walk, a kind of heavy-footed scurrying that had nothing to do with the rain. I pulled over and rolled
down the window. She stopped and looked at my car without moving
closer.

"It's me, Rita. Frannie."

Her expression didn't change. She shuffled to the passenger side
and got in. "Thanks," she said, although I hadn't offered anything. She
looked smaller, her hair wet and clinging to her shirt, some of the curls
turning to ringlets.

"What are you doing out here?"

"I was going for a walk."

"In the rain?"

She shook her head, drops of water splattering on the dashboard.
"I have a thing about rain."

"Oh," I said, smiling. "Too bad it's not a raincoat."

"Ha," she said. "What are *you* doing driving out in the country in
the rain on a Tuesday?"

"Driving to Charlotte, maybe. To see my parents." I wasn't going
to tell her about Hugh, or my practice engagement to Jude, since the
way it turned out, that's what hers had been, too.

"They flying in from somewhere?"

"No," I said. "They live there. My father's dying and my mother resents him and I don't know what to do to make things right." I surprised myself with that summary.

"Well, that's a big agenda for all of you."

"I just wanted to say it."

She looked straight ahead and said, "I was walking to the cemetery. Would you like to go with me?"

"To visit Evan?"

She nodded.

"Do we have to walk?"

"No," she said, "and this doesn't have to be sad and weird. I'm not the crazy lady who's going to stretch out on the grave and wail like a crazy lady who's sad and weird and crazy. And a lady."

"I think you just confessed to being a crazy lady," I said. "You said it too many times. Three times and you own it—that's the rule, you know."

"Then that would make me the official owner of hell." She lowered her window and stuck her hand out in the rain like she was trying to catch it, but she glanced at me to make sure I understood her metaphor.

I did. I pulled back onto the road. The rain had left puddles on the asphalt where the shoulder dipped. Someone had lost a baseball cap, the kind Hugh sometimes wore when he was working the kiln, the kind my father was collecting. I felt so sad and weighted again that I considered turning around and taking Rita back to Cornelia, the trip to Charlotte put off. But, for Jude's sake, I wanted to see where Evan was. It was a strange kind of wanting, though, because I knew it wouldn't end with joy or pleasure.

"I didn't know there was a cemetery out here. Where do we go?"

"Oh, it's not a cemetery," she said. "Just go straight and I'll show you."

"It's not a cemetery?"

She shook her head and fiddled with the radio until she found a bluegrass station. Then, about a mile further, she pointed to her right and said, "This is it."

It wasn't a cemetery. It was a shotgun house with a tin roof that looked like the original and a front porch that sagged—the way people do—from too much history and not enough support. The front yard was filled with random patches of monkey grass and moss, decorated stepping stones positioned in between. Rita paused on each stone, reading the date, all of them clearly art projects by Evan—smiley faces made out of seashells, chipped glass mosaics, peace signs made from old silverware, and even several round stones joined together and painted to look like a cat.

"That's my favorite," Rita said, stepping off one with two stick figures, a man and a woman, made of pebbles. And it occurred to me that Evan had died when Jude and Rita were still together. He only knew them together.

"Whose house is this?" I asked.

"It was my grandmother's," she said, over her shoulder. "My mother was living here, but she's gone now."

"She died?"

"No," she corrected. "She married her fourth husband. They live in Florida. The Manhandle, I call it. Every time she finds a husband, he seems to live in Florida."

She removed a key from her sock and unlocked the front door, wiping her feet on a dirty towel folded in front of it. I leaned back to look at the big, newer house next door, remembering that Evan had died during its construction. I followed Rita and wiped my feet too, not sure what I was going to tell Jude later.

We walked straight through the first two rooms of the house to the bedroom. Rita didn't pause except to run a finger over an old rocking chair and then give it a couple of gentle nudges. "Jude hasn't know about the room," Rita said quietly. "Of course, he has seen the grave, but he wouldn't like the idea of keeping Evan, you know, so close."

"He doesn't ever come out here?"

"Well, even if he did, he wouldn't go in the house. He thinks it's cursed."

I tried to imagine Jude thinking anything was cursed. To Jude, the whole world was the opposite of cursed, in a state of perpetual improvement. Jude, who thought call waiting was the purest form of democracy. Jude, who bought Girl Scout cookies because he wanted to encourage feminism.

"That doesn't seem like Jude," I said.

"It's because we were staying here when Evan died. Because it's my family's house. Because it makes it easier for him to relieve himself of any responsibility or aftermath."

"Do you think Jude was responsible?" I could hear my tone turn defensive.

"Jude was his father," she said sternly. "In some way or another, he was responsible for everything that happened to Evan."

"Just like you," I said, although I was thinking of my father's new and adamant need to protect me.

"Just like me," she agreed. "When you become a parent, you don't really have a chance to think about the hierarchy of duties. There's no time-out for thinking—it's all doing. I don't know if one quality is more important than the other, but I would say that responsibility and love are about the same thing."

"You don't believe in accidents?"

"Sure, I believe in accidents." Her tone was so dismissive that she could have just admitted to believing in breast implants or cable TV.

I didn't answer. I followed her to the next room, part den, part bedroom, with both a couch and a bed draped in worn cotton coverlets. On the wall were photos of Evan, all sizes, the baby photos mostly in black and white and then the older ones, where Evan wore an inquisitive smile, Rita's smile, in color. I closed my eyes, overwhelmed, and opened them again, letting my gaze travel down the rows so fast that it was almost like Evan was in movement. And I knew why Jude didn't come to the house. I didn't understand how Rita could.

She seemed to know what I was thinking. "My greatest fear is that I will forget what he looks like." With that, she opened a closed door, its clear glass knob cracked straight down the middle, and waited for me to enter first.

Inside was an assortment of piles, not unlike the way that Santa used to organize my gifts each Christmas morning of my childhood. Rita stood with her hand on the door and her back pressed against its edge. She didn't move, although her eyes were roving from one pile to the other, checking what she must have checked a thousand times, for I realized very quickly that each pile represented a year of Evan's life. She was doing the math, counting from one to six, reminding herself to stop there, not to expect seven, or eight, or nine.

I moved past her and bent down to sort through the first pile in a white wicker baby bassinette. Inside was a paper mobile, with four fish and an octopus in the middle. With it were a few bibs, stained orange, and an assortment of plastic cups and bowls. Tiny baby shoes were lined up in pairs down one side of the bassinette, and, tucked inside a pair of black Converse sneakers so small they could fit on my palm, was a key chain, the simple metal kind with the clamp that opened and closed, with only one key. I held it up to Rita. "This must be yours."

She smiled and shook her head. "No, it was Evan's. Jude gave him a car when he born. He figured it would be vintage before Evan got to drive." Her voice cracked.

"Now that sounds like Jude."

"He still has the car. A convertible Karmann Ghia. 1962."

"I didn't know that," I said.

"He's saving it, I think, rather than driving it."

"That also sounds like Jude." I doubted anyone had seen that car since Evan died. Rita's was more elaborate, but Jude must have had his own shrine.

Rita put the keychain back in the sneaker. "I know I was supposed to give away all his things. And I did give away some. But all that bullshit about their spirits staying with you or in your heart or whatever, it's not very useful to me. I want things I can touch. His spirit can't leave teeth marks on a pacifier. His spirit can't glue macaroni on a piece of construction paper or tie a shoelace. His spirit must be with Jude 'cause I don't think he's with me. What's with me you can put in a box and move. I want things that you can put in a box."

I didn't look at any of the other piles. I put my hand on Rita's shoulder and pressed. She let me, although only for a few seconds, after which she blew out a big puff of air and straightened her whole body, resilient again. Then we walked out of the room while the rain started back up and began to find a rhythm against the tin roof.

"He's buried in the backyard," Rita said. "Do you want to see?"

I shook my head. It was wrong to be here without Jude. "Jude should show me," I said, and I knew that I would ask him. I wasn't sure when, but I would ask him.

"That's fair," she said.

We walked through the house and out onto the porch. Rita slid the house key back in her sock and took a different stepping stone route to the car, with her palms turned upward. She got in the passenger seat and waved a hand outside the window for me to come. I stood on the porch and listened to the cars driving past, the sizzle-like sound of water between tires and road. I wondered why, as foolish as Jude might think it was, I was drawn to Rita, and then decided that it was her loneliness, as tangible as those piles of baby sneakers and picture books and macaroni-and-glitter-decorated Christmas ornaments.

Back in the car, I buckled my seat belt. Rita clamped her hands together and said, "Give me just a minute. I forgot something." She bolted out of the car and through the rain back into the house. I listened to two songs on the radio, worrying about my battery, before she returned carrying a plastic bag, her hair drenched. "Sorry," she said.

I looked at the bag, which she placed on the floorboard, but she didn't offer any explanation.

"Ready?" I asked, hiding my curiosity/

We were back on the road when she shifted in the seat, her legs crossed under her. "Jude should have brought you out here, but I figured he hadn't. Which is why I offered." She pulled her shirt sleeve down over her palm and rubbed the condensation off the windshield. "I would like to see Jude try and be happy."

"Me, too, Rita. Thank you."

"I don't know anything, really, about what I did to let go or not," she mumbled. "Maybe that's why I came back to this old place." She spread her arms, indicating what could have been the entire world.

"Nothing wrong with the South or its wounds."

"Nope," she agreed. "And if I sell enough vibrators, the South won't even have to rise again." She grinned, which made me feel relieved for the second time that day.

I drove her back into town, to a basement apartment several streets over from mine. Before she got out of the car, she reached into the bag and handed me a box the size of a bar of soap, wrapped in a piece of faded comic strip paper. It was solid but not heavy. "Please give that to Jude. He asked for it."

"Okay." I took it and put it in my purse, afraid to be curious. "So why don't you live in the house, Rita? Why do you live here?"

"No living in the homestead," she answered. "That would be too much of me at one time. I was born in that house."

"And was Evan?"

"Jude helped me choose the midwife."

"I never liked that word," I said. "The concept maybe, but not the word."

"Yep. Either you're a wife or you're not." She took several steps backwards and then turned to stroll around the side of the house.

I didn't go to Charlotte after all. I could visit my parents the next day, although I was afraid that I might never be able to visit Hugh again. I drove back home with the package on the seat beside me. I didn't open it. I had a feeling that Rita wanted me to, but, good or bad, whatever it was, the luxury was in not knowing.

Perhaps the unnamed curse followed me from Rita's grandmother's house to mine, hidden, ironically, inside the comic strip wrapping paper. It rained in Cornelia for two straight days, and my old roof couldn't take it anymore. The back part of the living room ceiling collapsed, avoiding most of the furniture but leaving puddles and plaster, turning my cats into looters. I watched them prowling, swiping little bits of debris across the room, patches of plaster or insulation sticking to their tails. Curse or not, my roof caving in was prophetic, the closest thing you could get to the sky falling, which was what losing Hugh still felt like.

I shifted some rugs and a lamp, made a few phone calls to handymen who were too busy being handy to take a call, and decided that I should spend the night at my parents', some place where the roof would stay on, some place with that level of commitment.

I took June Carter and Emmylou to the vet for boarding, knowing there'd be revenge later. I called Jude and told him I was going to my parents' house for the night. Then I went to Value City and bought three bottles of nail polish and a tube of a mint facial mask, and somewhere between the checkout and my car, I changed my mind. Rather than driving to my parents', I went to the Holiday Inn just off the interstate before Lake Forman. The room was $64.95 a night, even in off-season when there were no fish to hook, no sails to fill with wind. I took the key and climbed the stairs rather than take the elevator, in case Rita's curse should reassert itself somewhere between floors.

The room smelled like Pine Sol and soap. I turned on the television for the sound of the voices and sat on the bed, gazing out the window. Lake Forman was placid that afternoon, as usual. The streets bled into the distance, past the fast-food restaurants and gas stations, into Interstate 77, eight lanes of moving metal. Hotels were indebted to cars and roads, and temporariness. For all the sex that took place in hotel rooms, they were really just excuses to be somebody else.

Twice I had been to a hotel for the purpose of sex, once in college on a road trip to Washington, D.C., and then years later, in Charlotte, with a man I didn't know very well who called me Frances, not Frannie, even when I asked him not to. I was sure he was married, and I even traced my finger over the slight indentation his wedding band had left. After sex, we snuck into the swimming pool at 2 a.m. and kissed in the shallow end until our bodies floated to where our feet couldn't scrape the rough surface of the bottom. When we got out of the pool, I looked away from him, tightly wrapping my towel around my body.

The man never called me again, and I never called him. I assumed that he returned to his family that very night. I imagined children, televisions in his living room and kitchen, a wife who knew the score and could, in turn, imagine me. But there had been no repercussions. In the pool, the lights of the rooms trapped behind thick curtains, his breath had been warm on my skin, erasing the goose pimples from the cold water. Nothing more.

The Holiday Inn was too still and too quiet, so I did a few sit-ups and push-ups with a woman in a red warm-up suit on the public access station. I wandered down the hall and got a bucket of ice. I examined the toiletries and the thickness of the towels. Then I made a phone call, a local one that would cost me 85 cents since I had left my cell phone at home, and I waited, the bottles of nail polish lined up on the bedside table. I would be somebody else—not the easy version of Frannie, but the one Jude must have seen, the one that would take a village's help, or all of Cornelia, if it was offered.

When my mother arrived an hour later, she had been stopped for speeding and given a warning. She still looked flustered, a slight pink to her cheeks and startled eyes that wouldn't quite settle on me. "I might have been five miles over the limit but no more than that. I'm not a speeder, Frannie. You know that. I think of those numbers as the law, and I always respect the law."

"It was just a warning, Mama. Don't worry about it."

"I can only leave your father for a little while longer." She put her hands on her hips and then swatted at the bedspread. "Why did you come here? There are three extra beds in our house. You could have come and brought two friends."

"This could be a little slumber party here, Mama. But no prank phone calls. We can paint our fingernails or toenails"—I motioned toward the bottles—"and we can talk. I was a little lonely." I looked down at my bare feet. She had yet to warn me that walking around a hotel room without shoes would surely give me a fungus.

She sat on the bed and then pushed herself back so that she could stretch out her legs. I even caught a glimpse of her stomach, which I hadn't seen since I was a child, before she pulled her shirt back down. "What are we going to talk about?" she asked, as if she had already decided and was waiting for me to catch up.

I picked up the bottle of Precious Pink, but she shook her head.

I sucked in my breath. "Why did Grandmama knit me those ugly sock things with the pointed toes and itchy yarn every year? They looked like elf shoes."

"Because you do have rather pointed toes." She let her eyes travel to my feet. "And *good* yarn itches."

"Okay," I said. I inched down the bed closer to her. "Were you disappointed in my high school grades?"

She shrugged. "No, it was high school. And I didn't push you hard enough."

"Why," I asked, "did you never go to Spain? You always wanted to go to Spain. You know, to see the gypsies and everything."

She sat up on her elbows. "Frannie," she said, her voice lower, "why do I feel like these are more questions for your father?"

"Daddy never cared about Spain or gypsies."

She rolled her eyes, her code response to the buffoonery of the carnival, which usually meant that I was to roll mine, too, the both of us allied against something we didn't understand. "There were gypsies in the carnival, I'm sure. Why are you asking me all this now?"

"I've been thinking, that's all." I waited until she had settled against the pillows before I scooted beside her, our legs parallel, hers longer, both of us captured in the mirror across from the bed. "Why did you and Daddy stop loving each other?" It was the question that had lived inside me, unacknowledged and unattended, for so long that asking it made me feel old.

She turned, horrified, to look at me. "How can you ask me that?"

"Because I don't understand. And I need to understand before Daddy dies—"

"He's got some time left. The doctors all said it could be a good six months."

"Because then there's just going to be you and me."

"Don't," she said, her whole body now tense, "don't you worry about me, and don't you let any of this interfere with Jude." She stood up and clicked on the lamp. Her body was stiff, and she was angry, although, if she could help it, she'd never let me know it. I couldn't think of a single time when my mother had raised her voice to me, and it suddenly occurred to me that we had never learned how to fight.

"I'm not worried, Mama. I mean, that's not the word I would use."

"Good," she said. "I don't want you worried. You're Frannie. Worry never suited you."

The TV came on in the room beside us. I recognized the theme song from *The X Files*, the patient woman's guide to romance: aliens first, love later. I nodded toward the wall separating the rooms. "It used to be a Holiday Inn was a nice hotel."

She smoothed the end of the bedspread and walked to the bathroom to flick the lights on and off. "Used to, before they added the express part," my mother said, twitching her mouth.

"Everything works, Mama," I said. "They aren't rushing us that much."

She put her hands on her hips and nodded. "I left your father once. He doesn't even know it, but I left him."

I leaned forward and then pulled a pillow to my stomach to hug. "Left as in weren't going to come back?"

"You were at college, so I didn't feel like I was leaving you. Besides, in leaving him," she swept her arms out to her side, "I went straight to him."

"The carnival?"

"Aiken, South Carolina. That's horse country, you know—well, as horsey as the South gets. I say that because all those years I would think that if he had only chosen a normal hobby like being a cowboy, throwing some rope around a cow or two, then maybe I could understand. If he could just bring me home some barbeque, then okay." She sighed and leaned up against the dresser. "Anyway, I paid to get in the carnival, and I made sure that I looked as unlike myself as possible."

"Did you wear those huge sunglasses you used to wear, the ones that came halfway down your face?"

"Yes, and a pair of your jeans you left behind," she said. "I waited for the gorilla woman act, and I stood in the very back so your father wouldn't be able to see me. There were all these strange people standing around me, and when your father came out onto the stage, I could only think: *I'm married to that man. That man is my husband.* I wanted to tell the woman next to me. She had hair teased way above her forehead and a rose tattoo, but I wanted her to know that the man with the microphone was my husband."

"Were you mad at him?"

"I didn't know who he was. How can you be mad at somebody you don't know?" She looked at me to answer, but I didn't have one. She was slowly working toward her own anyway.

"What was the gorilla woman like?"

My mother thought for a second. "A woman turning around and around on the stage, too afraid to slow down and really be seen because she knows it's all a trick. It *looked* as if she grew hair, and then she kind of hunched over and made some grunting sounds. Then she ambled off, with her hands hanging down near the floor. I think she had some kind of arm extensions. God knows a woman, gorilla or not, needs them anyway."

"She didn't look like a gorilla?"

"She did and she didn't. Somebody behind me said it was done with mirrors."

"Mirrors don't lie," I said, pronouncing it "mere-ers" like my mother did and quoting one of her favorite shopping remarks.

"Hairy women who growl don't either."

"Do you think the gorilla woman knew something we didn't?"

"Oh, Frannie, I doubt it. That's probably what sent your father back home after only a few weeks."

"That, and he loves us," I said.

There was more to my mother's story. She never told my father about the visit to the carnival, about the huge suitcase she had pulled down from the attic to fill with underwear and socks and cotton clothes that would breathe, as if she were going off to summer camp, not leaving a life that she had built over the last twenty years. After the stop at the carnival that afternoon, never confronting my father, she drove to Virginia Beach, crossing two state lines and transporting a bottle of contraband chardonnay. The ocean did not speak to her the way it did to my father, but she hoped it might at least whisper something helpful, not about my father but about her. There were Melissa and the boy, and the carnival in all its tacky deceit. But behind it all was her.

She thought about cheating on him. It would have been easy at the beach, with real lives tucked away in other cities or states. Tourists were halfway to cheating. She could just walk down to the boardwalk and choose a man, a man who could invent a name for himself and forget any others that mattered. She could certainly still flirt, the simplest of tricks.

But she chose to buy a cheeseburger at a drive-thru and kept moving. She drove all the way to Maine, to the northernmost point of the country, and then she drove back, three stays in U-shaped motels built around pools out front. She looked at herself in the mirrors in those three rooms, thinner in one than in the others, and decided to go with the thinner version, since she had a choice.

My father beat her home. He was stretched out on the couch when she walked in. She asked him to get her suitcase from her car, and he did. They did not talk about where she had gone, but he asked her how I was, if I was studying hard, an assumption she didn't challenge. He told her only that the fire-eater had up and quit the carnival, and it was hard to find anyone else willing to take on that job for its literal-ness. A want ad was not an option.

"I never stopped loving your father, Frannie," my mother said as her story ended. "I wasn't very good at it, is all."

It was the perfect cue for telling her about my practice engagement, and I even dug down into the hard edges of my purse to find the green baggie twister that Jude had tightened around my finger, a practice engagement ring if there ever was one. I decided, though, not to disappoint her, knowing she would see the practice part for what it was.

What I did was unscrew the top of the Race Car Red nail polish and ask her to paint my toenails. "And I'd like the 'This Little Piggy' narrative while you do it," I added.

"This little *pointed* piggy," she reminded me and sat down on the bed.

She slowly dipped the brush in the polish and pulled my foot to rest on her lap. "Hold still," she said, concentrating so hard that I was worried she wouldn't be able to paint and talk, too. But she did a fine job, changing the little piggy's "roast beef" to "barbeque" and adding "organic" in front of market, until she got to the very last toe. She couldn't find the words, so I said them for her—"And this little piggy ran all the way home"—wishing my father were there to join in.

After my mother left the hotel, I locked the room, took the stairs back down to the parking lot, and walked to the gas station with the convenience store a few hundred yards down the access road. Shoved between twelve packs of beer, the one champagne selection was meager in quality but steep in price, and featured a strand of hair clinging to the bottom of the label. I bought it in honor of the gorilla woman.

Back in the room, I made another phone call, to Jude. I told him where I was, leaving off the "Express" after "Holiday Inn" so that he wouldn't get any ideas. All the ideas would be mine this time, with a little help from Rita. I wore pasties, no bra, underneath my UNC sweatshirt.

It took Jude almost two hours to get there. I suspected he was being coy, although he had sworn to me that they were busy doing inventory at the bakery, working late as all the employees counted jars and cans, ordering things like marzipan and fennel seed and almond paste. It gave me time. Without preparation, seducing a man in a hotel offered a limited supply of props. I had thought I could add to the effect of the pasties, but I couldn't wrap myself in Saran Wrap—the shower cap wouldn't count—or teeter on four-inch heels when I hadn't even brought slippers. The sewing kit was useless, although I did consider monogramming the pasties. Finally, I took those off and made do with just my red toenails and me.

When Jude arrived, I was wrapped in a Holiday Inn Express white towel, the logo running vertically down my body. "Whoa," he said, stepping back and closing the door behind him. "Not what I expected when you said your roof had caved in."

I smoothed the front of the towel so that he could read all of it. "Yeah?" I said, swiping my hand up and down my side for emphasis. "You like?"

"I like terry cloth as well as the next guy."

"There is no next guy. That would be wrong." I slinked over to him and kissed his neck right above his Adam's apple.

"I'm not going to ask any questions about the roof or anything else," he said, swallowing. "This doesn't seem to be a time to ask questions."

"Don't," I said. I pulled him over to the bed and gently pushed him down.

"Has something changed?" he asked.

"That's a question." I unbuttoned his shirt. I smelled the bakery on his skin, butter and cream cheese, and in his hair, the faintest trace of "his product," as he called it, which made his bangs and the square of sideburns over his ears feel bristly.

He unwrapped the towel and ran his hands down the side of my body, moving them to the small of my back. He pulled me toward him, and I sat on his lap, my knees pressed against his sides and my hips hitting below the round part of his stomach. He was warm and familiar. He tasted like Chapstick because he had stolen mine from the nightstand, kissing me in so many different places that I could almost imagine there being two of him and having to call the front desk for backup toiletries.

When we were both exhausted and Jude had muttered his trademark, "Let's do all that again very soon," I padded to the dresser and got my purse. I took the package that Rita had given to me and put it on the nightstand. "That's for you," I said, crawling over him to get back to my side.

"What is it?" He leaned over to peer at the comics. "*Calvin and Hobbes?*"

"It's from Rita, Jude. I ran into her today. She took me to the house."

"Her old house?" He shoved a pillow out of the way so that he could face me.

"She wanted to show me Evan's grave. She took me inside, but we didn't see the grave." His face tensed up, his hairline shifting forward, so I tried to beat him to his anger. "I want to do that with you. I have no right otherwise."

"You shouldn't have gone at all, Frannie." He threw the package back on the nightstand, and it bounced to the floor.

"You have to allow me to know Evan. You have to allow me that." I crawled back over him and picked up the box while he began kicking the sheets off like he had somewhere to go—at midnight in Cornelia, North Carolina, where the only thing open was the interstate.

"What is it?" he asked, hanging his legs over the side of the bed and sitting up. He tore the paper off before I could answer "I don't know" and tossed it to the floor. It was a shoebox and inside the shoe box a Russell Stover chocolate box and inside that a dark blue box, the kind that jewelers used to give away, the kind where my mother kept all of her "good" jewelry. Jude flipped open the lid and stared, the room so quiet that I could hear him breathe. Inside was Evan's key chain and car key from Rita's house.

"You know what it belongs to, right?" I asked. "Rita said you asked for it." I pulled on my sweatshirt again and sat beside him on the bed, letting my feet brush up against his.

"Yeah, I know what it belongs to," he said, dangling the chain. "It's to the car I bought for Evan when he was born."

"The Karmann Ghia."

"She told you about that?" He put the key chain back in the box and shut the lid. "But I didn't ask for it."

"She said you had asked for it, but I didn't know that's what was in the box."

He glanced at me, shame or frustration—I couldn't quite tell—in his expression. He held the box in both hands, turning it over, then opening and closing the lid. "You know what she's doing, don't you?"

"I think she's trying to encourage you to give the car to someone else. I think she's telling you to have another child."

"With you," he said.

"With me." I suddenly understood why Rita had taken me to the house.

He opened the nightstand drawer and put the box inside. "Don't let Rita and her theatrics upset you. She's not thinking clear. She's *interfering.*"

"It's okay, Jude," I said. I slid over and wrapped my arms around his bare torso. "She wasn't trying to hurt me. She doesn't know. If you think about it, it's really a generous thing she did."

"Maybe," he said. He pulled on his underwear and jeans and walked to the dresser, where he unwrapped two plastic hotel cups. "Do we have anything to put in these?"

"Check the ice bucket in the bathtub," I said. "I wanted to surprise you later, but now is good, too."

He smiled and ducked behind the door. "Bubbly bath," I heard him say before he reemerged, clutching the champagne bottle. He popped the cork, poured two cups full, and said, "Here's to those red toenails."

The champagne was bad, but we drank it anyway. I wanted Jude to ask me what we were celebrating, although he seemed to think it was simply this a night at a hotel.

"Want to watch something on HBO? It's free according to the sign out front."

"No, not really," I said. "I think we should talk more, you know. I like talking to you."

"Okay," he said, putting the remote back on the nightstand.

Later, I could blame it on the champagne if I had to. For now, though, I felt happy, thoughts of my father pushed back, replaced by something else. "The thing is," I said, reaching for his empty cup, "if we keep talking, we might not have to practice everything else."

He cocked his head and scooted closer to me on the bed. "Does that mean you're going to marry me?"

"Yes," I said. "It do."

"Does that mean for forever and ever?"

"Yes," I said. "It do."

Jude didn't care about my funny grammar. And I didn't care that it was a new truth, living side by side a new plan—for a baby—that began taking shape when he opened that jeweler's box, the two barely distinguishable for now.

Chapter 11

He never so much as said it, but about the same time I started thinking about my wedding, my father must have started thinking about his funeral. He would sit on the bench at the end of my parents' bed and begin the slow process of pulling on his socks and shoes, which seemed to take the little bit of energy he had. Then he would stop and stare at nothing, although when I told Jude about this, he said there was no such thing as nothing to stare at. My father would sit, maybe for two or three minutes, his lips moving every few seconds but no sound emerging. My mother thought he was praying. I was sure he was focusing. Jude said there was no difference.

The doctors maintained that my father could live a few more months, possibly longer, with continued chemotherapy and a lot of will. I had never thought much about will, since in my family it always seemed available, like paper towels or aspirin. It takes as much will, if not more, to keep things tucked away as it does to look at them straight on. My father had done his share of tucking away, but now he was looking at his death straight on, which put everything else, my mother included, a little more out of focus. I hoped I could help change that.

Two weeks into our real engagement, before Jude and I had decided any details of our big day, I headed to Charlotte to visit my parents. I used the half-hour drive to prepare myself for more discussion about my wedding, which I endured because at some point my parents were both bound to realize they were perfecting their own. More so than my mother, my father had been calling me with suggestions about where and how the service should be held. And he liked the word "service," although my mother didn't. My mother said the only wedding service I should consider was the caterer—everything else was a ceremony—but I suspected they were both right. I didn't care where Jude and I got married or even if self-imposed bliss in the form of a honeymoon took place anywhere but our imaginations, the only place bliss should be.

My father met me at the front door, looking the best I'd seen him in weeks. My mother was at the Y, taking her Saturday fitness class, so it was just the two of us in the den, sipping the herbal tea she had left on the counter with specific instructions for brewing. "Like a healthy witch," my father said, winking. It was fennel and licorice, which made me think of Rita, although it didn't take much for me to think of Rita ever since she had sent me back to Jude with the most ironic of messages.

"Frannie," my father said, "can I show you something?"

"Sure. What is it? Another animal from Brevna?"

He handed me his cup of tea and held up a finger. He disappeared down the hall, and I heard the bedroom door creak shut. I turned on the TV to get the weather but decided I didn't want to know. I heard my father pad back down the hallway and felt anxious about what he wanted to show me. While he remained very pragmatic about his death, I still couldn't accept it, especially on a day when he didn't need his cane for walking or my mother, the sentence-finisher, for talking.

When he returned to the den, he wore the top half of his old Navy uniform. It fit him again, although the buttons were dull and the blue flaps on the shoulders, which I knew from photos to have once been stiff and angular, were flat from neglect.

"How do I look?" he asked, throwing back his shoulders.

"Regal, handsome," I answered. "Where's the hat?"

"I can't seem to find that." He ran a hand over his bald head.

"You don't need it," I said. "The effect is still there."

He smiled sadly and sat in his recliner, his white sleeves extended along the armrests. "It's all about effect at this point, Frannie."

I could feel my brow begin to furrow, or, as Jude called it, "my borrowed brow," because I looked like someone else when I worried. I had always believed that my father's life had been defined by his years in the Navy, but I had seldom asked him about it. "So what did you like about the Navy, Daddy?"

"I liked how separate it was from everything else. Being out in a ship like that, on the ocean, it creates a kind of release." He nodded, approving his answer. "Other than your actual job, you can't do much about anything when you're out there. You can think, and that's about it."

"That makes sense," I said.

"There's a whole lot of space between thinking and doing." He looked at me over the top of his new reading glasses. It was the same look he gave me every year when he helped me with my taxes and I deducted gourmet coffee as a business expense. "A whole lot."

I thought, too. "I feel that way about being engaged."

"What's that?"

"It's just this stretch between thinking and doing."

"Maybe," he said. "They built drive-thru chapels in Las Vegas for people like you."

"I'll probably never go to Las Vegas."

"Me, either."

"I just want to go ahead and do it."

He cocked his head. "It almost sounded like you were going to say, 'go ahead and get it over with.' Were you going to say that?"

"No," I said. "Were you? I mean, thirty-eight years ago, would you have said that?"

He stood up, slowly, and walked over to the windows overlooking the backyard. My mother had moved the old cement planters that she filled with mums in the fall closer to the deck. They formed a semicircle around it, an amphitheater of waiting.

"There's only one reason to get married, Frannie."

"You're going to say 'love.'"

"What else?" he said. "You can invent lots of other ones, but it's the only one that matters."

"What if it doesn't last?"

"It only has to change, evolve. Nothing has to *last*."

"Memories? What about them? They last. Even the sad ones."

I had chosen my words carefully, but my father retreated all the same, the uniform unable to fortify him. He wouldn't say it, so I did: "Alice."

"Yes," he said, nodding. I wondered if he remembered those days when my mother was in the hospital as I did, empty and punishing, yet we were so contained in the house, so *there*. "Alice. But for right now, Frances. Only Frances."

"Okay, Daddy," I said, blinking away a tear. "Frances."

It was enough of a victory for both of us, so I reached in my purse and pulled out several bridal magazines I had bought at the grocery store. My mother would have been more selective, but I grabbed the first two I saw. "Well, there is this *other* bride you might remember. What about her?"

"Your mother, you mean?"

"Come on, say it with me. Made—"

He shook his head in mock disapproval. "Lane," he said, stretching the long "a" to make the nickname sound musical.

"Say the whole thing," I commanded. "Let's go all the way back to that day you married her. Before she became just Lane."

"Madelane," he said.

"She's the one," I said. I handed him the magazines, which themselves weighed more than some of the hungry models inside.

"She sure is." He studied the magazine covers and then turned them over, softly whistling.

"Lots of silly stuff I'm supposed to do as a bride, huh?"

He flipped through the pages, grimacing. "This doesn't look like you at all," he finally said.

"And I don't want any of it," I said.

"I say a tent in the backyard and a homemade dress."

"No elf shoes, though."

"What?" he asked.

"Ask Mama."

"I never thought you'd have a church wedding anyway," he said.

"I never thought I'd have a wedding." Not until I said it did I realize how much, and for how long, I had assumed that I would spend the rest of my life looking and looking until I simply ended up alone.

I ruffled through the pages of one magazine while my father, his breath warm against my scalp, peered over my shoulder to occasionally comment on a dress's decency or lack thereof. Any minute, my mother could return home and be annoyed that she had missed the most important wedding planning session. I knew what would happen. She would watch us, saying nothing, straightening the picture frames in the bookcase behind the sofa, afraid to claim any second-hand role, still waiting for my father to remember that long walk down the aisle.

The next day, Jude drove the Karmann Ghia to my house and parked it on the curb. I was proud of him. He sat inside it for a few minutes while I watched from the window, both sadness and joy tugging at my heart, one cancelling out the other. The Karmann Ghia was blue, which I didn't want to be, so I chose the joy—my plan for the car, for all of us, a large part of it—and went outside to tell Jude I was proud of him.

As I came down the steps, he honked, the black convertible top beginning to roll back, a strip tease if I'd ever seen one. When it settled, Jude popped up and leaned back on the headrest, his knees bent toward the dashboard. It was a classy toy-like car, low and round, barely wider than my couch, almost miniature, and seeing Jude in it reminded me of the first time I saw him—on the carousel.

"So this is it," he said when I planted both hands on the passenger door where the window would have been. "It has bouquet seats."

I looked inside. "*Bucket* seats."

"Your preference," he said, bowing his head, a smile creeping up both sides of his mouth. "But I was thinking that we could use it for the getaway car."

"Are we robbing a bank?"

"You said you weren't going to toss your bouquet, right?"

"I knew what you meant, silly," I said, smiling.

"We should use it for a celebration. It's time." He leaned forward and reached into the glove box, then held up the owner's manual. "The original," he said.

"No, that's you. In this car. Right now."

"Oh, yeah?" he said. "Well, anyway, what do you think of my plan? Want to ride off into the future in compactness?"

I walked around the car, making him wait for my answer in case he needed to revise his question to fit it. It was very blue, Carolina blue to be specific. The hood was smooth, but, when I bent closer, I could see gray specks where the color had chipped. "Yes, I want to ride off into the future in compactness. With you and all our baggage. I mean, luggage." I looked down at him and winked.

He took off his sunglasses and leaned up to kiss my cheek. "Okay then."

We looked at each other a few seconds, something settling in Jude before he reached back to put away the manual.

"So, it looks really good. Where's it been all this time?"

"A friend in Charlotte has an underground parking facility at his townhouse."

"That's called a basement here in Cornelia," I said.

He laughed. "Says Ms. City-Come-to-the-Country." He tossed me a pair of sunglasses with the price tag still attached. "So how do you feel about taking a ride?"

"Sure."

"I wanted to take you someplace."

"That trip you've been threatening?"

"Not the one where I accompany you into your future," he joked. "The other trip. It's a little closer."

"Right now?" I smoothed the top of my hair and straightened one of my earrings, but I knew where we were going. It didn't matter how well arranged I was.

"Right now," Jude said, so definite that I turned around to get my purse and lock up the house while he raised the top again, afraid to throw more caution to the wind.

A few minutes later, we were up against Cornelia church-hour traffic, which meant thirty or so cars and the van from the retirement community over near Lake Forman. Jude didn't go to church, but he respected those who did, allowing the Robersons and Daniels to pull out in front of him, all of us passing through downtown at twenty miles an hour until the Robersons' SUV pulled into the parking lot of the brand new McDonald's.®

"Want some chicken nuggets for the ride?" Jude asked.

"If you ever see me eating those chicken nuggets, please take them from me and read me their ingredients as my punishment."

"That's a no," Jude said, and shifted to third.

A few minutes later, the split in the road that became Highway 26 came into view, and I pointed to the right, Jude nodding beside me. We held hands a good half mile before Jude had to shift into second for a truck pulling onto the road, a man driving, with a woman sitting square in the middle of the seat beside him.

"How would you feel about a small wedding in my parents' backyard?" I asked Jude.

"Is that what you want?"

I nodded. "I don't want to go through all the hoops. I want it simple and small and soon."

"Soon because of your father?"

"Partially."

"How simple?"

"Short dress. Flat shoes. Braided hair."

"And for me?"

"A tux. My father would want you in a tux."

"How small?" he asked. "Can I come?"

I fanned my fingers up one by one four times over, alternating hands. "Forty-two," I said, "and that includes you."

"How soon?"

"How about the fall. In October."

"I always liked October. The light changes." He reached over and rubbed my ring finger. "I need to put something on that. But in the meantime, it's okay with me if it's okay with your parents. I'll call my folks tonight to see what they think. The only thing that might encourage them to leave Costa Rica is a wedding."

"I need to check with some people, too, I guess." I thought of Hugh, although I wasn't sure I would have the nerve to call him. I had not heard from him, and my father had not mentioned him either.

When Jude turned into the driveway of Rita's old house, he drew in a big breath and kept his gaze directly in front of the car. I reached down and pressed against the top of his hand where it rested on the gearshift. He parked at the end of the drive, tossing his sunglasses on the dashboard. We got out of the car, and he met me on the passenger side. "Evan would have probably been tall enough now so that I could see him over the top."

"He'd be eleven, so probably," I said. I cocked my head. "You okay?"

He nodded, moving in front of me and then reaching behind for my hand. He wore black Converse tennis shoes that he had bought at a thrift store for two dollars, the same kind in the first pile, the baby pile, of Evan's things. I suddenly remembered that Hugh used to wear them, too, years ago, the ones that came up to his ankles and made him look like the street kid he wasn't.

I followed Jude around the side of the house, sweat beading on my forehead from the July sun, already relentless at eleven in the morning. Then I stopped so suddenly that Jude kept moving, his hand pulling out of mine. I gasped and raised my hand to my chest, every inch of me filled with dread or shock or whatever the opposite of wonder was. The entire backyard was made of toys. It was more a dystopic film set than a yard; at least, it looked as if it had once been a film set and now was just waiting for someone to occupy it, to make it real. Five or six trees, oaks and what looked like a crabapple, grew tall above the yard, their limbs intersecting along the left edge, where rampant patches of weeds were poking through ivy. There was also a cleared spot that looked to have once had a pond, but it was now filled with fine, white sand and a very thorough collection of buckets, shovels, and scoops. I counted five plastic toy cars, the kind that kids propel with chubby legs, their speed completely dependent on enthusiasm. There were also three tricycles with wide Y handlebars, all lying on their sides and partially sunken into the ground. But there were four bikes, too, ranging from the two-wheeled version of the tricycle to a Schwinn 10-speed with a bottle clip rusted against the frame beneath what was left of the leather seat. Remnants of several kites hung from the lowest limbs of the one short tree, a huge crepe myrtle that grew lopsided, its inclination to the right, wayward shoots of new growth circling its wide base. One new kite, or at least it looked to be new, a dragon with fire on its tongue, was wedged between two branches.

I walked a few yards and stopped again. Just beyond the crepe myrtle was an area with every kind of toy truck, car, and motorcycle there was, some plastic and chipped and others metal and as rusted as the septic tank beside the driveway. One dump truck had been filled with dirt, and weeds spilled over the front of the cab. Beyond these was a mock garden, no flowers, just baseball bats, tennis rackets, ski poles, and hockey sticks stuck into the ground, tied to wooden stakes to hold them up. One of the oaks dangled a tire swing, the kind that would spin and spin with the right twisting, and another had a punching bag like boxers used. Yet another oak had small toys—a jack in the box, a bright yellow cash register, several action figures with missing limbs—tied to one of the branches, a row of bygone potential. To the right, two rusted pairs of roller skates were positioned under a skateboard, creating a low bench set into the ivy.

I felt my arms hanging awkwardly at my sides, transfixed by the eerie solemnity. I had never thought of toys as sad, but that was all I felt when I looked at these—a dark and palpable sadness. And I realized that while the inside of the house was a shrine to only the years that Evan had lived, the yard gave him a future. Some of the toys were for children much older than six.

"She wouldn't let him have toy guns," Jude said, watching me. "So you won't find any toy guns." I could hear a tinge of anger in his voice, but it wasn't directed at Rita. We stood for a few seconds, a passing car with the bass pumping against its windows the only sound breaking the silence.

"Would you have let him have guns?"

"I don't know," he said. "You can only keep the world at bay for so long. Eventually, it creeps in."

"Not here. The world has not crept in here."

"Rita won't let it," he said.

"How long has this been here?"

"She started doing it right after he died and maybe for two, two and a half years longer. So it's almost five years in the making. And now unmaking." He sighed. "You can't even see half the stuff. A lot of it has disintegrated or gotten covered over with dirt. Some things were stolen."

"Who could steal from here? That's so many crimes at once that his conscience would be a bag of bricks."

"Some people don't have a conscience, Frannie. You know that." He bent down and dug around the top of what turned out to be an old Play-Doh can, the letters barely readable.

"Oh, Jude." I kissed his shoulder, the rounded part that couldn't quite forget those years of high school wrestling. "I don't know what to say."

"She's unpredictable, Frannie. I told you that. Evan's death made her needy and weird. She's not a bad person, but you can't know what to expect from her. Like sending me the car key as a way of saying 'Get Frannie pregnant.' That's a little much."

I let my eyes scan the yard and then settle back on Jude. "But I get it," I said quietly.

"Get what?"

"I get this. I understand it. I understand why she had to do it."

"Because she can't let go," he said.

"No," I said, shaking my head. I thought about the baby food jars hidden in my closet until Brevna found them, the stacks of baby clothes and bibs that my mother carried all those years ago to the Goodwill donation center, her jaw set and her eyes the hollowest I'd ever seen them. She regretted giving those things away. She was so angry when she got back that she locked herself in the car and stayed in the driveway until suppertime had passed. "No, Rita's afraid she's going to forget something about him."

"I have that fear, too. She doesn't get to own that."

"I know you do, but I think Rita is afraid that she's going to forget herself. I can't explain it, Jude, but I understand it." I also understood why she sent Jude the key. The message, no matter how ironic, was for me.

He started walking, slowly, then faster. I followed him to the other side of the ivy, a cleared area about the size of a patio. Beyond it was the beginning of property that was better maintained, the grass cut short, the plot edged with creeping jenny. Four tomb-stones were spaced equidistance from each other, the farthest with Evan's name written in square, chiseled letters.

"I let Rita bury him here because we had never talked about it. You don't usually lie in bed at night and discuss where you would bury your six-year-old child, where he most belongs."

"Rita said he was born here."

"He was."

"And you won't go inside?"

"I won't."

"I'm sorry," I said. "I wish I could make the pain stop. I want to be able to do that."

"That's not your job," he said.

"I didn't say it was a job."

Next door, a dog started barking, and then a car started, three doors slamming in quick succession. Jude kicked a small green ball and watched it land beside the porch. "Let's just go home."

On the drive back to my house, Jude spun the radio dial, bursts of static the closest thing to conversation between us. And that was fine. Whenever he reached a patch of road where he wouldn't have to shift gears, he rested his hand on the top of my thigh. And that was fine, too.

"October twelfth," he said as we pulled into my driveway. "The second Saturday of the month."

"I'll check the *Farmers Almanac* about the weather."

"I'll check the married box on my next tax return."

I smiled. "What if," I began slowly, taking the opportunity I had been waiting for, "you could also claim another dependent? What if we found another way, not the traditional way, to have a baby? Would you want to do that?"

"You mean adopting?" He didn't sound interested, much less convinced.

"I mean a surrogate."

He mouthed the word, landing hard on each of the syllables. "I've heard of that. It's an interesting alternative for some couples." He was so far removed from the idea that he would have been the last person to guess, I wanted our surrogate to be Rita.

It was my father's idea to make my simple wedding dress. He had my mother bring down the old black Singer from the attic, and he practiced threading it while we watched, squinting, his body bent and his new bald head shinier under the light. "I haven't sewed in years," he said.

"Me neither," I said.

He tried to look stern, so I knew he understood the reference to my forced participation, years earlier, in Girl Scouts. My mother insisted. I, however, resented the entire system—the ugly green uniforms and the annual cookie campaigns that had me ringing the doorbells of strangers—so, to mock the system, I set out to earn every badge there was. And I did, sewing each onto the green sash with tiny, neat stitches, adding badges one by one until only the top right corner was empty, awaiting the final badge, the cooking badge. To earn it, I had to prepare a full meal for my parents, documenting the recipes, the nutritional content, the preparation time. One Tuesday night, I planned to make lasagna, homemade rolls, and a salad, but that afternoon my boyfriend Lloyd dumped me in a note he had slipped into my book bag, a dog (I had a cat) drawn at the bottom.

He wasn't really my boyfriend. He was a boy that wasn't Hugh. Hugh could be put off. Hugh gave me updates about my father. Hugh was sequestered, in the hallways of our school, in my imagination. But Lloyd Taylor was so visible, so real. He already wore suits, with ties and polished saddle shoes (as my mother called them). He was thin, studious, and had hair that was stacked, like stairs, down the sides of his face, a decade ahead of the '80s. He favored animals over people, other than me. He was devoted to me. He knew the genetic difference between chimpanzees and humans, and he said I was the best justification for evolution that he could think of.

I didn't know there was trouble between us until I opened my book bag for a pencil so that I could document, as required, my final Girl Scout victory. I read his note so many times, my hip pressed into the pull knob of my mother's spice cabinet, that the lasagna burned. The lettuce wilted, becoming the same green of the uniform that would mock me, and never got chopped. The dough for the rolls remained a lifeless lump beside the rolling pin. I never earned that cooking badge. But then, a few weeks later, someone found my defeated Girl Scout sash and added a homemade cooking badge, a piece of white cotton twice the size of an official badge with a pan of lasagna drawn on it. My father's stitches were tiny and precise, easily distinguished from mine.

"I'll trade you a pan of lasagna for a wedding dress," I offered my father.

"Draw me a picture first," he said, which I did with great concentration, wanting to dismiss the notion that the dress should be complicated and elegant, some kind of omen about married life to come. But I failed. I drew flouncy and puffy and swishy and sleek, nothing on the page matching what I saw in my imagination. I drew eleven pictures until I got it right: a tea-length dress with cap sleeves that was tiered and swirly only at the bottom.

"Good," my father said. "I can go from here."

A week later, he had made the pattern, his belt one notch closer in than when he started. And a week after that, the dress was done, hanging on a padded hanger that he had taken from my old bedroom closet.

"Men get uniforms; women get wedding dresses," he said seconds later, as I stepped out of the bathroom wearing the dress, barefoot, hoping not to disappoint him. "But you get a Frances dress."

"That's right," I said. I twirled for him, the silk bouncing just enough against my calves. "The dress is perfect, Daddy. Really. Perfect."

He scrunched up his face and then pinched the fabric above the waistline. "Maybe a little more gathered here," he said. Then he stepped back, wincing, which he did more and more each time I saw him. "What a treat to be able to see you this ready," he said. "You're lovely."

I smiled and looked away.

"Your mother always said you'd be the perfect bride."

"Mama?"

"That's right," he said.

"That's funny because I don't think she and I have ever had a conversation about me getting married."

"Oh, she's been talking about it for years." He sat down and bolstered one hand on each side of him against the couch. "Melissa, too. She always liked hearing about you."

I stared at him, trying as quickly as I could to filter my thoughts. "You know that makes me mad, Daddy."

"I thought it might. It was wrong of me, and now I'm trying to apologize. But don't be mad." His tone was just shy of pleading.

I sat beside him, ignoring the row of straight pins around my waist. "So tell me about Melissa. Tell me now, while I'm a little mad and confused, but very pretty."

He looked past me, toward the backyard, and sighed. "I felt like I owed her. That's all. Or maybe it was that I was compensating."

"For what?"

"Hugh's father. Davies. I never wanted him or his mother"—he looked hard at me—"Melissa, to know. That responsibility turned into something I never intended. But I couldn't let Hugh turn out like his father."

"I don't understand."

"There was one time when we were docked in Cuba, way south of Havana, but Havana was where the clubs were. So a bunch of us found a guy that would drive us, four hours, if I remember correctly, and we went for the drinks and the dancing. And the other thing that sailors are famous for. Davies and I were the only two married. A few of the other guys organized meetings with, well, prostitutes. Only they weren't prostitutes; they were just girls. Fifteen, sixteen years old. They worked the club. Girls in clingy dresses and high heels. Red lipstick, all of it. Hugh's father, Davies, did it, too. They even had the girls get up and dance with them."

"Does Hugh know this?" I asked.

"No. I mean, I never told him. What would I have said? Your father cheated on your mother again and again, at least once with a mere girl? I watched those girls and thought about how they were somebody's daughters. They could have been you, although you were just a hypothesis at the time. But nobody else thought it out. Davies didn't. Melissa was already pregnant. He bragged about it all the time."

"But Melissa knows?"

"She knew. Maybe not about the girls, but she knew, even if I didn't want her to."

"You owed Hugh and Melissa because Davies set a bad example?"

"Something like that. There's more to it, though."

I wasn't expecting a story, but my father had one anyway.

It was a Wednesday, and the ship had been at sea for three weeks with only one docking. He and my mother were newly married, and he missed her. But Davies was the sad one, pining for Melissa so bad that the other men teased him. After the night with the girl in Havana, Davies confided in my father: too much water, too much time, too many other men who had gotten away with it, too many questions about how his life with Melissa was going to play out. It was, then anyway, a fixed, permanent world of which he could only see the surface.

Davies had been assigned kitchen duty that week, and he left a pot of boiling water to settle down on the stove. He climbed the metal steps to the bow of the ship. He stood, his hips against the railing, and, as he told my father, wondered how he would ever face Melissa again.

My father only saw Davies's back and the long green-gray stretch of ocean beyond it. When he grabbed Davies from behind, they both fell back to the deck, each one earning an elbow bruise they could each easily explain away.

"You almost slipped up," my father said, sitting up before he added, "again."

"You read it all wrong," Davies said to my father. "I just needed some air." He looked hard at my father, who believed him, and then got up.

My father needed air, too. He carried with him the image of Davies in his crisp white uniform, the bright colors and lights of the club swirling in front of them, Davies's hand playfully tugging the fringe-like ends of the girl's hair. And then a crowd of people pushing them from behind so that he lost sight of Davies as he was propelled into the mass of dancers, women in sequined sleeves and men with their hair slicked back, each strand distinct. He didn't try to stop Davies. He didn't try to help the girl. He didn't judge if she was pretty or gaudy or maybe even plain. But he didn't try to help her.

Before Davies disappeared back down the galley stairs, he offered a "Thank you anyway" to my father. It sounded sincere.

"For what?" my father asked, a question meant to sound humble, to dismiss the whole incident for Davies, more so for himself.

When he arrived at that part of the story, my father stopped. He looked sheepish but not sad, and he seemed to be done with talking. I, however, was busy thinking—about how my father wanted to make sure I was taken care of, about how he was trying, in the best way he knew, to die gradually so that my mother and I could get used to the idea, about how he came to me first with his prognosis because he knew my mother only had him while I had Hugh. Hugh, who was always there to fall back on and who, perhaps thanks to my father, was one of the best people I knew.

"Oh, Daddy, you've been policing the world. Trying to make it better."

"It's a father's job," he said, with assertion, "to protect his daughter."

I nodded, turning slowly so that my wedding dress held together, the straight pins poking me up and down my left side. "Does Mama know all this?"

"Little by little," he said, patting my shoulder, "bit by bit." He wouldn't say any more than that, so I thought better about asking if he had told Hugh I was getting married.

An hour later, when I got back home, I had my answer. A message from Hugh on my answering machine said, "Congratulations, Frannie. I heard about the wedding. I wanted you to know I'm happy for you. You might not believe that, but I am."

I didn't quite believe him, although he sounded earnest, even on tape. I knew what it was like to have a cracked or, in my case, a divided heart because on some deep, dark secret level, I loved him back.

Chapter 12

Although it is the bride who is supposed to be slender and sincere at her wedding, my mother was the one who began a fitness regime that she stole from Jane Fonda, her hand weighted by a dumbbell, mine weighted by a ring. As promised, Jude had given me an antique emerald circled by a row of tiny diamonds. It had been his grandmother's. While the emerald was small, and the diamonds closer to chips than to carats, I awoke every morning aware of the ring, as if my dreams had settled between the stones. I dreamed about my parents now. Many times, they were new to each other, walking into empty rooms and discussing furniture, curtains, updated wiring—the last always my father's concern—their hands not quite touching and the windows beyond them, clear but empty. I couldn't control my dreams, and I didn't pay them much mind, reality being meaner, and tougher, and real.

My father's hospital visits totaled six now. Each time, my mother drove him, checked him in, and settled herself, sometimes for days, into the huge recliner in the corner, claiming the remote as her own when he dozed, the beeping of the monitors seeming now to come from somewhere within him. He had endured two blood infections, near kidney failure, and severe anemia, not from the cancer but from the drugs meant to stop it.

His most recent visit, less than a month before the wedding, he had gone back for severe dehydration, an ambulance carrying him away, my mother and I following in her car. After she clicked the odometer, we had driven in silence until we reached the hospital parking entrance, at which point she announced, "Five point three miles. Every time we come, it feels farther and farther away, but it's still only 5.3 miles."

"I thought at least 5.4 miles. I really did," I said, trying to joke, but it wasn't funny.

I had my own trick for avoiding reality, or at least making it better: I closed my eyes and saw my father return home, as he had each hospital stay before, walking on his own and asking, optimistically, what would be for supper. And his very last hospital stay, when he would finally have to opt for the wheelchair, my mother would push him out through the electronic doors and to the Buick, which would be decorated with shaving cream and tin cans tied to string. They would drive to the Outer Banks and camp on the beach, which was illegal but romantic. I wasn't sure why it felt good to assign my parents a life of soft crime, but I did—replete with camp fires and s'mores and sex, all of it a domino effect. I wasn't sure why it felt even better to assign my parents a life of sex, but I did—replete with children and dreams and loss, all of it a domino effect. And maybe my trick worked—because my father was released after only one night, IV fluids fattening first his veins and then his cheeks, and that very same day, Rita appeared.

An hour before I was to meet my mother in Charlotte for a yoga class, she dropped by my house on her way home from work, if you could call it that. My neighbor three doors down actually hired her for a sex-toy party. I hadn't been invited, still too new to Cornelia for that kind of inclusion, although *Cornelia* was too new to the modern world for that kind of inclusion. I was working in the front yard, pulling weeds and scattering mulch, when seven or eight women, pink gift bags in hand, filed down Sarah Brody's sidewalk and straight home to show their husbands just how well Tupperware kept things fresh. Rita spotted me, turned left at the sidewalk when she should have turned right, and handed me a package of chocolate-flavored condoms, which I took because no one else, not even Willy Wonka, handed out chocolate-flavored condoms on the desperate, smutty streets of Cornelia.

"I don't want you to feel excluded," she explained, dropping the package into a crinkled pink bag she dug out of her case.

"Thanks," I said, sitting back on my heels, dirt grainy under my fingernails. "I'm out of those, so good timing."

"They're defective," she said, cocking her head.

"Really?"

"No, not really." She playfully shook the bag. "You can taste the chocolate."

"Good to know," I said, standing. I could tell she was fishing for information, but then, so was I. "You've probably already heard this, but Jude and I are getting married. A couple of weeks from now."

"I figured you would. Jude doesn't like to be alone, and you—" She stopped, kicking a small clump of mulch back into the flower bed I had been bribing with fertilizer and compost all summer.

"And I what?"

"You suit him." She looked pleased with herself for saying it.

I shrugged and picked up the mulch bag, crumbling it into a plastic ball. "I hope so."

"You do."

"Jude got the Karmann Ghia out of storage, you know."

She smiled. "Well, it's going to have to go right back in, for at least sixteen or seventeen years, don't you think?" She looked imploring, not that she didn't always look imploring.

"Something like that." I wanted to be less cryptic, but I didn't know how. Soon, I would have to tell her that I would never give that car a new driver, not on my own anyway. And then I would ask her to be our surrogate. For now, I could size up her hips—wide enough—and her breasts—intact—and her willingness—hopefully intact.

"You can go visit the house anytime you want, if it helps, to feel closer to Jude," she added. I knew she was talking as much to herself as she was to me, and that's what kept me hopeful, another trick for facing reality.

"If your father's body can't be strong, ours should be," my mother said on our way into the yoga studio, which was really just an exercise room at the YWCA. That meant I wasn't underdressed, even though I was the only woman in sweat pants with road-worthy white stripes up the side and a T-shirt with a tiny coffee stain. Everyone else, my mother included, wore Spandex. I knew she needed to get out of the house, my father's sickness more and more replacing my father, so I didn't judge her panty line.

I gave up after the first downward dog. The instructor was too young and too serene. My T-shirt bunched up over my ears, my entire torso exposed. I offered my mother an apologetic smile and went to sit in the lobby beside a vending machine. My mother followed me, however, rolled purple mat in tow.

"I don't get it either," she said. "Pilates, I get. It was invented by a man in prison trying to stay fit, so I understand the commitment to this thing." She lifted her mat. "But yoga, I can't get the breaths right. I'm too tired to pose. I've *been* posing." She sat down, squeaking against the orange vinyl seat. "You're getting married and your father is going to die. Who will I be?"

It was the first time my mother had admitted that my father was going to die, so even though I had been saying it for weeks, it was the first time I fully believed it myself. "I don't know, Mama," I said, so much rushing into my head from my heart or maybe into my heart from my head. I thought of Hugh, or more specifically, I thought about myself if I had never known Hugh. He didn't define me, but he had *predicted* me, the Frannie who relied on Jude.

"I don't know either," she said, slowly.

"Well, you do." I scooted forward and draped an arm over the back of her leotard. "You'll be my mother. That's never going to change."

She rested her head on my shoulder for a second or two, her hair spray leaving its faint odor of alcohol. "Frannie, you don't have to go to any more classes with me or pull your hair back or wear a fancy wedding gown. It's okay."

"I'm not wearing a fancy wedding gown, remember?"

"I was using that as an example only. I meant that you don't have to try and please me. It's fine."

"Thank you, Mama. But maybe I haven't done enough of that." I slid back on the orange vinyl seat and watched mothers, tote bags over their shoulders, corral their children down the hallway toward the pool, flip-flops slapping and towels trailing like capes behind them. "Mama," I said, trying to start slowly, "you know Hugh, Melissa's son? He's a good guy. Like I told you. Daddy was a positive influence in his life."

"I know," she said. She stuffed her arms into her jacket and wrapped it tightly across her body, pulling the zipper up to her chest. "Your father was adamant about that."

A woman across the lobby knocked a stack of magazines to the floor, and her kids started laughing, tempting me to tell them not to. I thought of my father's request in the grocery store: that my mother and Melissa be friends.

"Maybe Melissa was a good mother, you know, to raise someone like Hugh."

"With your father's help."

"With Daddy's help," I agreed, surprised how adamant *she* sounded.

"Maybe," she said. She pulled the elastic handle of her mat over her shoulder and stood up, her car keys in the other hand. "Frannie, I have one piece of marriage advice for you. Years from now, after you and Jude have had a long and happy life together, want more. Always want more."

I knew exactly what she meant: it was going to be hard living without my father.

On October 12th, on the date approved by both sets of parents and the *Farmer's Almanac*, it rained on the morning of my wedding, big drops that hit the ground hard and kept coming. I stood at my living room window and looked out onto the street, rivulets of water floating the bags of leaves waiting for Monday's pick-up from one house to another. My dress would dry, I decided, but it would take some effort to dry out a crepe, or Hugh. He had surprised me by calling from a bar to say that he would be at the ceremony, but he planned on being drunk if I planned on being married. "I plan on it," I told him. "And I hope you'll be there, drunk or not."

"I choose drunk," he said, but his voice was clear and full of Hugh, not beer.

"Eat something and find a blue sports coat and make your mother come pick you up," I said. I wasn't sure he'd be there, which was exactly the opposite of our entire past, so it felt right to be anxious and uncertain for a change. If he did show up, Jude wouldn't have to arm wrestle him or spit further than him or bake better cookies than him. But, then again, I had never told Jude very much about Hugh.

I had six hours before the wedding. I didn't know what else to do, so I decided on primping. It was warm for October, even warmer in the sun. I sat in one of the ornate iron chairs, part of the patio set Jude's parents had sent from Costa Rica as an early wedding gift. The yard was completely fenced in and the street quiet for a Saturday, so I decided to tan topless, lawlessly exposing my breasts to Cornelia before lawfully sharing them with Jude. I got up and changed into an old pair of Jude's shorts and a T-shirt, drug one of my old teak recliners to the back of the yard, in front of the row of daylilies that had been a brilliant orange just a month before, and threw the shirt on the ground. I looked at the light as it filtered first through the thick clouds and then the trees and onto the grass, the yellowish tones still caught somewhere between summer and fall, what my father used to call half-sun as he stood on the porch on weekend mornings. I lay there, cupping my breasts to my body, glad for them, which was silly, but true.

I hadn't cried when the doctor's office called to give me the news about my reproductive problems, and that news had remained abstract for so long. It must have been the wedding, the usual sequence of marriage and parenthood that goes along with it, making it real. So I cried then, the beautiful, blushing bride turned up a few notches to nearly naked and neurotic.

Exposed breasts were one thing, tears another, so I walked across the yard, back to the house, my arms crossed against my breasts, determined to distract myself with clearing out the guest room closet so that Jude could hang his four nice shirts and one pair of trousers. I opened the back door and threw the T-shirt into the laundry basket on top of the washer, sending the cats, to whom I had not yet broken the news that Jude was moving in the next day, scampering behind the dryer.

Rita stood in the kitchen. I saw her before she saw me, although she must have heard the door creak open. "Oh, no," she said, covering her mouth with her hand. "You forgot to get the white dress."

"What are you doing in my kitchen?" I crossed my arms over my chest and backed into the laundry room, where I grabbed a shirt from the drying rack and pulled it over my head, my back to her.

"The door was wide open," she said, her voice growing fainter. "I didn't mean to be rude."

"It's okay," I called. I rubbed my eyes and blew my nose on the towel that Jude had stolen from the Holiday Inn Express as a souvenir of the night we were engaged.

When I walked back into the kitchen, she sat on the stool pulled up to the counter, looking dejected, as if I had punished her. "I'm sorry," she said.

"It's okay. Really. You just surprised me." I closed the door and looked hard at her. "I have a dress, by the way."

"Good," she said, wiggling to the edge of the stool and then pushing herself back to the floor. "Because I brought you something." She beat me to my own question, adding, "Jude told me about the wedding, that it was today."

I nodded, and she pulled a pair of shoes from a brown paper bag. They were ivory-colored, clearly very old, slightly crinkled across the widest part of the toe, and with a thin Mary Jane strap. They were the kind of shoes that should have been ceramic, sitting on the bureau of a woman just past her prime, but who wanted it back. "They're antique," she said.

"And symbolic," I added.

"Oh, no," she said again. "This is not a 'see if you can fill my shoes' kind of thing."

"Do you want me to wear them?"

"No, they're different sizes, and one of the heels wobbles."

I gave her a quizzical look. "Why?"

She cocked her head and thought. "I don't know. I like to think that the woman who wore them almost a hundred years ago or whenever was like the rest of us."

"Asymmetrical?" I pointed to my breasts, since she had just seen them.

"Imperfect," she said. "Besides, they came that way." She shrugged and offered a weak smile. "They're something old."

"You skipped over the something borrowed and something blue and went straight to something old?"

"*You're* not the something old. You're what? Thirty-eight?"

"Thirty-seven."

She laughed. I looked out the side window over the sink and saw that someone had tied a bouquet of white balloons and silver ribbon to my mailbox. One of the balloons was in the shape of a wedding cake.

"Listen, Rita, I don't know if this is the right time or not to bring this up, but I have to ask. It seems like you're really pushing for Jude and me to have a child. Why is that?"

She didn't flinch. "Jude should be a father again. It's what he wants."

I didn't know why she hadn't said it sooner.

"Okay," I said, not wanting to let on that this was new, or at least accurate, information. "But the thing is, I can't have kids. I can't, and Jude knows. So the Karmann Ghia is a little ironic, huh? It's certainly something blue, now that I think about it. Only we both know it's got nothing to do with tradition."

She widened her eyes, an expression somewhere between surprise and concern that made her look like one of those little girl cartoon characters. "Never?" she asked. "You can never have children?"

"Never."

She leaned back against the stool and looked down at the linoleum that Jude and I were going to replace, our first weekend project. I had no idea why she had come, if she had an ulterior motive, if, as Jude still believed, she couldn't handle the memory of Evan alone. I barely knew her. Maybe it should have been my mother there with me on the day of my wedding, adjusting hems and advice, promoting me. But, trying to make up for too many years of not knowing how to do so, my mother was at home taking care of my father. Everything was askew. If a wedding was a beginning, mine was going to be a jumbled mess of endings headed in the wrong direction.

"That's very sad," Rita said. "I'm sorry about that."

"Me, too. Jude won't say it because he's too nice, but he's probably disappointed, too."

"Well, he's still marrying you," she said. Then she added, not quite a whisper, "And he might be relieved."

I let her think about that for a minute while I rinsed out my coffee mug with my back turned toward her, trying to earn what I was about to say. Then I turned around and dried my hands on my shirt. "So, I can't *carry* a baby, but I can make one. With Jude. If that's what we decide to do."

"Ahh," she said, figuring it out. "A surrogate." She ran her fingers along the metal edge of the counter. She looked smug, maybe because she was remembering that she could do both or that Evan had been created under the best circumstances—there was no doubt that Rita had loved Jude and probably still did. "A hired womb. That'd take a certain kind of woman."

"The surrogate and the mother," I said, and shooed her home so that I could break the family tradition of nearly missing my own wedding.

&

I drove myself, no more bronzed than before, but surer of something, as if I had seen myself at a distance. Or maybe I was confused, thinking instead of Rita coming toward me that day on Highway 26, the rain announcing her. So I turned off Oak Street, the traffic light unusually long for a Saturday in early fall, and took the back roads to Charlotte, where I could see the clouds moving across the sky without the interference of billboards or overpasses. I would pass Rita's shotgun house, and I would pass Evan.

As I drove, I watched the balloons bobbing from the antennae. I had retrieved them from the mailbox and tied them there, convinced that attracting attention on the front side of being married—when there was still time to back out—was more important than on the backside. Jude and I had agreed to have none of the fanfare of bachelor/ette parties or garter belts, rice, and decorated cars. We would leave the wedding the same way we had arrived, only married.

When I passed Rita's house, the Karmann Ghia was in the driveway, pulled over to the right as if to leave room for another car to pass. I put on my blinker and turned. It was only a couple of hours until the wedding, and I didn't want a late groom, or a sad one.

Jude sat on the front bumper of his car, in cargo pants even more wrinkled and pathetic than my own shorts. "Aren't we lovely?" I said as I came around the side of the car. I stood in front of him and held out my arms in a T, in homage to the fanciest thing either of us had on.

"Am I supposed to see you before the wedding?"

"I don't know."

"You don't believe in that whole bad luck thing?" he asked, standing and then turning so that I was out of view.

"Curse, you mean?"

"Whatever."

"Well, what if I were a mail-order bride and the whole thing was built on complete speculation and someone had to come get me at the airport to take me to the church or wherever and I knew no one else but you because I had spent my whole life in a tiny village in…" I threw my hands in the air, searching for a country.

"Virginial," he offered.

I cast him a non-approving look. "That's more a state, but okay. I've spent my whole life in Virginial, and now, with all confidence and desperation, I come to your country to give myself completely and utterly and dirtily to you, an unknown man with a credit card."

"And a fetish."

"And a fetish."

He clapped his hands together. "Let's see. How would some of those details work? I'd pick you up at the airport and we'd drive directly to the church? The church would offset the fetish, you see."

"I'd be hungry, so we'd have to stop at a drive-thru." I sat on the bumper beside him, my leg against his.

"Chicken nuggets," he said, nodding his head. "Dipping sauce, too."

"Oh, so you'd go for the tainted mail-order bride who likes junk food?"

"I meant Virginial to be ironic."

"It always is," I said, laughing.

Jude wrapped an arm around my shoulder and hugged me to him. "Don't be mad at me because I'm here."

"Why would I be mad at you?"

"I don't know," he said. "Most people might think 'wedding' should be the only word written on their day planners."

"Jude, forty years of your life is not erased just because you're marrying me. I understand that."

"I know you do."

"Have you been back there to talk or to think?" I nodded toward the side of the yard where Evan's grave was.

"Yes," he said.

"Good." I rubbed his leg. "I think you need to visit him anytime you want."

"I can't always make myself come out here, even when I want to."

This time I wrapped my arm around his, like all that kudzu and ivy setting an example beyond us, and studied his forearm, the slight ridge of veins at his wrist and the three deep creases that ran parallel to his hand. Then I kissed each of his knuckles. "I'm ready for the honeymoon." I said. "The reason being that I am not tired."

"Why are you not tired?"

"Because I don't have to figure you out. At least not anymore." I gestured to the house and, by implication, to the yard of toys and the grave beyond. "You have never really needed deciphering, and so I have all this energy from not having to decipher you that I can apply to other things." I wiggled my eyebrows.

He sat for a second. "Are you just now realizing that?"

"I just now am," I said.

"Do you still want to get married?" He asked the question word by word, as if he were typing it out in Morse code.

"Well, I have the afternoon set aside. I have a dress and a new bikini wax that took seven layers of skin and half my soul with it. And I have the best groom in town. I might as well."

We stood and looked each other up and down. Then we both started to laugh. "That is the worst outfit I have ever seen you in," he said.

"They're *your* shorts."

He looked at them again. "Yes, they are." Then he turned around and saw the balloons, which were beginning to look defeated, the cake rethinking its third layer and the silver ones settling for gray. "Where'd they come from?"

"You, I thought."

"Not me."

"You didn't leave them on my mailbox?" I asked.

"I'd never advertise a cake like that," he said, smiling. "It's ugly."

"Ah, a mystery," I said, suddenly thought I knew who had brought them. I considered telling him that Rita had stopped by, but didn't.

My parents' house stood at the end of a street lined with huge oak trees and mailboxes built into stone columns. Most of their neighbors had lived there while their kids were in school and then moved to smaller homes or to Florida, that huge peninsular waiting room, when their kids left home. My parents had stayed long after I left, although, before my father got cancer, they had talked of moving to a condo. But neither of them wanted to relinquish the backyard. Mostly, it had grass and a few laurel bushes, and pine straw where the shade made it solemn. In October, the liriope would still have a few purple flowers, and the mums would be popping up. That was one reason I wanted to get married there: it had always been a patient space, waiting for its moment.

My mother had insisted on taking care of all of the wedding decorations. We had talked about flowers, how hydrangeas, sweet Williams, and sunflowers would dominate, roses being for lazy brides with no imagination. "I want fresh flowers," I said to her. "No plastic or froufrou stuff stuck in with them, though. And especially no plastic figures on top of the cake. Just lots of flowers and color everywhere. You know, like a gypsy would do it." She liked that idea. There was no discussion beyond that, although my father had called me several times to offer a secret report on her progress.

"She's found a band with a fiddler," he whispered into the phone. Later, he reported, "She's got wisteria planted to trail the deck railing. And sweet potatoes. Who knew they had foliage? The natural area in the back corner will be full of planters with all kinds of flowering things." The two times I had been to visit him after his last hospital stay, my mother allowed me only in the front of the house, the three of us sitting like strangers on the living room sofa, the Chinese porcelain side lamps turned on, day or night.

I followed the Karmann Ghia up my parents' driveway, taking deep breaths. I let Jude park first and pulled my car up beside his. "You are to change upstairs in the guest room," I said through the lowered window. "Remember?"

"And change I will." He got out of the car and then kissed me on the cheek, careful not to knock the side mirror out of position.

"Well, not too much. I want to put the ring on the right man."

"Did I mention that I baked myself a huge cake for some cheap woman to jump out of last night, but she never showed up?"

"You mean she's still in there?" I gasped and thumped my chest.

He grinned and climbed the stairs to the porch, a beige suit bag slung over his shoulder. "It's gonna be great," he called.

My mother emerged from the garage, dragging an old hose with duct tape wrapped around several places. She was still in jeans and the striped blouse I had given her last Mother's Day. "Well," I said, spreading my arms.

She stopped and looked at me. "Oh my goodness, the bride." Then she stepped over the coiled length of hose and hugged me. She smelled like grass and lemons, although for a second I wanted it to be gardenias, the scent of the perfume she had worn when I was a child.

"How's Daddy?" I asked.

"He's weak but feeling pretty good. Excited."

We stared at each other for a second. "I'm afraid that once I get married, he'll just keep getting worse," I finally said. "I'm afraid this will be his last decent day."

"I'm afraid of that every day, Frannie."

"I know."

She stomped her feet, releasing some mud from the green plastic clogs she had bought when she began the wedding project. "Do you want to see?" she asked.

"Finally," I said, and followed her through the garage and around the side of the house to the gate that opened onto the patio. She unclicked the lock and let me pass sideways in front of her, not saying a word, standing with one hand held to the latch.

I walked a few feet down the stone path and stood at its edge, where four steps led down to the yard. I turned to smile at my mother. It was perfect.

Down the steps, she had created a walkway bordered by rosemary bushes planted in mosaic pots, tall beyond the norm, each draped in a garland of red poppies with black teardrops in their center. Beyond this border, the brick patio was filled with shrubs and topiaries of all heights and shapes. Always good at following directions, my mother had avoided all plastic figurines, but in their place was a woman and a man figurine cut from bushes, potted separately, their shoulders touching just below their mouthless, eyeless, noseless faces—sensory deprived but beautiful. Behind them, forming several arcs around the patio, stood large cement planters overflowing with a mixture of herbs and hydrangeas. Although the wind was not co-operating, I spotted mint and basil, parsley, and lemon verbena, which explained my mother's new scent.

Past the steps, rows of chairs faced the arbor under which Jude and I would stand. I counted eight rows on each side of the aisle. While the seating was simple—straight-back, folding white chairs—all around it were the flowers I had requested, long stalks of sunflowers standing erect in ceramic containers and bunches of sweet williams tied to ornate iron stakes with golden ribbon. The arbor itself was wrapped with garland made with snapdragons and gladiolas. Behind it, on new, bright green grass, were five tables covered in layers of cloths, white lacy ones overlaid with bright floral ones. None of them matched, which must have been hard for my mother, since most of her life had been defined by pattern. A huge blue tent stretched over all the tables, its flaps tied back with gold rope.

"The tent was your father's doing, of course," she said, coming to stand beside me. I tilted my head, then took my finger and traced the outline of the tent against the sky, which was beginning to clear, its grayish tone outdone by the red cording of the tent's edges.

"The gypsies do the same thing," I said, smiling. "Sometimes just for cooking."

She smiled back sadly. "Well, I never thought about that." She turned around to look at the house. "Your father and I agreeing about a tent."

I hugged her. "Thank you, Mama."

"Well," she said, and turned away.

Half an hour later, there was a knock on my old bedroom door, and I recognized my father's entrance, the slow turning of the knob and then fingers wrapped around the door edge as he peered inside before entering. He looked better than the last few times I had seen him, with more color in his face and straighter shoulders. He wore the blue suit we had selected when I couldn't talk him into jeans and a tie with purple polka dots. He smiled and waved, still partially hidden behind the door.

"Are you leaving before all the fun starts?" I asked.

"No," he answered. "I wasn't sure who you were for a second and thought I'd welcome you. Whoever you are." He squinted. "Are you wearing eyeliner?"

I nodded. "Put it on myself, but I don't like it."

He wiggled his nose. "Lemon?"

"That's Mama rubbing off on me. Literally. I kind of like it." I hugged him, careful not to let myself worry about how thin he was.

"She's proud of you, Frannie."

I pretended to adjust my earrings, not looking at him. I knew what was coming. "I'm proud of her," I said.

"I'm proud of you, too. And I'm glad that I get to see this part of"—he stopped, looking for the word—"your evolution."

"Thank you, Darwin."

"I probably won't be here to see any other big events that—"

I put up my hand. "No, Daddy, no. We are not going to have this conversation. It would be a cliché, and it would be silly when there's about to be a gypsy wedding out there. A tent overseeing the whole thing." There was no need to let him finish his sentence, and he would only be disappointed if he knew that the only big event I could guarantee was Jude and my cats all staking out their territory.

"Okay," he said quietly, patting my back.

"Besides, Daddy, look at this dress." I twirled.

"It did turn out like the picture."

"It's perfect."

"Frannie, be happy."

"Yes," I said, still determined that my wedding not turn into a sentimental event. "Of course." If he could give me such a big directive, then I decided I could give him one, too. "Today, though, today I am getting married, and when you walk me down that aisle, I want you to *keep* me. *Keep* me."

"I'll keep you," he said, smiling.

"And keep Mama, too."

He kissed me on the forehead. "Thirty-eight years," he said, more a tally than an answer.

"Thirty-eight," I repeated. "And counting."

I made him leave the room while I fought tears, redid my makeup, and sprayed my hair, which was gathered in an updo with too much ambition in contrast to my bangs. I looked haphazard, so I let it fall to my shoulders, pulling a few strands away from my face and resecuring them with the pearl clip, a gift from my mother. I almost liked what I saw in the mirror.

Only five minutes later than they were supposed to, a fiddle and mandolin started up. I met my father on the patio and locked my arm in his. We stood, surveying our audience. The guest list had grown to sixty-five once my mother saw it, and I was surprised to see that all of the seats were full. "Eight rows times eight seats is sixty-four," my father confirmed. But my eyes were already traveling past the folding chairs. I saw the minister. I saw Jude, in blue jeans and a tux jacket, under the arbor, and he was smiling. I saw the back of my mother's head, her hair in perfect waves.

"Hang on," I said to my father.

I let go of his arm and walked quickly down the aisle, careful not to look at anyone but feeling their stares, somebody muttering, "Wasn't there a rehearsal?" I stopped beside my mother, bent to lift the hem of her yellow chiffon dress off the wet ground, and whispered, "I need you on the patio." She looked puzzled, then worried, neither expression good on the day of a wedding, and followed me without a word, no doubt thinking that something had happened to my father. And something had: her. But thirty-eight years was a long time—a reminder was in order.

I positioned her next to my father. He shrugged, and she squirmed, both of them confused. Then I said, "Excuse me" as I wedged myself between them. I stuck out an elbow for each to take, which they did, finally looping their arms through mine. I commanded, "Walk with me," and stepped a few inches out in front, a place so new to me that I felt giddy.

"What an exhibition we are," my mother said, trying not to sound happy.

"More a wide parade," my father corrected her.

"Come on," I said under my breath, "I don't want Jude to get bored up there and leave."

We crossed the patio, my ballet slippers noiseless against the brick but my mother's pumps tapping, and descended the steps, slowing for my father's sake. I could smell the herbs my mother had potted, especially the mint. I smiled at Jude, who was now shuffling, looking suddenly nervous, and kept walking, keeping my parents in step with me and allowing myself a few glances into the rows of guests. I saw my cousin Debra and my childhood best friend Sandra, in a pink blouse and big earrings. I saw Brevna and her husband, who must have taken a day off from the pet store to verify the stories about my family that his wife no doubt brought home. I saw Hugh's parents and two sisters and didn't care that they looked baffled, especially when we reached the fifth row from the back and I added two more people to our wide parade.

Hugh, clean and sober, was first. I motioned for him to join us, but he shook his head, shoving his hands into his sports coat. My mother whispered, "That must be Hugh," and I answered, "Yes," my eyes still on him. I mouthed "Come on," which he answered by mouthing "No." Jude was about to offer me the biggest yes I had ever gotten, which I might not have been able to accept without knowing Hugh, so I stood, staring him down, knowing it's hard to refuse a bride with that much leisure time on her walk down the aisle. He finally rolled his head and slowly edged in front of my mother's friend Betty, who had the seat by the aisle in order to claim the best view.

I added Melissa last, not that I thought of her as last, or least. Mostly, I thought of her as Hugh's mother, Davies's widow, someone who had more in common with my mother than most people. I didn't have to ask her twice. She stood slowly and edged sideways past my former neighbors Ben and Brandon to the aisle, glancing nervously from me to my father and then my mother. They exchanged a glance, my mother adjusting her string of pearls and then moving her eyes back to me. The five of us shuffled and bumped elbows, my parents and I in formation and Melissa and Hugh trying to figure out which side of us they should stand on, finally settling for behind us. I gathered them all as best I could, and we proceeded down the aisle as one clump of intimately disconnected people.

I kept Jude centered in my gaze. He had traded his serious posture—legs slightly apart, hands folded together in front of them, back straight—for arms folded loosely across his chest as he leaned forward, perplexed at best.

When the five of us stood facing the minister, Jude's bohemian friend from college who may or may not have had any theological training, Jude turned, too, and stepped beside me. "That was interesting," he whispered. My father kissed my cheek as my mother took her seat on the front row. Melissa and Hugh returned to theirs, bumping shoulders and hats as they edged down the row. "I'll explain later," I whispered back. It felt good to be up there with him, exhibited, with onlookers who knew our good intentions before we even said them.

Then the minister asked, exactly as we had rehearsed over the telephone, "And who has come today in truth and with confidence to be married?"

"Judson Lance Dawson," Jude said.

"Frances Marie Lewis," I said.

When I looked proudly over my shoulder at my parents to show them how fine I was going to be, I saw who could only be described as a wedding crasher, late, uninvited, overdressed, accepting the chair the mandolin player graciously offered because there wasn't another. It was Rita. She perched on that seat like she wasn't sure if she was going to stay, but maybe that was only my doubts taking over—because after our homemade vows and the clapping and my father taking my mother's hand to walk with her down the aisle again, Rita was still there to congratulate us, some new glint in her eye.

Chapter 13

Jude and I left our reception in the Karmann Ghia, with the top down and only the sticky residue of cake icing on our fingers and lips announcing our nuptials. Jude had made the cake, three layers of white swirled, like sunshine, with lemon cream and topped with chocolate icing, inspired by a recent episode in my bedroom. He had decorated it by hand so that the bottom layer was a carousel, horses attached to poles circling the outside; the middle layer was covered with different flowers, mostly red, of course; and the top layer, the smallest, had a folksy man and woman drawn with icing, both of them in diapers—or at least that's what Jude said they were wearing. Everyone else thought he had simply run out of white icing.

As requested, no one had decorated the car, although my mother left a bag of food, some blankets, and a US atlas in the back compartment, as if we were driving off into a Montana snowstorm instead of back up the interstate to Cornelia.

"Did you have fun?" Jude asked me once we were down the driveway. If I had answered no, I now had to stay until I could answer yes, and it occurred to me that all of marriage might be like that, at least on certain days.

"I did have fun. It was really fun."

"The opening procession might have been my favorite part." He reached over and tugged my braid, which I had asked my mother to do midway through the reception when it looked like I would dance. It turned out that Jude had some moves, which made me wonder what else I didn't know about him, so I tried to keep up. My mother kept up better than I did, though. He dragged her out on the patio, the official dance floor of the reception, and they did two more couples dances than she did with my father, who, looking more tired as the afternoon wore on, swayed along the best he could.

"I did it for my parents, mostly my father."

"I know," he said. "But back to those other two. And by other two, I mean Hugh."

"I told you. I've known him forever. He's Melissa's son."

Jude nodded. "When he looks at you, Frannie, you're backlit. Like a soap opera star."

"When have you ever watched soap operas?"

"Okay. When he looks at you, Frannie, it's like the sun parting clouds and shining down only on you."

"When have you ever parted clouds?" I asked, knowing I was losing the fight.

"It's like you told me, I can't blame you for having a past. I just hope he knows that you and I are serious." He held up his left hand, the silver wedding band on full display.

"He knows," I said. "He and I go way back. But you don't have anything to worry about."

"Well, there was the other small-in-a-floral-dress elephant in the room."

"Rita?" I asked, playing dumb. I was sure she had shown up because of our conversation about surrogacy, her interest piqued.

"Yep," he said. "Rita."

We let her name hover. I tucked my dress up under my knees so that the hem wouldn't drag against the floorboard. I would wear the dress again, I had already decided, with my turquoise necklace, maybe for date night anytime I felt Jude needed a reminder of this day. He must have read my thoughts. He moved his right hand from the gearshift to the top of my thigh, back and forth, all the way through Charlotte traffic until we got to the turn-off for the interstate.

We were a mile closer to Cornelia, the afternoon sun dipping below the tree line ahead of us, when Jude said something I never expected. "Rita is kind of pitiful."

"Because she showed up uninvited or because she didn't join the conga line, which you so clearly value?"

"She wasn't uninvited, Frannie."

"You invited her?" I turned my body to better face him.

"I should have told you, but to be honest, it wasn't a real invitation. I mean, she didn't get the paper one like everyone else. I mentioned when she was in the bakery that she could come, but I didn't think she would."

"It doesn't bother me, Jude. I like her, and I don't think she's pitiful."

"She's pitiful for coming."

"I don't know," I said, thinking. Rita was broken but fierce. I suspected that fierceness came from still loving Jude, fighting to find some way to stay connected to him. I didn't think our wedding day was the time to tell him that I had one solution already figured out, so I fought harder for her honor instead. "Maybe she thought it was a way of showing you that she's happy for you. Maybe she thought she owed it to you, since she's the one who left."

"The only thing Rita owes me is letting go, Frannie. I thought our wedding would encourage that, but time will tell."

I fidgeted in my seat, careful not to let Jude see my worry. Time told a lot of things it shouldn't. Jude and I disagreed about Rita. I needed her connected, to Jude, to us. And no matter how much Jude thought he had moved on, I couldn't share his grief the way Rita could.

"Let's just get to that honeymoon, okay?" I reached behind his neck and tickled.

He smiled. "I sure hope they have the champagne waiting at that fancy resort."

The fancy resort was Jude's loft, which would be rented the very next day to a young woman with an art degree and a pierced eyebrow. Most of Jude's things had been moved to my house, cluttering all the rooms, scaring the cats, and making me rethink first my closet space and then Jude's furniture aesthetic. We had decided to stay at the loft as a kind of ritual, some closure for Jude, opting against a honeymoon out of town. I didn't want to leave my father when it was clear that he was getting sicker, and Jude said he didn't believe in assigning marital bliss a geographical location.

The loft was practically bare. Jude had left behind only some towels, candles, and a futon on which we slept that night, all of the day's expectations exhausted and receding into dream.

Within a week of the wedding, when Jude and I were still getting used to two cars in the driveway and I started writing thank-you notes for wedding gifts, my father gave up reading. He called my mother into the den, where he was propped up on two pillows on the couch, an afghan over the lower part of his legs, and asked her to remove the stack of detective novels that grew bigger with each birthday and Christmas. "What should I do with them?" my mother asked, and he said only that all those words were cluttering his thoughts. The next day, he had her box up most of his cookbooks, all the possibility for Mexican mole and Turkish pastries and West African peanut soup to be left at the bottom of a Salvation Army receptacle (although my mother never took them there). Then it was his toolbox, which he gave to the mail carrier, shuffling down the front walk in sweat pants and his rubber beach sandals to hand it over, completely intact, all the screwdrivers turned in one direction and the pliers in the other, as he liked.

"I keep waiting for him to give up the carnival," my mother said, by telephone, her voice lowered to a near-whisper.

"He's not talking about going back, is he?" I asked. "It's been years and years."

"No. How could he?"

"By remembering," I said.

"I can't stop that," she said, and she was right.

Several days after that, my father stopped listening to the weather. I found his weather band radio, the cord wrapped around it and held down with duct tape, in the garage, on top of the recycling bin. Jude and I had come to visit on Sunday, leaving boxes of his clothes, our weekend project, unpacked in our hallway. My father had sent me out to the garage to find his golf clubs, which I suspected he was going to give to Jude, who hated golf.

"Don't you want to know the temperature in Sioux City?" I asked my father, holding up the radio when I came back in.

"No. Do you want that?" He nodded toward it, tightening his face as he did so.

"Why would I want the weather band radio?"

"To go with that fancy atlas your mother got you and Jude."

"Jude wants to buy an Airstream to give the atlas purpose." I sat on the footstool and lifted the afghan to see if he was wearing his beach shoes or the same old pair of suede slippers he'd had since I was a girl. It was the suede slippers, along with a pair of argyle socks whose elastic had given up.

"I've always wanted one, Duncan," Jude said. "They're classic."

"Put some water around one of those and you've got yourself a ship," my father said.

"I would prefer a nice, big ship," I said. "Only *men* don't mind sleeping on a kitchen table that converts into a bed."

Jude grinned, but my father arched his eyebrows at me. "On a ship, you just notice the water."

"I believe you," I said quietly. "All that space between thinking and doing."

"That's right," he said. "Did you find the clubs?"

"No."

Jude sat back against the thick embroidered pillow and fingered the tassels, obviously feeling awkward, so I sent him out to the garage to look for the golf clubs.

"I found the carnival because of golf," my father said matter-of-factly. He adjusted the afghan and kept talking as if he were never going to stop, once and for all telling his story. "I started driving to the country club for a game one Saturday morning—you were at basketball practice, I believe—and the golf bag was in the trunk and the cleats were on the floorboard where your mother's feet would normally be and I just decided that I hated golf. Everything about it."

"You taught Hugh how to play."

"I didn't want to," he said, shrugging. "So anyway, that Saturday, I drove past the country club and kept going north on Morehead Boulevard and then I was outside the city limits, downtown and the bank in my rearview mirror. The buildings looked like those pictures you used to draw me when you were a little girl. And then I drove, straight up the middle of the state. I ate lunch at a steakhouse, sitting at a table near the hallway to the bathrooms. And I kept driving until I was behind this caravan of trucks and trailers. I could see animal eyes in the openings of the last one, but I could never get close enough to see what kind of animal it was."

I heard my mother, the familiar flapping of her clogs, come to the doorway and then stop. If my father noticed, nothing in his face or tone showed it. I wondered where Jude was.

"It was one of those little vagabond carnivals, and I followed it off the exit ramp to a big empty field outside a little town called Sparrows, and I sat in the car with the weather band on, listening to rain accumulation in Washington state and watching all these people and animals emerge from those vehicles." He stopped for a breath. "It was like some kind of updated Noah's ark in reverse."

"Minus the water," my mother said from the doorway.

"Madelane, I'd wish you'd come sit down," my father said, without turning his head.

My mother didn't move, but my father kept talking anyway.

"So I kept watching this red pickup truck pulling one of those white trailers. A girl not much older than you at the time, maybe eighteen, got out, and I just wondered what someone that young was doing at whatever get-up was unfolding in front of me."

"The gorilla woman," I said.

He nodded. "After that, I had to see for myself what drew everybody to her."

"Did you?" my mother asked from behind us.

"Over the years, there were ten or eleven of them to watch. Not one of them stayed for more than half a season. They all left."

I shifted my body to look at my mother. She should have asked, but she didn't. "Why did you keep going back if *they* didn't?" I asked instead, expecting a philosophical answer, or at least an answer.

"I don't know," he said. "It was easy, maybe. But really, I don't know."

He sighed and didn't say more. And then I realized that he wasn't going to say anymore. And "I don't know" was far from satisfactory, far from the best thing, the one thing, that had to be said. It wasn't mine to say, and I wouldn't say it for him. I heard my mother's heavy footsteps fade into the kitchen and then the sounds of water running and glasses clinking against each other. She was mad. So was I.

I got up and went into the kitchen, my heart smack up against my chest and trying to get out. "Come back in the den, Mama."

"I'd rather not," she said.

I reached in front of her and turned off the water. I took a dishtowel and dried her hands, feeling both biblical and domestic. She let me. I could see, literally see, her anger make its way to her face, which became flushed and tense. I pulled her by her elbow into the den and made sure my father didn't have to turn his head to look at either of us.

"Daddy, say it. Finish the story."

"Frannie," my mother started, "he's weak today. Let's not—"

I shook my finger at her. "You, too, missy. He's going to say something, and then you're going to say what comes next." I bent over my father, so insistent that Jude, who had stopped in the doorway with the bag of golf clubs over his shoulder, turned and went back into the kitchen. "All that time, she blamed herself. Please say it, Daddy."

His eyelids fluttered a few times. Then he looked at my mother. "I'm sorry for putting you through that, Madelane."

"And Mama?"

She shifted her eyes toward the backyard and bit her lip.

"Say it. You've been here taking care of him for over a year and getting all organic on us and going to yoga because you don't know what to do with what's happening, so just say it like he was offering a piece of good advice or a party invitation."

"I accept," she said, staring first at me and then at him, "your apology, Duncan."

I pressed a hand to my chest and stood so still that Jude came behind me and whispered, "Frannie? You okay?" I couldn't speak yet, so I pressed back against him. In the doorway, the golf bag fell over, and the clubs clattered to the floor.

"I need to go home," I said to both of them. "Behave yourselves."

I picked up my purse and took Jude by the hand. He had never seen me so done.

It took my father five more days to finish dying. Each of those five days, I called my mother in the morning, hoping she would tell me what I knew wasn't going to happen, that my father had eaten an entire meal and then performed his once-normal stretches in the den, a thin layer of sweat accumulating on his forehead, his ancient track pants gathered at his ankles. Or that he had climbed heavy-footed to the attic in search of something, which he used to do at least weekly, usually not finding it, descending the stairs smelling of stale air and cedar. But of course, those things had not happened. Now my father only slept.

Each of those afternoons, I drove into Charlotte against the flow of commuters returning home and watched him sleep, just a few gray hairs on his head, along with a scattering of whiskers on his chin. Each night, I drove back to Cornelia to find Jude stretched out on our bed, watching the news, fully dressed, on top of the covers. It was his way of trying to share my suffering, although all it did was appease the cats, who were convinced that as long as he kept his shoes on he might actually leave.

Finally, my mother asked that I come stay with her so we could take shifts sitting with my father through the nights. "I always thought he would die in the hospital," she said, "but now he wants to die at home. Does that make any sense to you? That someone would have to die in the very room where they ate popcorn or wrote the checks?" I wanted to ask her if she would be able to live there after he died, but I knew she didn't share my belief about houses and spirits. Even so, she would have preferred the sterility of a hospital, the practical lines of hallways and medical charts. As much as my mother needed her, she didn't trust the hospice nurse, who arrived along with a hospital bed that had to be carried in sideways, like a bride, through the back door.

I had been waiting for my mother to ask for my help, so I told her I would be there in a few hours. I stopped editing an article about the impact of technology on agriculture, cooked lasagna for Jude, wearing my not-yoga pants with the stripes up the sides, and then I cleaned, unpacking five boxes that he hadn't and storing his enormous record collection under the guest room bed beside the dust bunnies with a lifetime lease. I cried the whole afternoon. When Jude got home from the bakery about six, he said I had frog eyes. Then he sat me down on the couch and rubbed my shoulders.

"What's the update?" he asked gently.

"The doctors think in the next few days. I'm going to stay over there so I can help Mama. So I can be there."

"Okay. Do you want me to come?" He straightened my collar and blinked several times.

"If you want to. At least for tomorrow when you can get away from work."

"You got it," he said.

"Jude?" I sat up and tucked my legs under me.

"Yeah?"

"I want us to have a baby. We can get a surrogate so it'll be really ours. I want us to do that, and I want us to do it soon."

"Frannie, I think maybe you're just upset about your father and this is a distraction. If you—"

"No. I want a baby. I want you to admit that you do, too. Even if you married me thinking it wouldn't ever happen, I want you to admit that you do, too."

"I won't say it," he whispered.

"Why not?"

"Because I feel like it would be a criticism of you."

"It's not a criticism of me. It's not. You won't say it because you can't admit it. You can't admit that you want another child because you think it proves Rita right in some way."

He stood up and kept his back to me, and then he marched into the bathroom. "You just take care of your father, Frannie," he called. "And forget the thing you said to me. Just take care of what you need to do for your father."

I followed him to the bathroom. He tried to close the door, but I stuck a foot in the way. "You can't be mad at me right now. You're going to have to help me get through this. Because you know how. So don't be mad at me right now because I've told you the truth."

I saw his arms stiffen, the angle of his shoulders sharpen. When he spoke, the words traveled across the room like slow bullets. "If your father dies, Frannie—"

"When, Jude, *when* my father dies."

"When your father dies, Frannie, I'll hold you and comfort you to the best of my ability." He jerked his toothbrush from the holder on the vanity. "And by the way, I don't know how. Nobody does."

"Okay," I said, hanging my head because I believed him.

And I still believed him the next day, when my father died, at home, one hand resting on the top of his left thigh and the other to his side, brushing against the metal bars of his bed, his palm turned up and his fingers curled as if he were cupping water. It was after three in the morning, and my mother was asleep on the couch, lightly snoring, her face turned toward its back. I would have woken her sooner, expecting the death rattle to alert me, but it never came. He only made a strange whistling sound, his last breath a long one. I took his hand and wrapped it in both of mine. I called to my mother. She came and stood beside me, the outline of the sofa's cording on her cheek. I placed his hand in hers and left them alone. I climbed the stairs to my old room where Jude was asleep and crawled in bed beside him, and as always, he kept his word.

Three weeks after my father died, my mother packed her two biggest suitcases, one of which contained the negligee from her honeymoon, my father's favorite, and went looking for the carnival that had borrowed him all those summer weeks. She took the negligee because, even though it still fit her, she would never wear it again—it was a reminder of my father and, in some ways, of the person she had once been. She took my father's Buick because it smelled like him and because she was convinced that cars, not houses, retained their owners' spirits. She even draped one of his suit jackets over the top of the passenger seat, as he had done every day of his thirty-seven years as a loan officer. She wore blue jeans, and her makeup was soft, just a hint of color that wasn't her own. Using her cell phone, she called me twice with a progress report.

After she left Charlotte, she followed a map to Blue Ridge, Georgia, below the North Carolina state line, in the middle of a national forest that spread across two hundred acres. At the sign announcing this expanse, she pulled over and turned off the Buick. She got out and sat on the bumper, her eyes shut in intense concentration. She imagined she and my father starting over, but then quickly dismissed the thought. She would not allow herself to regret anything about their marriage.

A few minutes later, she stopped in the drugstore in town to ask directions to the fairgrounds and bought a small gift. Then she drove on. When she began seeing the cars lined up to enter the graveled lot off the two-lane, she felt her pulse quicken. She waited her turn in line, then parked the Buick in front of a blue-and-white-striped tent, put her shoes back on, and bought a ticket for seven dollars that would get her into all the events and exhibitions. "Thank you," she said, politely to the woman in overalls who sold it to her, her face enshrined behind the window. "What a deal."

"I'll say," the woman responded.

Once inside, she bought a corndog and ate it without sitting down. She was not overdressed, she noted, surveying the people standing in line. They, like her, were prepared for the possibility of wonder and awe, and only casual clothes would do. Wonder and awe. Those must have been what Duncan sought, what she had stopped being for him. But he had stopped being that for her, too. If she thought about it, most people had.

Except for me.

She pushed her way through the waiting crowd to the very front, where she stood against the fence that barricaded the stage. It was warm for mid-November, the smell of trash everywhere. Behind her, a father told his little girl that what she was about to see was only pretend.

When the show began, my mother watched only the surface of the stage. Consequently, she saw the announcer's feet first, packaged in black wingtips with worn-down heels. Allowing her eyes to finally travel upward, she noted he was young and had long hair, perhaps secretly jealous of the gorilla woman's excess.

Just as my father had said, the gorilla woman turned out to be young, too, and skinny, with dark hair cut into long layers. For all the audience muttering she created, she stood alone in the middle of the stage, spinning around and around like a hapless leaf. Off to the side were mirrors, maybe a series of forty in all, which flashed image after image of a gorilla onto her so quickly that the eye couldn't keep up. My mother couldn't see the mirrors, but she had heard about them.

As she stood on the tips of her toes, like a dancer, to get a better view of the performance, my mother was not impressed. When it was over, she checked her compact once again, pleased that her hair was still neat. She clicked the case shut, rubbed a finger over the *MNL* embossed in thin, gold letters, and sighed. Turning around, she shoved her way back out of the crowd as the gorilla woman sprouted hair from the tops of her hands.

She spent the rest of the afternoon people watching: not the carnival people but the ones, like her, who had taken in the thrills as she had done. "There's where the show is," she told me over the phone, "and the mystery. Everything else is just filler."

On the way back to the Buick, she saw the gorilla woman emerge from the back of a smaller tent with plastic windows cut into the sides, and her opportunity finally arrived. The young woman wore a denim miniskirt and sandals that tied around her ankles. A bandana dangled from her purse strap.

"Excuse me," my mother said, waving a hand at her.

The woman looked over her shoulder, then stopped as my mother approached her, breathless, her own purse flapping against her hip.

"I know how you do it," she finally emitted, patting her chest to indicate her inability to breathe.

"Okay," the woman said. She put a hand on a hip.

"The act. I know how you do it."

The woman didn't flinch.

"I know," my mother repeated.

"Everybody knows how you do it," she said, turning away to point in the direction of the stage. "*You* could do it if you wanted to earn a little extra money. How are you at turning around and around and turning into someone you know nothing about?"

"Better than I used to be," my mother said sadly.

"I bet," the woman said.

"Why do you do it?"

"It's a job. That's what I call it. A job."

"Do you like it?"

The woman stubbed her toe in the mixture of dirt and grass. "I like it okay. Nobody's ever really asked me that before, but I like it okay."

My mother smiled at her. It was the smile that had originally attracted my father as she selected lettuce in the produce aisle of a grocery store.

"Why are you so interested anyway?"

"Do you have children?" my mother asked her, ignoring the question.

"What business is it of yours?"

"You must be in a hurry to get home. I'm keeping you from your family maybe."

"I travel with the carnival. Children are not recommended. They break if you're not careful."

"That's why you have to be careful," my mother said, thinking suddenly of a few things that she wished she had done differently with me.

"Do I know you?" the woman asked. She cocked her head, not in contemplation but more in judgment.

"No," my mother said, continuing without a pause. "It looks very mysterious from the audience's perspective. I wonder what it's like from yours."

"What are you talking about?"

My mother arched her eyebrows. She glanced at a group of passing people who no doubt assumed that they were mother and daughter, arguing, the carnival worn off. In a way, they were right. "The act. Your act."

"Lady, from up there all I see is the tops of people's heads. I see a lot of hair. And sometimes I get to thinking about why hair is on the head and not on the feet, and other times I think it's just fine on the head 'cause it covers up some pasty-looking skin and gives people variety. Mostly, I just see hair."

"That's exactly what we see when we watch."

The woman tugged at the top of her boot. "So you don't believe?"

That's it, my mother thought. Duncan wanted to believe. But believe in what? She still wasn't sure.

As the woman walked away, my mother strapped her purse across her body and got out her car keys, ready to drive back and tell me all she had seen and learned. But she wanted the woman to remember her, maybe one day suddenly recalling their conversation as she shopped for groceries. "Excuse me," she called again.

The woman stopped but didn't turn. My mother walked to stand in front of her, the toes of their shoes practically touching. "I didn't tell you earlier that my husband used to work with your act. Just in the summers for a few weeks. Duncan. Ever heard of him?"

"No, lady, I never did."

"Oh," my mother said, wondering if a woman with that much attitude might not deserve being a gorilla. But she smiled again and reached for the bandana on the woman's purse strap, straightening it, wanting to make it into a bow but deciding that she shouldn't. Instead, she stood as the young woman rolled her eyes and walked away.

After that, my mother gave the gift to the woman at the ticket booth. It was a bottle of perfume. She watched the woman set it on the counter behind her and imagined that someone completely in the carnival frame of mind might wonder if genies smelled like gardenias.

Back out in the parking lot, for the first time since my father's death, the full range of her emotions surfaced. My mother did not want strangers seeing her cry, so she, an almost-gypsy, drove the Buick behind the village of tents and back onto the road, then pulled off onto the shoulder, and sat, with the hazards blinking and my father's spirit crowding her in the front seat.

Chapter 14

On the morning that I stood in the guest room and imagined a crib against the far wall, a purple envelope with hand-drawn flowers found its way to my mailbox, ironically sequestered between the most recent announcement of a missing child and an advertisement for an all-inclusive travel package to Disney World. It was from Rita, addressed only to me in small, fringed letters that looked like she had cut them out of one of those children's books where the font is as pretty as the story. Inside was a change of address card, also hand-decorated. She had drawn a picture of a house, a road, and trees, above which an airplane in the shape of an arrow that pointed down and was pulling a caption that read "I Am Here." She had moved to the house with the toy garden, or at least that's what I assumed the address to be. I stood at the mailbox and read the card several times. Her last name, something I had never considered, was Phillips, so she must have changed it back to her maiden name, although I didn't like that term. I put the card back in the envelope and decided that she had something to tell me, which was good because I had something to ask her.

I wondered why she had moved back to a place filled with grief. I didn't understand grief. The day of my father's funeral, I felt almost nothing. My mother and I stood shoulder to shoulder in the church pew, our dark colors blending into each other. Neither of us cried. My mother tucked a Kleenex into the wristband of her shirt, but she only used it to polish the buckle of her purse, absently rubbing until I stilled her hand, covering it with mine. Jude wore the one suit he owned and a tie with green stripes that made his neck look short and his chin fleshy. He sat between the two of us in the hearse, answering the driver's questions in a hushed tone, opening the car doors for us, his eyes cast to the ground. "This must remind him of his son," my mother whispered to me. "Do you think it reminds him of his son?"

Minutes later, when the urn was lowered into the ground, Jude gripped my hand and whispered, "It's not him. Remember that he's already someplace else." He was right—the urn was empty. My mother had my father's ashes beside her bed, not ready to settle on a date to cast them to the ocean but working her way toward it.

For nearly a month, ever since my father's funeral service, Jude had stayed home from the bakery in the mornings, waking before I did to fix the coffee, which he slowly carried to me in bed with his arms stretched out in front of him, as if it were an explosive. Then Jude would look hard at me, as if he wanted to pull my sadness to the surface, but I couldn't find it. With all those long hours together, we got in each other's way, and the house began to feel like a spaceship, our bodies floating around, not knowing what to attach to.

After Rita's card arrived, out of newlywed obligation, Jude and I had sex in the shower; it seemed orchestrated and wrong.

"So this is marriage?" I asked as I began dressing to go to Rita's, although I didn't tell Jude my plans.

"Marriage with tragedy thrown in," he answered. I studied his back, the three moles on the left side that my fingers had connected again and again. I didn't want our lives to be defined by getting through tragedy. When he left for the bakery a few minutes later, his first morning back, I took the keys for the Karmann Ghia from the wooden holder by the kitchen door and then changed my mind and put them back.

I waited until ten o'clock, the time my mother had taught me was appropriate for visiting. Then I drove to the house with the toy garden and found Rita sitting in a rocking chair on the front porch, the wooden boards creaking beneath her. She didn't stop rocking but offered me a stiff wave.

"You moved back?"

"I suppose I belong here. In every room, I meet myself."

I sat on the top step, avoiding the rough spot where the wood had splintered. "I think I know what you mean," I said. "Ever since Jude moved in, I have to remind myself that my house is his house now, too. I can't be frustrated because under *his* ugly couch is *my* beautiful Persian rug inside *my* house that is so full of me."

"I meant Evan," she said, her tone flat.

I sighed, feeling stupid. "I know you did. I just wanted to get Jude in the conversation as soon as possible." I threw a pebble into the yard and watched it bounce off one of the stones.

She chuckled. "Once you marry someone, they're always in the conversation. Unless you're Jude and the conversation is about Evan."

"Even so, you still love him."

"Did you drive over here to tell me that?"

"No, but I think it's true."

"I won't disagree," she said. I was surprised that she conceded so easily, but then again, less than a month ago, she had watched him marry me—I didn't think she had ever wanted a reconciliation, which would have been a useless desire now. "If I knew how to un-love him, I would."

"I wouldn't ask you to."

"He would," she said. "He'd like me to pack up again and be gone, but I'm not going anywhere. This is home. And there's bound to be a nursing position at Tradewinds opening up soon. Nurses are even more in demand these days than sex toys."

I smiled, still trying to build my courage to say what I had driven over to say.

"I'm sorry about your father, by the way," she said. "I read the obituary."

"Thank you," I said, standing. I hadn't put on a jacket before I left my house, and I was going to suggest that we go inside until I remembered that going inside was an exercise in fortitude I didn't want to take on.

"Did I offend you?"

"No," I answered, trying to sound friendly when I was nothing but anxious, sliding my heel up and down inside my boot. "Rita, I came to ask you something. Just hear me out. Okay?"

"Okay."

"I'm looking for a surrogate so that Jude and I can have a baby. And I would like her to be you."

She slowly shook her head. "You are one gutsy girl."

"It's not easy to ask," I agreed.

"No, I mean that you must be doing this without Jude knowing, or otherwise he'd be here with you. That's pretty gutsy."

I shrugged, not wanting her to know that she was right. "It's a big decision. But please think about it."

"If I do it, will you do something for me?" She wrapped her sweater tightly around her body and crossed her arms over her chest.

"We would pay you, Rita. It would be a legal arrangement."

"Forget legal arrangements. The district attorney could appear on the side of this house alongside the Virgin Mary and it would still be a lot more than a legal arrangement." She smiled, as if she liked the idea of the Virgin Mary choosing a cursed shotgun house on Highway 26.

"It's more personal than that, that's true, but we'd make sure all the legal terms were clear," I said. "We would be fair." As soon as I said it, I couldn't decide which word, "we" or "fair," was the biggest lie. If there was one thing I had learned from my parents, it was that secrets eliminated any chance of a "we." And how could I be fair to Rita if I wasn't fair to Jude?

"If I agree to do it, will you do something for me?"

"What?" I asked. I had expected that Rita would have her own terms and that they'd be like Rita—bold, clear, a little nervy. On the drive over, I had even let myself imagine that she'd demand an ongoing relationship with the baby, holidays included. Jude and I would have to learn to share the camcorder but could blame some-one else for the inevitable slip-up about Santa. I couldn't decide how I would feel if Rita did ask for that kind of inclusion, but now I realized I wouldn't know unless I talked it over with Jude. And I hadn't talked anything over with Jude.

"Don't ever leave him."

I was so stunned that I braced one hand against the porch rail-ing. "What? I'm not leaving Jude. Why would you say that?"

She stood and reached back to still the rocker. "I don't mean next week. Or in three and a half years. I mean don't have a child with Jude and *ever* leave him and take the child with you. He couldn't handle it."

I only had to look at her to know that she wasn't threatening me or trying to intimidate me. She was a woman who had lost just about everything, and she was speaking from experience.

"I'm not leaving Jude, Rita. And even if I did, it would have nothing to do with you. It just wouldn't."

"Okay," she said, her long silver earrings bobbing against her neck.

"Okay what?" I asked.

A dog bolted out of the house next door and ran, barking, to the edge of the driveway that forked into Rita's, and then a woman's voice, cracked with age, called, "Bobo, Bobo, you mean old thing, get back in this house." Rita leaned over the railing and clapped her hand a few times, and the dog barked louder.

"Okay, I'll do it."

"I didn't hear you say yes, Rita. I want to hear you say yes."

"Yes," she said, with a quick nod.

"Thank you." I felt my hands flutter uselessly at my sides, but I knew I couldn't hug her. "Thank you." I took the steps back down to the pathway, wanting to feel happy or victorious. But I couldn't. I suddenly understood the shame and confusion my father must have felt during all those drives home from Melissa's and my mother's embarrassment after she stole baby Hugh. What would they have said to each other back then?

"Frannie?"

"Yeah," I said, turning.

"Make sure Jude's on board. This should be his plan, too." Her tone wasn't critical or harsh, and it was good advice, even if I had already given it to myself. I should have gone to Jude first. I was so sure I knew what he needed that I forgot I needed him more.

I felt so guilty that I accidentally drove home ten miles in the wrong direction, under a sky covered with thick, gray clouds that never did what they threatened—heavy rain, minus the water—all the while wondering if Jude would accept my apology.

After her carnival trip, my mother spent a few weeks feeling sad, during which she wrote her own thank-you notes to everyone who attended my father's funeral, and then she woke up the morning after I visited Rita, and decided that being sad would not honor my father. Or rather, she called to say that honoring herself would best honor my father. I thought it was a good idea. To cheer her on, I told her about my plan to hire a surrogate, although I didn't mention Rita. To cheer me on, she said it was a good way to honor myself. We were a fan club, small but devoted, lacking only Jude. After an entire day, I had still not found a way to tell him about my talk with Rita, and when I did, I doubted he'd be a fan of mine.

Maybe because of my mother's new focus on herself or maybe because I had called Hugh, who considered thank-you notes elitist, to finally thank him for coming to both my wedding and my father's funeral, I began to think about Melissa. My father had wanted my mother and her to be friends, and although I wasn't ready to throw them a luncheon, Hugh said something that made the possibility of their friendship more realistic. "He was a good man, Frannie," he assured me when I said that there was so much my father would never know about me. "Also, know this about him," he added, "When he was around, my mother was happier. She was home. She was a better mother. I look back and see that now. He was a good man. That's all you need to know." I had hung up the phone, missing them both—my father and Hugh—and thinking even more about Melissa.

Recently, I couldn't have a thought without my mother having the same, it seemed, so I wasn't surprised that afternoon when I pulled into my driveway behind my mother's white Lexus. She sat on the front steps, wearing flat shoes I had never seen and a trench coat. "Detective Lewis?" I said, meeting her on the sidewalk. "Or is that your real name?"

"It's only been three days since you've seen me," she said, dodging my humor. "You shouldn't have forgotten my real name."

She hugged me, tight. Since my father had died, she hugged me when she first saw me, when she told me good-bye, and sometimes, with no warning, in the middle of a conversation. We sometimes had a new ritual for phone calls, too. I'd say, "Bye, Mama," and then there'd be a long pause, after which she'd say, "I just sent a hug over the telephone lines, is it there yet?" I always said yes, even if it had gotten stuck somewhere along the way.

"June Carter's on the back of your sofa sharpening her claws." She pulled a piece of lint off her suede jacket and looked empathetic. "I peeked in the window."

"You don't have to peek in the window, Mama. You're family—you get to come in."

"I was waiting for someone to come home."

"Jude must have gone back to the bakery. They're doing catering now, you know."

"Frannie," she said, grabbing my arm, her voice low and solemn, "it seems that honoring myself is harder than I thought. It's an ongoing business." She smiled. "But there's something I can do right now, and it's tell you about Melissa."

"I've been thinking about her," I said.

"Your father died not knowing something, and I need to tell you because I don't want to own it any longer. It's Melissa's story. But, in the end, it's about me."

"I figured your story didn't end with returning Hugh after you stole him," I said as she followed me inside, pulled out one of my grandmother's tapestry dining-room chairs, and started talking before I could even sit down.

Nine days after my birth, nine days after my father left her apartment, Melissa stood at the window and studied the parking lot of her complex. "Not that parking lots were complex," she would later try to joke with my mother. On that day Melissa had turned twenty-one, a milestone age that meant nothing to girls who had babies before they reached it.

Still, she wanted to celebrate.

It was out of the question to expect my father to join her. And she really didn't know anyone else well enough to ask. Davies had moved her to Charlotte just a few weeks before Hugh was born, and then he had died, leaving her with a newborn and the South to learn all at the same time. She thought the South was sullen. All those manners were just prettied-up anger hidden in the folds of a handkerchief. She wondered why my father was so polite to her. Most men were not that polite. Most men asked for something. Now that he was dead, Davies asked even more of her. Hugh assured that. With motherhood, someone would always be asking. Some days, that was good, but today it was not.

She thought about calling the woman who lived in the apartment beneath her. Sheila. She had two children and a drunk for a husband. She wore the same two pantsuits almost every day, alternating the striped with the Swiss dot, and always the same worn blue Keds. Her kids whined, and her husband shouted. No, Sheila wasn't the one to invite to a celebration, even if she deserved one.

Melissa was still sorting through the few people she knew— maybe the other cashier at the drugstore?—when she heard Hugh begin to cry. She shuffled to the bedroom, imitating Davies's walk, as she sometimes did for reasons she hadn't figured out, that boyish gait, toes pointed slightly inward and knees tightened. It was the first thing she had noticed about him when she met him at a high school dance back in Iowa. It was silly to begin to fall in love with a man because of his walk, especially when so many of them found it easy to walk away.

Hugh's room smelled like baby powder and Lysol. He was standing in his crib, his chubby hands clamped around the bars, one foot hidden beneath the baby bumper with the elephants and gi-raffes. Melissa sighed. Then she reached for him, the thin layer of sweat he always had after waking up the first thing she felt. She had a date for her birthday. She had a date for every birthday to come. She had a date for every *day* to come. Maybe she was lucky.

She carried Hugh into the den and watched him toddle to the blanket spread out in front of the window. She watched him, the girth of his stomach pulling him forward. She liked looking at him, but she wasn't good at just sitting. She had to stand up to keep from feeling sleepy. Hugh had woken up three times during the night. She was used to being tired, but she couldn't get used to being rest-less. She felt so god-awful restless.

That was mostly why she did it. Restlessness was why she had done most of what she had done wrong, Davies included. She couldn't include Duncan. She had secretly hoped that Duncan might come around, but it was wrong to wish someone out of a marriage. It was wrong, even though you were lonely and ten pounds fatter than you had ever been in your life, including the summer of waitressing at Big Boy. It was wrong, even though your new husband died far too young, died a cheater and a liar, and chose a job that allowed for more cheating and lying, and with interna-tional flair. It was wrong because you loved him anyway, loved him and resented him all at the same time.

By the end of the day, the idea had crept into her mind on lit-tle spider feet. Itsy bitsy spider feet climbing up the garden wall, although in her case it would have been a cinder-block wall around a concrete balcony barely wider than one of the metal folding chairs she bought for $3.99 at the drugstore.

While she fed Hugh a supper of applesauce and hot dogs, she decided to do it. It would be only for an hour or so, and everything would be fine. No, you couldn't count on fine. So she called Sheila. She told her she had found a babysitter but she was young and new, which worried her. As she held the phone to her ear, she hoped Sheila would offer to watch Hugh, but she didn't. "Will you be home tonight?" she asked. "I would feel better knowing that you're going to be home tonight." Sheila was going to be home—where else would she be?

At 7:30, with Hugh sound asleep in his crib, Melissa left the apartment. She wore her green dress with the cap sleeves and brown pumps left over from her senior prom. Her hair was pulled back in a ponytail with a tortoiseshell barrette. She would have a quick dinner of steak and tossed salad, with a glass of Rose wine, and then return home. She would smile and flaunt her freedom. If she was lucky, she would meet a man. Maybe someone as lonely as she was, or maybe not.

She locked the door and felt her heart grow heavier in her chest. Something in her body, a current that ended in a sharp point, slowed her. Stop worrying, she told herself. Hugh was safe and would never know she was gone. She descended the stairs and heard the television from inside Sheila's apartment. She started Davies's car, checking the rearview mirror as she backed out. By the time she had reached the restaurant ten minutes later, she was light-headed and giddy. The parking lot was nearly full, but she found a space near the back door where one of the cooks was having a quick cigarette. As she walked past, he whistled, and she asked him if she could have a drag. The smoke felt like velvet in her lungs; it seemed to fill her, to eliminate all other possibilities for pleasure. She thanked him and turned to run back to her car, her heels clicking against the pavement. She drove home without thought, barely conscious of the changing colors of the stoplights.

When she hurried up the concrete stairs to her apartment, a woman, holding a small package wrapped in shiny blue paper, stood on the landing. Although she had only seen her once before, she knew it was my mother. Her mind raced for what to say. She couldn't let her inside because then she would know. On top of everything else, she would know how Melissa had failed at motherhood. She tried to smile, suddenly glad that she had a run in her pantyhose because it was the kind of thing a busy single mother would let go unnoticed. It was the kind of thing that should not happen on her twenty-first birthday when all she wanted was some assurance that her entire life was not contained in apartment 42E.

"Melissa?" my mother said.

Melissa didn't answer. She merely stood, the last hour of her life spinning around in her head like a conglomeration of radio stations. "Madelane?"

My mother nodded.

"Don't tell me you've brought me a birthday present?" Melissa nodded toward my mother's hands.

"Well, actually, I brought you a very late baby present. Is it your birthday?"

"No," Melissa lied.

"Where's your baby?"

"With a neighbor," Melissa lied again.

"You've been out?" My mother's tone was beyond curious, not yet insinuating, but certainly beyond curious.

"I just went..." She stopped. "Did you come to spy on me? Because there's no reason to spy on me. Duncan and I are just friends. He knew my husband."

My mother looked at her, even circled her once, without speaking. As they stood, Melissa heard Hugh crying from inside the apartment. Her hand rose instinctively to the doorknob. She stared back at my mother long enough to see that she had already been judged. She had nothing to lose. She unlocked the door and rushed down the hallway to find Hugh as she had left him, on his back with his arms flung out to his sides, but awake. She leaned on the side of the crib and covered her face with her hands. My mother watched from the doorway.

"Is it the first time?" she asked her when they met in the den after Hugh had quieted.

"I was gone maybe fifteen minutes."

"Is it the first time?" my mother asked again.

Melissa turned to face my mother, who had taken her first excursion since my birth. "Yes, it's the first time. It's my birthday. I just wanted an outing, something to celebrate. Alone." She started crying, although it was the last thing she wanted to do. "My neighbor downstairs is home. I made sure of it."

My mother sat the blue package on the carpeted floor and walked toward the door. When Melissa followed, she said, "I might have to call someone about this. You've forced a huge decision on me."

"Please don't...Madelane...Please don't. It was stupid. Please don't."

My mother didn't say anything else. They stared at each other for a few seconds, one in judgment and the other in desperation. They stood, and the world, at the least the one that Hugh would know, waited.

My mother left without saying good-bye, but as the door was about to close behind her, Melissa suddenly realized something. "Did you have the baby? You obviously had the baby."

My mother didn't answer. Melissa watched her shadow pass outside the window. She knew that she should go hold Hugh, pull him close to her, his head finding the curved hollow between her neck and shoulder. Instead, she stood at the window a long time and then fell asleep on the couch.

When my mother finished her story, I swallowed the lump in my throat and asked the obvious: "And you never told anyone, Daddy included, about this?"

"No. I promised Melissa, later, that I wouldn't, although I thought about it. I never told anyone, and she didn't either. Why would she?"

"She wouldn't," I said. And I wouldn't. There was no need to add to what Hugh had already lost.

"I don't think she ever did it again. Leave the baby. Hugh." She looked at me, a trace of sadness back in her eyes. "She couldn't."

"Because she was afraid you'd find out?"

"No, because she was afraid your father would." She gave me a wizened smile, the kind that's hard earned, and bent her elbows to rest on the table. "He was the one who mattered most."

I nodded. I didn't know how long my mother had known that Melissa loved my father, and I wondered how and when she had made peace with that fact. "But like I told you at the Y that day, Mama, Hugh, in spite of all this craziness, turned out just fine."

"That poor baby," she said, shaking her head. "It's a good thing your father checked in on him."

And then I realized that she hadn't accepted Melissa's feelings for my father as much as she had accepted Hugh's need to have my father in his life. "It's a good thing you let him," I said, squeezing her hand.

"So," my mother said, her new catch-all word for when a conversation had gone her way.

"So." I sighed and then remembered what I had wanted to ask her as she was telling her story. "What baby gift did you bring Melissa?"

"A gift card for a day at the salon," she answered. "But I never actually gave it to her. I kept it for myself."

After my mother left, I went immediately into my office, sat on the futon beside the cats, and did the best thing I could do to honor myself: I started practicing my confession to Jude about secretly going to Rita. I got through the part about *why* I had chosen Rita without a hitch—I was so convincing that June Carter even rolled over and went back to sleep—but it was harder to explain the secrecy. What had I wanted to control? And what would I do when Jude got angry with me, as I knew he would? He was bound to be so angry that whatever trace of Rita's curse still lived in our house might consider moving on.

"I'm sorry," I finally said aloud, because it was the only thing that would matter. And it was the truth. Agreeing, Emmylou stretched her front paw toward me. Normally, I would have given her a high five, but honoring myself hadn't yielded as big of a celebration as I had expected.

I leaned over and looked at the travel clock I kept on my desk. Jude would be home from the bakery in about two hours. I didn't have any urgent work deadlines, so I decided I would spend the time reading about surrogacy. I got up, turned on my computer, and went straight to the Internet, 1998's shiny new answer to the library. The first article I found argued that "wombs will soon be inconsequential. Like electrical outlets or commutes." That wasn't the science I wanted to know, so I changed the search terms and started reading about people instead. I read story after story of women who had been surrogates. Some were single women. Some were married. But all of them had children. Another article confirmed that agencies required surrogates to have had at least one child—it didn't say anything about their eligibility if the child had died. Another discussed counseling for both the couple and the surrogate. Yet another article explained that surrogates liked being pregnant; or they needed the money; or they wanted to help siblings or friends. One of the last articles I read included an interview with a woman who saw surrogacy as a "happy loss," which seemed so close to my perception of Rita's motives that I read her story twice.

Then I considered the fathers, searching for their stories and finding only sketchy anecdotes. One man in Texas wrote that he was glad his wife wouldn't have to endure pregnancy. Another man said surrogacy was both too little and too much biology. Someone had written an op-ed piece that argued surrogacy equalized marriage, eliminating both parents from pregnancy, as if parenthood or marriage could ever be so academic. I skimmed a few more articles, but they more or less repeated what I had already read. Where were the fathers? There were too many other things not said. I hoped Jude would have the chance to say them.

Finally, I searched for articles that discussed why women chose surrogates and found the same answer over and over again: they couldn't have their own children. Those who used in-vitro fertilization, as I would, were grateful that the child would be biologically theirs, and those who had no choice but to use the surrogate's egg were grateful, too. All of them simply wanted to be mothers. It was such an obvious truth. Nothing that obvious should have been that painful. But that's what it was—painful. I sat with my fingers hovering over the keyboard, my eyes blinking. How could I be a good mother if I was so selfish that I didn't even let Jude in on the plan?

I turned off the computer and went straight down the hall to our bedroom. I stood with my hands on my hips in front of the closet, so full of my clothes that Jude had to keep his in the guest room. I started with the items I hadn't worn in years. In one of the leftover moving boxes, I placed three pairs of pants and two dresses. Then I took the gray coat from its hanger and folded it into a square. I threw in the purple negligee, one that I had bought years ago but had never worn for lack of courage. And then it was flannel nightgowns followed by two pairs of faded jeans, eight blouses, five pairs of shoes, and one pair of not-yoga pants that still tried to mock me. Then I found an old pair of white dress gloves I had worn to the one debutante party I attended before I quit being a debutante. Before they went into the box, however, I pulled them over my wrists, working each finger into its slot. I walked around the house, touching everything I could, somehow amused that there would be no fingerprints left behind. I could wear the gloves all day, not answer the phone, not venture outside to be seen by the neighbors, and there would be no new proof of my existence until Jude came home from the bakery, calling out in his husbandly voice, "Honey, Molasses, and Cane Sugar, I'm home," and I, luckily, was required to answer.

I moved on to the household items cluttering the shelves built on both sides of the clothes rack. I filled a second box with a stack of old record albums, their covers thin and frayed at the binding, a set of bookends in the shape of seashells, a miniature television no bigger than a radio, and an assortment of sports equipment. When I finished, the closet was only half full, so I marched down the hall and gathered an armful of Jude's shirts, fleece jackets, and jeans, which, totally out of character for him, he kept on coat hangers, even the Levi's from the 1970s. I moved every single hanger to our bedroom closet, which was now so full I could never go shopping again. But the guest room closet was so empty I could stand inside it, which I did, shouting to test the acoustics.

I had made room for someone else.

When Jude got home from the bakery, five boxes filled the hallway, lining the wall. "What's this?" he asked. "Are you kicking me out?"

"Nope. I kind of like having you here." I kissed his cheek and took the loaf of French bread he had brought home for dinner. "I'm giving some stuff away. Every year my mother and I would go through my clothes and give things away."

"It's an odd assortment," he said, digging through the heaps, stopping to smile at the Ouija board. He picked up a flashlight and clicked the on button. "This works fine, Frannie."

"I don't need it, though. I have two others, and I don't want to be selfish."

"Okay," he said, tossing it back into the box.

I took his hand and led him into the guest room. "Look," I said, opening the closet door and sweeping my arm to the side like I was hosting a game show. "I moved all your clothes into our closet, trying not to be selfish."

"Well, look at that," he said, leaning in to look from side to side.

"You're not a guest, so your clothes should not be in the guest quarters." I sat on the bed and looked around the room. "Although one day I hope this is a nursery. This would make a good nursery."

"Any room with a window and something happy painted on the walls would make a good nursery," he said, and shut the closet door.

"The thing is, Jude, I did something that was very selfish."

"You kept three other Ouija boards?"

"No." I took in a deep breath that made me sit up straighter. "You know that I suggested we get a surrogate. Well, I found one." He stopped moving, and I said the next part even more slowly. "Rita. She already agreed." I turned my head to the side, afraid to look at him full-on.

"You're kidding, right?"

"No," I said. I turned my head back toward him and saw what I expected: Jude, still, his body rigid, his fingers tapping the front of his thighs. "It was wrong, Jude, and I'm sorry. I'm so sorry."

Then he started moving, shuffling toward the bed and then backing away, opening and closing the closet door again, flinging his arms up in the air and then letting them drop as he tried to speak, never achieving more than a series of comments that all began with "You actually..." and then tapered off into awful silence.

I stood up and reached out to touch his arm, but he backed away.

"You have to forgive me, Jude."

"Let me get this right," he said, his voice louder and louder as he continued. "You concoct this far-fetched plan to have my ex-wife carry our baby and, without telling me a goddamned thing about it, go to her and ask. And she says yes, which is the craziest thing yet. And *I'm* the one who has to do something. I don't have to do anything, Frannie. Not a goddamned thing." He stomped out of the room, and I listened first to his heavy footsteps down the hallway and then the slam of the back door and then the faint clicking of the cats' toenails as they ran for cover.

I didn't move for a few minutes. The phone rang, but I didn't answer. The guest room, the whole house, suddenly felt huge, and it was all I could do to start making the journey through the living room to the front door. I left, in the hope that Jude would be more likely to come home if I wasn't there, a plan that didn't make much sense. Not that anything did right now.

I walked for over two hours. I discovered two side streets that I didn't even know existed in Cornelia and an old well in a vacant lot that had been covered over with scaly wood. I met three children on bikes, one on a skateboard with metallic letters, and a golden retriever whose tag read "Ike," who followed me until I was no longer interesting: not even a block. I jaywalked fourteen times. I carried five newspapers still wrapped in plastic from the curb to front steps, wondering where the owners had gone for the weekend, if their lives would seem different when they returned. I stood beside the train tracks where I had seen my father what seemed like years ago and listened for a whistle. I felt like I had done some kind of permanent damage to Jude, to us, when all I wanted was to finally be honest with him.

As I suspected, Jude was still gone when I returned home, so I walked some more, finishing a blister on my left heel. I went back to the bakery, which I had passed an hour ago, its windows as dark as the night. Now, though, the lights in the dining room were on, and I could see Jude sitting at the back table, his reading glasses on and his head bent toward some papers stacked in front of the napkin dispenser. I stared, rudely, shamelessly.

Suddenly and completely and wonderfully, I could not imagine the world without him in it. I wanted to stretch that one little spot he occupied to the very edges of all the continents and across the surface of all the oceans so that I would never have to miss him, no matter where I went.

I tapped on the window. He looked up and shook his head, no trace of his usual quick smile. When he didn't get up, I tapped again, and then I moved sideways in front of the bench to jiggle the door handle. It was locked. We stared and stared at each other, through the glass, waiting for the other to act, two halves of one sad mime. A group of pedestrians passed behind me, their conversation halted and then resumed as they crossed the street at the light across from the old mill. Out of ideas, I started reciting country music lyrics, louder and louder, until Jude opened the front door and pointed me inside.

"I was going to do 'Stand by Your Mantle' next. It's what would happen if Tammy Wynette sang the Pottery Barn catalogue."

He didn't laugh. "I thought about leaving you," he said. "I did. Some of the boxes are still unpacked. The car's all gassed up. It wouldn't have been hard. All that convenience on top of your fucked-up news. It wouldn't have been hard."

"Okay," I said. "I wish you hadn't thought about it, but okay."

"But what came after it would have been hard."

"I just want you to understand that—"

"Instead, I called Rita." He stopped to gauge my reaction, which was to stop slouching and shove my shoulders back where they belonged. "She's coming over tomorrow night to talk."

"What?"

"The three of us are going to have a talk."

"What changed your mind?"

"I didn't say I changed my mind. That was a terrible, terrible moment back at the house. You can't expect me to have changed my mind."

He zipped up my jacket. I let him, dangling my arms at my sides, stunned and on the verge of something that had been a long time coming, or maybe just a long time being recognized. If I didn't love him, then nothing would rise in the morning, not his blueberry scones with the beaten egg whites glazing the top, not the water level of Lake Forman, released of weekend visitors and too many boats with too many motors going nowhere but in circles, not even my father's stubborn Southern sun inching over the Mason-Dixon Line, otherwise known as the horizon.

So, I said it—"I love you"—knowing that our baby would be a perfect, even practical, repercussion of that fact. If only Jude could forgive me.

Chapter 15

That night, while Jude's clothes were co-mingling with mine, we both slept in our bed but with enough space between us for June Carter and Emmylou and all of their cat friends, had they been outdoor cats with a lot of friends and not indoor cats that were stuck, quite possibly, with only me. In fact, I wasn't surprised when Jude woke me by tapping my shoulder, wanting to talk. I thought he regretted being in the same bed, even the same room, as me and was going to discuss who should move into the guest room.

I rolled over to face him. He wore jeans and a white undershirt and was clean shaven, although the clock showed that it was not quite six in the morning. "You have some toothpaste on your chin," I said, knowing better than to try to wipe it away.

"We can talk about my sloppy hygiene habits later," he said, and I sat up, heeding his serious tone.

"Okay," I said, hugging a pillow. "What are we going to talk about now?"

"What you did."

"It was horrible, Jude, I know. I told you I was sorry."

"Tell me how you feel," he said, still standing over me.

"I feel horrible. Guilty. I feel like—"

"No, I mean, tell me why you want a baby. Why it's so bad if you don't get one and it's just you and me paddle-boarding into the future." He sat on the bed and moved a lump of bedspread between us. "Tell me that."

"Well, it's not because I need a baby to complete myself or anything like that. And it wouldn't be *bad* if it were just you and me"—I flashed him a smile—"parasailing into the future. Our baby wouldn't be filling some kind of gap." I inched my hand closer to his.

"Then why?"

I looked at him, trying to buy some time because I didn't know the why part as sure as I did the why not. I had wanted a baby for so long that the yearning had replaced the baby. And then I thought about those hours last night when I wasn't sure that Jude would come home.

"My mother had a stillborn baby when I was twelve," I finally said. "A little girl. Alice would have been her name." When I saw his expression soften, I put up my hand and added, "It was a long time ago, but I'm telling you now because I think at first I wanted a baby because I didn't get a baby sister, and then much later I wanted a baby to give my father a grandchild so he'd die more slowly, but now…" I folded my arms across my chest.

"Now what?" he asked, his voice quiet.

"Now I want a baby because I know what it feels like to love. And I want to keep doing it. I mean, I want to see how far I can go with it. Love, that is."

"Have you joined the Hare Krishnas?"

I shook my head. "I'm too sappy even for them."

"You're not too sappy," he mumbled. He got up and went to the closet, shoving hangers apart to find his favorite green shirt, which he put on, followed by his belt and his watch, always in that order. And when he left for work, he would pause at the end of the driveway, bend for the paper, and then tuck it under his arm. The first few times I had watched him do all these things, they fascinated me. Everything I discovered about him made me wonder about ten other things: Was he nice to telemarketers? Did he like penguins? How many state capitals could he name? And the best thing was that when I discovered something about him, I usually discovered something about myself, too, but only if I wondered out loud. I was certain I could spend the rest of our lives exploring him, only if

I shared that wondering with him. And with the baby, who would offer plenty of wonder in return.

"So, do you still want me to be the mother of your child? Flawed, sappy me?" I sat up on my knees, feeling completely exposed, and toyed with the drawstring on my pajama pants.

"You're flawed but not sappy." He slid his wallet in his back pocket. "And you're right. About the love part. Evan was only six when he died. Besides wondering about the person he would have become, I'm curious about me. Who knows who I would be if he had lived? And Rita, too. Who knows who she would be?"

I nodded and crawled to his side of the bed. "So, do you still want me to be the mother of your child?"

"Yes," he answered, "but that doesn't mean I'm agreeing to Rita getting involved." He softened his tone. "And just so you know, Frannie, I'm sorry you lost a sister. I'm sorry your parents had to go through that." He reached to ruffle my hair.

"Yep," I said. "Me, too." I took his hand and tugged. "Do you want to get back in bed and do what other people do to make a baby?"

"No, Frannie," he said, pulling back. "No."

It was the first time Jude had ever rejected me, and it stung. "Okay," I said, and moved the pillow back in front of me.

He looked embarrassed and then turned to pull a jacket from the closet. "I'm going to the bakery and then I'll be home around four. Rita's coming at seven."

"Why is she coming? There's no reason for her to come if you're against the surrogacy."

"She's coming," he said, tension back in his voice. "We'll give her a Triscuit and a glass of wine, and she'll be fine. We can settle this whole thing." He gave an awkward wave and turned.

"Jude," I said, as he reached to close the bedroom door behind him, "I'm sorry about—"

But he only nodded and clicked the door in place so quickly that he didn't hear "Evan," the last, and most important, thing I said.

That afternoon, I was cleaning the bathroom, Jude's anger and Rita's impending visit casting a critical eye over everything, when the telephone rang.

"Soft serve," a familiar voice said when I picked up.

"What? Who is—? Mama?"

"That was the answer to one of your father's worst jokes: What do old tennis players and Dairy Queen have in common?"

"And is that a truck in the background? Where are you?"

"The Appalachian foothills. I couldn't stay in a house that isn't mine. I'm on a road trip. I stop when I see a place I want to stop." She was calling from the parking lot of a Dairy Queen off Interstate 46, where she was eating a vanilla cone dipped in butterscotch.

My mother, in further honor of herself, had sold the house where she and my father had lived without even putting a sign in the front yard or planning where she would live next. When my mother was at the mailbox, a woman in a green SUV had driven by and questioned her about the asking price. The woman had frosted hair, which my mother considered gaudy. But she didn't hesitate, coming up with a number that seemed reasonable and hoping that some of her lingering sadness could be left behind. When the woman accepted and said, "Well, I'm glad I asked," my mother responded, "You should always ask."

The closing wasn't for another three weeks, but the house, as far as she was concerned, was no longer hers. Not that it had ever been. My father talked her into buying it when he saw the bay window at the far end of the den. A tacky woman in an oversized car had convinced her to sell it. In the thirty-eight years between, she had lived most of her life. But not all of it.

I shut the toilet lid and sat down. "The gypsy trick, Mama," I said, "is to take your house with you."

"That's the part I haven't figured out yet," she said. "But you know the gypsies, they—"

"Move around because they have no home," I finished for her. I had heard her say it a hundred times. "You, though, are not a gypsy."

"I'm practicing," she said. "Besides, I'm in your father's Buick. Like the gypsies, I'm not traveling alone."

I smiled when she mentioned my father. I missed him every day, all day. "Okay, so maybe you're *on your way* to being a gypsy. Get it?" Feeling a tension headache coming on, I stood up and took two aspirins from the bottle in the medicine cabinet.

"Maybe," she agreed as I gulped the pills. "I did just drive seventy miles for an ice cream cone."

"We could romanticize gypsies all day long, Mama, but I know you'll find what you need."

"I don't like that word."

"There's nothing wrong with needing."

She laughed, which I hadn't heard her do in months. "Oh, my stars. This from the duchess of independence who has never asked for help from anybody."

I pressed my jaw against the phone and held it to my shoulder, my hands free so I could wipe the mirror. My frowning face became clearer with every swipe. "That is not me, Mama." I couldn't tell her about Rita, especially since it seemed more and more likely that Jude had invited her over to dismiss the possibility of her as our surrogate. I dreaded the evening, and despite the cleaning, I didn't feel very hospitable. It would be all I could do to offer some Cheese Whiz for the Triscuits. I added, "Not me. Not at all. Not anymore."

"Okay, missy," my mother said, not convinced. "I'll call you when I get someplace."

A few minutes shy of four, the house cleaned and my headache tamed, I sat on the front steps waiting for Jude. I wrapped my arms around my body and hugged myself because I was the only one available. Then I went inside and changed from my sweatshirt to a blouse to make myself feel noticed. When Jude arrived home ten minutes later, smelling like the bakery, it was clear he didn't want to hug me. I hadn't expected any different.

"I tidied up the house," I told him when he met me in the kitchen, his keys landing hard on the table.

"You don't have a lot of editing jobs coming in?" he asked.

I shook my head. "Not right now. It'll pick up."

He put his hands on his hips and stared at me. "So why Rita? Why not someone else? Some woman named Suzanne who already has kids and is parenting them? Which, by the way, is an agency requirement."

"But we wouldn't be using an agency." When he rolled his eyes, I said, "Okay, so Rita would be turned down by an agency because she's not parenting a child. But *we* know her, Jude. You know her best and maybe she left you, but we both know it was the grief over Evan. She feels useless and a little lost, and I understand that."

"You do? Why would you feel useless?"

"Sort of useless. A little bit useless," I said. "Because I can't do the most natural thing in the world. Because I can't give you what I know you want. What if it were the reverse? What if Mr. Mister didn't work?" I asked, pointing to his zipper.

"You mean when I'm seventy?" And then he smiled, which made me optimistic that he would forgive me after all.

"If you think about it, Jude, it's a very generous thing she's doing. Or would have done."

He opened the refrigerator door, looked inside, and shut it. Then he took three wine glasses from the shelf and rinsed them, handing each to me to dry, which I did, still unsure why he was worried that Rita's wine glass might have spots if he was going to reject her.

"I made a bunch of phone calls while I was at the bakery," he finally said. "I talked to some lawyers. And my friend Todd. He and his wife used her sister as their surrogate."

"Oh, yeah?" I said, tossing the dishtowel on the counter.

"Apparently, North Carolina has more laws about relocating old cars than embryos, if I may be blunt."

"It's hard to think outside the womb," I said. "Trust me."

He leaned over and said, "I'm trying to trust you, Frannie. That's what this is all about."

"I know," I mumbled, feeling the awkwardness return. "I know that."

"If we're going to have a child, then we have to trust each other. Oh, and then there's the whole we-took-some-vows-in-front-of-a-bunch-of-people-and-God thing."

I held up my hand and twisted my ring. "This, you mean?"

"Married," he said. "That's us. And I'm okay with that. You?"

"I'd do it again," I answered.

"With me or with someone else?"

"You." I nodded. He kissed the top of my head, which was appropriate since I needed to use it more if I wanted to stay married. "So why'd you invite Rita over? Can you prep me a little?"

"Well," he said, leaning against the sink. "Initially, I was going to tell her that your agreement was off, that *I* hadn't agreed to anything. But now, I want to see what she says, feel her out. We have to insist on counseling. There will have to be counseling, even without an agency involved. The lawyer agreed. *Our* lawyer. I hired him."

My emotions shifted from anxious and worried to relieved and hopeful so quickly that I was afraid anything I asked him might shift them back, but I had to know. "What made you change your mind?"

"I remembered something your friend Hugh said to me at the wedding reception."

"Which was?" If I needed to explain Hugh again, the evening was off to a bad start.

"He said I was a lucky man."

I couldn't help it: I hugged Jude. If Hugh had been there, I would have hugged him, too.

৵

Rita showed up late, carrying a box of wine. Jude met her at the front door. "Are you about to mail that wine somewhere?" I heard him say as I walked into the living room.

She laughed and handed me the box. "It's Sunday. I couldn't buy a decent bottle, so I brought what I had. I'm sorry. I know it's tacky." She looked from me to Jude. "I guess you have glasses."

"We have glasses," I confirmed.

"I figured you did." She leaned to look into the dining room. "And you have a table. For eating. Will we be eating?" Jude shot me a look. "I'm not inviting myself to supper. I just don't understand why I'm here."

"To talk about the surrogacy," I said. "Jude knows, Rita. We've talked about it."

"Oh, good," she said, slumping her shoulders with a little too much drama. "That's good. And smart, too."

"Sit down, Rita," Jude said. "We didn't mean to confuse you."

I put the box of wine on the coffee table beside the bowl of nuts and a plate of Jude's cheese straws from the bakery. I figured they were a bettering offering than Triscuits. Rita chose the winged-back chair and crossed her legs, a red clearance tag visible on the sole of her cowboy boot.

"Thanks for coming," I said, sitting beside Jude on the couch. It occurred to me that I had never seen Jude and Rita together, and I wondered if they would be more or less comfortable with each other if I weren't there.

"Yes, thanks," Jude echoed.

Rita slapped both palms on the chair's arms and uncrossed her legs. "Listen, I know this is awkward, so I'll start. In case you were wondering, I have not changed my mind. I will be happy to be your surrogate."

"We'd pay you, of course," Jude said. "And there'd be the legal details to work out."

Rita looked at me, fighting a smile, amused that Jude was repeating what I had already told her. She waved her hand in the air. "Legal sshmeagle," she said, in mock impatience, "but okay. And by the way, I'm not doing it for the money."

Jude took a nut from the bowl and tossed it up and down in the palm of his hand. "Why *are* you doing it?"

She could have come up with just about any answer, but she said what I expected her to. "I'm willing and I'm able. If it's a loss—some people might think of it like that—it's an easy kind of loss, one I can see coming," she said, shrugging. "Besides, I can't lean on the memory of Evan forever. If I do, I'll be buried a tilted, useless woman."

I watched Jude swallow, his eyes on the bowl of nuts. It took him several seconds before he could nod, lifting his gaze to meet Rita's. Two, maybe three more seconds, and the tiny connection that might have been a memory itself had passed. I pushed the cheese straw plate toward Rita, allowing myself to think about how I would never be a part of their history. I need the practice.

"We've done some research," I said, glancing at Jude, "and everyone agrees that the three of us should go to counseling. Whatever fertility clinic we choose will probably require it. Are you okay with that?"

"Of course," she said. "I expected that would be the case. They're going to want to know what kind of relationship I expect with the baby after the birth." She smiled and shifted in the chair, tucking a leg underneath her skirt. "I did some research, too."

"Good," Jude said, his business voice restored.

"And I would want to see the baby. After the birth. Regularly."

"It's Cornelia, Rita. You couldn't not see the baby," I joked, but she didn't even smile.

"I don't want weekends and holidays. Just an hour or two here and there."

Jude stood and picked up the box of wine. "That's what the counseling is for." He took a few steps toward the kitchen. "I'll get us all a glass to toast."

Rita untucked her leg and leaned forward to reach for the plate. "That's okay," she said before popping a cheese straw in her mouth. "I should be going. And it's never too early to start practicing for pregnancy, so enjoy the wine."

Jude and I walked Rita out to the front porch. He put his arm around me and whispered, "I accept your apology," while we watched her walk to her Volvo. In response, I leaned my head against his hand resting on my shoulder. The night was chilly, with what my father would have called "connect the dots" stars overhead. Up and down the street, living room lamps were turned on. I could hear Mr. Burns from two doors down rolling his trash bin to the curb, even though the collection wasn't until Tuesday. Across the street, the Simpsons' Christmas wreath still hung on their door. It was a quiet, even a predictable, life that I had chosen. When I thought of the future, I looked forward to the ways Jude and the baby would change all that. Rita hadn't brought up her request that I never leave Jude, and maybe she had realized how ridiculous it was. Even if I had agreed to it, the truth was that none of us could control the future.

As Rita's headlights disappeared around the corner, Jude shoved his hands in his pockets and sighed. "I think we have to let her see the baby," he said. "It's a risk, Frannie."

I knew he only meant Rita carrying our child, but I answered, "Every day is a risk and it always has been." I was hopeful that we could be scared—just a little—of everything, together.

At the time, my father's process of dying had seemed methodical—giving away his things, abandoning his hobbies, telling his secrets—the same way his process of living had been. Now that I was going to become a mother through surrogacy, I had to believe in methods and process, but I suspected most of what happened in anyone's life was accidental and based on luck (thank you, Hugh). The best you could hope for was that death would be a kind of mirror, somehow reflecting the people you kept in your life, those people who watched you change, and stayed.

Maybe going to counseling helped me understand this, although counseling itself was a process I didn't necessarily enjoy or endorse. In ten sessions, sitting with Jude, Rita, and the psychologist in a circle like we were kindergarteners on a cookie break, I grew more and more bored with the psychologist's gentle, coaxing tone. By the middle of the second session, Jude and I had agreed to everything Rita wanted, payment of her medical bills and an ongoing but limited presence in the baby's life, and she had agreed to everything we wanted: a healthy baby. The other hours that followed were devoted to the logistics of the embryo transplant and Rita's understanding of how this pregnancy would differ from her first. The psychologist's concern, of course, was Evan, so Rita went into great detail about how the shotgun house and the toy garden, though extreme, had helped her move through her grief. She was ready, she argued.

Jude kept reminding me that the counseling was only one part of *the process*. "We won't know anything until the baby starts moving and becomes real to her," he said, and I knew that he spoke from experience.

When the fertility clinic sent the final papers with the psychologist's signature, Jude and I stayed up late and drank half the box of wine that Rita had left, sitting on the front steps in the dark, all of Cornelia asleep. Jude had insisted that we celebrate before calling Rita with the news, so we drank too much and made fun of couples who used sex to get pregnant when there were perfectly good turkey basters and petri dishes and plastic "sample" cups. Then we went inside and had sex, finally calling Rita the next morning.

"Let's do this," she said when I told her the clinic had approved, the phone angled away from my ear so that Jude could hear, too. "Womb is me."

"We put the 'us' in uterus," I said. It was the standard routine Rita and I used to end all of our conversations about the pregnancy. Jude rolled his eyes every time he heard it, but I liked how Rita and I could joke. Ultimately, we were all mad scientists anyway.

"She almost sounds happy," Jude said when we hung up.

"Well, she starts the shots tomorrow, so let's hope it lasts," I said.

Before her body could accept an embryo that Jude and I had made, Rita had to endure a series of hormone shots, synching her cycle with mine and fortifying her "lady parts," as Jude called them. So for three weeks, she called us every night to say that she had taken the shots, and every night we thanked her for putting up with the pain and inconvenience, although she said we were too earnest—pain and inconvenience were part of the agreement.

At night when I undressed, I would run my hands over the tops of my own thighs, wondering if Rita kept a tally of the puncture wounds in hers. Sometimes I dreamed about them, connecting the dots, which made strange figures—animals with cabbage for heads or stick men with enormous genitalia, a whole different kind of ball and chain. Other times I dreamed that as Rita slept, babies emerged from all the injection sites, dozens of babies with pink, puckered mouths and Jude's dark eyes and droopy lids. In my dreams, all the babies would watch Rita sleep, and when she woke, they would merge into one huge baby conglomeration and she would have to spend hours sorting out the chubby bodies, looking for matching ears and legs with the same number of knee creases.

Meanwhile, I hoarded eggs like the Easter bunny turned criminal. Or I liked to think I did. After two monthly expeditions into my lady parts, the lab confiscated only four useful ones. Jude did his duty, the requisite dirty magazines and plastic cups included. He didn't tell me much about what went on behind the closed door, but once he said, "Maybe it's the baker in me, but I really think they should hand out measuring cups. Make it more of a challenge."

"It's not a bake-off," I told him. We both knew that I could be involved with his end of the commitment, but he never invited me. He seemed determined to make our contributions as similar as possible, which meant keeping them separate.

The day the lab called to say we had made three successful embryos, Jude answered the phone. When he hung up, he padded into the kitchen and braced his arms in the frame of the door, pushing his torso forward and smiling. "There's been a merger."

I stopped washing a coffee mug and let the water run for a few seconds before I turned it off. "Really?"

"Apparently," he said. "My people called your people. There was chemistry—or rather biology—and there was mutual admiration and enhancement. A willingness to work together. An agreement was made, and now some off-site real estate is being negotiated."

"Well," I said, "Off-site real estate. That's a whole new way of looking at it."

He dropped his arms from the door. "We should be excited, Frannie."

"I know."

"We have created embryos. You and me."

"You and I," I corrected him.

"You and I."

"And with someone else, a baby," I said.

"Are we excited?"

"It's too soon to be excited without wine," I said. I kissed him on the cheek.

He wrapped his arm around my arm. "Come on. We're going to act it out." He pulled me toward the hallway. "Let's do sex the old-fashioned way."

"What do you mean?"

"In reverse. The egg and sperm are already hooked up, so let's start with sex and end up with foreplay. And dessert. Sex in reverse."

"It did all start at the bakery," I teased.

"The carousel," he corrected me.

I followed him down the hallway, the newspaper still wrapped in plastic on the coffee table and three loads of laundry overhanging the sides of the bathroom hamper. I wondered if I would ever tell our child about this day, or if it would be the part of history defeated by conventional details, like birth weight and first words.

I remembered some of the "reversal," as my mother once called it in sad sarcasm, of my baby sister Alice. My mother had wall-to-wall blue carpet installed after the nursery was restored to a guest bedroom, and it smelled like the fabric store where my father sometimes took me. My father seldom went into the guest room after the carpet was laid. He used to go there to do his household budget, but after Alice, he moved his desk to the back workroom, which was directly under my bedroom. In the months after her birth, often at night, before the house became completely still and quiet, I would hear him talking. At first, I thought he was talking to himself, perhaps consoling himself in the way that my mother seemed unable to do. After several nights, I realized that he was reading aloud, and it seemed to be a book, a long book about the ocean and an old fisherman. Two years after that, when we read *The Old Man and the Sea* in sophomore English, I recognized some of the passages and decided that my father was simply reading to the baby he never knew, filling in her absence with a story about the ocean.

Now, though, I suddenly realized that my father was not reading to the baby he never got to know. He was reading to the child who had grown into himself.

After three more months, in June, when Jude and I had written dozens of lists—of baby names, of good universities, of things our parents did to us that we would never do to our child—Rita was pregnant. Her body had rejected the first two embryos, but the third one—a miracle, not a charm, she argued—was implanted on a Monday, confirmed two Fridays later, reconfirmed after three weeks, and announced on a Saturday. She showed up at the house while I was working on an article and Jude was at the bakery. I opened the door, and she smiled. "May 21st. It's a Thursday. I hope that's a good day for you." Later, I discovered the clinic had called us, too—its due date more optimistic by twenty-four hours.

I stood, frozen, looking at her. "Thursdays are usually good days," I said quietly, thinking how my father would be pleased about a birth in the middle of the week and wanting to process the news for as long as I could, the victory slow and sure. "Really?" I nearly squealed. "Really?"

She stepped into the house without being officially invited and handed me one of two plastic bottles of milk. "Congratulations," she said. "Cheers." She unscrewed the lid of her bottle and took a swig.

"Cheers," I repeated, my entire body on alert.

"Go on," she said. "Chin up."

I checked the expiration date on the lid and then took a long sip, keeping my eyes on Rita. Then she took another small sip, raising her eyebrows as she swallowed. We tapped the lips of the plastic pints together.

"I would have preferred champagne, but then I would have to reprimand you for not being healthy and not taking care of…the baby."

"Go on and say it," she said, wiping the corner of her mouth.

"Say what?"

"*My* baby."

"It *is* my baby."

"You see?" she said. "You're already thinking like a mother."

When she drove away, I saw a yellow "Baby on Board" sticker on her back window, announcing the transition from possibility to reality. I didn't want to admit it, but I was jealous she had beat me to it.

I could have called Jude, or stopped by the bakery, or hired an airplane to advertise the news across the sky. At the very least, I should have been relieved and very happy. But I wasn't. I felt a sense of dread, and it took me two hours of watching sitcoms to know Rita and that sign created the dread. I fought it, standing in the guest room for twenty minutes arranging and rearranging imaginary baby furniture, and then I fought it harder by putting on a show.

I changed into a denim skirt and sandals, pushed the sides of my hair away from my face the way that Jude liked, and brought up from the basement the stroller we had bought, impulsive and hopeful, at a yard sale several weeks ago. From the refrigerator, I pulled the bottle of champagne purchased the same day and then found the two plastic champagne flutes I borrowed from a neighbor's pool party years ago. I put these in the large pocket on the back of the stroller and then placed inside the stroller a piece of pottery I had bought from Hugh years ago. He had tried to give it to me, but I insisted on paying for it, full price plus my eternal dependence.

I pushed the stroller down the sidewalk of my street and crossed Main Street, headed toward the bakery. I moved quickly, with my shoulders tilted slightly forward and both hands clamped to the metal bar, the way I had seen mothers do when they had an agenda.

Jude was only a few minutes ahead of me on his way home, so our paths converged not halfway but in front of the Methodist church, where the girls' basketball team was letting out of practice. He almost didn't recognize me behind the stroller, but then he stopped, looked from it to me and grinned. "Did it take?" he asked, fidgeting the hand that held a pie box.

"Due date March 21st," I said, cocking my head, then lowering the stroller canopy so that he could see the champagne. I was still fighting a sense of dread that wouldn't go away.

"Ah, plastic flutes. We are going to have the fanciest baby." He came around the stroller and hugged me so long and so hard that I thought I was going to wet my laciest pair of panties.

"We are going to have the smartest, kindest, fanciest, bestest baby ever," I said, and took the pie box so that I could then hand him the tiny ceramic carousel Hugh had made, each pony no bigger than my thumb. "For his or her nursery."

"The starter room," he said.

We could have stood on the corner, showing off to all of Cornelia, and I could have hurried Jude home and called my mother with the news. It could have been a celebration with no dread creeping in. Only it wasn't. As I turned the stroller back toward home, I saw Rita's brown Volvo station wagon glide past us, its backseat piled high with boxes and a plastic luggage container on top bumping over the ruts and making the kind of noise that someone running away for the second time should have considered more carefully.

"Tell me that's not Rita," Jude said, his voice hollow, his chin following the car.

"Okay, that's not Rita," I said, watching the taillights fade, already feeling the distance between my child and me. I made a pact with myself right then and there—even with a lie fresh off my tongue—that I would never allow such distance again.

Chapter 16

"The car was packed," Jude said. "To the roof. And you know she saw us. She had to have seen us. Everybody in Cornelia is always watching everybody else. You can't tell me she didn't see us."

"I'm not sure she did," I lied again, my hands still glued to the stroller handle.

"She's leaving. With the baby. I should have known this would happen," he said, his free hand swinging in the air. "I should have known."

I didn't blame Jude for his reaction. I knew that you don't give someone who's already left you once the benefit of the doubt—if you've already seen it, a turned back is definitely a changed mind. So I let him take the pie box from my hand and place it in the stroller beside the champagne and Hugh's carousel.

He jerked the canopy back up and started pushing the stroller down the sidewalk, so fast that he had turned the corner before I could even move. Someone who didn't know better would think he was a proud daddy with a baby he needed to get home to mama.

I followed Jude, the dread growing more physical, slowing my legs while my heart beat faster. When I caught up to him, he turned and glared at me. "We're calling the police."

"Jude, we've got a stack of papers with a bunch of legal babbly-gook that says we've got nothing to worry about. She's not running away. She can't, really."

"She just did, Frannie. You saw her. She just did."

"We don't own her, Jude. We don't know where she's going."

He stopped. Three girls in blue and white uniforms scurried past us, all legs and long hair, laughing about somebody named

Gwen, a wannabe Goth who had apparently worn purple lip liner to school. I turned to look back at the square, telling myself that Rita might have made the first turn and then kept turning, circling a square as only Rita could do. It wasn't my best lie to myself, but it was good.

When Jude started walking again, he left the stroller behind, so I gripped the metal bar with both hands and kept my eyes focused on his back all the way to the house, where we did not drink champagne.

Instead, Jude called Rita. He held the phone away from his ear so that I could hear the rings. I counted eighteen before he hung up. He called back, this time with nineteen rings, then it was a third time with twenty rings, and I was afraid he had invented a new form of torture, more so for me than for Rita. I took the phone from him and hit the redial button. When her voice mail finally picked up, I simply said, "Rita, it's Frannie. Please call us," which was when I regretted our uterus joke.

"You got some kind of connection with the robot man in the voice mail system?"

"I have a friendly voice is all," I said.

He frowned harder and started pulling things from the refrigerator while I watched: a bottle of hot sauce, olives, baby carrots, a jar of almond butter. He bent to get a chopping board from the bottom cabinet, his right knee creaking as he stood up to study the assortment. "Do you feel like spicy olive and carrot salad with a dollop of almond butter for dinner?" he asked sadly.

"Sure," I said, taking an olive from the jar and offering it to him before I slid it in my mouth, not ready to give in to panic yet. "If I was going to have cravings, it would be that. What you just said."

He planted his hands on the counter behind him, elbows facing back, and watched me swallow. "We'll give her until tomorrow, Frannie. Maybe she'll call. If not, I'll go over to the house, and if she's gone, we'll see what the attorney says. Or the police." He threw his hands in the air. "Did I just say 'police' for the second time tonight?"

I nodded. "And it's only 8:30."

He thought about this for a minute, and then he grabbed his keys from the basket on the counter. "I'm going over to her house. I'll be back."

"I should go with you," I said, but he shook his head and was out the door before I could name all the reasons I should go with him: none, unless you counted the fact that he had left his wallet, driver's license included, on the kitchen counter. Rita was now his fight, and I knew it. When he came home forty-five minutes later, with nothing to report but a dark, empty house, he knew it, too.

The next afternoon, Rita still had not called. Jude took off from the bakery and rode with me to the house with the toy garden. It was just as Jude had described—empty driveway, curtains pulled tight across all the windows, and the screen door locked from inside, the back door obviously Rita's exit strategy. Jude walked the entire circumference of the house, trying each window, grimacing when it wouldn't open. I didn't know what he thought he would find inside—Rita wasn't there. Then I realized he wanted to know if she had taken Evan's things with her, if Rita was *that* gone, his original prediction, as good as a curse, coming true. He couldn't go inside to see them for himself, but he needed them to be there.

We could have broken a window and entered, although it would have felt like vandalizing a church. It *was* a church, of sorts, so I looked up to spot a small, round window made from an old vent. Somebody with the right tools but an odd aesthetic had said, *Let there be light,* which was a hard command to follow, but I would try. I had Jude get down on all fours, and then I stood on his back and inched my way to the closest side of the window, the pane so dirty that I had to spit on my hand to rub it clean. And there they were, the piles of tiny sneakers and comic books and backpacks, and along the wall behind them, the one long line of photographs of

Evan. I closed my eyes. I had to shift back onto my heels to keep from falling. Jude didn't know it, but in our guest room closet, behind his brown coat, hung the first piece of clothing our child would own: a navy blue pea coat. If I opened my eyes, there was Rita's house, Evan's history organized and finite, but behind my closed eyes, there was only the one tiny coat.

"Is it empty?" Jude called.

"No," I said, stepping slowly back to the ground. "It looks like everything is still there." In the backyard, too, all the toys were in the same spot, and the model airplanes, wings missing, cockpits empty, swung lazily from the branches of the oak.

"That's good." He reached up and guided me back toward him. I tilted my head to rest under his chin, my ear finding his collarbone.

"I'm sorry, Jude," I whispered. "I'm sorry about Evan. Maybe that was all you've needed me to say this whole time."

"He was an incredible kid. He loved being outdoors." He pressed his lips to the top of my head and added "thank you" so that I felt the words, his breath, on my forehead.

"She's coming back, Jude." I turned around and gave him the best Southern eye of the tiger I had. "And the baby is still ours. Wherever that baby is right now, it's ours."

"What if she doesn't believe that?" he said. "What if she doesn't?"

"She has to." And I meant it.

On the ride home, I let my eyes wander outside the car window. The new high school, still under construction, already had its name, Iredell County High, poking its elbows out in both directions, to a body shop on the left and a shotgun house like Rita's with a vegetable garden on the right. They'd both probably be bought up and turned into tennis courts or a track, but for now, I could imagine our child's generation being the segue between the North Carolina I had known and the one that would replace it.

As soon as we returned home, Jude called our lawyer, who assured him that it was too soon to call the police. Rita wasn't a missing person yet, and the contract said nothing about shutting up your house or renting a luggage container for your car or driving your anger, grief, and fear from county to county, state to state until they became too road-weary to count. It wasn't a strategy that worked for most people, but it never stopped them from trying.

It certainly hadn't stopped my mother from trying. She appeared the next day, unannounced, back from her third road trip, 1,078 miles thus far clocked on the Buick, five state maps, and ten disposable cameras full of photos that would remember the things she didn't. She already had some of them framed in the apartment she rented in Charlotte. She knocked on my door, handed me two boxes of saltwater taffy, and hugged me, patting my back three times in quick succession and then once again as she pulled away. "That's once for every Southern state I've driven through." She sliced a hand in the air. "Cut through them like they were soft butter."

"The taffy tells me you made it to the beach."

Her smile disappeared, and she let her purse fall to the crook of her arm. "The ocean is better at making a car stop than a red light ever was."

"And that's why there are boats," I said, borrowing my father's muse.

"I found the spot where we'll scatter your father's ashes. We'll take a boat out…his last trip to the sea." She flipped her hand and drew an invisible line down the edge of her palm. "Here's the Outer Banks," she said. "And here's where the ferry leaves for Ocracoke."

"Is that the place?" I asked, bending to look more closely to humor her.

"That's the place." She sounded not only sure but determined, as if my father had given his approval from the Buick's passenger seat, the window cracked an inch for fresh air.

"When?"

"Soon. I feel like it should be soon."

I turned to search for my day planner in the roll-top desk that Jude had brought from the bakery, but changed my mind. "Let's not plan an exact date. Let's just go when it feels right. I'll call you if I feel it first, or you can call me if you do. What do you think?"

"It sounds like not a plan," she said, smiling. "That will be a hard day, but we've had our share of practice in hard things."

I took her purse and put it on the sofa, gesturing for her to sit. "I have some news, Mama. It's mostly good. Do you want to hear?"

"Mostly good?"

I had already told her that Jude and I chose Rita to be our surrogate, so I began by explaining how it was done—the injections and the embryos that had formed, literally, during our last attempt. I named our attorney. When I got to the part about the baby nearing two months, I described him or her as a soulful tadpole, which made my mother gasp until I added "but only for now." I confessed I had bought a book on raising a teenager because it was the part that scared me most.

"The thing is, Mama, Rita's disappeared." When I said it, I felt the panic I had fought so hard to hide.

"She's taken your baby?"

"I think she'll come back, but for now we don't know where she is."

"We should go find her," she said. She stood up, her hands on her hips. "Let's go. There's got to be places she'd run to, places you can check."

"We've already driven out to her house a few times, but—" And then I knew. I knew where Rita was because she had done everything but send me a second handmade "I've Moved" announcement. I practically jogged to the kitchen, nearly tripping over June Carter, as my mother called out, "Frannie, what is it? What did you remember?" I grabbed my keys and slung my purse over my shoulder, checking the lock on the back door and trying to breathe normally so I wouldn't alarm my mother.

"I have to go," I said when she came to stand in the doorway. "I've got to go talk to Jude and tell him to get Rita. You can stay here if you want, but don't let the cats out. I've got to go." I didn't give her a chance to ask more questions. She watched from the front porch as I backed out of the driveway, and I hoped all of Cornelia appreciated the chance to view a gypsy-in-progress.

Jude was standing behind the register when I got to the bakery. He arched his eyebrows as I zigzagged through the line of late lunchers waiting to pay. Then he pointed to himself, mouthing, "Do you need me?" I nodded. He gave a woman her change without taking his eyes off me. He knew I had come about Rita. He studied my face so hard, trying to figure out if I had good or bad news, that a few other people started staring, too. I had to look away, embarrassed from all the attention.

After two more people paid, Jude nodded to one of the other bakers to take over the register and moved down behind the pastry case. I leaned over the glass above the few cookies and scones that were left, careful not to get any fingerprints on it, and whispered, "I know where Rita is."

"She called?" He said it with enough volume and alarm to turn a few heads, so I steered him out front, but away from the bakery's entrance where somebody would surely stop to discuss the mushroom soup lunch special or the high school fundraiser.

"There's a motel off the interstate, exit 47 or 48, something like that, where you and Rita stayed. That's where she is."

"How do you know this?"

"She mentioned it to me months back. It's where she thinks Evan was conceived, but then you probably know that. She's there, Jude. I know it." I took his hand and put my car keys in it, curling his fingers around them.

"You want me to go?"

"Go get her. Tell her it's all okay. Just go get her." I untied his apron, lifted it over his head, and crumbled it in a ball. "And don't send her running further." I pointed to the car.

"Okay," he said. He glanced back at the bakery but didn't take a step toward it. "What will you do until I'm back?"

"Worry."

"Me, too."

After he drove away, I should have put on his apron and gone back into the bakery to see how I could help. Without Jude there to supervise, a customer was bound to get overcharged or under-charged, and there would be smudges all over the pastry case—Jude used to threaten a bakery database of fingerprints in order to trace the culprits. Instead, I started walking back home to my mother.

When Jude called a half hour later, she and I were sitting on the front steps, waiting for what I hoped would be a caravan, Jude in my car out front, leading Rita in the Volvo, the Baby on Board sign no longer in sight. The call, however, was a summons. Rita was at the hotel. The baby was fine, but Jude said that I should come. "She's asking for you," he said, like she was helpless in a hospital room and I was one ahead of the priest. That was fine—I knew what to say.

My mother insisted on coming and then on driving, so I agreed. I locked up the house, and we got in my father's Buick, moving a collection of seashells and a box of Kleenex from the front to the back seat.

We drove though Cornelia without speaking, my knee tapping my anxiety against the dashboard. My mother had her mouth drawn tight, but it wasn't until we got to the ramp for the interstate that she finally said what she had been thinking. "I'm not sure I like this Rita."

"You don't have to like her, Mama," I said, my voice sounding as ragged as I felt. "You only have to get me to her."

"And after that?" She put on her blinker to merge onto the in-terstate and then clicked it off again, a habit she had picked up from my father, who never turned into his own driveway without the same precaution.

"After what?"

"If she comes back home, then what? Will she run off again?"

"She won't run off again," I said. If I had told her that Rita still loved Jude, she'd only want more details, and I was tired of details.

My mother slid her hands around the steering wheel, not convinced. "Well, if she does run off again, I have a few places I can recommend that she visit to send her straight back home. Meanwhile, get her to yoga so her feet are one with the earth."

"One with North Carolina," I corrected her. "The earth is a big place." I paused for a second. "I thought you quit yoga?"

"I went back," she said matter-of-factly. "I quit because I wasn't good at it, but any parent should see the foolishness in that." She nodded, accepting her own advice.

The Hilltop Motel sat more than a mile off the interstate. Either Rita's memory was bad, or it had moved itself away from the noise and non-celestial lights of eight lanes of traffic. It was old-fashioned, one of those in a U-shape, with a pool in the middle and 1950s aluminum chairs in front of all twelve rooms, right beside the silver A/C boxes jutting out of the front windows. It didn't look like a place you would choose for its Wet & Wild suite, which I had a feeling Rita invented just for me.

My Honda was parked next to Rita's Volvo, the only two cars in the small lot. Jude stood in front of the reception office, but he jogged across the pavement to hug me. "She's in room 4, and she's fine," he said. "She promises she'll come back to Cornelia if she can talk to you."

"Did you argue with her?" I asked.

"Nope." He made his fingers into either a V for victory or a peace sign. I wasn't sure which.

"Okay, I'm going in." I took his hand and swung it a few times, acting as casual as I could. Then I crossed the parking lot and told my mother I would be right back. I pointed to the door of room number 4.

"I'll go with you," she said, getting out of the Buick. "For backup."

"It's not a hostage situation, Mama," I told her.

"It kind of is." Since she was right, I let her.

I knocked on the door, and Rita, pale and anxious-looking, opened it. She wore old Levi's and a thick cotton shirt with the sleeves pulled down, dwarfing her hands. As soon as she saw my mother, her expression turned to shame. She lowered her eyes as we walked past her into the room, which was neither wet nor wild—only a normal motel room, outdated but clean, with a sink outside the bathroom for those who liked to separate their bodily rituals. And one more thing—a mirror over the bed for those who didn't. But any romance the room might have held years ago had checked out, no remorse, no license plate number, a bad check written in red felt-tip.

"Are you okay?"

"Yes, and so is the baby. You don't have to worry about that." She offered a wave to my mother, who nodded and smiled. We were all so polite that there should have been applause.

"Were you leaving? Or were you just coming here with a luggage carrier to take home the TV and all the towels?"

"Both," she said. She rubbed her toe in the carpet, which made my mother wince. "I need some towels."

"What are you afraid of?" I asked, not smiling at her joke. I put my purse on the bed and unzipped my jacket to show her I was prepared to stay, if that's what it took to get my baby back within a small radius of me.

"Everything," she answered.

"Can we please use complete sentences?" my mother asked, not unkindly.

"Okay." Rita sighed. "I wanted to leave because I was scared of everything. I was scared that I might or might not end up loving the baby and so I started driving and then I got as far as here and I stopped." She looked at me, earnest and pleading. "I didn't want to make you and Jude worry or give that counselor something to regret. I only wanted to feel it—you know, feel the baby and not think about anything else."

I could have drawn a thick black line between Jude/me and Rita, a line bolder than the one where she had written her signature, but that was not what I wanted. "Please come back to Cornelia, Rita. Please come back and be part of our lives."

"It's really hard, Frannie. After Evan, even the happy things are hard. *They're* the hardest. Five years, and I can just now say that."

My mother, who had pulled a Kleenex from her purse to hand to Rita, leaned down to eye level with her. "I want a grandchild," she said, like she was making either a confession or a threat. "So stay put. And by the way, you're lucky if it took just five years." She gave Rita another Kleenex before she smiled at me and walked back out into the sunlight.

"My mother," I said, my voice quivering, "knows what she's talking about."

Rita swallowed and rubbed her nose with a Kleenex. "I threw up both mornings here."

"The curtains are awful," I said. "They'd make anyone throw up."

She leaned back on her hands and bent her knees up to her chest, sullen. "It was definitely morning sickness."

"I know," I said, sitting on the edge of the bed. "And if I could, Rita, I'd be sick for you."

"But you can't," she said quickly. "That's what you're saying, right? That you can't do any of it."

"No, I meant that I'm sorry you're sick." I stood up and smoothed out the bedspread, suddenly so tired that I wanted to wrap myself up in it and sleep until the baby was born.

"I'm sorry," Rita said. "I'm sorry, Frannie."

"It's okay." I could see Jude outside the window, suddenly peering in and then not peering in, saying something to my mother and pointing away from the motel. I picked up my purse. "I'm going home now. But we'd like you to come for supper tomorrow night. And all this will be forgotten."

"Jude doesn't forget anything," she mumbled.

"And lucky for all of us that he doesn't," I said, not wanting to use Evan's name.

But she knew better than I did how Evan lingered in the room. She inched herself down until she was lying flat on her back, her hair fanned out around her and her arms and legs turned out to the corners of the bed. She stared up into the mirror, so I looked up, too. She waved again. "Hello, hello, hello," she said to all three of us.

When Rita was about five months along and the baby was moving more and more, she called me to the house with the toy garden to see and feel the kicks. "You need to experience this," she said. "I think she'll know it's you." For weeks, Rita had referred to the baby as a girl, although Jude and I agreed that we didn't want to know the gender, that with all the strategizing and scheming it took for us to make a baby, the very least we could do was to be pleasantly surprised. Still, Rita insisted, and I wondered if she hadn't secretly called the ultrasound technician for confirmation. He was a little sweet on her anyway.

That afternoon, I found her seated on the couch, her stomach jutting out like a fish bowl and her hair, which had grown even curlier with pregnancy, falling in tendrils against her shoulders. Still small, Rita's body had become bold. Besides her stomach, her calves had rounded, and her breasts, too, were full and heavy. Yet she never slowed down. She practically skipped around town, one hand resting on her stomach, and every time I saw her, from the other side of the street or through the bank window, or the few times she sat across from Jude and me for dinner, I would imagine where the baby's head was, and the hands.

I liked to think that the hands had formed first, ten fingers with big plans, ten fingers that knew how to mold things into shape, how to make sense of the world, like a certain potter I knew. Hugh's ceramic carousel waited on the dresser in the nursery. A few days ago, when I had stood too long in the little room, imagining the baby's routine, I thought I had seen it turn. "There's not a secret motor?" I asked Hugh when he called to see how I was, but he only laughed and said, "Love, or at least that's what all the poets say."

"Feel right here," Rita said, pointing to just below her breasts.

I bent down and placed three fingers against her cotton shirt. I had bought a used medical book and studied the pictures representing the stages of pregnancy, all the while wondering how anything so utterly miraculous could be explained in such cold terminology. Whoever had written that book had never felt their child kick from inside someone else's body.

"He/she dances like Jude," I finally said.

"You mean without any inhibition?"

"Or pride."

She laughed, and I felt a definite ping beneath my fingers. And then the goose pimples, spreading up my arms like tiny, tickly feet. "I don't think I've ever heard you laugh like that," I said.

She leaned back and looked at her stomach. "Maybe not," she said. "It must feel like one of those bouncy houses to the baby."

"Nah," I said. "It's all water in there. I bet it feels like a bunch of waves."

Rita rubbed her hand over her belly and closed her eyes, her head resting on the back of the couch. "I'm trying really hard not to love this baby."

I knew that later I would tell Jude about my visit, so I spoke for both of us. "You just keep trying," I said, "but not too hard."

We smiled awkwardly at each other. I walked back out to my car, my heart pounding and full. I drove directly to the bakery and went in through the kitchen door, the way my father had all those months ago, and told Jude to come with me. I was surprised that he did, since it was still the lunch rush and he had lost another employee, this time to college.

"Something's happened," he said. "I can see it in your face."

"I felt the baby kick. We're going home," I said, and I drove him there, his white apron still tied around his waist in tiny knots that would take nimble fingers to undo. I led him to the backyard and pointed to the far left corner. "The swing set will go there."

"Okay," he said hesitantly.

"You'll have to put it together because I'm still not good at assembling things."

"You're a girl. You're all good at it when you want to be."

"Well," I said.

"Well," he repeated.

"And if the baby is outdoorsy, which I think is likely, the pup tent will go there." I pointed to the other corner. "But for now, let's just pretend." I led him behind a patch of trees and bushes that had grown far beyond our intentions.

"Well, look at that," he teased. "Someone should spread a blanket of leaves right there and do the nasty."

"Someone should," I said, reaching for those apron knots, lowering my voice to avoid summoning the neighbors to any kind of tawdry exhibition.

But in the months ahead, I was proud of the exhibition we became. The pup tent moved from speculation to reality when my mother gave us one as a baby gift. Jude and I, and sometimes Rita, would take the baby out in the backyard and place her in the tent, centered, so she could look up through the peephole overhead and see the sky. Once her eyes were able to focus, she'd stare and stare, following the clouds and fluttering her lips, impatient for words.

"Do you think Lane is going to tell a story one day about her crazy parents who left her in a tent?" Jude once asked.

"She ought to," Rita answered, and I had to agree.

My parents shared the same birthday, a fact that neither could deny, one that sometimes found its way into tense moments and made them stop to consider the power of coincidence. Born just minutes apart, they felt obligated toward each other. It's what prompted them to believe in the order of the world and to want so much to accommodate their differences.

My birthday missed theirs by three days. My father refused to believe such a near miss was inadvertent on anyone's part, so to celebrate my first year he put up a red-and-white-striped tent behind our house that ran the width of the backyard. It went up on their birthday and stayed for three days, until mine, stretching, he said, to connect those dates just seventy-two hours apart. I crawled around his feet, pulling at his shoestrings and drooling rivulets down my chin. "Under the tent," he said as he told me the story, "three days are one day."

"Numbers," my mother had said, shaking her head in mock exasperation but smiling nonetheless.

For three days at the end of my first year of life, the rule was to live outside as much as possible, which was fine with my mother because she had read that the gypsies did the same. My father grilled out everything, from hamburgers to squash, and the smoke rose between the tent stripes like mysterious script disregarding the ruled lines of notebook paper.

My mother brought out the plastic baby bath I had long outgrown, the one suited only for little, pink newborns, and let me splash as much as I wanted, although I was squeezed in tight as memory. I crawled on green carpet that offered an enormous array of insects to study and taste. The neighbors watched and talked.

My father loved the novelty. He loved the fresh glow so much outdoors gave my mother, and he admired the way I gravitated toward the two puddles just beyond where the big top left off and the regular world began. Once, racing to get me before I unraveled the cord that kept the tent upright, when the darkness, too, stretched between the poles, my mother remarked that the only thing about so much vinyl overhead was that it obscured the view of the stars.

"We'll have to fix that," said my father, the product of months suspended between ocean and sky, as he reached for that very same cord.

And he did.

Acknowledgments

Thank you to Mercer University Press for believing in this book. To all those who have supported this book by reading early drafts—Marshall Klimasewiski, Linda Tillman, Janet Stephens, Sarah Larson, Frank Hubbard—thank you. And to the editors of the literary journals *The Southern Women's Review*, *The Chattahoochee Review*, *Necessary Fiction*, and *Free State Review*, who published portions of this book in different form, I owe you. Thank you to my mother and my sisters, Bess, Ruth, and Gail, for sharing my love of books and making me want to write them. Thank you to Caryn Karmatz Rudy for her generous and good advice. Thank you to the sweetest of all sweet things, Joshilyn Jackson and Karen Abbott, who worked with me on draft after draft of this book and whose presence is so much in these pages that I want to build them a house in Cornelia. And to Denver Butson, Michael Carroll, and Patrick Ryan—what can I say but that you were there from the beginning, keeping the fearless faith? Thank you, thank you, thank you.